THE GOVERNESS AT ST AGATHA'S

'Mistress, what are you doing?' Miss Chytte asked quietly.

'What do you think, Miss?' I bent over the sofa and lifted my skirts, then lowered my wet panties so that my bare bottom was raised high. 'I am to blame for the spoiled uniforms, Miss Chytte,' I said faintly. 'The whole thing was my idea. You will please fetch my new birch and deal with me.'

Miss Chytte smiled thinly and obeyed. 'I am sure that every one of us girls would be only to happy to deal with you, Mistress,' she said as she raised the flogging instrument. 'Don't you agree?'

The cruel twigs hissed through the air and lashed my naked rump, sending streaks of white flame across my skin.

'Oh, yes, Miss,' I grinned fiercely, squirming as my clenched buttocks smarted with pure, beautiful fire. 'Yes!'

By the same author:

MEMOIRS OF A CORNISH GOVERNESS
THE GOVERNESS AT ST AGATHA'S
THE GOVERNESS ABROAD
THE HOUSE OF MALDONA
THE ISLAND OF MALDONA
THE CASTLE OF MALDONA
PRIVATE MEMOIRS OF A KENTISH
　HEADMISTRESS
THE CORRECTION OF AN ESSEX MAID
THE SCHOOLING OF STELLA
MISS RATTAN'S LESSON
THE DISIPLINE OF NURSE RIDING
THE SUBMISSION OF STELLA
THE TRAINING OF AN ENGLISH GENTLEMAN
CONFESSIONS OF AN ENGLISH SLAVE
SANDRA'S NEW SCHOOL
POLICE LADIES
PEEPING AT PAMELA
SOLDIER GIRLS
NURSES ENSLAVED
CAGED!
THE TAMING OF TRUDI
CHERRI CHASTISED

A NEXUS CLASSIC

THE GOVERNESS AT ST AGATHA'S

Yolanda Celbridge

Nexus

This book is a work of fiction.
In real life, make sure you practise safe sex.

First published in 1995 by
Nexus
Thames Wharf Studios
Rainville Road
London W6 9HA

Copyright © Yolanda Celbridge 1995

This Nexus Classic edition 2002

The right of Yolanda Celbridge to be identified as the Author of this Work has been asserted by her in accordance with the Copyright, Designs and Patents Act 1988

www.nexus-books.co.uk

ISBN 0 352 33729 X

All characters in this publication are fictitious and any resemblance to real persons, living or dead, is purely coincidental.

This book is sold subject to the condition that it shall not, by way of trade or otherwise, be lent, resold, hired out or otherwise circulated without the publisher's prior written consent in any form of binding or cover other than that in which it is published and without a similar condition including this condition being imposed on the subsequent purchaser.

Typeset by TW Typesetting, Plymouth, Devon
Printed and bound by
Clays Ltd, St Ives PLC

Contents

1	Veronica's Chastisement	1
2	A Tight Corset for Miss Chytte	17
3	Dinner at St Agatha's	28
4	Swish	43
5	An Impudent Visitor	56
6	Open Day	77
7	Leopardskin	91
8	A Dip in the Thames	104
9	The Rules of Swish	127
10	A Naked Duel	134
11	Connie in Leather	142
12	The Governess Bound	155
13	To Worship a Queen	172
14	The Dungeon of St Agatha's	190
15	In the Steam Bath	205
16	Silk Stockings and Panties	223
17	Masquerade	241
18	Kisses for the Governess	254

1

Veronica's Chastisement

'Well, Veronica,' I said in a stern but kindly voice. 'It seems you have been a naughty girl.'

Veronica Dove bowed her head, her raven hair cascading prettily over her white starched blouse.

'Yes, Miss de Comynge,' she murmured.

'Only the second week of term, and already Madame Izzard has occasion to send you to the governess. Tut, tut, Veronica!'

I looked at the note from the French mistress, its delicate lilac script familiar to me from the days, not so long before, when I too had received my instruction at St Agatha's. It seemed an age! Yet, outside, the playing fields and the broad expanse of Wimbledon Common beyond lay as familiar as ever under their crisp white carpet of snow. A silent, beautiful world whose stillness was interrupted only by the occasional bicyclist criss-crossing the dazzling canopy like a slow insect. It was warm in my study and I felt an inner glow too, at the satisfaction of being the owner and governess of the institution which had nurtured me.

It was three years since I had taken control of St Agatha's. As I watched my girls exercising on horseback, or at tennis, I felt a glow of satisfaction at what I had achieved. For they were no longer girls, they were young women. I had used my ownership of the place to turn it into a finishing school for young ladies who, though they piquantly wore the traditional blue skirts and knickers of schoolgirls, nevertheless boasted the ripeness of grown-ups. Most were not that much younger than my own twenty-three years, yet my stern black governess's costume – usually of the purest shantung silk – emphasised the difference in rank that a governess enjoys; as did the governess's cane which I carried proudly as a symbol of office.

My girls were generally obedient, although sometimes a governess must be obliged to chastise, as will become apparent.

'Hmmm ... for three days running you have neglected your French studies, Veronica,' I said.

'Yes, Miss,' said Veronica, biting her lip.

'Any excuse? Although you know how I hate excuses.'

'I ... I try to do my best, Miss.'

'At St Agatha's, we require more than a girl's best. Your papa, Major Dove, is keen for you to gain a place at Girton, or Somerville, or one of these new ladies' colleges which have lately embellished our ancient universities. A St Agatha's girl aims at higher things in life than mere housewifery, Veronica. A command of the French language is an entry into the world of diplomacy, culture, art, and society in general. How will you flirt with a rich young beau in Biarritz or Monte Carlo if you cannot tease him in the language of *amour*? Why, you are almost nineteen, and it seems you cannot attend to the simplest studies!'

Veronica's face was pink with embarrassment as I, although not five years her senior, roundly upbraided her. In this life, as I constantly remind my girls, clothing makes such a difference in the demarcation of social station. Veronica stood humbly before me in her crisp school uniform: white blouse, against which her very full young breasts swelled most fetchingly, with a dark blue necktie; dark blue pleated skirt, flowing to the ankles; sturdy black boots with white socks peeping coyly above. I, her tutor, was fiercely resplendent in shiny black satin, frilly white ruffs at my neck and wrists, and my waist pinched in by sharp laces, as though I were wearing a most severe corset, although to my secret pride I had need of none. Neither did my derrière, which gentlemen have been kind enough to compare to soft ripe peaches, require a bustle or similar artifice to exaggerate its prominence. Thus accoutred, I seemed many years Veronica's senior, and she only a slip of a girl, although a girl whose figure excited me to a certain envy.

'It seems that Madame Izzard has already given you a mild chastisement,' I said thoughtfully, 'which obviously had no effect.'

'Why, it was scarcely mild, if you please, Miss.'

'Describe it.'

'Oh ... I was spanked, Miss.'

'That is certainly a mild punishment.'

'But in front of the class!'

'Yes?'

Veronica was becoming rather agitated, and her flushed face did not seem to express shame, but a curious excitement. She licked her lips.

'I had to bend over Madame Izzard's knee, lift my skirts very high, and receive a spanking from her – yes, on my panties, Miss! Just like a little girl!'

'Like a naughty little girl,' I replied. 'How many did you take?'

'Ten, Miss. And very hard. How they smarted!'

'Obviously not enough, Veronica. Here at St Agatha's we are rather old-fashioned, and believe that learning must be instilled by sound discipline. Don't you agree?'

'Yes, Miss.'

'Please make yourself comfortable on the sofa,' I said, gesturing to the heavy leather Chesterfield which I remembered only too well from my own trembling visit to the former headmistress, my sweet vengeance upon whose person I have described in my previous volume of memoirs. (Suffice it to recall that, having cheated me of my rightful inheritance, she was obliged, on pain of being unmasked, both to give me sole ownership of St Agatha's *and* bare her bottom to my vengeful cane; to this day I cannot think which revenge was the more pleasing.)

Veronica perched herself nervously on the sofa, her skirt raised slightly so as to bare her calves to the merry log fire. I took my place beside her and put a friendly hand on her knee, smiling as I made myself comfortable, for it was *my* sofa now.

'You are a fine girl, Veronica. Handsome like your father, and I – we – have great hopes for you.'

'Thank you, Miss,' she said happily.

'But what are we going to do with you? Slacking just isn't on, is it, Veronica?'

'No, Miss. I suppose I deserve a beating.'

'I suppose you do. You realise it will have to be a caning.'

She looked at the pretty rack of instruments of chastisement which adorned my bookcase, and swallowed.

'I understand, Miss.'

'Yes,' I added cheerfully. 'Sometimes a sound lacing is the only way to bring a negligent girl to her senses. When a tight caning tickles her bare bottom, it concentrates her mind wonderfully.'

'The . . . the *bare* bottom, Miss?'

'Of course. It is the way of St Agatha's.'

'Mayn't I even keep my panties on?'

'You certainly may not. It shall be your unclothed buttocks that I flog, Veronica, for there is no point in doing things by half measures, is there?'

'Oh . . . no, Miss.'

I took my hand from Veronica's knee, after giving her a reassuring squeeze, and rang the bell to summon my maid, Tess.

'After I have beaten you we shall have some nice tea and cakes. Would you like that?'

'Yes please, Miss!' cried Veronica, her eyes alight. How feeble is the vaunted bravery of men compared to the fortitude of a woman who has tea and cakes on her horizon!

Tess duly appeared, her sulky country face illumined by a pouting smile as she realised that Veronica was to receive a beating. I ordered her to bring us a nice tea in fifteen minutes time, after the chastisement had been effected. The afternoon was drawing to a close, but I had no doubt that Veronica's appetite for tea proper, with the other girls, would not be spoiled; the excitement of pulling down her panties to show off her glowing bottom to her awed sisters (which I knew she would be persuaded to do by those curious little minxes) would undoubtedly increase her avidity for food tenfold.

Tess departed, grinning at the thought of one of the 'la-di-da' London girls baring her bottom for the same punishment that one was frequently obliged to administer to her own rustic Cornish globes.

'Well Veronica, to business,' I said briskly. 'I know your father is strict in matters of discipline, so I take it you are no stranger to the cane?'

'Why, of course, Miss. I mean, no, I am no stranger. Papa used to lace me quite frightfully when I was bad.'

'How frightfully, Veronica? How many strokes would you take?'

'Oh,' she said, flustered, 'I'm not sure. Lots and lots.'

'I see,' I replied gravely. 'Well, please bring me a cane from the rack. That yellow one there, that's right.' She bent over to pick it up somewhat gingerly. 'It's a nice supple yew, a springy little thing, and I think it should make you smart quite nicely.'

Veronica looked abashed as she handed me the shiny cane, feeling its unexpected weight and thickness. I took it from her and swished it smartly through the air, which made her blanch a little.

'Good,' I said. 'Now, I think I shall take you on the back of the sofa, Veronica. Would you please bend over and make yourself comfortable.'

Shivering slightly, she obeyed.

'Bottom high in the air please, and lift your skirt well over your back. Then slide your panties down to your knees, or, if you prefer, take them off altogether, for I want your thighs well parted.'

Veronica bent over, and numbly raised her skirt to reveal a gorgeous full bottom tightly swathed in a no less gorgeous pair of frilly silken panties. They were bright turquoise and covered in all sorts of charming adornments: gold stars, little pink butterflies and silver moons.

I grinned, and said, 'Since it is your first lacing at St Agatha's, we shall let you off lightly, I think. You'll take just a Cornish dozen and, since you are so used to the cane, I dare say you won't feel more than a tickle.'

'A Cornish dozen?' she murmured uncertainly.

'Eleven, of course,' I answered.

'Eleven ... Oh ...'

I slapped the cane on the back of the sofa with a satisfying *whip*!

She trembled, and I was sure she had dissembled: Miss Dove was quite inexperienced in matters of chastisement, which was why her tender papa had sent her to St Agatha's in the first place.

'And one more, I'm afraid, for those panties of yours are in flagrant breach of the rules. They are quite magnificent – such delicate workmanship, I am quite envious – but you know that only the regulation dark blue panties may be worn. A St Agatha's girl must be obedient in all things, you know.'

'Oh, Miss – papa gave them to me specially. A whole set of panties in all the colours of the rainbow, which he brought back from India. Surely these are *nearly* blue?'

'Nearly is just a weasel word for *not*. Off with them, if you please girl, and take your punishment.'

Trembling, she obeyed, and folded her luscious silk panties neatly before placing them on the sofa. I suppressed a sigh of delight at the spectacle of her magnificent bare fesses revealed to me in all their smooth nudity, full, lean and delicately muscled, yet with skin as soft as a baby's. 'You have a fine sturdy derrière, girl,' I said, stopping myself from adding, just as juicy as your papa's. Then I continued: 'I must say you remind me a little of myself at your age, Veronica. Would it surprise you to know that I was once bent over this same sofa to receive a caning on my naked bottom for the crime of wearing improper panties?'

'Really? What colour, Miss?'

'Red, I think. A very fetching satin, though not as nice as your Indian delights.'

'You know, then, Miss, that a girl needs to feel exciting and pretty.'

'Of course I know, you goose, and that is why I am going to cane you, for our need for excitement must sometimes be thrashed into a useful direction.'

'I know, Miss,' she whispered.

In truth, I was becoming excited myself at the prospect of lacing that sweet bare bottom with my springy cane, and felt a giddy hint of moisture seeping between my thighs. How well I remembered my own girlish longings, my nightly escapes from St Agatha's to dance under the stars, naked and alone, and the fervour with which I would caress my young sex as I pleasured myself, bathed in the divine moonlight ...

I took a deep breath and brought the cane down quite viciously towards Veronica's trembling bare buttocks, but delivered the cut to the back of the sofa, where it made an awful crack, causing her to flinch deliciously.

'Miss ...' she cried, bewildered.

'You are a silly,' I said. 'Did you think I would give you a dozen? Tell the truth – you haven't been caned before, have you?'

'No, Miss,' she stammered in an ecstasy of embarrassment. 'Papa used to spank me, but he wouldn't cane me, even when I really deserved it. I think he was frightened to see my poor bottom all pink and glowing.'

'And are you frightened by that? Even though now you must feel the smarts rather than view them.'

'No, Miss,' she said stoutly, and I knew she spoke the truth.

'Your punishment is three strokes,' I said, smiling. 'And one extra for wearing improper underthings. That makes four, and they will be four tight stingers, I assure you. Ready?'

'Yes,' she said, with some relief in her voice. 'But ...'

'But what?'

'I would have taken a dozen cuts, without flinching ... from *you*, Miss.'

'You are a silly,' I said, and proceeded to give her the tightest, juiciest lacing I could.

I delivered the strokes with tantalising slowness, being careful to place each one in the same spot, right in the centre of those smooth bare buttocks, relishing the delicious clenching as the cane stroked them, and the sweet blush that rapidly suffused her naked skin. All the while I spoke to her in a bright and friendly voice:

'You see, Veronica – one! – you must be obedient at all times – two! – and in all things. You must obey the rules of St Agatha's above all, and you must obey without question the senior staff – three! Miss Chytte, Mr Whimble the Chamberlain (I had given my lordly slave Freddie this impressive, if meaningless, title, for his boyish vanity) and of course myself. You do understand.'

'Yes ... Miss ...' she hissed through clenched teeth.

'Splendid! Four!'

I delivered the final stroke with splendid ferocity, and she let out a little moan. It was all I could do not to plant my lips on those quivering globes and cover them with tender kisses. I was panting and my sex was quite wet. As I reluctantly laid the cane aside (I could have lashed those sweet fesses until Veronica leapt to embrace me, sobbing for mercy!), there came a knock on the door which I knew was Tess.

'Well!' I gasped. 'Now for some tea! You may put those panties back on, just for the moment, dear. I must say you took your punishment well, and your bottom scarcely squirmed at all. Your papa will be proud to know that his daughter has such pluck.'

'Thank you, Miss,' said Veronica happily. And when she had composed herself, I bade Tess enter with the tea things.

The wench entered, saw Veronica's flushed face, and smirked broadly at me. I met her impudent wink with a chilly frown, and wondered, not for the first time, if I had been right to accede to Miss Chytte's wish that her Cornish serving girl, for all her insistent physical charms, should be brought to the metropolis to serve us in our new domain. However I had agreed in the knowledge that Tess's sportive country vitality would serve me well in purposes that transcended the merely scholastic, and it would have been churlish to deny that I took as much pleasure as Miss Chytte in the many festive hours we spent with Tess as our willing and unabashed plaything. Nevertheless, the girl had to know her place here in London, away from the brutish democracy of the lustful shires. It was improper of her to smirk at a lady and, more important, a lady who was a paying customer. Tess wore a maid's uniform, albeit a rather pretty one, complete with bustle, corset and a rather pleasant décolletage which allowed a tempting view of her ample Cornish bosom, and that uniform obliged her to submit to exactly the same instruction in good manners as my paying young ladies. It was time to give her another lesson.

Tess put the tea things on the little table by the fireside, and I noted with approval that there were plenty of scones, a variety of scented jams, and of course the ubiquitous clotted cream without which no Cornish repast is complete. My time in that fogbound duchy had not been entirely without instruction, and I had learned that, as a sound business practice, my girls at St Agatha's should be as well fed as they were well disciplined, for anything less would lead to inefficiency and would not be cost-effective. Nothing besmirches the reputation of our English boarding schools as much as the insipid food, which many girls carry into life as their sole, dismal memory of their alma maters; whereas a well-fed body frees the spirit to concentrate on useful things such as fashion sense, *haute cuisine* and business administration.

The silver teapot steamed merrily atop its little oil burner, while Tess, with undisguised glee, ogled Veronica's bottom as it shifted uncomfortably inside her skirt, and winked nastily at the red-faced girl. I decided that this was really too much.

'You have something to say, Tess?' I said coldly.

'No, Miss de Comynge,' she chirped, wide-eyed with dumb insolence.

'Then wipe that smirk off your face, girl.'

'What smirk, Miss? I wouldn't smirk just because a highborn young lady got her comeuppance with four juicy lashes on her bare rump, not me, Miss.'

'How did you know?' I thundered. 'How dare you listen at my door, you slut!'

'I may have heard something by accident,' she said sullenly. 'You cane very hard, you do, as I well know, Miss.'

Veronica's sheepish blush had become suffused with an indignation as strong as my own.

'You will curtsey and apologise to Miss Dove,' I said icily.

With a surly grimace, Tess did so.

'I'm very sorry, I'm sure,' she said, somewhat grudgingly. 'May I go now, please, Miss?'

'Certainly not, Tess, for your apology isn't complete. Insolence cannot be excused merely by a sullen curtsey, so you'll get just the same as Miss Dove.'

'Lor, lumme,' said Tess.

'And,' I continued sternly, 'you'll take them from Miss Dove herself. Bend over the sofa, Tess, lift your skirt and petticoat, and take your knickers down.'

'I'm not wearing any knickers, Miss.'

'Why, you slut!' I cried, omitting to mention that I was not wearing any myself, having given them that morning to my dear slave Freddie. I always pretended that I made him wear my tight, frilly panties as a mild discipline, although I knew very well he loved to.

I selected a cane, a stout ashplant this time, and handed it to Veronica. She took it with a gleam in her eye which I had not seen before, and which pleased me, for I intended to test her worthiness to play her part in my schemes for the future.

'I hope you have what it takes to be a St Agatha's girl, Veronica,' I said, as I pushed Tess's head down over the sofa and made her spread her bare thighs in a position to which she was quite accustomed.

'Oh! Please, no, Miss!' she protested, without protesting too much. The flounces of her dress and petticoat muffled her cries, and I gazed with satisfaction at the sturdy bare bottom exposed to our view.

'No knickers,' I snorted. 'How filthy!'

'Us Cornish girls are too poor for city dainties such as knickers and that,' grumbled Tess untruthfully.

In fact, I was beginning to wish that I had worn my panties, for the sight of a second bare bottom, ripe for a lacing, had the effect of increasing the flow of hot wetness from my sex; it was now a determined trickle, which I could feel seeping down the soft insides of my thighs towards my silken stocking tops, which I feared would be marred.

Veronica advanced, holding up the ashplant, with shining eyes and flushed cheeks.

'I'm ready, Miss,' she said quietly.

'A full four then, and as hard as you can. Let us see if there is some muscle in that croquet arm.'

Veronica said nothing, but suddenly lifted the cane and brought it down on Tess's naked buttocks with a swiftness and ferocity that surprised even me. It certainly surprised Tess, for she jumped and clenched her trembling bottom, giving a sharp cry.

The second stroke graced the same spot as its forerunner, and Tess began to squirm most prettily. At the third, she squealed, her bottom writhing madly in an effort to dissipate the stinging, and as the fourth cut took her, the tender globes were frantically pulsating as though in mimicry of some rutting beast. My sex was quite wet by now, and it was all I could do to not to plunge my hand to my tingling lips and frig myself there and then, in defience of all rules of scholastic decorum. I noticed that Veronica was panting, her bosom thrusting proudly against her sweat-damp blouse, so that her generous nipples clearly protruded, swollen and hard against the fabric of her shirt and the bodice underneath. To my delight, I saw that she too was as excited as I was at the spectacle of the girl's naked buttocks smarting under the crop! If it had not been for the cruel, though necessary barriers of social position, I should have embraced her, touched and caressed the sweet plums I had so recently laced, and penetrated her sex myself, knowing that she would be as wet as I was. Veronica's face had the ferocity of a huntress, and for a moment I saw her as my revered Selene, the cruel moon goddess who was the object of my girlish worship as I danced naked under the stars.

'I am well pleased with you, Veronica,' I said coolly.

'Now, let us take tea; I think we have earned it. Tess, you may stop your snivelling and serve us.'

'Yes, Miss,' snuffled Tess, and philosophically smoothed down her skirts, then applied herself to her duties. Soon Veronica and I were sitting cosily by the fireside, trying to wolf our delicious scones, jam and cream as daintily as possible.

'Tess,' I ordered, making quite sure my mouth was not full, 'you will go to Matron and get a pair of regulation panties. No, two pairs, for I expect you to wash one pair every now and then. They cost eightpence halfpenny each, so I shall deduct one shilling and fivepence from your next wages.'

'Oh, but Miss de Comynge,' whined Tess, 'that leaves me but . . . but . . . two shillings and fivepence!'

'No it doesn't, it leaves you four shillings and sevenpence, you clot! And six shillings a week for a girl of your talents – plus full board, mind – is a handsome remuneration in this metropolis.'

'But all my brothers and sisters and cousins . . .'

'Who are all figments of your Cornish imagination,' I interrupted. 'I know very well you spend your wages on cheap scent, tuppenny ale and omnibus rides. Off with you to Matron! I shall telephone her this instant!'

Tess cast a fearful eye on the wonderful instrument of Mr A. G. Bell's invention, as though it were some daemonic juju from the wilds of Bodmin Moor, and departed hurriedly. I picked up the receiver and asked the girl on duty at the board, a nice lass from Woking named Phoebe Ford-Taylor, to connect me with Matron's telephone. My call was not strictly necessary, but I was still in love with this marvellous new toy with which, I was assured, I could now communicate with over twenty thousand souls throughout the metropolis! A few seconds later the telephone at the other end tinkled and clicked, and Matron answered.

'Hello there, d'ye want the business?' crooned her soft Irish contralto.

'Deirdre, it is Miss de Comynge. Haven't I asked you to

answer the telephone as follows: "St Agatha's Academy for Young Ladies, Matron speaking"?'

There was a pause.

'St Agatha's Academy for young Young Ladies here, Miss de Comynge, Matron speaking, d'ye want the business?' said Deirdre.

'Deirdre,' I sighed, 'please remember you are no longer strutting on Praed Street.' When I explained the business of Tess, Deirdre chortled.

'Why, the dirty young whelp. Do you want me to give her insides a good hot cleansing with one of Mr Izzard's new machines?'

'No, Deirdre, I'm sure we can arrange that later. Just the panties, please.'

'Well, I'll give her them two sizes too small. That'll learn her!'

Smiling at this mild prank, I replaced the receiver. 'Well, Veronica,' I said at length. 'Are you comfortable?'

'Yes, thank you, Miss.'

'Are you sure you wouldn't prefer to take your tea standing up? It is all right, you know, for I expect your bottom stings just a little.'

'A little, Miss. But it is all warm and tingly, too. It is nice in a way.'

Our eyes met, and she blushed most attractively.

'I must find out, though, why you have been remiss in your studies. The academic discipline is no less prized at St Agatha's than social discipline. These days are full of promise for women, you see: the great professions and universities are open to us; married ladies may own property in their own name and we are free to hone and strengthen our bodies in these new sports like lawn tennis and bicycling. There are already some lady automobilists, of which I am proud to be one, with my splendid new Panhard-Levassor outside this very door. Why, when the twentieth century dawns, it is certain we shall have the vote, although for myself I think that a very mixed blessing. But to take advantage of our newfound freedoms, we girls must do twice as well as boys, at everything, especially our studies. So what can be the reason for this slacking, Veronica? Are you unhappy at St Agatha's?'

'Oh, no, Miss,' she cried. 'It's the best institution I've ever known. Already I have lots of super chums – there's Prudence Proudfoot, and Amanda Nightingale, and Phoebe Ford-Taylor, and –'

'Yes, they are all sound girls,' I interjected. 'So whatever can the matter be?'

Veronica sighed deeply.

'Why, nothing, Miss.'

I took Veronica's hand, which was trembling, and looked into her eyes. 'Come, Veronica, I know that sigh,' I said softly. 'There is a young gentleman, I fancy.'

'Oh, Miss, papa is very strict. I have never ... I mean, *you* know, I mean ...' She broke off in sweet confusion.

'Who is he, Veronica?'

'Oh,' she blurted in a rush, 'he is the finest and most handsome of all the cavalrymen. One day papa, mama and I were walking in the park, from our house in Curzon Street towards the Knightsbridge Barracks, when he passed us. He saluted papa, of course, and then when papa wasn't looking he turned back and tipped his cap to me and gave a little bow. And oh, Miss, he smiled! Second Lieutenant Arbuckle is his name and honestly, Miss, he smiled at me!'

Her voice trembled; it seemed that she could take four strokes of the cane on her bare bottom without blinking, yet the thought of Second Lieutenant Arbuckle's smile had her on the verge of a swoon. Truly, we women are tremendously unfathomable, as gentlemen are never tired of pointing out.

'Veronica,' I said tenderly, 'you are young and ripe with love and beauty. It is normal to direct these feelings towards the person of a fine young man. But your heart must not rule your head, I'm afraid. When you have matured a little, you will find that there are plenty of fine young men, and that you may pick and choose amongst them at will.'

'But Miss de Comynge, I love only Second Lieutenant Arbuckle!'

'Aren't you secretly happy to pine thus, to feel such sweet melancholy? You are in love with love, Veronica, not I'm afraid, with Second Lieutenant Arbuckle.'

'I cannot believe it,' said Veronica doubtfully.

'Of course not. That is why your papa sent you here, so that rigorous discipline may turn you into a woman. Do you want to disappoint your papa, Veronica?'

'No! I love my papa more than anyone in the world!'

'And what about Second Lieutenant Arbuckle? Suddenly he is not quite so important, eh?' I said rather brutally.

'Oh ... well ...' said Veronica miserably, and reached for her handkerchief.

I took the opportunity to give her a tender hug and a soft kiss on the cheek.

'So,' I said, 'we must be brave and give your papa,' – I was going to say 'value for money' – but instead I whispered, 'a girl to be proud of.'

'Yes, Miss,' sighed Veronica. 'I shall make him proud of me.'

'Good,' I said briskly. 'Now, as to these delightful undergarments that your papa gave you, they must be given up and will be kept safe for you. Your papa was very naughty to give them, for he knows our rules. I must speak to him about it – he has a telephone in Curzon Street – and I'll tell him that if he were one of my pupils,' I had a roguish twinkle in my eye, 'I should chastise him most severely. Yes, most severely.'

I rolled the words round my tongue with relish, for I was feeling quite ticklish for another meeting with the doughty Major Dove and his mysterious wife Thalia, Veronica's rather prudish (I gathered) mama.

'Yes, of course, Miss,' said Veronica. 'It is just that Second Lieutenant Arbuckle was in India with papa, and wearing them reminds me of ...' Her sentence tailed off helplessly.

'Well, if you have finished your tea, you may attend to that errand,' I said. She got up to leave. 'Veronica,' I said suddenly. 'Do you lie awake at night, unable to sleep, thinking of Second Lieutenant Arbuckle?'

'Why yes, Miss. How did you know?'

'And do you find that you caress yourself – there, you know, in your lady's place?'

'Well, sometimes, Miss.'

'Wearing these panties, that remind you of him?'

'Surely there is nothing wrong in it?'

'No, it is normal and healthy, in *my* opinion, which is the opinion of St Agatha's. But in future, when you tickle yourself there, and make yourself all hot and wet and tingly –'

'Oh, Miss!' she cried, with a furious blush.

'We are all girls, Veronica. When you do this thing, and I know how sweet it is, please wear your regulation panties. I'm sure you have not even unwrapped the package in which they were issued to you, but when you do, I think you will be agreeably surprised. I designed them myself; they are high-waisted, and err perhaps on the skimpy side. In short, they are rather fashionable, perhaps even . . . daring. Stroke yourself, Veronica, through the regulation blue satin, and you will understand that while you are here, your love must be for St Agatha's.'

Veronica smiled. 'I understand, Miss,' she said, looking me coolly now in the eyes. 'Really, I do.'

2

A Tight Corset for Miss Chytte

'More hot water, please, Miss Chytte,' I said, nuzzling into the scented foam that lapped my breasts. 'And some champagne, too. Well chilled. I take it the iceman came this morning?'

'Yes, Mistress. But the ice block has not been broken.'

'Well, chip it with your fingernails, Miss! Get a bucketful and chill my champagne. Or have some girls do it. Yes, that shall be added to our menu of punishments: miscreants shall break ice for an hour.'

'I'm proud to obey, Mistress; you are a veritable slave-driver!'

'No cheek, slave, or I'll dress you in the girls' uniform, even though you're my aide. How would such democracy suit you?'

'Would I be beaten like the other girls?'

'More, I imagine.'

'Then I should like it very much, Mistress.'

'Ha! One day I'll devise a punishment that you won't like at all.'

'I should like that too.'

I flicked the leash which tethered Miss Chytte, and she trembled as the thong tugged at her nipples and sex-lips, which were prettily pinched and attached by little golden lockets. Apart from these adornments and her black ankle boots, she was naked like myself, though somewhat colder. Gravely I handed her the leash, and she wrapped the thong carefully round her waist before donning her coat. She then departed on her errand, snug in the symbol of her servitude. I lay back in my bathwater and began to soap my breasts lazily, not for the first time, and smiled as I reflected upon my good fortune.

How pleasant the realisation of a young girl's dream, to be headmistress of her old school! Although my plans for St Agatha's had more to do with the pleasure houses of Paris or Stamboul than the groves of Academe. My eventful sojourn in Cornwall had led me to this: young Freddie Whimble, my erstwhile pupil at Rakeslit Hall, was now my devoted slave and factotum, whom I honoured with the title of 'Chamberlain', as befitted the son and heir of Lord and Lady Whimble. Lord and Lady Whimble were now happily reunited by my good devices, which had rescued his Lordship from a long period of – well, eccentricity; Marlene and Deirdre, the sturdy gay girls I had plucked from their unstructured self-vending in the purlieus of Praed Street, became respectively, my Manciple and my Matron; then there was faithful Mr Izzard, known to me of old, since, as a schoolgirl, I would barter my used panties for sweetmeats or playthings at his pharmacy in Wimbledon High Street. During my days in Cornwall, Mr Izzard's inventiveness in the matter of curious disciplinary and hygienic appliances did much to help me tame young Freddie's rampant male vigour, and to gain the devoted allegiance of the Sapphic Miss Chytte. Now, happily married to the former Mlle Solange Gryphe of Aix-en-Provence, my old French mistress, he was enrolled with my partners in my plan to create, within the starched confines of a girl's college, the finest house of pleasure that London had ever seen! His devotion to his hygienic art and his enthusiasm for the regulation of the various intimate bodily functions of both male and female, ensured a steady supply of devices both to heighten pleasure and, in the case of a lady, to nullify the inconveniences caused to her body by pleasure's pursuit.

Although I was sole commander of the establishment and its operations, we regarded ourselves as partners, thanks to a profit-sharing scheme, a novel but extremely sound business practice and one which I thoroughly recommend to all ladies embarking upon a business career. Miss Chytte, whom I had rescued from her tea-shoppe in the glum Cornish village of Budd's Titson, by Rakeslit Hall, proved an admirable administrator, and my reforms were proceeding with delicacy and stealth. If a lady can manage a tea-shoppe in Cornwall, she can manage anything.

I looked at my reflection in the ceiling mirror, and permitted myself to think my body beautiful. I caressed my full breasts, bringing the big plum nipples to a delicious tingling stiffness, and then idled my fingers in the forest of auburn curls that was my generous mink.

I teased myself slowly and thrillingly, allowing my fingers to play on the lips of my sex, prominent even when flaccid, but now swollen most proudly. I saw myself as a queen; a goddess even: the cascade of hair framing my shoulders and breasts, the ripe teats themselves, a flat belly leading to a Mount Pleasant of striking fullness, which many gentlemen had been kind or besotted enough to kiss and stroke with awe; smooth long legs, delicately but sturdily muscled. My whole skin was glowing with golden health, my honey colour being due to my distant Mediterranean origin (or so I puffed myself!). Only my bottom was hidden from my view. The buttocks and back are the only parts of our bodies we cannot easily contemplate, and therefore, to me, are the most mysterious and most beautiful. I am proud of my bottom, perhaps inordinately so, although I must rely on the compliments and caresses of others to make me conscious of the power of those firm, smooth globes. With what rapture have Freddie and Miss Chytte nuzzled me in the cleft of my naked buttocks, smothering my skin with kisses, fervently tonguing my proudly standing anus bud itself, or, when my commands are harshest, making those centres of pleasure tingle at the caress of a cane or sweet whippy birch ...

As I caressed my gently wriggling body, I daydreamed of a future in which I should rule an empire of wealth, power and beauty. Every girl dreams such dreams but I had made a reality of them. Wealth, to me, means not the vulgar opulence that is the limit of most gay girls' horizons, but the musky aura of copperplate bank statements, thick carpets and closed carriages in Berkeley Square at twilight. In the midst of this dark, enthralling world, a bright shimmering beacon: St Agatha's, a temple of pleasure where rich men could doff their robes of propriety and become happy little boys again, where the loveliest flowers of English maidenhood would relieve them of their anxieties and their lucre. I should be the Andrew Carnegie of lust, my good works knowing no frontiers!

In Cornwall, far from the constraints and complexity of the city, I had made myself, or discovered myself to be, a country whore. I liked it: enjoyed my power over those sturdy yeomen, as I perceived the lusts and longings that boiled beneath their rough-hewn respectability. So many successful men long to be humiliated and punished for their success. Ashamed of their 'filthy lucre', they long for the flutter of a woman's eyelid or the swell of a shapely breast, to remove it from them! Business consists of giving customers what they want, even if they don't know they want it. And what most of my customers truly want is to be treated like a beastly little boy (a little boy who possesses oodles of cash), and be punished for it with a damn good hiding. When a man is stripped naked and thrashed by a lovely woman, he is made to feel appreciated for himself, not for his money. Too many transactions between gay girls and lustful gentlemen are unsatisfactory, because the vendor imagines that the client is paying to use her body, whereas in fact he is paying for her to use his.

I had observed that Marlene, in her businesslike Scotch manner, had in Praed Street a tariff for various lustful services; a sort of erotic menu. While sound, this is not the practice at St Agatha's. With me, a man pays – oh, how he pays! He begs to pay, he sobs until I take his bawbees! And in return he may have everything he wants, or he may have nothing at all. His Mistress may be cross with him; or she may refuse to be cross with him, administer the most savage of chastisements or the tenderest of endearments. Either way, she is giving him what he wants, which is the thrill of uncertainty. A client may leave St Agatha's sated with the most delirious poking, or his bottom glowing from the sternest of lacings; or he may leave in an agony of frustration because his Mistress is 'not in the mood'. In return for his guineas he has only the promise of more, 'next time – if you are good'. Seething, he vows that there shan't be a next time, but as the sap begins to course in his balls – his Mistress has forbidden him to remove his restrainer and relieve himself of his aching tension! – he begins to long for his implacable paramour again. His cock longs to stand stiff for her, and he returns humbly, his pocket full of guineas, begging to be punished for his impudence.

The important thing is never to undercharge. Men like to boast of their profligacy, how much they have lost at gambling or in drinking bouts, and to squander money on women is a great source of pride. In this way can a kindhearted businesswoman do wonders for the male ego.

I was so pleased with my musings on the science of marketing that when Miss Chytte returned with champagne on ice and a bucket of hot water I invited her to join me in the bath and take a glass of wine, before we joined the rest of our company for dinner. However I frowned when I saw that she had allowed her fingernails to become unseemly from chipping at the ice block, and to show my disapproval, I ordered her the mild chastisement of lacing herself in one of the corsets I kept for such purposes. She doffed her coat, and nude, opened the closet, from which I selected a yellow satin corset, with severe whalebone stays in the former fashion. Still trembling from the cold in the ice room, she laced up the corset as tightly as was possible, on my instructions, so that her breasts were pinched up and swelled very fetchingly over the stiff corselet, while her waist was severely constricted in a wasp shape, to her noticeable discomfort. 'Oh!' she panted. 'It is so abominably tight, Mistress! I couldn't help getting my nails chipped.'

'Then you'll know better next time, slut,' I said harshly, and made her bend so that I could clip her leash back onto her nipples and sex-lips. Then I gave the thong a healthy tug, and she squeaked as the corset bit into her flesh. I made her open the champagne – deriding her clumsiness – and pour a trembling glass for each of us. Then I said that she might join me in the tub. 'There is plenty of room for two.'

Of course there was room! It was Miss Chytte herself, in her dainty apartment atop her tea-shoppe, who had awakened me to the delights of a sumptuous bathroom, and I had installed for her a glittering array of mirrors, basins, bidets and hygienic devices such as the colonic irrigator. In pride of place was a splendid set of *évacuateuses à la turque*, twin commodes upon which ladies may squat and enjoy a friendly chinwag as they attend to their business, in the manner of the harem. These I had been obliged to order from M. Cornichon's shop in the Rue St Denis in Paris, since such things were unobtainable in London, our English middle classes believing that the evacuation of food must be as glum as business as its ingestion.

'Why did you make me corse myself, Mistress? The garment will surely shrink.'

'Get in, you bumpkin!'

When Miss Chytte had lowered herself with much bubbling into the suds, I told her of my musings on the subject of selling pleasure.

'It is part of a girl's education,' I concluded, 'to learn the realities of life, that is, love, power and money. It is better for a woman to be her own whore than society's. Look at the splendid marriages that are made between great courtesans and men of substance! Do such men care for the footling cult of purity? No, they are proud to own a woman who has known a hundred men before, secretly thrilled to fuck in a place where so many of his comrades have already been tried. A St Agatha's girl, Miss Chytte, will in later life be a happy girl!'

'I believe my corset is shrinking!'

'I dare say it is.'

'It is so tight, I think I need to squat!'

'You will control yourself, if you please, Miss,' I said harshly.

I took hold of Miss Chytte's nipples between my thumb and forefinger and gave them a cruel, playful squeeze, as though mocking her.

'Oo!' she said, grimacing.

'One day, you will marry a rich man, Miss,' I said.

'I! Marry?'

'You will wish it. I shall make you wish it.'

'Then I shall obey, of course. I shall want to obey you, Mistress,' she murmured shyly. 'As long as you will still have me for your slave.'

Her nipples were quite stiff and stood up like thimbles. I rasped them hard with my fingernails, and she sighed softly.

'Remember that we women can take our pleasures joyfully, Miss Chytte. But men are little boys. They want their pleasures to be naughty, and they want to be thrashed for taking them. It is every man's fantasy that he is uniquely sinful, and our job is to assure them that they are special, even though half the men in creation profess the same tastes, and the other half won't admit to them.'

'Ouch! This corset is damnably tight! But tell me –'

'You wish to be released from it?'

'Oh, no! But what about the men who love to chastise ladies, who dream of caressing our bare bums with a sturdy tawse or birch?'

'They are punishing the woman for her failure to punish them, Miss Chytte. And they are the ones who, having delivered the lustiest thrashing to a lady's naked fesses or back, will take ten times the punishment in return, and be tearfully grateful that their Mistress has wisely understood their desires. That is called psychology.'

'How wise you are.'

'I am more than wise, I am selfish,' I replied, and suddenly my fingers touched her labia, stroked the sex-lips tenderly, then plunged into the soft recesses of her lovely wet quim.

'Oh, Mistress ...'

'You have a sweet lady's place, and I shall never tire of it, not even when it is the preserve of a man's cock, Miss Chytte. It is so silky, so nice to touch, and to kiss.'

'Oh, Mistress, you make me tremble. How tight this corset squeezes! I think I'll burst, it crushes me so. It ... it's adorable!'

The thought of Miss Chytte's tummy squeezed by that

stern whalebone, and her warm oil that seeped from her cunny over my probing fingers, caused my own sex to moisten and my belly to flutter with desire. I swept the foam from the surface and looked down into the clear water, where I saw a little shiny pool floating from her crimson slit, and looking between my own parted thighs, the same. I wriggled closer to her, clasping her thighs with mine, and saw our love-juices mingle in the water. Miss Chytte gazed too.

'Oh,' she said, blushing prettily.

I took her hand and put it on my sex. The lips were quite red and swollen beneath the auburn hairs of my mink, which swayed and danced in the water like pretty sea flowers, while Miss Chytte's mons was shaven and gleamed bare like a rock.

'What a lovely water garden we make,' I said, as her fingers penetrated my slit. And then it was my turn to cry out in pleasure. My clit was stiff and tingling now, and I made her caress me there while I stroked her quivering belly through the wet fabric of the corset, which clung to her like a second skin. Teasingly, I gave her clitty little taps, making her moan and wriggle for more.

'Please kiss her, Mistress,' she whispered. 'Kiss my clit, all stiff for you.'

The water swirled around us as our bodies writhed gently.

'I should love to, Miss Chytte, but I should get my hair wet. You, on the other hand, have nothing to fear with your short, boyish coiffure, so you will please oblige me with your lips and tongue on my own nympha. I'm quite as wet as you, my dear, and my cunt longs for your mouth to caress her.'

My eager slave squirmed in our bath and positioned herself for this tender homage. While my hands rubbed her hard little teats, flicking the stiff nipples with sharp fingernails, she plunged her head below the water and I felt a delicious tonguing of my clit, as though I were being nibbled by a shoal of little fish. I placed a hand on her neck and pressed her to me, moaning in soft delight as her tongue darted in and out of my wet slit.

She wanted to come up for air and with a powerful squirm she burst from the water like a dolphin, her breasts heaving. I clasped her hard to me and fastened my mouth on her right teat, chewing the nipple with my teeth and rubbing my nose against her breast skin. At the same time I clamped my fingers on her swollen cunt, and frigged her stiff clit very vigorously, until her gasps had turned to sighs of pleasure.

But her caresses had brought me to my plateau, and I knew I must spend to turn the tingling of my every nerve end into the warm glow of orgasm.

'Again, Miss!' I commanded, and obediently she slipped her head beneath the foam. I clasped her head tightly against my quim and to encourage the impassioned flickering of her tongue, I got my toes to her own lady's place, and with a vigorous thrust, penetrated her oily slit. Groaning, she parted her thighs to ease my passage and my toes thrust vigorously in and out of her quim, my big toe slapping her clit at every stroke. Her tonguing redoubled in vigour and it was not long before the tickling in my belly became a fire, and I knew I must spend. I pressed her head tightly to my cunt, her mouth soft and wet against my sex-lips, and cried out as my body churned the water in my rush of pleasure.

At last, when my spasm had subsided into glowing happiness, I remembered to release Miss Chytte's head, and she came up, quite crimson from holding her breath.

'Please don't stop, Mistress,' she panted, clamping her thighs firmly against my foot so that it was sweetly trapped inside her. 'It is indescribable, it's so lovely. Oh fuck me with your little tickly toes, sweet Mistress!'

In the distance, the gong rang for dinner.

'There's no time for that,' I said cruelly. 'There is scarcely time to manicure your nails with an emery board so that you are presentable.'

I abruptly withdrew my foot from her sex and reached for a nailfile from the toilette table. Then, taking her hands, I began to rasp at her jagged nails. Still she moaned; I saw she rubbed her thighs together, hoping the friction on her clit would make her spend.

'Sit still, slut,' I said, 'or do you want me to tighten your corset?'

'I don't think it's possible,' she replied. 'It is so tight already, but awfully exciting in a strange way.'

'Sit still,' I said. 'My, you are a slut!'

In annoyance, I pressed the nailfile against her erect nipples and slid it roughly across them, as a reminder to behave. The effect was electric. Her mouth opened as if to scream, and she yelped loudly, closing her eyes tight and shaking her head vigorously. I ceased my rubbing, fearing I had hurt her, but she moaned, and pressed my hand to her trembling breasts, making me rub the nailfile across her bare nipples as hard as I could.

Suddenly her groans turned to a howl, and she convulsed in a breathless spend, her belly heaving under its cruel corset.

'Well!' I said, as I got out of the bath. 'I learn something new about you every day, Miss Chytte.'

She took hold of my fingers and kissed them, then got out of the bath and, dripping with water, pressed her lips to my feet. Taking my toes into her mouth, she sucked and tongued them until I was all ticklish again.

'And you will learn something new and gorgeous,' I continued rather brutally, 'when your lovely tight cunt feels the hot, stiff pricks of men fucking her.'

'Oh, Mistress,' she murmured shyly.

'Come, Miss Chytte! I know you had a rude experience in Cornwall. But I rescued you from your beastly seducer, the Rev. Turnpike, didn't I?'

She nodded.

'Here in London, you will learn to crave a man's naked body pressed to yours, his arms and lips on you, his hard manhood bathing your womb with his hot, creamy seed.'

'I ... I could come to like it, Mistress – if he would properly flay my bare bottom first!'

'Have no doubt of that,' I said, kissing her full on the mouth, and smiling. 'We are all St Agatha's girls now!'

The second gong rang.

'We must dress quickly, Miss,' I said. 'I expect you are

glad to be released from that wet corset. My! How it has shrunk, you poor thing, it must be agony.'

Her face fell.

'Mayn't I go corsed to dinner, Mistress?'

'Why, you will be dripping all over the dining room!' I laughed.

'But in the closet, I see there are others, dry ones. Mayn't I? Please?'

'You are indeed curious. Very well, then, but hurry.'

Her eyes lit up.

'Thank you, Mistress! Oh, look! That lovely pink one! It is just as handsome as this, so lacy and frilly – please let me wear it?'

'You may.'

She hurried to strip off the wet yellow corset, revealing vivid red strap marks on her flesh, and took the pink corset from the closet.

'You see?' she cried in delight, as she struggled to strap it on.

'It is quite lovely!'

'But even smaller than the yellow one,' I said, puzzled.

'Oh, yes, Mistress! It is adorable! It is far, far too small.'

3

Dinner at St Agatha's

My dinner table was alive with the gaiety that youthful vitality, the electricity of success and the finest wines can so wonderfully create. Freddie, resplendent in white tie and tails, looked so handsome that I wished he were sitting in my lap instead of at the end of the table, for I wanted him as my dinner! Around me sat Miss Chytte, Marlene and Deirdre, and the Izzards, all in their finery, eyes and lips shining as we toasted the good fortunes of St Agatha's.

I remembered Mme Izzard as my French mistress Mlle Gryphe, when it seemed she had been at St Agatha's since the crusades. She had been a shrewish spinster in the French mode, excessively rouged, hair in a tight bun, lips always puckered in a frown, and her prominent nose gave her a hawklike aspect. But since her marriage to Mr Izzard the pharmacist (which surprised everyone but me), she had blossomed into a veritable flower. Gone were the daubs of maquillage; her cheeks and eyes glowed with health, and her body seemed to possess a new, lissom softness. Men, of course, have cruder ways of explaining the beneficial effects of marriage on a female. Her husband, too, had taken on a pleasing rotundity, no doubt due to the sound cuisine of Aix-en-Provence, and it was charming to watch the two eye each other amorously as they sipped their wine at my dinner table. It was Saturday evening, and so our dinner could be more leisurely than usual.

'A fine body,' said Mr Izzard solemnly. 'Velvety, but with a hint of iron; a bouquet both flowery and severe; a vigorous growth, fruity but tough, with plenty of muscle in the right places. As we oenophiles say, plenty of hair round the bottom.' He nodded at Mme Izzard, who looked into her glass and nodded back. 'The wine is good too,' he added, and we all laughed, causing his wife to blush furiously. I looked at Mme Izzard, and was curious to know how hairy her bottom was! Sometimes the most unassuming ladies sport an astonishingly luxuriant mink. Mme Izzard was slim, with small, pretty breasts, but she had a large bottom and wide hips in sturdy peasant fashion, and I suspected that between her legs there grew a veritable jungle of curls. I wondered what she looked like naked. I had never thought of a teacher being naked before, but now that I saw her as a woman, I wanted to see her nude, and compare her body with mine. I also wondered how she and Mr Izzard looked when at amorous sport, now that I saw him as a man, not merely a pharmacist. In my profession, I have learned to keep dossiers on everyone I deal with, information being the same thing as power (my library of dossiers on my distinguished clientele would make a passable substitute for *Who's Who*), and while my dossier on Mme Izzard was very meagre, I had learned to my surprise that she was well the right side of forty.

Miss Chytte, lovely in pink taffeta over her tight corset, laughed delicately. Marlene and Deirdre hooted and slapped their thighs. Freddie looked perplexed. Tess paused in her service to frown, thinking we were mocking her, but a slap on the rump restored her to bovine locomotion.

'So Frenchie has a hairy minge,' said Marlene, *sotto voce*, although things said in her Glasgow accent tended to be more voce than sotto.

'Decorum, Marlene,' I murmured.

'Och, I'm just jealous Miss, for I've only a wee scrub of a mink myself, and I've had to spend a fortune on falsies from Mrs Danziger's shop on the Bethnal Green Road. Many of the gentlemen like a hairy girl, you see.'

'Falsies?'

'Rugs, you know, for your lady's place, Miss.'

'Good heavens,' I said.

'The thing to do,' added Deirdre, her mouth full of potage bonne femme, 'is to shave your mound bare – some gentlemen like it that way – then keep a choice of minks to suit the client. Curly ones, thick ones, coloured ones, or in funny shapes like butterflies.'

'Ah,' interrupted Mme Izzard, 'I do believe you are talking about *le vison d'amour*, the mink of love!'

'Well, we are among friends, Madame,' I replied. 'And I think we all know what business we are about here.'

'Why, in France we are not shocked by such things,' said Mme Izzard gaily. 'We gladly discuss, how do you say, pubic matters, over our dinner plates.'

In truth, I was not sure how much Mr Izzard had actually told his spouse about our plans. I knew that she admired his ingenious 'urogenital' appliances, but then the French are all obsessed by such things. I hoped to enlist her as one of our inner circle – mistresses to guide and instruct the chosen girls who would be our 'special' class. Enlivened by wine, I decided that now was perhaps the time to find out.

'Oh,' I said casually. 'Deirdre was telling me that gay girls, you know, have whole closets full of false minks for their lady's place, which they keep shaved. It seems this attracts gentlemen.'

'I have worn them myself,' chimed in Miss Chytte. 'Although normally I keep my mons quite bare.'

It was in fact Miss Chytte who had introduced me to the thrill of shaving my pubis, although at the time I had assumed it was a practice made necessary by the hygienic conditions prevailing in Cornwall.

'Ugh!' cried Tess, 'that is unnatural and cruel! Why shouldn't the poor little crabs have their own cosy home?'

'It itches, fool,' said Miss Chytte, her former mistress.

'Doesn't everybody itch?' said Tess, puzzled, as she retreated to fetch our main course.

'Tess is just jealous,' I said artfully, 'because she thinks she is being left out of our plans.'

'Plans? What plans?' cried Mme Izzard. 'I think something is on foot, Miss de Comynge. I am intrigued.'

'Mme Izzard doesn't need any wig down there,' said Mr Izzard proudly, 'for she has got the biggest –'

'Albert! You make me blush!' said his wife happily.

Tess returned with our main course. Maxence, my new Belgian chef, had done us well with a succulent filet mignon and pommes frites, which occupied our attention for some minutes, after which I remarked nonchalantly to Mme Izzard:

'I believe, Madame, that you administered a spanking to Miss Veronica Dove in front of the whole class.'

'Why, yes. But it did the lazy girl no good, so I sent her to you, Miss, for a more impressive chastisement.'

'You don't think it immodest to expose a girl's intimate apparel, and give her ten slaps on the bottom?'

'Ha! English modesty! The girl cannot even count, for it was twelve slaps! And I should never administer any punishment with which I myself was unfamiliar. Mr Izzard, I am glad to say,' she blushed most charmingly, 'is a strong believer in the virtues of wifely correction.'

'I say, Izzard,' blurted Freddie, goggle-eyed. 'D'you mean to say you spank your missus?'

'A vigorous stimulation of the gluteal nerve endings increases the affectionate propensities of a married lady towards her spouse,' said Mr Izzard scientifically.

'Super!' cried Freddie. 'On the bare bum, I hope?'

I tried not to laugh at his boyish enthusiasm.

'Of course!' replied Mme Izzard, her eyes twinkling. 'A spanking that is not on the bare flesh is like a kiss without a moustache.'

Freddie's fingers strayed unconsciously towards his hairless upper lip.

'As for modesty, Miss de Comynge,' she continued pointedly, 'I dare say you gave Miss Veronica her caning on the panties?'

'Why, no,' I said. 'Canings are given on the naked bottom.'

'Well now, that is severe.'

'Like you, Madame,' I said coolly, 'I should not administer a punishment with which I myself was unfamiliar.'

In the ensuing silence, all eyes were on me, and I knew it was time to broach the delicate matter of business to Mme Izzard.

'Madame,' I said. 'You are aware that I, ah, inherited St Agatha's from my predecessors Mr and Mrs Lowe. But there is slightly more to my story. You see, in Cornwall, I was in contact, for business purposes, with Mr Izzard. His services enabled me to offer . . . services of my own to the gentlemen of that place. In short,' – I took a deep breath – 'I was a –'

'Mr Izzard has told me everything,' said Mme Izzard, with an impish smile.

'In the interests of scientific verisimilitude, of course,' added Mr Izzard.

'Deirdre and Marlene,' I went on, 'are –'

'*Filles de joie*, also. I know.'

'Then you must know of our plans.'

'Miss de Comynge, I have been longing to be included. It is so exciting; it makes me feel young again. Oh, my gay days in Paris, after I was thrown out of that *saloperie* of a convent! So many handsome officers! I had my customary place – the best place in Paris! In the Rue St Denis, the very elegant doorway of Cornichon the bidet merchant. I would be clad all in black; silks, lace and leather, and I would flick my crop in the air, and click my spiky silver toecaps at the hussars and dragoons in their fine uniforms.'

'Gosh!' said Freddie. Miss Chytte looked at Mme Izzard with new interest, while Deirdre and Marlene grinned knowingly.

'And Mr Izzard was aware of your past, Madame?' I said politely.

'Aware, and scientifically fascinated, Miss!' said Mr Izzard proudly.

Tess shuffled in with the dessert trolley, coffee, and liqueurs.

'Well, then,' I said, helping myself to profiteroles with cream, 'I suppose we should get down to business.'

St Agatha's was – is – a monument to centuries of English art and practical ingenuity. She contains bits of almost every style and every period, skilfully woven into a fabric of timber, brick and stone whose aspect impresses the eye and whose intricate whimsy impresses the mind. The oak-panelled dining room in which we sat was evidence of a past not to be tampered with lightly. The refurbishments I had in mind – the provision of private rooms and bathing chambers for the pursuit of pleasures no less antique than St Agatha's – would fit nicely into the labyrinth of halls, corridors, bedrooms and secret staircases which the founders had thoughtfully bequeathed to us. At our convivial table, we discussed these and other matters: the need to attract the right sort of girl, and indeed the right sort of parent, who expected their offspring to receive sturdy English discipline, and who would, in time, be eager to pay for sturdy English discipline for themselves. I emphasised the importance of discreet publicity, word of mouth and well-placed social contacts (I mentioned the plans I had to use Major Dove in this respect).

'What about a handsome brochure?' chirped Freddie. 'You know, printed on thick cream parchment, with lots of tasteful lithographs, historical language and suchlike. That would be topping!'

'But just a little vulgar, Freddie,' I replied. 'We do not wish to tout for business; rather the opposite. Our product, you see, depends on its exclusivity.'

'Eh?'

'There are certain things that everyone wants because not everyone can get them.' I mentioned the name of a famous gunsmith in Bond Street. 'You must wait five years for the privilege of paying two hundred guineas for a pair of shotguns, and their order books are full into the next century! And look at the gentlemen's clubs of St James'. It is almost impossible to beg or bribe your way in, and for that reason, men will make utter fools of themselves to do so! The more inaccessible, dangerous or expensive something is, the more desperate people are to have it.'

At that moment, Tess appeared, holding a bundle of fresh newspapers, which she handed to me.

'This came by messenger, Miss, for Mr Izzard's attention, from the office of the Sunday . . . the Sunday Intenser.'

'Well, give them to him, Tess,' I said.

'Tomorrow's Sunday Intelligencer,' cried Mr Izzard, gleefully. 'Hand them round the company, please, Tess. I think what we want will be on page three.'

We all turned to page three, and read:

NO MERCY FOR SLACKERS AT COLD COMFORT COLLEGE
By N. B. Izzard, Court and Social Correspondent

Through tears of shame, beautiful heiress Lucinda Charmley-Boddis expressed her heartfelt regret at the disgrace to her family (the Berkshire Charmley-Boddises), caused by her sudden expulsion from the elite St Agatha's Academy for Young Ladies, in Wimbledon, Southwest London. She complained, however, of disciplinary practices draconian even by the standards of the sternest military academy, of cold showers, unrelenting pressure to achieve scholastic excellence, and a regime of severe corporal chastisement, frequently administered to the unclothed body, as the punishment for the slightest infraction of discipline.

'After frequently subjecting me to the most painful canings, the Governess, Miss de Comynge, finally said that my moral fibre proved impossible to stiffen, and that I was not fit to be a St Agatha's girl.'

Unable to gain entrance to the jealously-guarded privacy of St Agatha's, our reporter managed to contact Miss de Comynge by telephone (the number, obtained with great difficulty, is Wimbledon 11), but she refused to comment on the distressing case of Miss Charmley-Boddis.

'St Agatha's trains girls to be unmatched in charm, intelligence, and social grace. We believe in the efficacy of strict discipline and corporal punishment to achieve this aim, and any girl not up to scratch must leave.'

Asked if parents willingly paid fees which are alleged to be ten times those of Eton or Harrow for such an education for their girls, Miss de Comynge replied:

'Excellence costs money. St Agatha's is one of the most exclusive finishing schools in Europe, and our waiting list is full. As for what you call our regime, St Agatha's girls are proud of being special.'

Invited to deny the accusation that St Agatha's girls were flogged on their naked posteriors, Miss de Comynge actually laughed, and said:

'Why should I deny what is true? I told you, St Agatha's

girls are proud of being special', upon which she discontinued our telephonic interview.

'Splendid work, Mr Izzard,' I exclaimed, as the others read with puzzled frowns.

'Yes, that should do the trick. Good old Nobby – that's my cousin, N. B. Izzard,' he explained.

'You have talked to these people?' said Miss Chytte.

'Of course not. I have anticipated matters a little, to give you a surprise.'

'I don't remember any Lucinda Charmley-Boddis,' said Deirdre.

'That's because there isn't one,' I replied.

'You mean it's all tosh?' cried Freddie.

'It is called marketing, Freddie. Who needs brochures, when the newspapers are so obliging?'

'But it makes St Agatha's sound like a dungeon!'

'Correction, Freddie. It makes St Agatha's sound like a wildly expensive dungeon. Just wait,' I licked my lips. 'By tomorrow lunchtime, a place at St Agatha's will be more sought after than an invitation to the Royal Box at Ascot. As Mr P. T. Barnum put it in his colourful American idiom, "There ain't no such thing as bad publicity."' I touched my lips, and blew a kiss at my boy, and he blushed sweetly. 'Marketing, Freddie,' I said.

After the company had departed, I found myself excited and unable to sleep, so I decided to take the night air. I wrapped myself in my sable coat, and let myself quietly out of Headmistress's House – I was still unused to thinking of it as my house – into the walled flower garden, beyond which a path led through the woods to the snow-clad common. The garden was pretty with snowdrops, the air was crisp and still, and a bright moon gleamed on the shroud of snow that stretched north to Putney Heath. In the clear air, I could easily make out the ramparts of 'Caesar's Camp,' and the stark silhouettes of Shadwell Wood and Lady Jane's Wood. All was magically still, and I felt a powerful urge to throw off my clothing and dance under the moon, as I had when studying in this same place. But

35

now I was Governess, and had to mind my decorum! So I lit a Turkish cigarette instead.

It was then that I noticed some curious tracks on the snow, like footprints, but jumbled, as though their owner had been pirouetting, and barefoot. I followed the tracks, with the snow crunching like seashells under my boots, to Lady Jane's Wood, where they disappeared into clumps of bracken. I thought of some wild animal, a faun, or (my imagination running riot) a satyr, as in the Greek legends, and suddenly I was startled by a glowing pair of eyes which stared at me from the dark wood.

They were brown eyes, no less startled than my own, for they at once disappeared and I heard a crashing of branches as the beast stumbled away from me, perhaps frightened by the glow of my cigarette. I quickened my pace, and entered the wood. The trees were sparse at the edge, but thickened into a dense clump at the centre, and towards this clump the beast was scampering. There was a gap in the forest, a glade lit by the harsh moon, through which he was obliged to pass, and there I saw him. He stopped at a distance of fifty yards or so, and turned to face me.

It was a young chap. He was tall and slender, with a mane of unruly russet hair over a golden skin, and he was nude. His frightened eyes flashed warily in the moonlight. I could see his body quiver as he panted from his exertion, and, at his waist, russet curls framed the long branch of his manhood which, under my gaze, trembled and stiffened slightly, thrilling me with power. To my surprise, I saw he had white snowdrops set in his hair, and petals peeped too from his thick mink, where he had braided them prettily into his pubic bush. He stared at me as if mesmerised, until his penis had risen to full, gorgeous height, gleaming in the moonlight like a shaft of ice. And then he smiled, a lovely smile that was shy and yet at once arrogant, the smile of an erect male animal. We stood still, each strangely in the power of the other's gaze. At last, I made a move towards him, breaking the spell. In an instant he was gone, leaping south towards the village.

Naturally, I was annoyed at this invasion of my territory, and also curious to see more of that lithe young body, the pretty coltish bottom he had shown me as he scampered, and the cock which had thrillingly risen for me. I lit another cigarette with trembling fingers, and set off back to my house. Entering the garden, I noticed for the first time that the snow was disturbed there, too, and there was an empty swathe where my snowdrops had been plucked. Now I felt less sleepy than ever. I hurried to my chamber, and quickly undressed, and when I was naked between my silken sheets, I tugged the bell pull that would ring in the room at the far end of my house, which was Freddie's room.

When Freddie arrived, prompt and excited, I sat up in bed and allowed the bedcovers to slip nonchalantly down, revealing my bared breasts. I said nothing, but nodded to him, and he lost no time in removing his nightshirt. He stood before me wearing nothing but his leather restrainer, with my silken panties over it, and I could see from his flushed expression that his penis was already straining against its confining pouch. I ordered him to come to me and bend over. It was my custom to oblige him, on occasions, to wear his restrainer and, as a treat, I let him wear my panties as well. This practice had started at Rakeslit Hall as my method of disciplining his rampant youthful ardour – that is, the tendency of his cock to spend most of the day in a state of excitement – and I thought it even more necessary now that he was the Chamberlain of an establishment richly scented with the fresh bodies of women.

I unfastened the straps from his waist and balls and the 'disciplinary tongue' slid easily from his tight anus, where, Mr Izzard assured me, it had a wonderfully controlling effect on wayward impulses. I myself found that wearing such a device fuelled, rather than dampened my erotic ardour, but I supposed boys to be different. In any case, his cock sprang at once to a splendid stiffness when I had released him from his prison.

'I haven't visited you in ages, Mistress,' he moaned as he knelt by my bed and laid his lips reverently on my naked breast.

'Two days, you rampant, silly goose,' I said. 'Now stop saying your prayers and get into bed with me.'

He obeyed, and soon we were locked in a tight embrace, my thigh between his, firmly stroking his balls, and his stiff cock tickling my bellybutton. I caressed his lovely bottom, my fingers rubbing on his cleft and his trembling little anus bud, which I teased by putting a fingernail slightly inside, making him sigh and wriggle. His powerful chest crushed my breasts, making me giddy and my sex hot and wet. And as our lips pressed in a sucking kiss, I darted my tongue against his. My sex was so wet that I wanted him to enter me without further ado, and I parted my thighs; my quim nuzzling his balls so that he would take the hint and poke me at once, but instead he drew away and looked down at me with soft eyes.

'You smell so lovely, Mistress,' he said. 'You have bathed.'

'Well, of course I've bathed, you chump. Hurry, and fuck me with that big hard cock of yours – my cunt hasn't tasted him for two whole days, and she is thirsty for his cream!'

'You have bathed with Miss Chytte. I smelled her, and you have the same perfume.'

'You are very impudent,' I said softly.

'I am impudent, Mistress,' he said, and turned over to lie across my thighs. I clasped his balls, holding them tightly, and then began to spank him. I spanked his naked buttocks until they blushed a fiery red. I could feel him quiver, his stiff cock bucking at every blow to his bottom. When I saw the first droplet of spend appear shyly at his pee-hole, I squirmed to be underneath him and, still slapping his jerking bum, I squeezed his balls between my breasts, while my mouth closed on his swollen bulb and gently sucked him until the hot spend spurted over my lips and tongue. When his moans had faded to a whimper, I kissed his mouth with my glistening wet lips and tickled his balls, as though to thank them for their gift. My own sex was flowing with love-juice, longing to feel his cock inside me, and I knew that Freddie would not stay long in a flaccid state.

I kept tickling and kissing and stroking, and his cock never became limp at all, but was soon standing erect and proud once more.

'You certainly need your restrainer,' I murmured. 'All these girls to excite you ...'

'Only you excite me, Mistress,' he said fiercely as I stroked his hot buttocks. I clasped his head to my breasts.

'I excite Miss Chytte too, you know. She is my friend, and we like to bathe together.'

'Am I not your friend?'

'You are more. You are my slave.'

'As is Miss Chytte.'

I held Freddie by the shoulders and looked at him intently.

'Do you want to fuck Miss Chytte, Freddie? We could be three in a bed – I should like that. You have the power of a stallion; imagine loving us both, time after time.'

'If it would give you pleasure, Mistress.'

'Don't be coy! Remember when you went with Marlene, in Praed Street? That certainly gave you pleasure.'

'Because you had ordered it, Mistress. Anyway, Miss Chytte is Sapphic. I think she would find a man's caress unwelcome.'

'Oh, you are jealous, is that it? Is your silly male vanity wounded? Well, my buck, I don't care for your vanity, I care for this hard cock of yours and nothing else!'

Without more ado I climbed onto the boy and straddled him, then plunged his penis right to the hilt into my swimming love-slit, and rode him like the stallion he was; bucking and squeezing his rigid penis so that my belly shuddered with spasms of tingling pleasure. I rubbed my clit against his glistening shaft, feeling his little downy hairs tickle her. Joyfully, my bottom squirmed on his manhood until we were both at the plateau of climax. I could tell by his moans and gasps, and the shivering of his cock, that his sperm was longing to bathe my womb, so, almost at the last moment, I slackened the pressure of my muscle and raised my buttocks a couple of inches from his thighs. Then I took his penis at its base between my thumb and forefinger and squeezed hard, checking his ardour.

When I sensed that he was calm, I rode higher on his prick and positioned my sex right at the tip and then began to rock back and forth so that my engorged, heavy lips lapped against his swollen bulb, teasing him to a frenzy. His ardour was so great that he was ready for anything. Deftly, I rose from his prone body, with a little plop as my cunt kissed his cock goodbye, and moved up, turning smartly around, to squat on his face. The whole weight of my body rested on his head, with his mouth pressed quite ruthlessly against my wet quim, and his nose deliciously tickling my anus. He needed no prompting; I heard myself squeal at the strokes of shivering pleasure from his tonguing on my hard nympha.

At the same time he rubbed his nose against my anus, which filled my belly with a delicious tickling warmth, and I squirmed against his face with a slow, heavy writhing of my hips. I drew up my legs and clutched my shins, so that my feet were off the bed, and thus his face bore the entire weight of my body. He clutched my buttocks, scratching them hard with his fingernails, and tried to draw me even more heavily down on him as his sweet tongue wriggled inside my slippery wet cunt. I shut my eyes as I felt my climax draw closer, and thought of Freddie with flowers in his hair, as I had once adorned him in Cornwall, on the morning we went to the wood to collect twigs for the birch with which I was to flog him. But now, in my fantasy, the flowers in his hair were snowdrops.

Opening my eyes, I saw his cock standing so stiff and shiny wet from my love-juice, that I had to take him in my mouth. I lowered my knees back onto the bed, and bent all the way forward, which had the effect of raising my sex slightly from his mouth. This gave him space to fuck me in my slit with his darting tongue, which he held as firm as any prick. I grasped his tight balls and directed the shaft of his cock towards my own lips, then, with a swift gulping motion, I thrust the massive hot pole right to the back of my throat, and began to suck with short pumping motions as my head bobbed over him.

Freddie cried out, and his loins began to jerk and buck

as he fucked my mouth, his foreskin sliding back and forth against my tongue and palate.

'Oh, Mistress,' he sobbed, and pulled my hips hard down onto his face again, smothering my cunt with kisses as though her lips were the lips of my face. My own loins were jerking now to his rhythm, and the tingling of my clitty felt like strokes of lightning fusing through my whole body. I was on fire; gasping, I rose to straddle him once more, and this time I turned so that his glans was pressing against my anus bud. I squatted firmly astride his hips, and placed his hands, one on each of my buttocks. His strong fingers forced my cheeks to spread wide, stretching the tender skin between cunt and anus and I lowered myself onto his prick, squirming at his painful entry into my unwilling folds of arse-skin. I wriggled and he thrust, inch by inch, until my tender anus gave way to his pressure and with a lovely thrust, as though unlocking a secret door, his cock slid all the way inside my intimate passage.

Now I leant forward again, this time to kiss him on his lips, my arms around his broad, muscled back, as his loins pumped his cock in and out of my writhing arse. I shuddered with pleasure as he fucked me slowly, drawing his shaft all the way out to the wrinkled bud before thrusting in anew, so that each sweet penetration seemed like the first. With my sphincter, I squeezed his cock, milking him, and then I placed his palm on my swollen clit and with his four fingers in deep caress of my soaking quim, he frigged me there until I could no longer hold off my spend, and allowed the spasm to overwhelm me. The sweet fullness of my nether hole and the surge of tingling electric pleasure from my tickled clit made me cry out like an animal! As I spent so gloriously, my anus squeezed Freddie's cock with all her strength, my buttocks slapping his thighs, until to add to my pleasure I felt his hot spurt of sperm inside my intimate place. Panting, and soaked in fragrant sweat, we lay back in each other's arms.

'It was lovely to ... you know, to do it – that way,' said Freddie after we had snuggled for a while.

'Heavens, why so coy, Freddie?' I laughed. 'You mean you like to fuck in the bumhole, with the lady on top.'

'With you on top, yes, Mistress. To feel the weight of you on me, and to kiss your mouth as you spend. You are so heavenly! It must be lovely to be a girl, and take such pleasure.'

'It is lovely to give you pleasure, Freddie. My sweet, you are the manliest buck in the world!'

'Sometimes I wonder what it must be like to be a lady, so smooth and smelling so sweet – to be like you, Mistress.'

'Do you want that? Remember when I made you a girl once, in Cornwall – when I fucked you in the bumhole with one of Miss Chytte's clever toys?'

'Yes, Mistress. God, it was lovely.'

'I shall do it again. The next time you deserve a whipping.'

'Thank you, Mistress,' he murmured.

'You could be a girl, in a sort of way,' I mused. 'You could be my maid. I could bathe you and scent you, and shave your whole body smooth like mine: your legs and bum, of course, and your prick and balls too. I could dress you in petticoats and silk stockings, a garter belt and straps, perhaps a nice tight corset, and my frilliest panties, and you could serve me. Would you like that?'

I suppose my tone was slightly mocking, for he replied:

'You are teasing me, Mistress.'

'Not at all,' I said.

'Then I should like that.'

I kept Freddie with me that night, for I wanted my man beside me. I dreamed a strange dream, that Freddie and I were naked in the snow, in the moonlight, and he was fucking me. His muscles shone with sweat as he bucked. So hot was he that I felt no cold, and the snow melted around me, lapping my bare buttocks with a bath of hot water. Freddie's hair was snowdrops, and his penis was a giant oak tree, with a bouquet of green leaves for his mink. But the face was not Freddie's face: it was the face of the young man I had seen in Lady Jane's Wood.

4

Swish

Sunday was a quiet day at St Agatha's, with many girls fetched by their parents for a day's exeat; the others, after church at St Fiacre's in Calonne Road, would amuse themselves as they pleased. That Sunday I proposed to visit Miss Chytte in the house I rented for her at 323 Worple Road, down Wimbledon Hill from the village, and perhaps take a glass of sherry wine and a biscuit with her.

After breakfast, I despatched Freddie to do muddy things at his beloved stables, afterwards no doubt to mingle with the whip and saddle set, for manly pints of beer at the Dog and Fox. I blew him a kiss as he set off, and smiled, for my bottom still glowed with the fiery effects of his buggery the night before. How I love to take a man in my arse! It makes me feel so naked and beastly; so wonderfully used. And the sensation of a powerful cock sliding ruthlessly in and out of that tight passage makes me quite breathless with joy.

I went to my study to fetch my gloves for my walk, and suddenly the telephone rang. I picked up the receiver, and the mellow South African lilt of Dotti van de Ven (I made the girls take turns at switchboard duty) informed me that there was a Mr Bozer on the line, calling from Eaton Place.

'I do not know any such person,' I said, puzzled, and a trifle apprehensive, for it was always possible that Mr and Mrs Lowe, having been justly displaced from their fraudulent ownership of St Agatha's, would try some chicanery to harm me.

'He says it is about his daughter,' said Dotti.

'Ah,' I said, remembering N. B. Izzard's piece in the Intelligencer. 'I will speak to him.'

'Hello!' barked a voice somewhat nervously. 'Can you hear me with this strange contraption?'

'Yes,' I said in my frostiest voice. 'Miss de Comynge speaking. How may I help you, sir?'

'Bozer here. You've heard of me, of course. Godfrey Bozer, of the Wiltshire Bozers.'

There was a crackling pause.

'Yes, Mr Bozer?' I said.

'It is about my girl Emily. Dashed annoying business – had to come up to town – hate the place, really, I'm one of the Wiltshire Bozers, don't you know. And so is Emily. She prefers the country, too, that is, er . . .'

'Wiltshire?'

'In a nutshell. Good. We understand each other. I'll bring the girl round straight away, and I hope you can knock more sense into her than her last place. She needs plenty of the crop, take my word for it.'

'Sir, there is a misunderstanding. I am unfamiliar with your family – you must know that the waiting list for St Agatha's is full.'

'The thing is, Ma'am –'

'Miss.'

'Well, Miss, one of the servants left this tuppenny paper lying around, and I happened to see the piece about the Charmley-Boddis girl. I know her, of course – rum do altogether for the family – but what girls need is discipline; and none more so than my Emily. I've had to take her away from Dodd's Academy in Holland Park, because they were afraid to give her the strap, d'you see?'

'Mr Bozer,' I interrupted, 'I am afraid I am unfamiliar with your family, whether in Wiltshire or elsewhere. How do you spell the name?'

'Why, B-E-A-U-S-I-R-E, of course. Came over with the Conqueror.'

Now I recollected that there was a Beausire family who were reputed to own gold mines in Australia, cattle ranches in Canada, railways in Argentina, as well as large portions of said Wiltshire.

'Oh, those Beausires,' I said. 'How old is Emily, sir?'

'Just seventeen. A firebrand, takes after her late mama, who fell off her nag at a rodeo in Texas. Rotten luck.'

'I am so sorry. Well, there might just be a place in the lower form for Emily. But I want to point out that the article, however scurrilous, was factual in this: we are strict, we are exclusive, and we are very, very expensive. Before we accept Emily, we must interview both the girl and the parent. Today is quite out of the question; therefore I shall expect you at our open day, the Wednesday of next week. A cheque for a hundred and fifty guineas, as your deposit, will have cleared by then. If she is accepted, the sum will be credited to the cost of the first term. I am afraid it is not refundable should our standards fail to be met.'

'I say! There's style for you!'

'I must advise you, Mr Beausire, that the severity of our discipline is legendary.'

'Plenty of the rod, Miss! That is the way we Beausires are brought up!'

'And that not only must parents consent to our disciplinary methods, they must approve of them as well. We hold that children take after their parents' example, sir, and vice versa. An erring daughter indicates an erring father, and both require correction.'

When he spoke again after a pause, his voice was softer and curious.

'I'm not quite sure I follow.'

'I think you do, Mr Beausire.'

'You mean, if Emily cuts up, it's sort of my fault too?'

'There is a special tariff for extracurricular discipline.'

'Why,' he laughed nervously, 'you make it sound as though you'd thrash me as well! And make me pay for it!'

'It does sound like that, doesn't it?' I said drily. I paused to let the import of my words sink in, and heard him breathing heavily.

'So I think you know what to expect. When I receive your cheque by first post tomorrow, I shall send you confirmation of your visit to our open day. And remember to be punctual; bad timekeeping carries a most uncomfortable penalty here at St Agatha's.'

'You shall have my cheque, Miss!' he cried eagerly, like

a small boy. 'And I'll try not to be late, honestly I will, for I would hate to earn a thrashing!'

'Would you?' I said.

After that, the telephone did not stop ringing. The same conversation, with slight variations, was repeated two dozen times or more. By lunchtime I had 'bagged' a fine selection of fathers most concerned for their daughters' good behaviour, and eager to guarantee it with their own persons. All of them were wealthy, learned or noble, and both Houses of Parliament were well represented (mostly by the Conservative interest). Curiously, all the callers had in common the extraordinary carelessness of their servants, who seemed to leave scurrilous newspapers all over the place. All in all, a morning's work on Mr Bell's wonderful invention, the telephone, had netted me enough to buy a Daimler automobile, or pay the stipends of twenty vicars!

There had been a fresh fall of snow during the night, and the dazzling whiteness under an icy blue sky gave Wimbledon the aspect of a fairyland. I took my thick fur hat and mittens, and a knobkerrie walking stick which I swung gaily as I walked through the village. Mr Izzard's shop had its familiar window full of ingenious appliances. On the corner, at the Dog and Fox, I spied Freddie at ale with the suburban classes, deep in horsy conversation and surrounded by dung and straw and similar homely items. As I looked at his boyish face I suddenly felt all happy and melting.

As I went down Wimbledon Hill, I noticed for the first time a rusty old gateway, half off its hinges, in the middle of an unkempt hedge and overhung by branches. There was no driveway, just a worn track between the trees and, in the near distance, the outline of a large house: a ramshackle affair of not more than three storeys which spread over the hillside as though it had grown there like moss. One of the charms of Wimbledon, indeed of London in general, is the constant discovery of the unexpected, even in a place one knows well. The leafy hills and byways of Wimbledon are a charming labyrinth.

I peered at the house, and saw no sign of life. Then I saw a rough board nailed askew to a tree and covered with snow. I brushed off the snow with my stick, and read in faded gold letters:

ST ALCUIN'S ACADEMY
AD MDCXII

Another institution, so close by, and of which I had not even heard! I resolved to investigate, not least because I was curious to know their acreage. By St Alcuin's situation, it seemed that they owned the dank forest which brooded on the far side of our own trim lawns, and if the establishment was as decrepit as it looked, or had fallen into total disuse, then a knockdown price might buy some expansion of my own demesne.

I proceeded down to Worple Road, and was soon sitting before a roaring fire in the drawing room, sipping a glass of chilled fino sherry. Miss Chytte was all smiles that I had graced her with a visit, for, although I kept a room for myself at 323 just in case, as there was a room for Miss Chytte at St Agatha's, I tended to stay at Headmistress's House, where I had Freddie's services on call. Miss Chytte knew this and pretended not to mind.

'And how is Freddie?' she asked jovially.

'You saw him at dinner last night, Miss. Do you really mean, what happened in my bedroom after dinner?'

'Oh, no. Mistress, I didn't mean –'

'Well, I shall tell you anyway.' And I did, in loving detail. As I described my embraces with Freddie, I saw her blush and frown and fidget, crossing and uncrossing her legs.

'Why, you are all red, Miss Chytte. So the naked embraces of a man and a woman excite you! I believe you are not as Sapphic as you think.'

I then proceeded to tell her about my morning's profitable work. 'Just think, Miss Chytte! Men – rich, charming, virile – a source of pleasure and enrichment for all of us, demanding neither commitment nor responsibility! Men who shall pay to be your slave as you are mine! Wouldn't you like to exercise your corrective skills on an array of gentlemen's bottoms?'

'To whip men ... to make them squirm? Yes, it might be rather exciting.'

'And afterwards, when a man's cock is well stiffened, to take him inside you! To feel his hot prick stabbing so sweetly in your belly, as you buck and moan? Your sex wet with desire! It is the best pleasure in the world, Miss Chytte. The second best being the purse of gold sovereigns he will present to you in appreciation of your charms. Your womanly charms, Miss Chytte.'

'Oh,' she said. Then: 'You will stay to luncheon?'

'At such short notice?'

'Why, Verity, you know, the new maid I took, can make us a beefsteak and a nice salad, with a bottle of burgundy. And there is some trifle for pudding. She's an expert. London girls have to be versatile, unlike dear Cornish Tess, whom you have seduced away from me!'

I responded to her playful accusation:

'Tess amuses me, but you have probably got the better bargain. I'll stay, with pleasure.'

I was curious about this Verity. The girl duly appeared, curtseyed to me nicely, and took her orders. She was a pretty little cockney, with pertly jutting breasts and a bottom that looked ... energetic. She smiled sweetly showing surprisingly white teeth, and went off to make our luncheon.

'A nice girl,' I said. 'How much are you – are we – paying her?'

'Seven shillings a week, all found. I got her from the agency in the village.'

'Hmmm,' I said slyly. 'She must be worth it, then. I take it you have already put her through her paces?'

Miss Chytte reddened.

'Come, Miss, you know I am not jealous. But I'm insatiably curious. Have you diddled her?'

'I may have done, once or twice.'

'May have done!' I laughed. 'She was willing, then.'

Miss Chytte smiled shyly.

'I was quite satisfied,' she said.

'Tell me, then, have you had occasion to discipline her?'

'Quite frequently, as it happens,' she replied coquettishly.

'Now it is I who am jealous. Does she take it bare bottom?'

'Skirts over her head, Mistress, and buttocks naked, begging for the cane. And not a squeak out of her, more's the pity.'

'That is excellent,' I said, and proceeded to tell her of my newly-hatched plan for St Agatha's open day, when prospective parents would have a grand tour of our establishment, to be shown the workings in their entirety.

'That means everything, Miss Chytte,' I said.

'You mean, including . . . ?'

'Especially that.'

When our meal was over, and Verity had served our coffee, I stretched lazily and said that it was always difficult to find ways of passing the long Sunday afternoons.

'Well, Mistress, I can make a suggestion, but I think you know what it is. The flogging stool is dusted and polished, and my bottom is already bare for you.'

'You are a lustful minx, Miss Chytte,' I replied. 'I suppose it will be instructive to punish you, and I'll get an appetite for my tea.'

Her eyes sparkled.

'I'll send Verity out on an errand.'

'No, I mean it will be instructive for Verity to watch as I lace you, Miss Chytte. Won't it?'

'Yes, Mistress,' she said, and happily began to lift up her skirts.

On Sunday evening, the snow began to melt into slush, which was washed away by gloomy bouts of rain. That night I sat in my darkened study and watched for my naked young faun to appear on his strange errand, and was irritated that he did not. Nevertheless the demanding work of running an institution such as St Agatha's and supervising its complex population had to go on, and I have never shirked hard work. But each night, when all was still, I kept my lonely, fruitless vigil. On Wednesday, I held an intimate staff meeting to explain my plans for the open day a week thence, and also to outline my little scheme for organising the real business of St Agatha's: creating a 'school within a school', as it were.

'All elite establishments,' I explained, 'have elite societies within them. At Eton, there is a society called "Pop". Here at St Agatha's, we shall start our own elite, composed of girls sympathetic to our aims, and eager to participate in them.'

'Gay girls, you mean,' said Marlene.

'In a word, yes. I need your suggestions; the candidates must be from the upper level, and by now you should have some idea of which ones have the right outgoing personalities. I, for example, have hopes of Veronica Dove, whom I had occasion to cane only last Saturday. And – this is, of course, amongst ourselves – young Tess cheeked her, and annoyed me so much that I was obliged to give her a lacing there and then. Only I permitted Veronica to wield the lash as she was the one who had been insulted. The girl beat Tess as though it was her very vocation!'

'Mmm . . .' murmured Miss Chytte.

'Now I have noticed her set of friends are all handsome girls with, I think, great potential for, ah, gaiety. Girls like Phoebe Ford-Taylor or Amanda Nightingale.'

The others joined in enthusiastically.

'Prudence Proudfoot?' said Mme Izzard.

'That American girl, Connie Sunday?' said Miss Chytte.

'Florence Bages, certainly.'

'How about Vanessa Lumsden? And Dotti van de Ven, the beautiful Boer.'

'Imogen Gandy is rather nice,' said Freddie, and promptly blushed.

'There is Jane Ruttle, I suppose,' said Deirdre.

'I find her a little too reserved; there's something funny about her,' said Miss Chytte. 'Although she seems wholesome enough.'

'She is not religious?'

'Oh, no. C of E like the rest of us – no offence intended, Mme Izzard.'

'Well, leave a question mark by her,' I concluded. 'The main thing for all of us is to ease these selected girls gradually towards our way of thinking, so that when the opportunity for lustful pleasure presents itself, the initiative to take it must come from them! There will be social events at the Academy; gentlemen will visit, and it may be that suggestions of friendship will be made, or perhaps confessions of naughtiness to a trusted lady; naughtiness which she will feel obliged to punish, according to our tariff. Perhaps it will be she who makes the suggestions; our task is to create an atmosphere of luxury, an appreciation of the finer points of physical chastisement, so that our pupils will come to share the appetites of their mistresses.'

'Then it would be logical to test all of them as you have tested Veronica,' said Miss Chytte.

'Agreed. You are all empowered to cane, so I suggest you find reasons to punish, and see how they take it. Most important, if they are keen to give it to others.'

'Well, Miss,' said Deirdre. 'Chastisement is no great shakes, I mean every girl's had a lacing or two, but what about more delicate matters?'

'She means poking,' said Marlene helpfully.

'I think we know that,' I said. 'Surely they all study biology? And Mme Izzard's rather daring French textbook of my own authorship is clearly an aid to lustful thinking.'

'It is all book-learning, though,' said Deirdre. 'They need a practical demonstration.'

'A splendid idea!' I cried. 'We will have nature study, in the raw! You, Miss Chytte, will organise a nature ramble, and take a party of girls to the woods near the southern fence, where that unkempt forest grows outside our land. There is a little summerhouse there; you will take a picnic lunch; yes, it shall be a lovely day out.'

'But I know nothing of nature,' she protested. 'I come from Croydon.'

'Nonsense, Miss, you have lived in Cornwall, which is

full of the stuff. Why, after these rains, there will be all sorts of things to see: mice and voles and snails, and whatnot.'

'We can eat them!' said Mme Izzard.

'And grass snakes,' I said. 'Very English, grass snakes. It is most important to know about grass snakes.'

'Will they be poking?' asked Marlene, puzzled.

'Probably not, but it doesn't matter.'

I smiled.

'You see, when Miss Chytte arrives at the summerhouse for the girls' picnic, it will not be unoccupied, and the girls will be entertained to an instructive little spectacle. Their reactions to it will be most illuminating.'

I signalled that the meeting was over and crooked a finger at Freddie, ordering him to stay.

'By the way,' I said, before they left, 'there is the question of a name for our elite group of girls.'

'Ah!' exclaimed Mme Izzard. 'I suggest something with the French glamour – "Le Cul En Rose", perhaps?'

'Lovely, Madame, but we are an English establishment, I'm afraid. I have thought of a name. Eton has its "Pop", so St Agatha's shall have something equally elegant: we shall call them "Swish"!'

My decision was greeted with enthusiasm, and when we were alone, I explained to Freddie what he was to do in the summerhouse.

'Snakes! How absolutely horrid!' cried Vanessa Lumsden.

'Ugh!' agreed Florence Bages.

'They are English snakes, girls,' I said.

'And voles! Pooh!' declared Phoebe Ford-Taylor.

'What is a vole?' asked Connie Sunday in her soft American drawl. 'Is it like a skunk?'

'It's nasty, anyway,' pouted Imogen Gandy. 'And snails!'

'Ugh!' chorussed all the girls at once.

'You will jolly well enjoy yourselves, girls,' I said firmly. 'Anyone not enjoying herself will be thrashed. Got it?'

'Yes, Miss.'

'Very well. After morning coffee, you'll meet Miss Chytte in the vestibule. And don't forget to wrap up well and wear your rain-boots, for though it's a lovely day, it is still cold and damp. And after your instructive nature ramble, you'll have a picnic in the summerhouse, with lots of cakes and clotted cream as a Saturday treat!'

Mollified by my last phrase, the girls chattered excitedly, making sniffy comments about the 'drippy wets' who had not been chosen to go. I smiled, sensing the esprit de corps of 'Swish' already in the making. They were gleeful as I watched them march off at the appointed time behind Miss Chytte, who, ever fond of dressing up, was accoutred with sun hat, net, binoculars and jam jars, while the muscular Dotti van de Ven was entrusted with the all-important picnic hamper. I watched as they traipsed into the shrubbery, where their investigatory path should bring them to the summerhouse in an hour and a half, when the sun was high.

I then returned to my study and summoned Freddie. He arrived promptly, rather gorgeous in grey frock coat and pinstripe trousers, with a red silk cravat and gleaming white spats.

'You look sublime, Freddie,' I exclaimed, but spats! They will get all muddy.'

'Mistress?'

I had forgotten that muddiness, to Freddie, was a desirable state of affairs.

'Never mind. You have money?'

'Yes. But, Mistress, I am so nervous!'

'Come, Freddie, you know you had a "pash" for Tess back in Cornwall.'

'That is why I am nervous.'

Agitated, he fingered his upper lip, and I noticed a little growth of downy hairs.

'Freddie, what is that fungus underneath your nose?'

'Oh ... I must have forgotten to shave.'

'Freddie! Don't dissemble! You are growing a moustache!'

'Well, Mistress ... Mme Izzard said that a kiss without a moustache –'

'I do not recall giving you permission. Are you proposing to kiss Mme Izzard?'

'No, Mistress.'

I nodded to my rack of correctional instruments.

'I have a nice new birch, Freddie. *Betula pubescens*, the young hairy twigs, very supple and very painful, a punishment for the most serious of offences. I'm longing to try it out. Don't you think growing a moustache without my permission is a most serious offence?'

He gulped.

'I'll shave it off at once, Mistress.'

'No,' I said, stroking my chin thoughtfully. 'Leave it – we'll see how it develops. If it turns out to please me, I won't birch you.'

He looked at me with longing, not knowing whether to be sad or grateful.

'You shall be punished, though.'

'Thank you. Thank you, Mistress.'

I looked down and saw that the excitement had caused a noticeable swelling of his manhood.

'Well!' I said, tapping his bulge playfully. 'You are in a state for your Tess! But will you have the endurance to pleasure her? Looking at you, I think you'll go off like a rocket.'

'If she agrees,' he said in a forlorn voice.

'What do you mean, if? You have a shilling for her, haven't you? Money opens all doors, Freddie, and much else besides. Didn't you seduce me with a shilling back at Rakeslit?'

'That was different, Mistress.'

'It is never different, boy.'

With that, I speedily unbuttoned his trousers; his prick sprang out for me, as stiff as an oak.

'Mistress?'

'Hush, boy. I am making sure you are fit to perform.'

I lowered my head and placed my lips on the swollen bulb of his penis, then, with one swift movement, engulfed the whole shaft until his glans was tickling the back of my throat. Very gently I applied my teeth to his balls, and he drew his breath in sharply. Bobbing my head, I sucked his penis very firmly – already I could taste a drop of sperm that had crept from his pee-hole – with my teeth softly biting the pearls of his manhood. He groaned softly, and clutched my hair to him. His penis shuddered and, as he whimpered, I swallowed every lovely drop of the hot spend that spurted to my throat.

'Oh, Mistress!' he cried. 'You possess me!'

'Good,' I said brightly, licking the spend from my lips. 'And now that you are not so excited, it is time for Tess to do the same.'

I kissed his mouth tenderly with my shiny lips.

'I wish it could be you, Mistress. It would be awfully thrilling, if I knew others were watching.'

'I am the Governess, chump. It is all right for Tess, for she is a maid, and for you, because girls know that all men, whatever their station, are rampant beasts. But not for me, just at the moment. Now button yourself and be on your way, and remember that I shall be watching you, and I am the severest of drama critics!'

Immediately afterwards, it was Tess's turn to attend me. She had dressed for the occasion, meaning she had discovered a clean blouse and even allowed a washcloth to hover near her luxuriant armpits.

'Here is your shilling, Tess,' I said. The coin disappeared like lightning into the region of her panties. 'Now remember, Mr Whimble does not know of our arrangement. You must be kind to him, for he is inexperienced, and let him think he is seducing you. You must protest, sigh, moan, and so forth, in short, play the part of the reluctant virgin.'

'Eh? What does that mean?'

'Reluctant: shy, unwilling, timid.'

'No, Miss, the other word.'

'Go on, Tess,' I sighed, with an affectionate pat on her bottom. 'I just know you'll do well.'

5

An Impudent Visitor

Beneath Tess's crude but sultry Cornish exterior lay a crude but sultry Cornish interior. She breathed with the naked vitality of the land: sex was like the weather, a fact of existence which might bring pleasure or discomfort, but which it was impossible to avoid. If a man wanted her, he had her, just as the heavens rained if they wanted to. When she was Miss Chytte's maid, she had been introduced to the joys of uranism, or love between women, and that too was a fact of life. The only thing that would upset Tess would be for no one to want her. She even enjoyed feeling exploited by low pay, although in fact I treated her quite generously, at a time when a labourer with a family to feed was glad of twenty-one shillings a week. Feeling used reassured her that she was valued.

She certainly gave, and had, good value in the summerhouse that day. The little sugar cake confection of white and pink boards stood a few yards from the boundary fence, between our pretty woods and the unkempt forest of, I suppose, St Alcuin's. It had a verandah, and large windows with shutters but no glass, and was easily reached from the main building of St Agatha's by a discreet shortcut through the shrubbery; a distance of about five hundred yards. I watched as Freddie and Tess solemnly embarked across the lawn, arm in arm. How sweet! Each planning to seduce the other. A few minutes later I took the discreet path and followed them unseen to an observing post between the trees, where I had a good view of the house's interior. The windows were open, although it was winter, and I could see the meagre furnishings, including a rather fetching quilted divan, which would be the props for my drama.

Freddie and Tess entered by the back door of the house, and right on cue I heard the laughter of girls approaching from the other direction. They disappeared from my view, positioned as they were by the verandah at the front of the house.

'Oh!' cried Miss Chytte, as planned. 'I have forgotten the key to the front door! Wait here on the verandah, while I go and fetch it, girls, and no mischief while I'm gone!' Then I saw her stride across the lawns towards St Agatha's. The girls chattered excitedly, but abruptly their noise stopped as I heard Freddie's booming voice:

'What a pretty place! We are quite alone, sweet Tess. Sit on this divan, my dear.'

The was a stealthy shuffling of feet as the girls clambered up on the verandah to watch.

'It's cold,' said Tess.

'But we have a splendid view of St Agatha's don't we?'

'It's warmer there,' said Tess, rather unseductively.

'But I shall make you warm in here, Tess,' cooed Freddie. 'You know I have long admired you, from afar. How many nights have I tossed and turned, dreaming of your beauty! But I did not dare –'

He put his arm around her waist.

'You being a lord and all,' said Tess helpfully.

'Yes – but now – a kiss, please, Tess. Just one kiss. No one will see, for we are quite alone.'

There was an excited rustle of skirts from the verandah that even I could hear. Tess opened her mouth to receive her kiss, then remembered her role and cried.

'Oh, sir! It ain't right!'

Freddie's hand was on her breast, stroking and squeezing.

'How can my love be wrong, gorgeous Tess? Here, I have a gift for you, a nice shiny shilling, to show I love you.' There were excited gasps from the audience.

'Well, sir, I suppose a kiss will do no harm,' said Tess, as the coin vanished into her underthings. Freddie embraced her and kissed her lips most convincingly, while placing her hand between his thighs, where his stiff cock was prettily bulging in his trousers. She did not resist, but stroked him there and returned his kisses with a fervent slopping of her lips. Freddie broke away, and cried:

'Oh, God, Tess, I must have you!'

'Have me, sir? Whatever can you mean?'

'Do not torment me, sweet Tess!'

I saw his hand kneading her naked breasts, revealed by the opened blouse whose buttons Tess had slyly undone.

'Such teats!' cried Freddie. 'As white as milk! Oh, I must kiss them!'

His head went to her big pink nipples and he bit and sucked them, to the accompaniment of Tess's half-hearted moans of protest, while his hand crept under her skirt, which she had obligingly raised, and between her parted thighs. Her body was indeed as white as milk, in contrast to her sunburnt countenance, and I found my sex moistening with excitement as I recalled my naked sport with Miss Chytte and Tess in Cornwall.

'God, Tess, you have no panties on! And your lady's place is wet for me, do not deny it! How slippery and hot she is! I mean to . . . to fuck you, Tess. Don't pretend you haven't done it with other gentlemen!'

'Oh, sir, I am innocent.'

'Another shilling, damn it! Just to take me in that lovely wet gash of yours! Oh, Tess, feel how hard I am for you! I will poke so sweetly that you melt with pleasure!'

My pulse quickened with enjoyment of this splendid theatre and, beneath my cloak, I parted my thighs and let my hand stray there.

Tess took the shilling, and lifted up her skirts to reveal her shining gash, peeping under her thick mink like a succulent oyster. Freddie fumbled with his buttons, revealing his hard and proud cock. All the girls sighed. I heard myself say 'Mmmm'.

'Sir!' cried Tess, putting her hands to her mouth. 'That engine of yours is so big! You can't possibly – I mean, he won't go into me.'

Freddie had his swollen crimson bulb nuzzling at the lips of her quim, but abruptly she closed her thighs to him.

'Please, Tess!' begged Freddie. 'I want to fuck you!'

'Oh, sir, he is bigger than other men's. I'm frightened he will hurt me. He's so stiff and hard and monstrous.'

'He won't hurt you, Tess, my lovely flower. He will spurt his seed amid your petals and you will have the greatest happiness you have known.'

'I just can't!'

'Here! Another shilling will change your mind.'

Tess simpered, and took the coin.

'Well, I suppose he is pretty, in a way, sir. If you please, I'll suck him a little, to see if he tastes friendly to me.'

There was another ripple of excitement from the watching audience. Tess bent down and took Freddie's cock between her expert lips, and her hair began to dance up and down as she sucked him. My own sex was unmistakably wet, and I felt my belly start to flutter.

Suddenly Freddie emitted a deep wail, and threw his head back. Tess took her mouth from his cock, but kept her lips lightly on the tip of his glans, where a trickle of white spunk had already appeared. I had underestimated just how much vitality those lovely balls of his contained! Firmly, Tess took the shaft of his penis in one hand and cupped his balls in the other, and with deft fingers rubbed his quivering shaft, while she squeezed the balls beneath and flicked her tongue over his wet pee-hole.

'Come, sir,' she teased, 'let me milk you. You are naughty to spend so soon, before I have had my pleasure. My cunt is all wet for your cock, and here he is going to spend in my face. Oh, you are naughty, and I think you must be punished for your boldness.'

At that, Freddie groaned deeply, and a jet of sperm made a fountain over Tess's lips and cheeks. She cooed softly as she milked his bucking penis, and lapped up the creamy fluid, smacking her lips as she swallowed.

I was swallowing too, as my breath came hard and panting. I took my hand away from my skirt and drove it beneath the waistband of my panties, across my mink to my swollen sex-lips, and began gently to frig my naked clitoris.

Suddenly, Tess leapt to her feet, leaving Freddie with his cock soft and dangling, and his trousers round his ankles.

'You have paid for a fuck, sir, but you haven't given me one! I'm disappointed!'

'Your beauty excited me so,' stammered Freddie.

'I am an honest woman, and you shall have what you paid for. I'll punish you for your boldness, until that cock is stiff again, sir! Look at that soft thing, that was so hard! Why, you're no better than a blubbing girl!'

Tess took a bamboo rod from a stack of gardening implements in the corner of the room, and the watching girls gasped in anticipation as they saw Tess crack the stick smartly over her thigh to break it in half. Breathing heavily, she stood over Freddie with two canes, each three feet in length, and with wicked raw ends. She switched them menacingly, and Freddie went pale; I did not think he was acting.

'No ... wait ... please, Miss,' he blurted. But with a powerful grasp on his neck, she forced him to bend over and bury his face in the divan.

'Will you take your punishment like a man, sir? Or must I dress you in my panties and petticoats, and put ribbons in your hair, and paint your face like a girl's?'

'Do what you must,' said Freddie, his voice trembling.

'And what is that?' she taunted.

'Beat me. Please, beat me.'

'On your naked bottom?'

'Yes!'

'Well, you must ask nicely.'

'Please, Tess, thrash my bare bottom.'

'Go on.'

'I beg you, whip me until my arse is crimson! Make me squirm, Tess! My bum's naked and helpless for you. Punish him, Tess, make him quiver!'

'That's better. But such hard work must be paid for, sir.'

'Damn it, take another shilling! Take two! Please, oh please, flog me, Tess, sweet Mistress!'

I pretended to myself that Freddie was acting, but I knew he was not. My fingers flickered inside the wet lips of my sex, each touch on my throbbing clit sending a spasm of pleasure through me. I was too excited to feel jealous of Tess, and I knew I was not far from a spend. My panties were thoroughly soaked in my slippery love-juice, and I longed to see Tess thrash Freddie's bare bottom. Tess lifted both the bamboo canes, and brought them down with a crack on the boy's buttocks, sending a giddy rush of hot pleasure through my belly. Freddie jerked violently, but did not make a sound, even though I could see bright pink on his naked flesh. Again and again his bared buttocks danced to the rod, and at each stroke he squirmed and gasped, but did not cry out. I felt myself at my plateau – my quim was a river of hot juice – I could not contain myself any longer, and as Tess delivered her final whistling cut to Freddie's bare nates, I felt myself shudder in the aching sweetness of a spend.

Suddenly, I had the feeling that I myself was being watched. I focused my blurred eyes, and there, on the other side of the boundary fence stood my faun, my 'snowdrop boy'! He wore a dark suit, like a uniform, and gave me a piercing look, his lips creased in a cruel smile. Then he turned on his heel and stole away – having seen everything, including watching me frig myself!

Tess threw the cane aside and beckoned Freddie to stand. He raised himself, and his prick shone as stiff and swollen as before, to the sighing delight of my girlish onlookers. Now, Tess positioned herself on the divan, her skirts up over her breasts, and her naked thighs spread wide. With her fingers, she parted the lips of her glistening gash, and murmured to Freddie:

'Now you are a man again, sir. Pleasure me, if you will. See how pink and wet my lady's place shines for you. She wants to feel your big stiff tool deep inside her.'

Without a word, but panting fiercely, Freddie straddled her. His cock plunged to its hilt between her swollen sex-lips, and now it was Tess's turn to moan, as, with the vigour of a beast, he stroked her so hard and powerfully that her own buttocks had to pump madly to match his rhythm, and she clutched his reddened bottom to her with sharp fingernails as though trying to push his cock into her very womb. It was gorgeous to see Freddie's muscled back arching and rippling as he took his woman to the brink of her pleasure, then slowed his strokes, teasing her and making her writhe under him with her thighs jerking madly, begging him to finish her and let her spend.

It seemed that he fucked her for an age, sometimes stopping altogether, to gaze at her with a cruel sneer as her pale body writhed like a caught fish on the end of his penis; then suddenly, his buttocks would clench and begin their maddened dance as he bucked her so hard that she wailed with rasping breath at each stroke of his cock, his balls slapping against thighs that shone with the flood of her love-juice. At last she could take no more, and her belly heaved as she howled in the ecstacy of her spend; she clutched Freddie to her, her lips on his, and only when he knew her spasm was convulsing her did he roar as he released his own flood into her squirming loins.

I was quite giddy with desire as I made my discreet way back to St Agatha's. I find it awfully exciting to watch my man fuck another woman, to see the animal thrusting of his loins as a female's body writhes beneath his. This may seem surprising, since women are supposed to be so jealous of each other, but a lover may, through years of familiarity, become a friend. To see him naked on another female is to be thrillingly reminded of his raw sexuality as a male beast whom I have tamed, and whose strength belongs to me. It also reminds me that I too must remain a seductive, sexual animal, if I am to keep him in my thrall. And there is the excitement of demonstrating my power over him: he is fucking on my orders, as my slave, and it is I who am in command of the lustful spectacle. Such scenes, if properly managed, ensure that a love affair remains intriguingly spiced.

How many men (as the reader shall see below) yearn to watch as their dear wives are vigorously fucked by a young, virile male! A man's wife – his dearest friend – becomes a stranger to him, as she cries out and takes into her sex that stiff young rod and the seed of those young balls.

It is as though he is watching himself from outside. He is that virile youth, it is he who thrusts so ruthlessly into his wife's cunt, now nothing more than the cunt of a nameless, rutting female animal, newly impassioned by young, fresh cock. He feels a new surge of manly vigour: this woman belongs to him, and he must show his own virility to secure his possession of her. The fucking is over; his wife is still sighing in the aftermath of her loving spasm, when he takes her, astonishing her with his passionate vigour. Her slit is still soaking from the young man's embrace, her body still glowing from his virile essence, and her husband knows that by fucking her swollen quim, so recently pleasured, the same virile essence will become his.

I sat in my study later, all flushed and dreamy and shivery. I wanted Freddie inside me; I wanted that strange dark boy too, as well as Freddie! I closed my eyes and dreamed of both of them, each fucking me and kissing me: my mouth, my cunt, my bumhole, all at once, somehow. I was panting – I knew that faun had seen me frig myself by the summerhouse, the cheeky beast, and that made me want him even more! I felt so tingly and confused!

My reverie was broken by a knock on the door. It was Miss Chytte, come to report on the success of our escapade.

'I waited until Freddie and Tess left by the back door, Mistress, before I returned with the key to the front. The girls were so flushed and excited! They all wanted to sit on the divan and feel the quilt which was still warm from their bodies, and they trembled so much they could scarcely eat! In fact, that is a bonus, for they all made a terrible mess, spilling their clotted cream all over their uniforms, so that they must be cleaned.' Miss Chytte smiled. 'Naturally, I told them they would all be punished for their carelessness.'

'Did they protest much?'

'Mistress, it was their suggestion!'

'Good . . . very good indeed. Where has Freddie gone?'

'I think he went off to the stables.'

'Damn!'

'Shall I fetch him?'

'Yes. No! Don't fetch him. Wait – Oh damn. Oh, Miss Chytte . . .'

'Why, Mistress, you are all in a tizzy!'

'Damn it, I am not in a tizzy! Oh blast!'

'Mistress, what are you doing?' she asked quietly.

'What do you think, Miss?'

I bent myself over my sofa and lifted my skirts, then lowered my wet panties so that my bare bottom was raised high.

'I am to blame for the spoiled uniforms, Miss Chytte,' I said faintly. 'The whole thing was my idea. You will please fetch my new birch, the *Betula pubescens* and deal with me.'

Miss Chytte smiled thinly and obeyed.

'I am sure that every one of those girls will be happy members of "Swish", Mistress,' she said as she raised the flogging instrument. 'Don't you agree?'

The cruel twigs hissed through the air and lashed my naked rump, sending streaks of white flame across my skin.

'Oh, yes, Miss,' I grinned fiercely, squirming as my clenched buttocks smarted with pure, beautiful fire. 'Yes . . .!'

It was a few nights later that I saw him again. I was very tired from my day's work, and had said goodnight to my company, desiring nothing but a sound sleep. I sat wearily on my bed and began to undress. It was only when I was stripped to my petticoats, I remembered to close the curtains. The rain had ceased, and the night was fine and clear, so I lingered for a moment by the window, not caring that my upper body was bare. And then I saw him! It was my insolent young faun, in my flower garden. The brute was quite naked, bending over to pick some early daffodils, and he had his back to me, affording me a view of his slender muscles and pert bottom, which in less annoying circumstances I should have found pretty. I wondered why he was naked. I myself, as a young girl, had adored dancing nude under the starlight on this very same turf, but then I thought I was alone. Here he was, positively courting discovery.

He turned slightly, and I saw that his penis was erect. Despite my irritation, I knew him to be beautiful. My heart thumped with excitement at the savage, insolent power of that nudity. And I lingered at the window, my naked breasts pressed against the glass, half willing him to see me.

Then my anger and curiosity galvanised me into action. I flung on my blouse, not bothering to button it, and wrapped a cashmere shawl around my upper body, and in my stockinged feet I stole from my room. I opened the door to the garden without sound, and crept painfully down the gravel path until I was upon him. I grasped his upper arm tightly, and to my surprise he did not start or flinch, as though my grip were the most normal thing in the world.

'Who are you? What d'you think you're doing in my garden?' I blurted.

Slowly, he stood up, and looked at me with lustrous eyes. His age must be nineteen or twenty, scarcely older than Freddie, but there was not a hair on his smooth brown body. I thought rather absurdly of Freddie's moustache! His sleekly-muscled frame was almost like a coltish girl's; I thought that there are many ways for a male to be beautiful.

'Well? Answer me!' I cried, and he smiled with teeth as white as a wolf's. My shawl slipped, as I was shaking in my agitation, and I released his arm to cover my embarrassment. Yet he made no move to flee, but stood there watching me slyly, hands on his hips, with that monstrous standing cock sucking my gaze towards him. His skin was a mass of goose pimples, but he did not shiver.

I grabbed his waist, and his smile faded, as though a game was over.

'Name,' I rapped sternly.

'Mordevaunt, Miss. Peter Mordevaunt.'

His voice had a curious musical lilt, and was a deep, thrilling bass that seemed at odds with that slender body.

'Where have you come from Mordevaunt?'

'Why, Jamaica, Miss.'

'I mean where, at this time of night, boy! Why, you are indecent! You'll catch cold, you . . . you silly!'

'From St Alcuin's, Miss.' He nodded towards the gaunt building hidden by the unkempt forest. 'I left my uniform by your boundary fence.'

'You came naked across our lawns? It is scandalous behaviour.'

'No Miss, through the bushes. I was careful not to be seen.'

'But I have seen you. And I've seen you before, in Lady Jane's Wood.'

I looked down at his engorged penis, and felt my belly flutter. 'You were indecent then, too.'

'I like to be naked, Miss. Only the stars can see me.'

'Damn it, boy, I can see you!'

His lips creased in a gentle smile.

'I don't mind that.'

I could see him shivering now, for the cold was crisp.

'Oh!' I cried, 'this is too much! You must at least keep warm!' And I took off my shawl, and wrapped his shoulders in it, forgetting, in my exasperation, that I left my bare breasts visible under my open blouse. Then, all flustered, I buttoned the blouse, getting the buttons all in the wrong holes, which seemed to amuse him.

'I suppose you found it amusing to spy on me the other day by our summerhouse?' I said, trying to sound accusing.

'I wasn't spying. I was watching you, Miss. Because you are quite interesting.' And he glanced insolently down at his penis, which, if anything, was stiffer than ever. Quite interesting! I almost exploded in frustration. A lady wants to be complimented – but to be thought quite interesting – the cheeky brat!

'Who is the principal at St Alcuin's?'

'Doctor Hamm, Miss.'

'Well, he shall hear of this. It is quite outrageous.' But my words were forced: I realised I wanted to take that cheeky brat into my arms and cuddle him, and stroke that lovely cock that stood so proud for me. But now there was alarm in his voice.

'No, Miss, please. I am truly sorry . . . I thought I would be undisturbed. I thought you wouldn't miss a few flowers. Dr Hamm mustn't know! Please!'

'And why not?' I demanded.

'It would be awful,' he said glumly.

'You are afraid of punishment? Of being beaten?'

'Oh, no,' he said scornfully, 'not that. But if he sent me down, I shouldn't get to Oxford. And Dr Hamm is capricious in his moods.'

'Well!' I said. 'You must be punished. You realise that?'

'Yes, Miss,' he said meekly.

'You know who I am?'

'Of course, Miss de Comynge.'

I bit my lip, and drew a deep breath.

'You will come to my study, then, at your morning break from lessons, tomorrow. What time is that?'

'Oh,' he smiled. 'At St Alcuin's, Miss, that is any time at all.'

'Hmm! Ten o'clock sharp, then.'

'You are going to beat me?'

'Yes.'

'And you won't tell Dr Hamm?'

'Perhaps not,' I said with a thin, coquettish smile. 'Now go, and take my wrap, for you would catch cold without it. You may return it tomorrow morning, when you come to me for your beating. Be off with you, boy!'

I watched him vault nimbly over the low garden wall, then disappear into the shrubbery, with my wrap trailing behind him like a pennant, and his cock still beautifully, maddeningly stiff. I returned to my room and went straight to bed, to be troubled by uneasy dreams, in which Freddie and Peter Mordevaunt somehow fused into one person. And every time I started awake, I shook my head and mumbled:

'Quite interesting! The nerve!'

I felt on edge in the morning, and did not want to face my colleagues, so I had Tess bring me my breakfast in bed. Tess wore a jaunty smile, and I asked her if this meant she was finding life in London agreeable.

'Oh, yes, Miss. There is so much to do.'

'You get on with the other maids? I mean, you are not bothered by jealousies, backbiting and so forth?'

'Swimmingly well, Miss. I think I have the measure of them, and they're not a bad lot, for townies, and Mr Whimble looks after me. He is a very kind gentleman,' said Tess as she flounced away, grinning.

For some reason, I had little appetite, but I drank a lot of tea, for my throat was unaccountably dry. Then I sat naked on my Turkish commode for a long time, trying to marshal my thoughts concerning the day's business, but found that I could not think further than my ten o'clock appointment. I felt much more chipper when I had bathed and put a dab of scent under my arms and on my mink, and donned my tightest and most severe black silk dress. Thus accoutred, I installed myself behind my desk and waited for ten o'clock.

Peter Mordevaunt arrived promptly. He was rather sheepish as he stood before me in his dark green blazer and grey flannel trousers, neatly pressed, with his boots brightly polished. he held out a package, prettily wrapped in gift paper, with a little pink ribbon tied into a bow.

'I brought your shawl back, Miss,' he said. I took the parcel and put it to one side, and smiled at him.

'Thank you. That is very thoughtful,' I said. 'Well then! You know why you are here.'

'Yes, Miss,' he replied, rather shyly.

'Sit down on the sofa by the fire for a mimute, Mordevaunt,' I said cheerfully. 'Before I bend you over it. I intend to make you tremble in a while, and I don't want you to blame the cold.'

He sat down nervously and I joined him on the sofa.

'So,' I said, 'you'd rather take my punishment than face the wrath of this Dr Hamm?'

'Yes, Miss.'

'He must be a tyrant.'

'Not really, he is just unpredictable. There are only half a dozen students at St Alcuin's, and we do pretty much as we like. Every so often, Dr Hamm loses his temper, and says we shall never get to Oxford, which would only be true if he expelled us.'

'You are all going to Oxford?'

'Why, yes. The founder of St Alcuin's endowed a dozen

tied scholarships, you see, at various colleges. They are exclusively for St Alcuin's pupils, no matter how stupid, and there are never more than a dozen of us, so unless you actually get expelled, you are guaranteed acceptance at the university.'

'I must call on Dr Hamm,' I said. 'I think we may have business to discuss. In the meantime, Mordevaunt, you and I have our own business, and you will find that we at St Agatha's are neither moody nor unpredictable. I'm going to give you the tightest thrashing you've had in your life.' I put my hand on his wrist and looked at him tenderly. 'It'll be a full six, you know. If you can't take it, just say so, and I'll stop, and you can go back to Dr Hamm with a little note explaining matters.'

'I'll take your punishment, Miss.'

'Bare bum, I'm afraid.'

He swallowed and nodded, his eyelashes fluttering.

'Good!' I said briskly. 'Please take everything off below your waist, Mordevaunt, and knot your shirt over your tummy.'

As he undressed, I made a show of selecting my implement of correction. I took one of my hardest canes, a thick yellow yew branch with a two-inch split at the tip and nearly four feet in length. With this, I had drawn gasps even from the hardy Miss Chytte. When I turned round, Mordevaunt had folded his clothing neatly and placed it on a chair; he was naked below his waist, and barefoot, his long slender penis hanging quite limp from a forest of thick, soft curls. I forced myself not to look at him there, and instead swished my cane through the air with a satisfying whistle. He eyes went wide.

'Ready?' I asked.

'I think so, Miss.'

'Right. First, you can oil the cane for me. It makes her just that much more painful.'

I took a jar of linseed oil from my cupboard, and gave it to him with the yew branch. Carefully, he rubbed the oil into the yellow wood, looking rather serious and composed.

'Good,' I said when he handed me back the cane. 'I'll

take you over the sofa, I think. Bend over, legs wide apart – that's right – and rest your hands on the sofa back, keeping your head high. Wipe your oily palms on your bottom first to clean them. The oil is good for your skin, and it will make you sting more.'

I watched, my heart fluttering, as his fingers rubbed the oil into the taut smooth skin of his buttocks, until they gleamed. Then he positioned himself as I had ordered, with legs and arms stretched wide, and his back arched.

'Stand high on your tiptoes, please. That way, you can't wriggle so much, to get rid of the smarting.'

He obeyed, showing me the pale soles of his feet, which made a pretty contrast to his brown skin. His leg muscles quivered tight, beneath the gleaming oiled buttocks. He looked so helpless and brave and adorable.

'Ready?'

He nodded.

'Right!' I said, 'we've got all morning, young Mordevaunt, so I'm going to skin you nice and slowly.' I brought the cane down with a sharp crack squarely in the centre of his naked buttocks. He drew in his breath sharply, and almost at once I delivered a second whistling cut in the same place, which made him jerk with pain and surprise.

'There! That's the first two out of the way,' I said brightly. 'I expect those were pretty tight.'

'Yes, Miss. My bottom's smarting ... quite a lot.'

'I always believe in giving the first two fairly sharpish, so you know what you're in for, and then I can watch you squirm as I take the rest nice and slow. Four more to come, so be brave. Well, we've quite a nice day for it, haven't we?'

He looked to the side and saw the pale winter sun shining through my drawn curtains.

'Don't worry, no one will see,' I smiled.

'It doesn't matter, Miss. I shan't cry,' he panted.

'So you wouldn't mind if someone were watching.'

'No, Miss,' he said slowly, 'I shouldn't mind.'

I laid the third stroke on the tender skin at the underside of his bottom, almost on the tops of his thighs, and that made him gasp harshly.

'You are from Jamaica, then,' I said.

'Oh . . .' he swallowed. 'Oh . . . yes, my family owns the Mordevaunt plantation just north of Port Antonio.'

'You are a long way from home. I suppose you miss your father and mother.'

'Yes, I do. But it is tradition, that the Mordevaunt boys go first to St Alcuin's, then to Oxford, and I am the only son, so it is very important that I complete my studies there. The founder was a Mordevaunt, you see.'

'Four!'

I delivered the fourth stroke across the top of his hindquarters, and was rewarded with a little sob in his throat, and a nice shudder of his glowing pink bottom.

'How strong you are, Miss!' he stammered. 'I don't think I've ever been laced so tight.'

'So tightly, Mordevaunt. You use the adverb,' I said sternly. 'Five!'

'Ah! Oh . . .'

I had returned to the place of the first stroke, and as I saw the delicious swathe of hot crimson skin, I became aware that my sex was growing moist and ticklish. He danced on his tiptoes, his buttocks trying to squirm and dissipate the smarting.

'You want me to stop, Mordevaunt?'

'No, Miss. Don't,' he replied throught clenched teeth. 'I can take the sixth cut, I promise.'

I looked down and saw that under that forest of glistening curls, his penis was standing stiff! His curve of erection was very high, almost parallel to his belly, and this excited me.

'Six!'

I put every ounce of strength into my last cut, and was panting as hard as he as I finally laid my cane aside. His reddened buttocks trembled uncontrollably, and his breath came harsh and rapid, like a puppy's. He swallowed repeatedly, with little sobbing sounds. My sex was now very wet, and I longed to press my lips to his flogged bottom and kiss those lovely red plums!

'That's it,' I said. 'You may get up now.'

'Please, Miss, I shan't for the moment. I am a little embarrassed.'

I looked again at his throbbing naked prick.

'I see,' I said thoughtfully. 'But you were far from embarrassed last night.'

'Last night, he stood for your beauty, Miss. Now he stands for my pain.'

'Well, take your time, young man, and I may admire my handiwork. My, how red your bottom is! I dare say you won't want to sit on it for a while. Do you always get an erection when you are beaten?'

'I have never been beaten by a woman as lovely as you, Miss.'

'So you are no stranger to a lady's cane.'

'Oh, no, Miss. The mammies on the plantation used to take charge of "the young master" if I was naughty. Which was most of the time, it seems. I got the whip quite a lot.'

'He seems to be as hard as ever,' I said. 'We shall have to do something. You will remain there while I call Matron.'

I picked up the telephone, and had myself connected to the surgery. When Deirdre answered, I explained the problem as delicately as I could.

'It is a case of the priapism,' she said. 'That is, when a gentleman's pole stands up and will not lie down. It is awfully difficult for me to come now, Miss, because I am just in the middle of giving the lower form their weekly enemas with Mr Izzard's colonic irrigation machine. My, you should see their bottoms! It seems some of them got quite a lathering from Miss Chytte after spoiling their uniforms.'

'Are they sullen, Deirdre?'

'Not a bit. They are proudly showing off their pink bottoms like a proper lot of little madams.'

'Well,' I said, secretly delighted at this information. 'What do I do about this young man's priapism?'

'The best thing is to put his balls in a bucket of ice, Miss. Oh! She's overflowing!' And Deirdre rang off before I could say that I did not have a bucket of ice handy.

'Well, Mordevaunt,' I said, my pulse racing. 'It seems that, ah, there is a remedy. But tell me something, does this happen to you frequently? I am speaking medically, on behalf of Matron. You must be truthful.'

'It does, Miss,' he answered.

'And what do you do about it? Do you young men play with each other's penises, to relieve yourselves? Perhaps make women of each other, and put your penises into each other's bums?'

'No!' he cried, his face scarlet. 'That is what some chaps do when they are young and silly, but now it is ... well, naughty.'

'No, Mordevaunt, you silly, it is not naughty, just rather lonely, that's all. You have done such things?'

'Yes, Miss.'

His poor face was redder than a beetroot! Into my mind flashed a picture of my faun, wrestling naked with another like him in a pretence of love, and the thought of such a spectacle was curiously thrilling.

So I suppose you diddle yourself, is that it?'

He nodded sheepishly.

'Is that what you were doing when you spied on the two at their private sport in our summerhouse? The truth, mind.'

'Yes, Miss,' he blurted. 'But you were doing it too!'

'What!'

'I know ladies do it,' he went on, rather desperately, 'for I've seen my sisters do it. Honestly! I meant no harm!'

Now it was my turn to blush. I saw that his gaze had strayed to my waist, and that now there was a sly glint in his eyes.

'Well!' I exclaimed, struggling to compose myself. 'It seems that the tropical sun makes very lustful boys! But this is England, and things are different, you know. We don't cavort around naked, diddling ourselves, and putting flowers in our hair and suchlike.'

'I know,' he said sadly.

'Stolen flowers at that!'

'I ... I wanted to make myself pretty for you, Miss, because I have dreamt of you.'

I longed to tell him that I was more touched than he could realise that he had made himself pretty for me. But instead I frowned at him.

'Enough of this. I propose to deal with your problem in correct medical fashion. Stand up, and fold your arms behind your back.'

He did so, still with that great penis standing so tall in front of him, and seeming so big for his slim body that I thought he would topple over! Again, that sly look came into his eyes. I followed them to my sex and saw that my satin dress was pressed so tightly against my panties that there was a wet stain clearly visible. I swallowed and blushed, and his eyes held mine.

'What are you going to do, Miss?' he asked, trembling.

'A hygienic operation, nothing more,' I blurted.

Suddenly, I wanted to hurry. I turned round and bent down, then lifted my skirts up to my thighs, affording him a generous view of my black silk stockings, and then I tugged down my panties. They were all wet, and I could see his eyes sparkling. I advanced to him, and laid my panties on the tip of his penis, then began to rub the throbbing shaft. He sighed.

'Hands behind your back, boy,' I said as I stroked his lovely stiff cock and with my other hand cupped and tickled his balls. How I longed to do more!

'This is what Matron told me to do,' I said as I tenderly rubbed his tense young manhood. 'It is therapeutic, to effect a temporary cure of your priapic condition, and I approach the task in a purely medical spirit.'

'Oh, Miss, it is lovely,' he sighed. Teasingly, I squeezed the engorged glans, rubbing my finger through my panties over his pee-hole, whose soft slit I could clearly feel. I tried not to look into his eyes, but I could not help doing so, and his stare transfixed me.

'I saw your bare breasts, Miss – like golden honey. I wish to see them again.'

'You are a demanding young whipper snapper,' I said, panting. I could feel my face burning and flushed, and my love-juice was trickling on my naked thighs.

'Please.'

I could not refuse him. I had not meant things to go so far, and I felt I was losing control. My sex was gushing wet, my belly shuddered, and I longed to have him, but I knew that now was not the moment. I had to keep command of him.

I took my hand from his balls and, still frigging his cock, unbuttoned my blouse all the way down to my waist, so that my naked breasts sprang out to his gaze.

'There,' I said, trying to sound brisk and matronly, 'will that help? I only show you my teats because I suppose it will make you spend faster.'

'Please let me have one touch, Miss. Your nipples are so swollen and stiff and lovely.'

I clicked my tongue. 'No, Mordevaunt, keep those curious hands behind your back'

But when I saw his face fall, I suddenly took my panties from his cock and knelt down before him; then I took his naked penis between my breasts. Holding my erect, tingling nipples between thumb and forefinger, I pressed my breasts against his cock and began to squeeze him hard, rubbing up and down and caressing my nipples as I did so. He shut his eyes and began to moan and his breath became heavier than when he had taken the cane on his naked bottom. He groaned and panted, now, and his hips writhed at the soft pressure of my naked breasts squeezing the shaft of his cock. I could not restrain myself; I lowered my head and flicked his pee-hole with my tongue, tasting a creamy little drop of spend already peeping there.

'Almost ready!' I murmured. And then I swallowed his whole cock between my breasts, pressing in so that the bulb was rubbed by my very nipples. His manhood shuddered and bucked as a great spurt of hot spunk washed my trembling teats, and he gasped in his joy.

I wiped his penis, and then my own breasts, with my panties, and put them on my desk.

'There! That's better, isn't it?' I said in a shaky voice.

He nodded, and began to dress himself, and when he had done so, he said gravely: 'Thank you, Miss. And thank you for my beating.'

'I hope you have learned your lesson.'

'I am proud to have received such a beautiful one.'

'Please give my compliments to Dr Hamm, and tell him I shall be glad to take tea with him to discuss matters of mutual interest.'

He bowed, and we shook hands. As soon as I had closed the door behind him, I went giddily to my desk and sat down. There was the gift-wrapped package containing my shawl. With numb, mechanical fingers I opened it, and saw lying neatly on top of my shawl, a delicate garland of spring flowers!

My heart melted, and my quim was a torrent of love-oil as, trembling, I lifted my skirts and pressed the garland of flowers between my parted glistening thighs. A snowdrop, one sweet snowdrop that he had picked for me, touched my stiff clitoris, and at that single touch I cried out in surprise and joy as the ecstasy of a glowing spend shuddered through my body.

It was quite a few moments before I reached to put on the panties I had left on my desk, and discovered they were no longer there.

6

Open Day

Freddie was quite divine at our St Agatha's Open Day. I had never seen him so splendid: immaculate in morning dress, his hair brushed and pomaded and the wispy little thing he called a moustache quite fetching. He was every inch a young lord as he joked man-to-man with the fathers and flirted outrageously with the blushing matrons. Miss Chytte and I had on our best black kit, swathed in tight satin with our hair in buns, so that the matrons would find us pleasingly stern and modest, while the gentlemen had a good view of our female curves. I mingled serenely, and overheard snatches of conversation:

'Young Whimble, eh? You take after your father ... knew him in India ... went to ground for a while, I believe. Oh, back at Rakeslit, is he? Splendid! And dear Lady Whimble is well? Awfully glad!'

'They wish me to spend time in the world, sir, to gain experience.'

'Splendid idea! On to Oxford, I expect.'

'Perhaps.'

'Splendid! And the Guards?'

'I do hope so.'

'Splendid, splendid!'

This conversation was repeated often, with Freddie indefatigably smiling, never more than when the trials of the unfortunate, if fictitious, Charmley-Boddis family were mentioned.

'Rum business, the Charmley-Boddis girl! Good friends of mine, but don't really like to mention it to them. Tact, you know.'

'Of course.'

'Still, that Lucinda was a bit wet, wasn't she?'

'You could put it like that.'

'Couldn't take the . . . you know!' (Motions of administering corporal punishment.) 'Ha ha!'

'We are very strict here, it's true.'

'Smack botty, that's the ticket! Never did a filly any harm! Ha ha!'

'I do so agree, Mr – Beausire, isn't it? And between you and me, I don't think any of us chaps has been the worse for a good tanning, either.'

'That's the spirit! Ha ha!'

Freddie was such a man among men! Little did they know that just that morning I had fastened him into Mr Izzard's tightest (number six) restrainer, most effective in channelling the vital energy of the manly parts to the brain, with the consequent blossoming of the social graces, especially where it was necessary to charm females. It caused me great amusement to think that with every sway of his delicious young bottom, Freddie was experiencing an unbearable tickling from that imposing tongue locked in his bum-hole!

The day began shortly after breakfast, when a shiny array of carriages and automobiles trotted or chugged up to our main portal, to be greeted by myself and Miss Chytte. The plan was to keep everyone well fed and watered, thus in a receptive mood. First, we served coffee. Tess was pleased as punch in a new frilly uniform I had got her. Her generous cleavage, French-maid style, did not escape the notice of the gentlemen, especially when she bent over to add a discreet noggin of rum to their cups. With equal discretion, Miss Chytte relieved them of their non-refundable cheques. There was to be a further break for elevenses, then a scrumptious Belgian lunch from Maxence's kitchen, and of course afternoon tea, with generous helpings of the clotted Cornish item. Tea was to be served shortly before the *pièce de résistance* of the day, a show which would leave them in no doubt as to the virtue of St Agatha's. Tess and the other maids were under strict instructions that at no time was a lady's plate to be left cakeless.

I moved regally amongst the assembly, maintaining a

steely hauteur which would, I hoped, impress the ladies of my moral seriousness, and excite the gentlemen in another way, as they mentally undressed me, as is the wont of gentlemen. The prospective pupils traipsed nervously after their parents, and I was careful to give them winning smiles, and make sure that like their mothers, they were force-fed with cream buns, though of course none of them needed forcing.

There was a ripe assortment of clients: military men; churchmen, including the bishop of somewhere in Africa; a few junior ministers of the Crown, distinguished members of the Bar, and various industrialists and landowners. All were rather pleasingly wealthy, including one tweedy gentleman from Essex with whom Freddie seemed to get on well, who was apparently the 'greyhound king of East London', whatever that meant. Freddie and he made manly talk, that is chiefly about breeding horses, training horses, and things you could shoot, trample or tear to pieces from horses. There was much thigh slapping, especially at the inevitable comparisons between the equine and human female.

'Course, a gel's like a filly, needs plenty of the crop, eh?'

'Whip her smartly, and she knows who's in charge, ha ha!'

'That is very much the St Agatha's way, sir,' I said with a sweet smile. 'And I think you'll agree that colts and stallions respond to the crop just as well as mares and fillies. A good hard thrashing on the rump of a wilful male causes him to buck marvellously, I believe.'

There was a wondering silence.

'Whatever can you mean, miss,' said a Member of Parliament with nervous jocularity.

'Oh, I think some of you gentlemen know what I mean,' I replied. And swept away with an imperious wiggle of my bottom.

Some of the parents of the Swish girls were there, including Major Dove and his lady wife. Thalia Dove was attractive in a muscular, rustic sort of way, with quite a good figure that she unfortunately concealed under dowdy rural garments. She seemed withdrawn and rather shy, although with a decent dressmaker and correct posture she would have been quite striking. Perhaps she thought that being an officer's wife entitled her to neglect the womanly art of pleasing. When I got Major Dove on his own for a moment – he seemed to know quite a lot of the people there – I said without smiling (but in a deliberately high voice, so that those who wanted could hear), 'I want a word with you, alone, Major, in my study after tea.'

'Alone?' he whispered eagerly.

'I think you know what it is about. Your daughter had to receive punishment for a misdemeanour of which you are the culprit.'

I referred, of course, to the exotic Indian panties, a pair of which I was at that moment wearing. They were of a luscious design in pink frilly silk, decorated with orchids and hummingbirds.

'I'm sure I have no idea, Miss,' he lied.

'Then,' I said, smiling, 'we shall see how long it takes to remind you, won't we?'

He bowed his head, and murmured: 'I shall be honoured to attend you, Miss.'

'And when you do,' I said, 'remember that you address me as "Mistress".'

This last remark did not fail to raise inquisitive eyebrows as a blushing and excited Major Dove rejoined the company.

The day proceeded most agreeably. As our guests were treated to a comprehensive display of St Agatha's at work, Miss Chytte and I made mental notes of the most likely prospects: those gentlemen whose eyes sparkled more lustfully in the presence of our older girls, or whose ears caught my frequent fond mentions of discipline and physical correction for both sexes. I gave a running explanation of the workings of St Agatha's, which were not much different from any other establishment, with its paraphernalia of classes and forms, rules, prefects, games, duties, privileges and punishments. I showed them the ice room, where girls clad in skimpy gym kits that clung sensuously to their sweating bodies, laboured to chip the huge block with little axes, and was complimented on my ingenuity.

We visited classrooms, laboratories, the refectory, and the games fields, where short-skirted young ladies chased each other in varying degrees of muddiness. The gentlemen in particular were most enthusiastic spectators. They were then treated to Mme Izzard conducting a French lesson, from the French primer of my own composition. The rather grown-up adventures of Albert, Henri and Yvette were intended to teach the students more than the dry, traditional textbooks. They were reading a passage where Yvette is being soundly thrashed by the brutal Henri for burning his *potage aux lentilles* (illustrating the use of the pluperfect subjunctive) and I was pleased to see that those parents who could follow the text were quite appreciative.

In the surgery, Deirdre met with general approval, certainly from the gentlemen, not least because of her short nurse's tunic which she had buttoned most carelessly, revealing an ample display of succulent breast flesh evidently untrammelled by corsetry. The approval became positive enthusiasm as she demonstrated the superb array of modern equipment for the care of the girls' health, including the ingenious products of Mr Izzard's science, such as pads, panties, bust improvers, various female restrainers, and the shiny new 'lavage' machine. This was a contraption by which colonic irrigation could be administered to several patients at a time, via a complicated series of tubes that could alternate pressure, temperature, or type of fluid, without removing the tube from the hygienic area. Deirdre described how a fractious or disobedient patient would find her warm irrigation turned to icy coldness at the touch of a lever, and everyone laughed. 'It works just as well on gentlemen, mind,' she added. 'One tube fits all, and sure down there everybody's the same.' At which everyone laughed even more, but especially the gentlemen.

'Then, of course,' I said nonchalantly as we wound our way through ancient corridors, 'there is the punishment cell. It's not really a cell, for there is no lock on the door, and it's not used for punishment either. I show it to you as a rather amusing curiosity.'

I led the company down a creaking staircase, and opened the door of the little cellar. There were gasps of prurient astonishment.

'It was actually a punishment cell, in the days when St Agatha's was a convent,' I continued. 'The old equipment is still here – I believe it has considerable antiquarian value, and is listed as such in the accounts – and, needless to say, it is in disuse.'

They gazed at chains, stocks, whipping posts, and a fearsome array of quirts and scourges. There were nervous murmurs of 'Well, well!' and 'Good gracious!' but the gentlemen I had my eye on simply licked their lips.

'Of course,' I said. 'In the bad old days, or some would say the good old days, the abbess of St Agatha's had considerable secular authority, so this place was frequently used to chastise unruly males of the locality. Or even from further afield, so celebrated were the disciplinary talents of the good sisters.'

'However, quite seriously, you must realise that our discipline here is indeed strict by modern standards,' I continued, as we made our way up the stairs. 'And that in consigning your daughters to our stern but loving care, you engage them to accept all correction we choose to administer.'

We ascended to my study, where I invited them to inspect my rack of caning implements and explained the varying degrees of severity. They thronged to look! The men nodded with grave approval, while the ladies almost all became flushed and excited, with much fluttering of eyelashes and handkerchiefs. Tea was then served, and vast barrelfuls of Cornish clotted cream disappeared down London gullets.

'Jolly good tuck, Miss,' enthused one military gentleman. 'You Cornish are hearty trenchermen.'

I was on the point of saying that my acquaintance with Cornwall had been mercifully brief, when I thought that I might as well exploit this supposedly glamorous connection. 'Why, indeed,' I replied. 'We have splendid old culinary traditions in dear Kernow. We are very close to our cousins on the "continong", the Bretons, you know, and share their love of cuisine. Why, I am half French myself, as my name suggests.'

The last was the only true part of my statement, and it seemed to satisfy my gourmand friend. I decided that my association with Cornwall, however tenuous, might serve to endow me with an aura of wild Celtic romance, should I have need of such a thing.

'Finally,' I announced, 'I propose to permit you all to witness a typical scene of correction, conducted of course with total modesty and propriety. However should any ladies or gentlemen feel that such a scene would cause them distress, they are of course invited to excuse themselves. Normally punishment is given in a private room, such as my study, but today, with the offender's written permission, the flogging is to take place in the great hall.'

'A flogging!' The excited whisper coursed around the guests. No one asked to be excused.

We filed into the great hall, where a muslin screen had been erected on the dais, with a wooden chair behind it, visible in silhouette. When all were seated, I nodded to Miss Chytte. She left and returned moments later with her maid, Verity, who was wearing a St Agatha's uniform, and was carrying a long yellow cane before her, upturned on her palms. They mounted the dais and their silhouettes appeared behind the screen.

'This young lady, whom I shall of course not name, was found at the unladylike practice of smoking. Her punishment is four strokes of the cane on the buttocks, and she has agreed to take it in front of your eyes. I might add that she has gained no remission of punishment by agreeing to this. The screen has been placed there for reasons of modesty, as will become apparent.'

The maid, Verity, kissed the rod that was to flog her, then handed it ceremonially to Miss Chytte. Then, Verity unfastened her skirt, removed it, and folded it on the seat of the chair. This was followed by her panties, which she placed on top of her skirt. These operations were clearly visible through the thin muslin, and there was an excited murmuring in the audience.

'Canings at St Agatha's have always been administered on the naked buttocks,' I explained. 'And we are proud to maintain this tradition.'

Miss Chytte raised her arm to its full height, and lashed Verity's bared bottom with four whistling strokes, at intervals of five seconds. Verity took her beating stock still, without uttering the slightest sound. The atmosphere in the hall was electric. When the beating was over, Verity replaced her skirt and panties, bowed to Miss Chytte, and followed her from the hall as serenely as she had entered. I scrutinised the faces of my prospective clients, and every one shone guiltily with pleasurable agitation; the most animated, I noticed, being the daughters themselves.

As the families variously took their leave, most of the gentlemen positively begged me to accept their cheques and their daughters.

'Oh, I have already accepted your cheque, sir,' I said with a winning smile. 'It remains to be seen if I accept your daughter, and indeed yourself.'

I was pleased to observe that many of the gentlemen winked and grinned at Major Dove, knowing that he had business with me. And when Mrs Dove had been despatched to chat with her daughter and Miss Chytte, I took him to my study and locked the door behind us. Major Dove and I were at last alone.

'On your knees, sir,' I rapped at once. 'You have some explaining to do.' He obeyed, and looked up at me like a puppy.

'Mistress?'

'I find you utterly despicable, sir. The panties, have you forgotten?'

'Oh! Yes, I admit I am wearing them, and proudly. On your orders, Mistress.'

Now it was I who looked perplexed.

'The panties you were kind enough to present to me when you visited me in Windsor last year, and corrected me for my insolent demeanour. You ordered me to wear them on parade, and, well, this is a sort of parade, isn't it? But if I have been amiss, of course I must be chastised.'

'Oh, those panties. Yes, of course you are to wear them, sir. I would punish you for not doing so, in fact. But I speak of the garments you gave your daughter to wear, in knowing breach of Academy regulations. These, sir!'

I opened my drawer and took out a selection of the gaudy underthings.

'Oh! But surely . . .'

'There are no "but surelys" at St Agatha's, sir. Victoria was caned for her wrongdoing, and I intend to punish you just as severely.'

'I see,' he said, smiling wanly and trembling a little, either in fear or excitement. 'May I ask how many she took, Mistress?'

'Four. But as you are ultimately responsible, you sir, shall take a full six – with the birch.'

'The birch?' he exclaimed, his face pale.

'Six on your bare arse, sir, as hard as I can lace you. If you can't take it, you may crawl out of here like the snivelling cur you are.'

'No! I'll take it, if you please, Mistress. Six on the bare arse, with your cruel birch!' he murmured, rolling the words on his tongue as though they were a magical incantation.

'Well, it is less than you deserve, you worm. Why, offenders at the Marlborough Street court are frequently sentenced to fifteen strokes of the birch, and convicts in Wandsworth Prison get the same with the cat-o'-nine-tails, for crimes less heinous than yours! And don't tell me that you officers don't flog your soldiers just as brutally!'

'Some officers still do, even though it is no longer permitted. But I would never do such a barbarous thing, for it is cruel, and I cannot abide cruelty – except yours, sweet Mistress!'

'Get up, you pathetic wretch, and let me have your arse bare at once. I intend to see if you are as brave as your daughter.'

Trembling, he stood and began to undress. I was quite amused by the sight of my own panties being peeled from his big cock, which was already stiffening healthily.

'I see you are afflicted with the same problems I was obliged to correct in our last encounter,' I said. 'Your manhood is standing up in front of me, sir, and I find it quite disgusting.'

'You know I cannot control him, Mistress, when he scents your beauty.'

I smiled. 'Happily, I foresaw this, and have a solution to the problem,' I said. 'It is a delightful little device which our Mr Izzard calls his "uro-spermatory inhibitor". I took a shiny steel metronome from my drawer, the type used by piano tuners. It was about half the weight of a London brick, and was suspended from two chains with heavy clips at their ends. Swiftly I clipped the device just beneath the shaft of his penis, then let it hang like a pretty ornament from his hairy ball-sac.

'I say,' he said wonderingly.

'Is it uncomfortable?'

'Why, no. But I might feel dashed delicate if . . .'

'If your pole was insolent enough to stand up without my persmission?'

'Yes.'

'Then we mustn't let that happen, must we?' I said brightly. 'And I'll know if you are naughty, because the metronome will alert me by its ticking! Now, sir, to business. Over the sofa, if you please.'

He was barefoot and naked from the waist down, and reminded me of my sweet young faun whom I had chastised not so long before, except that where Mordevaunt's body was slender and taut, the Major rippled with hard military muscle. He positioned himself with his bare bottom raised as though for an inspection. I took my birch, and gave her a practice swish in the air. The whistle made him start, and the metronome gave a warning tick-tick under his balls.

'Gosh,' he said with a grimace. I closed the curtains, and lifted my birch.

'Isn't it nice and cosy, Major, with the fire glowing so prettily on your naked bottom? He'll glow hotter than my fire, though, when I have thrashed him for his naughtiness.'

'Oh, Mistress,' he gasped. 'Please make him squirm, for he's the naughtiest bottom in the world!'

'Why, sir, I'll whip you till you dance like a monkey, and you'll think me the cruellest of organ-grinders!'

With that, I brought the birch down firmly on his hindquarters, making him groan softly. Then I cracked him again in the same spot, and his buttocks jumped, like pretty kittens awoken from their idleness. The metronome began to tick slowly.

'Three!' I cried, taking him aslant, so that there was a delicious crisscross of pink suffusing his squirming buttocks. 'It seems, Major, that your daughter Veronica is sweet for a certain Second Lieutenant Arbuckle,' I said nonchalantly.

'What! That bounder!'

'It was for him that she wore the panties, you know, because he was with you in India, and they reminded her of him thus.'

'I didn't know. I'm not sure what to think. God, Mistress, how it hurts! My arse has never smarted like this before!'

I could hear the metronome ticking quite briskly now.

'Four!'

'God, that's tight! Mistress, you are superb! Oh! Oh! And this thing is squeezing my balls, as though it is you! It is devilish lovely!'

'But your tough arse has quite worn out my birch, sir. She'll have to be replaced, and you know I must charge you for that, if you want to take your full punishment.'

The metronome was now rattling like a machine gun.

'Yes! I'll pay! God, thrash me, Mistress! Thrash my naked arse, please, please!'

I looked down and saw his prick well-throbbing and stiff, the balls squeezed like marbles by the clips of his inhibitor. Enthralled by the sight of the helpless bare buttocks of the male squirming under my lash, I felt my sex deliciously wet. Savagely, I delivered a fifth harsh cut, and his penis leapt to full, straining erection, with the balls beautifully outlined in their tight drumskin.

The metronome chattered furiously.

'Oh! Yes!' he gasped.

'I noticed, Major, that you are already acquainted with many of our guests today,' I said.

'What? Oh, I meet a lot of people. Hunt balls, regattas, and so on.'

'Well, if any of them are curious about our little meeting here, you must tell them you can say nothing.'

'Of course. There's one cut to go, isn't there? Oh, that will be the hardest and sweetest, won't it, Mistress?'

'I have already taken the birch with both my hands, sir.'

'It'll be tighter than I can bear!'

'You will make a point of telling your friends that you are not permitted to say anything. Understood?'

'Yes, yes. Oh, flog me, Mistress!'

To the crazed rhythm of the metronome, I raised both my arms and stroked him a sixth and final time, with a veritable whopper of a cut, which made him shudder and cry out with a squealing sob, and I saw a pearl of white at his pee-hole. The Major was about to spend!

'Oh, Major Dove,' I said softly, my own sex very wet now. I put my fingers to the swollen red bulb of his trussed cock and began to rub the skin very tenderly, flicking my fingernail across the slit of his pee-hole. His sighs became a hoarse, panting rasp; his cock trembled; the metronome clicked in furious staccato accompaniment; his hot sperm spurted in a creamy jet over my fingers, and he moaned in delirious joy as the fruit of his balls bathed my woman's skin.

Suddenly there was a loud crack as the metronome split in two parts, and fell to the floor!

'You are incorrigible, Major,' I smiled, as his sobbing became a satisfied mewling sigh. 'I think that in future, to control your impetuous manhood, you must wear not just my panties, but also what we call a restrainer.' I produced one of Mr Izzard's 'Number Fours', in a soft leather pouch but with an extra-large anal tongue.

'It acts on the nerve ends,' I explained scientifically. 'To prevent unseemly engorgement of the *membrum virile*, or priapism, and I command you on your honour to wear it at all times, except, of course, when it must be removed for obvious reasons.'

The Major looked disappointed that he had to remove the thing at all, and happily spread the cheeks of his arse for me.

'I've never done anything like this before, not really,' he said.

I did not care to know what 'not really' meant as I lubricated the tongue with his own spunk, then with three or four firm thrusts had the device deep inside his tight anus, the pouch strapped on his balls and cock, and the whole buckled round his waist.

'You'll wear it until I order you to the contrary,' I said. 'Except when inconvenient – during relations with Mrs Dove, for example.'

'Oh, I don't think there is much danger of that,' he said sadly as I helped him to his feet.

'You mean you don't . . .?'

'Not for ages.'

'Then you must take your pleasures with gay girls.'

'No! I am faithful to the marriage vow!'

I thought it a shame that this lovely hard soldier's body should fall into such cruel disuse.

'Perhaps dear Thalia needs a little correction herself, to bring her to her senses,' I suggested. 'In fact, I think I might soon have occasion to interview both of you together, Major. In the meantime, I order you to make sure, on whatever pretext, that she gets a good look at your bare bottom which I have made blush so prettily.'

'Very well, Mistress, if those are your instructions.'

'They are. And before you leave, there is your account to settle. Let me see . . . one broken uro-spermatory inhibitor: four pounds seven shillings and sixpence (I made that up). One number four uro-genital restrainer: three pounds ten shillings. Oh, and of course, one new birch, *Betula pubescens*: six guineas. Total, fourteen pounds, three shillings and sixpence, please.'

'Six guineas for a new birch! The cane I had to replace for you in Windsor was only a fiver!'

'It is called inflation, Major,' I replied curtly. 'And things in town are more expensive than in the country. Here,' I handed him the birch, 'you may keep this as a souvenir. And if your Thalia wants to know why your bottom is so proud, you may show it to her.'

'Oh thank you, sweet Mistress! I dare say she will be curious.'

'Then tell her the only truth which the curious need to know about St Agatha's, which is that naughtiness must be severely punished.'

I gave him a friendly, chaste kiss on his cheek, in farewell. 'You are a very naughty boy indeed, Major Dove, and your charming daughter can be a very naughty girl. Who knows, perhaps Mrs Dove is naughty too.'

7

Leopardskin

Not long afterwards, I called on Dr Hamm of St Alcuin's, ostensibly to pay my respects as his new neighbour. But as I passed through the gnarled corridors of the ancient place, with its lovely smell of young men, sweat and muddiness, I wondered whether my true motivation was to make some business arrangement, or to be closer to the lair of my young faun, Peter Mordevaunt. Dr Hamm received me cordially and served tea, then we made small talk about the trials of running an educational institution, the incurable muddiness of young people (I thought of my sweet Freddie!) and so on.

'So tell me, Dr Hamm,' I said, sipping my tea. 'Do you beat your charges often?'

'Well, I do when I get the chance, Miss de Comynge.'

'Bare bum?'

Dr Hamm raised one of his bushy eyebrows, followed by the other bushy eyebrow, and his weatherbeaten face creased into a rather coy smile.

'Yes, indeed. Strip 'em and whip 'em, that's what we say in Africa. But they keep running away. Slippery creatures, chaps.'

'Oh ... don't you have prefects? To hold them down while you administer punishment?'

'Why, they are all prefects! Or think they are. Just because they're going to Oxford! Damn cheek.' He sighed, and poured more tea. 'Trouble is, Miss de Comynge, the money is tight, tighter than any beating I could lay out to make 'em behave.'

'Young Peter Mordevaunt ...'

'You know him? He is the worst scallywag of all! But he takes his punishment without squealing, I'll grant him.

Gave him a swishing the other day, six with a strong willow, and not a murmur. My eyes aren't what they used to be, but I could have sworn someone had lathered him before me; his bum was blushing before I laid a stroke on him!'

I pretended to cough, to hide my smirk.

'But how do you know him?'

'Oh, the fences of our properties adjoin, sir.'

'Why, so they do. I don't get about much these days. So you're the new boss woman over at St Agatha's. Good luck to you. I didn't care for those Lowe people. Name suited 'em, ha!'

We sat in the doctor's book-laden study, every inch an antiquarian's den. I did not ask what he was a doctor of, although, from his library, it could have been any one of a dozen subjects. He was a handsome man of about fifty, with the tanned face common to those who have served the empire with sympathy in exotic places.

His study looked out on to a veritable jungle of overgrown trees and bushes, and the musty corridors of St Alcuin's echoed to the cries and war whoops of his unruly charges. I saw that his walls were hung with a variety of African curios – masks, head-dresses, robes, and a big leopardskin – and that his library contained many tomes of African interest. One volume caught my eye: 'Flagellation and Fertility in the Initiation Rites of the Upper Congo'. He saw my eye on it, and said shyly:

'Ah, I wrote that, you know. Rather proud of it, actually.'

'May I?'

'Of course.'

He handed me the heavy book and I leafed through it, dwelling on the copious lithograph illustrations which depicted various rather stimulating scenes. There were pictures of pretty, naked African males wearing strange masks as they endured hearty floggings from the equally naked females of their tribe, or else dealt out floggings to the lovely dark bottoms of the same females. In some pictures, young men and women were coupling in vigorous love-bouts under the kindly eye of the tribal 'mammas', who bore a striking resemblance to Deirdre, my Matron.

'Africa must be a very fertile continent,' I observed.

Dr Hamm smiled.

'I have very fond memories of the Dark Continent,' he replied. 'I lived the life of a native, you know, sharing all their rites and customs.' Tribal whoops and clatters rang outside in the jungle, and I supposed he felt quite at home here in St Alcuin's, but he sighed.

'I wish I could return. My heart lies there. Lack of money.' He shrugged sadly. 'I could find a wife of means, I suppose, but I could never happily marry here in England.'

'Surely, sir, you are a personable gentleman, of good position, and there must be many ladies who . . .'

He held up his hand, and smiled.

'No, it's not that,' he said enigmatically, and sighed again.

Suddenly I felt my heart well up with sympathy for this attractive gentleman, trapped here, and lonely, thousands of miles from what he thought home.

'What, then?' I persevered.

'I had a wife whom I loved dearly, but she died of one of the plagues that affect our poor Africa.'

'An African?'

'Of course. Shortly after her death, I acquired this pile by inheritance from a distant cousin and, having no other sources of funds, returned to England. I have tried to interest myself in European women, but I fear it is impossible. African women understand the male so perfectly, you see.'

'Why, sir, a woman is a woman,' I said archly. 'We are all the same in the places that count most for a gentleman's satisfaction.'

I must admit that my pride was nettled; and my concupiscence aroused, not least by the morsel of information that Dr Hamm actually owned St Alcuin's. I rose and approached him. Then I stood behind his chair and placed my hands on his shoulders, massaging them firmly. I could hear him breathing in my perfume, which I had applied specially for our meeting.

'Dr Hamm,' I said sternly. 'I too have known money worries, but by common sense have raised myself out of them. You can do the same. You possess St Alcuin's, as I understand?'

'Lock, stock and barrel.'

'Including the tied scholarships to Oxford?'

'Of course.'

'I suggest that the sale of St Alcuin's would provide you with passage to Africa and a living for the rest of your days there.'

'Would that it were so!' he groaned, and now I leant forward so that his head was cushioned by my breasts. 'In Africa, begging your pardon, dear lady, I was known for ... for my virile powers. To return to my people, I should be obliged to take a wife, or several. And I should be obliged to satisfy them. I have been so long alone that I fear I cannot any longer.'

Now my fingers crept down his neck and inside his loose collar.

'Come, sir, a thing once learned is never forgotten. I am a woman of the world, sir, and it grieves me to see a handsome gentleman denied female company.'

'I fear it is hopeless,' he sighed, but did not flinch from my touch, which had now become a caress of his manly breast.

'Hopeless is a word which at St Agatha's would earn a girl a thrashing,' I said softly. He turned and smiled, blushing quite sweetly. I looked him directly in the eyes. 'Yes, sir,' I said. 'I think you have given me serious offence.'

He nodded, shyly and hopefully!

'If, sir, you felt restored to your manly vigour there would be nothing to stop you from selling St Alcuin's and returning, solvent and a whole man, to your beloved Africa.'

'But who would buy it?' he said.

'St Agatha's will,' I replied briskly. 'After I have proved to you the efficacy of the St Agatha's way. First, sir, you will bend over your desk and lower your breeches, for I am going to cane your bare bottom for you, as though you were the naked African in the lithographs you have.'

'Oh, Miss! Very well! Yes!' he cried. 'But wait – first . . .'

Dr Hamm took down from his wall the leopardskin I had admired, and a curious mask of bones and feathers. I frowned, puzzled, as he handed me the heavy animal's skin.

'Please, Miss, put it on, I beg you!'

I almost laughed, but of course men do have such strange fancies where intimate punishments are concerned.

'This is rather unusual,' I said mildly.

'It is according to the ritual of my people. I must wear the flogging mask and you the robe of the vengeful leopard goddess!'

I was quite glad that I did not have to wear the mask, and said that I agreed. He sighed with happiness and put the mask over his head, giving himself a very fearsome aspect.

'Now, Miss, I must tell you – it is according to the sacred rite – that I must be fully naked for my beating.'

Muffled by the mask, his voice sounded like a tuba.

'Very well, sir,' I said. 'We must respect what is sacred.'

Dr Hamm began to unbutton his suit, removed his braces and cravat, then his spats and shirt collar, fiddling with the studs in agitation, and it struck me that men are just as cumbersome in their apparel as we women, though in different ways, of course. At last it was time for him to unroll his pantaloons, and he stood before me, his leathery body completely naked.

Naturally I inspected his manhood: a slender thing, but very long, like some Africans, and quite still. His body was tanned and well-muscled, and I supposed a life in the veldt, or bush, or jungle, had kept him limber. I was no stranger to older gentlemen – my lucrative experiences as a gay girl in Cornwall had taught me that age does not change the important part of a man – but I had never found one actually stimulating before. Even hidden behind his funny mask, there was something interesting about Dr Hamm. Yet I had never before seen a man's cock so limp in my presence! Normally, the sheer excitement of nakedness is enough to make them tremble.

'Well, sir,' I said. 'This is a fine leopardskin, but I wager the African goddesses did not wear a lady's black formal dress. So in the interests of verisimilitude' (I had learned this word from the lustful Reverend Turnpike, when he photographed me nude) 'I propose to disrobe for your flogging.' His mouth gaped. Smoothly, I divested myself of my black silk dress, my stockings, suspenders and shoes, and said coolly:

'Perhaps you will be so kind as to unlace my bodice, sir.'

He did so with trembling fingers, and with my back to him, I slipped out of the tight red bodice, then abruptly whirled to face him, making my heavy naked breasts bob before his eyes. With a flourish, I draped the leopardskin over my shoulders, and finally stepped out of my red lacy panties, which were rather full and billowy in the bloomer fashion. I threw them at him, and he caught them and blushed, then laid them carefully on the desk.

'You will please furnish me with a suitable implement, sir,' I said, as he stared in awe at the curly lushness of my mink. No doubt he could smell the scent I had dabbed on my sex-lips. In response, he fetched a fearsome switch of bound twigs, somewhat like a birch, but harder looking.

'They are the twigs of the banyan tree,' he said, 'that grows beside the great River Congo. That is what I used to flog my charges there, so it is right that I taste the same punishment. And what sweet punishment it shall be, for ... for you are very pretty, Miss, I ... I have never seen a white woman undressed before!'

'A strange compliment indeed! But thank you,' I said sweetly, as he bent over his big teak desk, with his bottom splayed for the kiss of the whip. I noticed that his nose was positioned only a couple of inches from the warm aroma of my discarded panties.

'I take it these rods have touched young Mordevaunt's bare arse?'

'Oh, yes,' he said. 'Many times!' And at that thought, I felt myself moisten in my sex.

'Well, let us get on, sir, with a nice tight six on your bare bum,' I said, feeling quite savage as I looked at those naked globes trembling nervously in anticipation of my chastisement.

I raised the whipping tool and brought it down with a whistle on his taut buttocks. He jumped, then, to my surprise, let out a great roar, which his mask made sound like the bellow of a wild beast. I found this curiously exciting, and responded in kind:

'So, you are a beast of the jungle, are you? I, then, am the beast that shall tame you!' And with my second cut I made a bloodcurdling yell which I imagined to be that of a leopard, or near enough.

'Yes! God, how tight you flog! My arse is on fire!'

Straight away, I delivered a third stroke, roaring lustily. I placed the stroke in exactly the same place as the others, and his poor bottom rewarded me with a vivid crimson blush. How it must hurt, I thought, and laid the fourth stroke again on those pretty blossoms.

By now he was indeed howling like an animal, and so was I. My sex was now gushing wet at my excitement, and in my giddy fury I imagined myself indeed to be a jungle beast. The leopardskin slithered sensuously across my back and buttocks, tickling me with its soft hairs, and my body was already glistening with sweat.

'Five!' I cried, lashing his squirming arse-globes with all my might.

'Aah!' he responded, his face pressed to my panties on the desk, breathing hungrily of their perfume. 'Oh, Miss. Oh my beautiful leopard mistress; your lash awakens me, you are all the scents of the flowers and trees, the strength of the wild beasts, the roar of the jungle ...'

I looked down and saw that his penis was half-stiff!

'Six!' I shouted, and with both my hands on the banyan rods, I laid a cut on his naked quivering arse so ferocious that I thought he must faint. But instead, his cock leapt to its full sumptuous height, and I felt my quim quite gushing with wetness. I was no longer a Governess, all prim and proper, I was a female animal, transported from the sultry tropics to flog my naked male into submission.

He sobbed into his mask, a low, crooning sound halfway

between pain and joy. I grabbed him by the neck and pulled him towards me. Then I tore the mask from his face and kissed him on the lips, while I put my hand on his balls and squeezed them gently. My fingers went to the tip of his throbbing cock, which I caressed for a moment or two, tonguing him in a mouth which was increasingly responsive to my caress.

'You are a man, sir,' I hissed. 'And you will pleasure me like a man. Sir, you will fuck me. My cunt is wet and gushing for you, and wants your stiff cock inside her, this instant!'

I lay down on the floor, with my silky leopardskin as a rug, and pulled him down to me, forcing his cock against the swollen lips of my moist cunny. Then, I guided him into me, gasping as that thick tingling tool filled me so warmly. I clasped his burning buttocks with my ankles, and directed him thus to thrust into me; bucking underneath him until, with sighs of joy, he understood, and responded to my rhythm. With one hand, I held his neck, so that I could press my mouth and tongue to his, and with the other, guided his own fingers to my stiff clit, so that he could frig me there.

What he had forgotten, he soon relearnt and was soon fucking me with the energy of a young lion. This excited me beyond endurance, and the pressure of his dry finger on my swollen clit, like a hunter's seasoned finger on his trigger, brought me surprisingly soon to a shuddering orgasm, which I think took him aback as much as it did me. Still he frigged my clit, quite gently now, and arched his back so that he could take my quivering teat in his mouth, sucking on it as though I were giving him milk. I was glowing in the aftermath of my orgasm, and felt just in the mood to get to the heart of the matter.

'Well, sir,' I panted as his hard cock thudded remorselessly into my hot wet quim. 'Now you see that you are fit to return to your beloved Africa.'

'Yes,' he gasped. 'I believe so. I so want to spend in your sweet body, Mistress, I know I shall spend! Then I shall be a man.'

'Let us agree then on a price for St Alcuin's, sir,' I said. 'And then I promise to milk you of all your lovely spunk.'

'Now . . .?'

'Of course. When may we converse more intimately? Now, St Alcuin's is not exactly in the best of repair, nor does it bring in much in the way of fees, I suppose. It will need a lot of work. To be honest, I think the best we can do is fifteen –'

'Oh Mistress! Fifteen hundred pounds. Well, it might be enough to let me live in Africa in adequate style, but to be a prince, a man with many wives, why, I should need twice that. I'm sure St Alcuin's has potential!'

'You drive a hard bargain, sir. But the magic of your hard tool is enough to sway a weak woman like myself. Shall we say three thousand pounds, then? It is agreed?'

'Agreed. Oh, thank you!'

The thought of money made his fucking quite merciless, and I responded by squeezing his cock with my throbbing quim to milk him of spunk, and in a very short time he cried out once more and shuddered as his sweet jet bathed the neck of my womb with all the hot creamy spend that he had stored for so long.

His fucking had made me hot again, even after my lovely spend, but I thought it best to take my leave, as businesslike as possible. On my way out, accompanied by my fawning African lover, we passed Peter Mordevaunt, who looked at me knowingly, making my cunt damnably, sweetly wet all over again. And I think he knew, for he smiled with those angel's lips!

'Ah, Mordevaunt,' bubbled Dr Hamm. 'Miss de Comynge of St Agatha's is to be the new Principal of St Alcuin's!'

Mordevaunt smiled, and I replied as coolly as I could:

'We have met, Dr Hamm. In fact I believe young Mordevaunt is in possession of an article of mine.' I referred of course to the panties which I knew he had removed from my desk after I had thrashed him. 'And we share an interest in wild flowers, especially the bright red flowers that a lady's birch makes blossom on the bare buttocks of an errant young man.'

And now it was his turn to blush.

I was exultant as I made my way back to St Agatha's, having agreed on a meeting with lawyers and accountants to sort out our transaction 'sealed with a kiss', as it were. I had St Alcuin's and those valuable scholarships to Oxford; I had young Peter Mordevaunt in my power, as well as his lusty young fellow students, and I had bought the place for three thousand pounds, when I had been about to offer fifteen!

The transfer of ownership of St Alcuin's to St Agatha's, that is, to me, was effected, and kept, without fuss or undue publicity. The students and staff of each establishment were informed, of course, but were assured that no dramatic changes would be made, except that henceforth I was to be Principal of St Alcuin's: any pupils worthy of severe punishment would be referred to me.

Apart from that, the two masters of St Alcuin's, Messrs Carter and Dobbs, were left to get on with beating a semblance of knowledge into their charges. Both were gin-soaked. One was a defrocked clergyman and the other a cashiered army officer, so I imagined them quite suited to the instruction of young men in an academic institution. I surmised that the students had long since learned to look after themselves.

It was the land, and even more the ripe young male inmates, of St Alcuin's which interested me. On that unkempt land roamed a dozen sturdy, lustful young whelps whose talents I proposed to awaken, as I awakened those of my swish girls: for it is wrong to assume that only gentlemen feel the stirring of the flesh, and are willing to pay for their secret pleasures. I had observed the demure wives of my new parents, and wondered how many of those splendid mares were being regularly and satisfactorily tupped by their stallions.

Dr Hamm departed with great and tearful ceremony on his way to Southampton, bound on a ship for Africa. I had said a private farewell, giving him a sound whipping with a willow stick, and then allowing him to reconfirm his virile powers with a swift rogering of my bumhole (this time sans leopardskin).

I then set about organising a little outing so that my girls and boys could get to know each other. This was to be a cycling trip to East Molesey, by the river, where we would enjoy a picnic, the weather having taken a warmer turn in recent weeks.

The young men of St Alcuin's were divided into those who knew all about girls, and those who considered girls soppy. Either way, they welcomed the chance of an excursion, and a respite from classes; of course my girls were thrilled, and talked of nothing but young men and clothes, but chiefly clothes.

The day before our outing, I invited the young ladies of swish to a rather copious tea, for it was time to be blunt.

'I have a gift for you, girls,' I said, not beating about the proverbial. 'It is a little brooch which you will wear proudly on formal occasions.'

There were oohs of pleasure as they unwrapped their presents: each of the seven girls received a disc of amber, set in silver, and inside the amber was a tress of my own hair, cunningly bound at the end with the tiniest little silver chain, so that it resembled a miniature birch! I had had the skilful Mr Izzard create these jewels, and was well pleased with the satisfaction of the girls.

'The eight of you are now members of the club known as swish,' I said grandly. 'St Agatha's is an elite, and you are an elite within her.'

Everyone was very excited, which pleased me enormously.

'You have not invited Jane Ruttle, Miss?' said Phoebe Ford-Taylor.

'No, Phoebe, I haven't', I replied.

'She's a cissie!' agreed Dotti van de Ven.

'Blubs when she has her bottom tanned!' said Vanessa Lumsden, and there was a murmur of general agreement.

'Very well,' I said. 'You have brought us to the heart of the matter.

Swish is, to put it bluntly, for girls who know how to take and administer punishment. None of you is a stranger to the cane or birch on your naked bottom, and all of you have taken a beating proudly. It shall be your task to teach others to do the same. You shall have powers, special powers, to administer punishment where required and, this is the nub of the matter, it shall not always be to the rear of a St Agatha's girl.'

'You mean, girls from other academies?' said Amanda Nightingale.

'I mean, young men from other academies, Amanda,' I replied coolly. 'And sometimes gentlemen, who are not in education at all, but whose naughtiness requires a sound thrashing!'

The girls blushed, their eyes sparkled, and there was a tinkle of nervous, excited giggles.

'Why,' drawled the American, Connie Sunday, 'it'll be just like when I had to whup my brothers back in Mesa Grande; tie 'em to the corral fence and tan 'em bare-ass naked, and I guess English boys are just as full of devilment as American ones.'

'How shall we find such gentlemen, Miss?' said Veronica Dove, with a serene smile.

'Oh, you won't have to find them, Veronica, for I shall find them. Or rather, they shall find me. You see girls, part of the duty of St Agatha's is to prepare you for your lives as women of the world. And that of course means learning to deal with men in all their exasperating simplicity. The most important thing to remember is that all men are little boys, and require frequent chastisement, even where we do not possess corrals to tie them to. St Agatha's has consented to absorb our brother establishment, St Alcuin's, partly in order to introduce you to the muddy world of the male. And to that end we are all going on a cycling trip tomorrow, to the pretty village of East Molesey, just by Hampton Court Palace, for a picnic by the banks of the Thames. At least, you shall cycle, while I follow in my automobile, "riding shotgun", as Connie would no doubt put it.'

'You mean, Miss,' said Prudence Proudfoot, 'that the girls of Swish will have to chastise naughty men?'

'Yes, Prudence. And you shall have the finest frocks to

wear, jewels and perfume, and there shall be little gifts for each of you when you have pleased me. Now, being a lady is demanding work, sometimes. If any girl does not feel up to it, then she is in no way obliged to be a member of our club.'

'Our club, Miss?'

'I am the Mistress of the club,' I said. 'But it is up to you to elect your own officers, devise a set of rules, and of course, punishments.'

'And we shall have to be entertained by gentlemen, and lace their naked bottoms?'

'Yes.'

'Ooh,' chorussed my girls, one and all. 'How exciting!'

'Good,' I concluded. 'Now, are there any questions?'

'Yes, Miss,' said Florence Bages, with a sly grin, 'the chaps from St Alcuin's that we are to meet tomorrow – have they been naughty?'

'I wouldn't be at all surprised,' I said, smiling.

8

A Dip in the Thames

Four chaps to eight girls! It was enough. Out of the dozen denizens of St Alcuin's the rest apparently thought that girls, picnics, cycling and cycling picnics with girls were 'soppy'.

We had three strapping young bucks, named Booter, Weldon and Phipps, and my faun, Peter Mordevaunt, who seemed, by the leonine force of his character, in subtle control of his colleagues. He had made sure they were all scrubbed and laundered. When the males learned that our destination was East Molesey, nothing would do but that we must visit the maze in Hampton Court Palace first, before settling down to our picnic by the river. I readily assented, curious myself to visit this famous labyrinth. Booter, smug at knowing the place, assured us that it was impossible to get lost under his guidance, and that even if one did, the wardens came round regularly to guide one out. I calculated our journey time, and saw that the maze would fill a comfortable hour before we settled down by our riverbank.

We set off, therefore, in fine spirits towards Kingston-upon-Thames. The morning was sky-blue bright, and the pretty cycling frocks of my Swish girls made a wonderful display as they swirled in the breeze, with an occasional glimpse of regulation blue panties that was missed by the boys as they huffed and puffed to stay in front of the pack. Freddie and I followed in my gleaming new Panhard-Levassor, both splendidly accoutred in goggles, gloves and crimson leathers. I was in fact able to drive the contraption, having learnt the mysteries of gears, brakes, chains and pulleys quite easily, but I let Freddie take the wheel, as a sop to his manly pride. The dear lamb! He was so grand as he raced along behind the bicycling girls at a shuddering fifteen miles per hour.

Bushy Park was glorious with spring foliage; through the gates, we saw the deer at play. Our mood was carefree when we arrived at the gates of Hampton Court, despite our exertions, or rather theirs, for I had enjoyed a lovely trip watching Freddie wrestling with gearbox and steering wheel. I meanwhile, sucked on a lollipop and occasionally amused myself by tickling him just where his cock bulged so seductively beneath the tight crimson leather, which caused our automobile to perform alarming swerves.

The delights of the palace itself were for another day; I had arranged a group rate to admit us all to the maze, informing my charges that a penny would be added to their fees. We paused for a glass of lemonade from the copious hampers Freddie had loaded in the back of the car, and in we went. All except Freddie, that is, who was deputised like a good chauffeur to mind our car and bicycles.

The maze was indeed guarded by serious uniformed men with moustaches and long flagpoles. It was explained to us that the maze was 'swept' every hour to pick up strays, and that to be rescued, it sufficed to stay put and call help! every few minutes. Thus encouraged, we ventured into the maze, where a disagreement took place. Booter said he knew the fastest way to the heart, and proposed to lead us thither; Mordevaunt, to my surprise (since he had not visited the maze before), said that he knew a quicker way. There was much good-natured argument, and it seemed the girls, being conservative, preferred to follow the knowledgeable Booter. Mordevaunt did not seem put out by this humiliation but looked at me coolly and said:

'I wager Miss de Comynge will prefer to come with me and see if I don't know the fastest way to the heart of the maze.'

'Ha!' I said, feeling a slight frisson of excitement. 'And what will you wager?'

'Well, that should be up to you, Miss,' he said meekly. 'Perhaps whoever of Booter and me is last to the heart should pay a forfeit, to be decided by the young ladies.'

The girls cheered excitedly, for all girls love a contest between young men, especially when they are allowed to choose the loser's penalty.

'I'm game,' I said.

We set off in opposite directions, with Veronica Dove in charge of the Booter expedition, and the proviso that we should in any event reassemble by our vehicles in one hour. Mordevaunt scarcely paid me heed as he plunged surefootedly through the corridors of the maze, startling wandering couples and families with his single-minded pace. I kept up with him rather breathlessly, and supposed him to possess some mysterious tracking sense from his exotic homeland. On and on we went, twisting and turning, until we had left everyone else behind, and came to an apparent dead end.

Mordevaunt turned to face me, with a strange smile.

'There, Miss!' he said.

'There what?' I replied, hot and cross. 'This isn't the centre of the maze.'

All around us, forlorn cries for help! rent the heavens, and I thought we must soon add to them.

'I said nothing about the centre, Miss,' he said solemnly. 'I said I knew the way to the heart of the maze.'

He approached me and I saw that under his skimpy cycling shorts there was a distinct swelling! Most impudently he caressed my chin with his fingertips. I swallowed nervously, as much in trepidation as at the knowledge that his caress thrilled me.

'I mean,' he said, 'the beautiful dark maze that is a woman's soul, Miss.'

For a moment I was too stunned to speak, yet felt myself weak with a strange, fearful desire that made all my limbs tremble.

'Mordevaunt,' I gasped at last. 'What do you want?'

'Why, Miss, I want you,' he said simply. 'Don't you see how much you excite me? You have always excited me, Miss; and when you flogged me, and – well, you know – my excitement knew no bounds, and I knew I must have you. I wear your panties with which you milked my seed, to be near to you. But it's scarcely enough, is it?'

'I suppose not,' I sighed, my sex seeping hot and wet with the moisture of my desire. 'Oh, Mordevaunt, you are impudent. This is madness. There are people everywhere, I have only to cry for help.'

'There are no people here,' he said with a lazy smile. 'And cry, by all means, Miss, just like all those others, who will be rescued by the park-keeper in an hour. Alternatively, if you find my desire in poor taste, you have only to walk back through the maze. No one stands in your way.'

How cruel he was to offer me the choice of freedom!

'Well, – I might get lost,' I said lamely, and he looked me in the eyes, and knew that he had won. My face was flushed; my sex gushing; my whole body shivering with desire, heightened by the extraordinary place and danger of discovery. He smiled coldly.

'Lift up your nice crimson skirts, Miss, and lower your panties, for I am going to make your bare bum just as crimson as your leathers.'

My heart thudded. 'What?'

He chose a long, thin branch, well studded with buds, from the yew hedge, and snapped it off so that the green wood was splintered into a jagged tongue.

'I intend to lace you, Miss. – Very hard.'

'It is an outrage! I am your governess, boy!' I cried, feebly.

'Your eyes tell me it is no outrage, Miss. Now lower your panties, for I am going to thrash your naked bottom, as you so cruelly thrashed mine. It is a punishment for all the sleepless nights I have passed with your image burning my brain.'

My breath came in sharp little gasps, as I melted before the quiet ferocity of his lust.

'Oh, Mordevaunt,' I blurted. 'I didn't know . . .'

'Yes you did,' he replied coolly. 'You knew, and loved my torment, Miss.'

'Well, then,' I sighed, after a long pause. 'I suppose I do deserve punishment.'

I lifted my leather driving skirt to reveal my white frilly panties, stockings and garter belt. He swished his cane through the air, and it whistled.

'Put your skirt well up, over your back, Miss, and lower the panties,' he said. 'Then bend over and touch your toes. It is the St Alcuin's way, and as our new principal, you should be familiar with our traditions!'

Numbly, I obeyed, and was soon clutching the points of my crimson boots with my skirt up over my shoulders, my naked buttocks exposed to the cool air. My panties were lowered across my thighs and I was afraid he would see the wet patch where my sex had flooded so copiously! I heard his breath now as hot as my own.

'Such soft, firm globes, Miss,' he whispered. 'What a shame to make them blush, but blush they shall, and hotter than you can imagine.'

'Please,' I begged, 'don't be cruel to me, Mordevaunt.'

I jumped as the first cut of the cane lashed my bare bottom, right across the centre, but I did not cry out.

'I intend to be as cruel to you as you have been to me, Miss,' he replied, panting. 'That is fair.'

A second stroke whipped most powerfully across my naked rump, and I quivered as the white-hot glow spread through my bottom.

'Oh, God,' I said. 'That is tight, boy! That is so tight! Where did you learn to whip so smartly? God, how it hurts! My poor bare bottom's on fire! Please be kind. Oh, how many must I take? How many ... Master?'

My quim, already wet with my love-juice, gushed so copiously at that thrilling word that I felt the hot fluid course down the inside of my thighs and into my stocking tops. Yes! He was, for this glorious moment, my master! My bare woman's buttocks naked to his rod, and naked, too for his manhood to thrust into my helpless wet cunt! How I adored the boy at that moment, adored the sting of his cruel cane on my defenceless bare rear, and longed for him to fuck me!

The caning continued in silence but for the whistle of the yew branch and my gasps, as that damnable splayed tip caught me again and again in the tender middle of my clenched bare buttocks. I gulped the fresh spring air, the scent of the flowers making my head swim with delight as the glow of my caned bottom suffused my whole body in a frenzy of delicious smarting pain. I shut my eyes and felt that green rod crack on my defenceless nates, and imagined it was his penis, hard and long and springy, hurting me unthinkably with each loving stroke. I lost count of his strokes; every one was laid with delicate force, almost with tenderness, to tickle the greatest pain from my bare flogged behind.

'Oh, Mordevaunt! God, it hurts so damnably, you beast! I never flogged you like this!'

'You did, Miss,' he panted.

'Oh, Mordevaunt . . .'

He did not need to answer, for he understood what my woman's moan signified. No sooner had the cane laced my buttocks with a final, fiery stroke than I heard it cast aside, and felt my quim-lips parted by gentle fingers and then, with a silent roar in my whirling head, his penis thrust into my soaking slit and he began to buck me with the hardest, most tender strokes imaginable, slapping his belly against my quivering bare bum with the utmost ruthlessness as though my whipping were continuing in another, sweeter guise.

I can keep silent under a flogging, but now I could not.

'Oh, Mordevaunt, fuck me!' I heard myself cry. 'Fuck my wet cunt. Feel how wet she is for you. God, you are so hard! Oh Master, fuck your slave!'

'You'll punish me for it later, you sweet bitch,' he hissed. 'But by God I'll fuck you now. I'll make that soft arse squirm for me.'

'She squirms already, she dances for you, Master! She is alive with your sweet flogging!'

And as he fucked so hard and so gently, I felt a new rain of blows on my reddened behind, as his hands cracked down to spank my hot, naked arse-cheeks.

My clit throbbed and my pussy gushed fluid over his stroking cock; I could not hold back from my spend. It came upon me as I felt his cock shudder. The spanking stopped and he gripped my hips tightly holding me to him as his glans pressed at the neck of my womb to spurt his powerful hot jet of creamy sperm deep inside me, and as I felt him spend, I howled in my own orgasm that washed my very heart in a flood of pleasure.

'Ah ... Ah ...' I panted, opening my eyes to realise that I was still bent over in the position of my beating!

Suddenly a tousled head appeared under my lips, and I saw Mordevaunt kneel and kiss my crimson boots, taking the points full in his mouth while I caressed his neck and hair.

'Thank you, lovely Mistress,' he gasped, as he sucked my shoe leather. 'I am your slave.'

'Get up,' I said at last. 'You are not my slave, you are my student. And make no mistake, you shall be well whipped for your insolence today.'

'Mistress, lace my bare arse until I cry for mercy, then show me none! For my insolence, I know!'

'Yes, Mordevaunt,' I sighed, smiling. 'Such sweet insolence must not go unpunished.'

At that moment there was a cough and I turned in alarm. One of the moustached wardens, waving his flagpole, stared at us. Luckily my skirts were down, and Mordevaunt had tucked away his naked manhood but he was still kneeling at my toecaps.

'Is anything the matter, mum?' he said. 'I heard a call for help and I have come to show you the way out of the maze. There's not many as gets this far.'

'Oh,' I said, wondering what he meant by that. 'No, there is no need. I was not calling for help; a stone got into my boot, and my student here is attending to it. We know the way back, thank you.'

'Oh, very good, mum.'

And the worthy departed.

Mordevaunt led me back to the maze entrance, both of us silent, not touching, though I think we both longed to. I remembered my fevered words in which I had acknowledged him as my master, however fleetingly, and in the height of passion. Yet I did not regret them! There are times when the sternest of mistresses longs to be a master's slave, and feel his cane caress her naked behind.

Strangely, there was no sign of Booter's party when we rejoined Freddie at the car. He looked at Mordevaunt with undisguised suspicion, even hostility, as I explained what had been organised. But I silenced him with one of my chilliest looks, which he knew was a warning of a savage beating if he persisted in his bad manners. At last the Booter group emerged from the grounds of Hampton Court, all giggling as they saw us.

'Well, Miss, said Booter, 'I think I have won the wager over my friend Mordevaunt, for we waited a time but saw neither hide nor hair of you at the heart of the maze.'

'Indeed,' I said, 'I must admit that –'

'Nonsense Booter, you chump!' cried Mordevaunt. 'We were there before you and got tired of waiting!'

'You expect me to believe that?'

'Well, I left a souvenir of our passage,' said Mordevaunt coolly. 'It was a yew cane which I plucked from the hedge, and used to amuse myself.'

The cheeky young pup! I thought. I would definitely beat him for insolence!

'And how should I notice that?' scoffed Booter.

'Oh, I noticed it,' said Veronica Dove softly, and held up the splayed yew cane at whose caress my bottom had so recently quivered. 'I thought it awfully pretty and took it as a keepsake. It will do for our Swish gatherings, won't it, Miss?'

Her eyes met Mordevaunt's, then she looked coolly at me, and I blushed! She knew . . .

'Yes, Miss,' said my young faun, as we prepared to continue our journey. 'I promised I would take you to the heart of the maze.'

Past the pretty village of East Molesey, a towpath ran a little way along the banks of the river. We saw a few families out for their pre-luncheon stroll; the gentlemen with merry straw boaters and the women gay with parasols and summer dresses, although it was as yet only a lusty spring. But ladies will take the earliest opportunity and brave every discomfort to bare their flesh!

I directed my party further ahead, until the terrain was quite deserted, and found a muddy track leading down to the riverbank, easily navigable by our vehicles, but unlikely to attract pedestrians. At the end of this track we found the ideal spot for our picnic, a secluded dell by a bend in the river, where we could imagine ourselves in the apple-blossom fastnesses of rural England, which, by London standards, we were.

The noonday sun was hot, and all of us were quite lathered with the sweat of our various exertions. Chirping with delight, the girls spread rugs and tea things, while the young men watched gawkily, marvelling at our charming female ability to set up home wherever we find ourselves. Freddie seemed more composed, although he still looked daggers at Mordevaunt, but he fingered his fledgling moustache with the satisfaction of owning something the other males did not. Old Father Thames flowed cool and serene, and longing eyes were turned to him. I voiced the unspoken thoughts of the company:

'Wouldn't it be nice to cool off in the water?' I said gaily.

The girls all cried with excitement.

'We have no bathing costumes, Miss,' said Phoebe Ford-Taylor.

'Adam and Eve had no bathing costumes, Phoebe,' I replied. 'And this is a veritable garden of Eden, I think.'

'You mean skinny dipping, Miss?' said Connie Sunday. 'Why, girls, that's what we do in Arizona – find a crick and jump in, bare-ass.'

'Quite, Connie,' I said. 'Although I am not sure "bare-ass" is a ladylike expression.'

The chaps were all blushing and pretending not to hear, and my lustful Freddie, no stranger to a woman's bare body, looked just as excited.

'Well, Miss,' said Veronica Dove, 'there is the question of Booter's forfeit, isn't there? We are supposed to decide it. If the boys turn their backs, we can bathe, and discuss the matter out of their earshot.'

'Ooh, yes!' chorussed the young ladies. I nodded my agreement and ordered Freddie to supervise the lads so that they should not peek.

'Better still, Mistress,' he said, 'I can take them to the other side of the bushes, round the river bend, and we can all bathe ourselves, for we are just as hot as you females.'

'I'm sure you are, Freddie,' I said, tapping him mischievously between his thighs, where, despite the leather pouch of his restrainer, a lovely bulge sprang all the lovelier for the discomfort I knew it caused. 'But won't you have some explaining to do, when the others see your restrainer?' He bit his lip.

'You can be very cruel, Mistress,' he said softly. 'But, Mistress, I am proud to wear it for you. They will be jealous when they see I am your slave!'

'So I'm not really cruel enough, am I? Now off you go for your bathe, Freddie,' I said. 'And afterwards you shall have a nice glass of wine with me.'

No sooner had they trooped off under Freddie's instruction, than my girls were scampering naked into the water! Their clothes, as if by magic, had been stripped and neatly folded on the bank, and soon they were splashing and laughing like so many Greek naiads in the paintings of Mr Burne-Jones. It is so lovely to see girls naked together, their minds freed from care as their bodies are freed of clothing. They splashed and giggled, caressed each other's hair, breasts and bellies, and playfully examined their bottoms for evidence of their most recent chastisements. Veronica Dove, who seemed to be emerging as their natural leader, huddled them into a whispered conclave, and I heard them discussing the forfeit to be dealt out to young Booter for his tardiness at the Hampton Court maze.

'His arse ought to feel the sjambok,' said Dotti van de Ven, gruffly.

'I'd like to tan him with a rawhide whip,' giggled Connie Sunday. 'Make him buck like a mule.'

'We have neither rawhide nor sjambok,' said Veronica, 'but I do possess the green yew cane, and I propose to give him sex of the best for his presumption.'

'On his bare bottom?' said Amanda Nightingale.

'Of course.'

'Ooh, I've never seen a chap getting a lacing before. And on his bare bum. Ooh!'

'Why,' boasted Connie. 'I've seen it and dealt it too. They squirm just the same as any gal, I assure you. All this stuff about men being strong is just hooey! And I tell you, there's nothing nicer than seeing one well tanned on his naked behind. How they wriggle, and try not to cry out! I'm getting all wet just thinking about it, and I don't mean from the River Thames.'

'That's settled, then,' said Veronica sternly. 'Six of the best for our arrogant friend, bare bum.' Then she turned to me. 'Aren't you coming in, Miss?' cried Veronica Dove. 'The girls of Swish invite you, our Mistress!'

'I?' I replied, pretending to be surprised. 'I have more serious things to do, girls. I am going to make a photographic record of our little outing!'

There were gasps of surprise as I removed from my car the photographic apparatus I had from Mr Izzard. It was the latest thing from America, he assured me, a small box which could snap pictures almost instantly, without the need for tripods, lights or other encumbrances. I began to take pictures, my camera clicking busily as the girls delightedly preened and pouted, thrusting themselves into my viewfinder. Such innocent, charming, vanity! And I have to admit that my purposes were not entirely recreational, for I proposed with the consent of Swish, to make an album in which my girls' charms would be presented in every aspect to potential gentlemen friends.

The sun beat down. Photography is as hot a work as any other and I sweated under my leathers. At last I could refuse their entreaties no longer and stripped myself to their ironic cheers, then dived naked into the water amongst them. The caress of the water was heavenly, and it was soon accompanied by caresses of a different kind, as bare hands stroked my bottom, back and even my breasts, to coos of admiration.

'Oh, Miss,' said Florence Bages. 'You are more beautiful than any of us! Your bosoms are so plump and your bottom so big and firm!'

'Nonsense!' I said. 'But thank you for the compliment. You are all beautiful, girls. Why, Phoebe's breasts are bigger than mine, Amanda's bottom more rounded, Dotti's arms more muscular, Veronica's eyes more lustrous . . .'

I felt a cool hand stroking my bottom, which sent shivers up my spine. It was Veronica, standing so close in the water that the tips of our breasts tickled. She smiled very knowingly at me.

'Why, Miss, I saw that the cheeks of your bottom are all pink and glowing, and your skin feels so hot! Anyone would think you had taken a lacing just recently.'

'Oh, it is just the irritation from my car seat,' I lied, blushing.

'One would almost think you had felt that green yew switch across your naked backside, Miss,' continued Veronica sweetly. 'But I suppose appearances can be deceptive.'

'Well, Veronica, they can indeed. And if we weren't all naked chums together in the sunshine, I'd say you had earned a caning for your cheekiness.'

Veronica swam lazily away, as if daring me to catch her.

'You know I can take your caning, Miss, and smile while you are thrashing me. I am a Swish girl, remember? And proud of it.'

I was so thrilled at her defiant words that I burst into rapturous laughter.

'We are all Swish girls!' cried the others. 'Swish! Swish! Swish forever!'

'Yarroop!' hooted Connie Sunday, presumably in her native idiom. She then abruptly swam out into the river, her tanned, leathery little body glinting like a goldfish.

'Be careful, Connie,' I cried. 'The current . . .'

'Yah!' She shouted. 'I've swum across the Rio Bravo to old Mexico! This ain't a river! I want to see what the others are up to!'

'Connie, that's rude!' I cried, automatically. But of course I was quite eager myself to learn what they were up to. Connie dived under the water and swam around the bushy promontory, to reemerge a few minutes later, gasping after her long period underwater.

'That lot!' she cried. 'Aren't they the rude ones, though!'

'Whatever do you mean, Connie?' I said.

'Why, they're playing with each other!'

'Well, so are we!'

'No, I mean . . . they're diddling, Miss. Aren't men just the rudest creatures?' All the girls pricked up their ears with curiosity.

'Diddling?' said Phoebe Ford-Taylor, and promptly went all red. 'You don't mean . . .'

'They've got their pegos out, and they are all stiff,' said Connie triumphantly. 'You go see! It's mighty pretty, rude though it is. Those stiff young limbs, like saplings, and their hands rubbing and tickling and stroking! It made me feel all excited, somehow!' And she too blushed.

'Mordevaunt – was he diddling, as you put it?'

'The one you went into the maze with? Why, no, Miss, he was swimming on his own, and kind of grinning to himself. And Mr Whimble was swimming too.'

Speedily, I climbed onto the bank and put on my leathers, not bothering to dry, so that I felt slithery and wet inside the soft skins, which was curiously exciting.

'I'll put a stop to it!' I cried, meaning it sincerely. I felt insulted. I did not want the chaps playing with themselves when my girls were there!

'Are you going to punish them, Miss?' cried Vanessa Lumsden.

'Booter's already getting six!' said Veronica.

'He'll have a dozen, then!'

This caused great excitement.

'A dozen for the lot of them!'

'On their bare bums!'

'Filthy beasts!'

'Wait!' I cried, feeling a little foolish as I stood there dripping in my fine leathers. 'I must verify Connie's report. There is all the difference in the world between innocent horseplay, and, well diddling.'

With that, I plodded round the bushy outcrop to the cove where the boys had gone. I heard their cries of merriment, and hid myself behind the foliage to spy on them. It was true: Booter, Phipps and Weldon were nude, the water up to their balls, and each had his hand on another's penis, which he was frigging with rapid, rather unromantic movements. Mordevaunt was away at the far bank, swimming on his back, with his own penis, that sweet engine whose pleasure I had tasted, floating softly like a big log between his downy thighs. And not far away, Freddie was splashing energetically at the crawl stroke, as though trying to taunt Mordevaunt into racing against him.

The cries of the others indicated that they were playing some sort of competitive male game, to see who should spend the soonest.

'Phippsy's coming! The beastly tyke!'

'No I ain't! You're a bleeding liar!'

'Booter's bloody well going to spurt!'

'I fucking ain't, not for a million years!'

I burst from my hinding place. 'What is the meaning of this?' I thundered.

'Oh, Miss . . .'

Hands were abruptly removed from pretty throbbing members, which with miraculous speed became sadly limp.

'We were just playing about,' faltered Booter.

'I am not talking about your beastly games,' I said icily, my hands on my hips. 'I am talking about your shocking grammar. Gentlemen do not say "ain't" like common guttersnipes!'

'Well, we got carried away, Miss,' said Phipps sheepishly.

'Is that so? Well, you'll be carried away when I punish you for your foul mouths! I should make you wash your mouths with soap, but I'm going to be decent, since it's such a nice day, and let you off with a thrashing. Follow me – no need to put your togs on.'

'But, Miss – the girls –'

'It'll be bare bum, Booter,' I said. 'And what have you got to be modest about? My other students have been bathing nude like yourselves.'

'You mean the young ladies will watch?'

'I mean the young ladies will tan you, boy! Quick march!'

It was a sheepish crew that followed me to my band of

117

naked naiads, all humming with excitement as they smelled chastisement.

Freddie and Mordevaunt watched quizzically from a distance, then swam round to our side of the bushes for a closer inspection of the proceedings, both keeping their distance from each other, and Freddie ostentatiously treading water in the best place; showing that he was Mr Whimble, the Chamberlain of St Agatha's, and Mordevaunt a mere pupil! I looked to see if Freddie was holding his restrainer, but no: he must have kept it on for his swim, and I mischievously hoped the leather would shrink round his balls.

I hoped he was out of earshot, so I called the girls around me, while the boys stood miserably with their hands cupping their manhoods, though unable to resist gaping as my nymphs emerged nude and adorably dripping from the waters of the Thames.

'Now, ladies,' I said. 'I must tell you as members of Swish that I know a few of your secrets.'

'Secrets, Miss?'

I wagged a reproving finger.

'I know what you saw in the summerhouse,' I continued, 'for Mr Whimble made a clean breast of things. Would it shock you if I said that Swish girls might be asked to behave in just such a way as Tess, with certain gentlemen?'

Uncertain frowns gave way to smiles, then giggles, and all the girls portentously shook their heads, except for Connie Sunday, who smiled with a wide, happy grin as big as her Arizona sky. I felt that there was more to Connie than met the eye and resolved to quiz her later on.

'Right,' I said briskly. 'For the meantime, these particular gentlemen have incurred a severe punishment. Not for what Connie calls diddling. I should like to meet the girl who has not diddled with her friends! No, their offence is to have used the most frightfully vulgar language within earshot of ladies. For that, they shall each receive six strokes of the cane on there bare bottoms.'

The trio of miscreants groaned loudly.

'Miss, Booter is already to get six, as his forfeit,' said Veronica in a tone soft as butter.

'Why, so he is,' I said brightly. 'Well then, he shall take twelve, won't you, Booter? Eh? Speak up.'

'I'll ... I'll take the punishment, Miss,' he bleated.

'Splendid! Well, there are eight girls, and three boys to receive a total of two dozen strokes. That makes three strokes per girl. Booter shall go first, with a nice hard six, then he can watch as his chums are punished. And finally, enjoy six more for his forfeit. Each girl to deliver three of the tightest strokes! Veronica has the cane, and may start.'

'The one with which Mordevaunt was – amusing himself, Miss?' said Veronica innocently.

'Quite so, Veronica.'

'Oh, Miss, I've never been caned bare bum before,' wailed Phipps. His two friends rounded on him.

'Liar! Liar! Pants on fire!'

'Silence! There is always a first time, Phipps, liar or not, for now that you are under the tutelage of St Agatha's, you should know that canings are always administered to the naked buttocks, of male as well as female.'

'I can testify to that,' said Mordevaunt quietly, emerging from the water to the gasps of admiration of all the females, not least myself, for his sleek brown body with its huge, menacing manhood dangling so soft and cuddly between his legs, was a truly thrilling sight.

'I suggest you tie 'em, Miss,' he continued. 'I don't think they'll be able to take it otherwise.'

Glumly, the victims allowed themselves to be seized by their wrists and lashed firmly, each to a tree trunk, with thick tendrils. They were obliged to stand arms apart and backs to us, like sailors awaiting the cat-o'-nine-tails. It was a splendid sight, those juicy male bottoms, lyrical in their gentle nudity, about to squirm under the cruel thrashing of my charges!

'Well, I think you may begin, Veronica, I said. 'And then, after a robust lacing has exercised your forearms, you shall all have a good appetite for luncheon.'

There was a loud cheer from the girls as Veronica deftly sliced Booter's bare arse with the yew cane, and I knew myself how much that young branch could hurt! Booter groaned, and I ordered him to keep a strict silence or he would get the cut over again. Veronica stroked him again, wickedly finding exactly the same spot on his tender flesh, and he jerked and writhed in his bonds, but made no sound. The third stroke took him there again, and this time his dance of pain was a joy to behold. I saw that my young ladies were open-mouthed and flushed, and held their hands to their naked breasts, unconsciously caressing their stiffening young nipples.

I had my camera busily clicking. My sex tingled and seeped with excited moisture, and I wished I could be naked again, and take my turn at flogging the bare young men. The spectacle of my students eagerly accepting the quivering yew cane to make the helpless male bottoms smart was superbly thrilling to me. Their own bare bums danced with eagerness quite as much as their victims' with discomfort!

Soon the trio had taken six strokes each. I had made sure they were on tiptoe, so that the muscles of their backs and thighs were well stretched, and quite adorable as they manfully bore their floggings, their naked bodies wriggling softly like eels. The proud Booter seemed to take it the worst, and I felt sorry for him choking back his sobs. All the girls had taken their turn at the stroking except Connie and Phoebe Ford-Taylor, who was positively trembling with excitement. She had the largest, ripest breasts of my band, fine sturdy melons that were now topped most deliciously with the hardest, stiffest nipples I had seen! Connie's teeth shone in a hard, laconic smile, her mouth open and raw, with a faraway, glazed look in her eyes. I knew that look, and I knew that her quim was as wet as my own.

'Well, now, it is time for Mr Booter's forfeit,' I said. I passed along the row of tethered males, stroking their inflamed bottoms with the palm of my hand, like a slave-mistress. 'We have made them blush prettily, haven't we, girls? A fine hors d'oeuvre ...'

'Yes, Miss!'

'And now for our main course, we shall see Booter tak-

ing another six, for his impudence at Hampton Court!'
Lovingly, I stroked the boy's arse, as crimson as my driving leathers. He was a fine specimen, with a musculature not as pronounced as Freddie's but still rather enticing. Mordevaunt saw my fingers linger on the crack of his arse, as I played with his reddened buttocks, and his eyes narrowed. Booter was whimpering at my touch, and still shaking. Then another hand touched his smarting bottom. It was Mordevaunt's.

'Miss,' said Mordevaunt quietly, 'I don't think Booter can take any more. He may be a silly arse, but a full twelve – well, it's not fair.'

'Nonsense!' I cried. 'He is a strong young man, and will take it.'

'Six! Six on his bum!' chanted the girls, and I was obliged to order silence with a frosty raised eyebrow.

'Miss, I'll take the six for him,' said Mordevaunt. 'It was my fault, in a way – this silly forfeit.'

'There is nothing silly about six of the best, boy,' I said, unable to look him in his sweet eyes, for I was blushing so much. My heart melted; I could not bear the thought of hurting my lovely faun, and yet part of me longed to see him thrashed again, his naked bottom writhing under the cane. There was something about the nudity of them, which lent an innocent, pastoral air to our otherwise stern proceedings, as though we were sporting in the bucolic glades of ancient Greece, and I was reminded of the vicar's garden in Cornwall, where I had enjoyed my naked Graeco-Roman wrestling bouts with Mrs Turnpike, the vicar's buxom wife.

'Very well,' I said at last. 'Veronica, tie Mr Mordevaunt beside Booter, and Phoebe will begin his chastisement.'

Meekly, Mordevaunt allowed his wrists to be trussed and soon he was on tiptoe beside the others.

'Thank you, Mordevaunt,' groaned Booter.

Mordevaunt looked at me as Phoebe, her heavy breasts swinging, lashed his bare bum with the whippy little green cane. He shut his eyes and grimaced but said nothing, and I felt my sex all wet now, as his body quivered under

Phoebe's powerful strokes. After the third, she passed the cane to Connie Sunday, who laced Mordevaunt as though she were wielding a peppy bullwhip. She grinned savagely as she made his bare bottom dance. She was an expert. No doubt the leathery life of the Wild West contributes largely to a girl's disciplinary skills. Mordevaunt took his beating without a sigh.

It was with a trembling hand that I touched his flaming buttocks after Connie had ceased her flogging. His breath was hoarse and panting. I longed to take him in my arms and kiss him but Freddie was watching from the river, glowering at this discovered intimacy.

'Well, sir,' I said, 'your friend is in your debt, I think, for you have taken the fiercest lacing of the four of you.'

'I wish it had been from your hand, Mistress.' he whispered, and I whispered back to him:

'You shall have it, Mordevaunt, I promise.'

The flogged fellows gradually came back to life and, grimacing, climbed back into their clothes. We were all dressed now (Freddie's restrainer having indeed shrunk most uncomfortably round his poor balls!) and as an extra frisson of punishment, I made the St Alcuin's lot serve us our luncheon. It was a delightful repast, with lots of cold meats, salads and shrimpy things. Maxence had done well by us. I sat beside Freddie with a cool glass of chablis, but he seemed to be in a sulk.

'What's the matter?' I said. 'Didn't you enjoy seeing those fellows get a whipping? And all my girls so ripe and naked?'

'That chap Mordevaunt . . .' he said eventually. 'Are you sweet on him, Mistress? I thought I was your slave!'

'Oh, so you are jealous?' I cried. 'Well, my fine buck, you know how I hate jealousy! Miss Chytte is my slave, too, and does she complain?'

(Actually, she did, but in gesture rather than word.)

'Major Dove, Veronica's father, too! As your Mistress, Freddie, I may have as many slaves as I like, and don't forget, when the business of St Agatha's begins to expand, I shall have many more. Why,' I said, cajoling him with a sly tickle of his balls, 'you may even have your own slaves – female ones. Ladies of a certain age who will pay for the exercise of your virility on their persons.'

'I, have slaves, Mistress?'

'Didn't you see the way the ladies eyed you at our open day? Perhaps it is that moustache of yours.'

'Oh! You like it?'

'They will. As for Mordevaunt, yes, I have had occasion to chastise him. I caught him stealing flowers from my garden.'

'Whatever for, Mistress?'

'Why, for me, you chump!'

'So you are sweet on him!'

'It is perhaps the other way round, Freddie,' I said. 'Even so, my body is mine, to dispose of as I please. If she is mistress of a thousand others, it may not concern you.'

He sat brooding darkly. Did he suspect what had happened in the maze? A woman well fucked cannot easily hide the fact. How glad I was that he did not know of my passionate Sapphism with his own mother, Lady Whimble! And yet, I thought, perhaps, in the interests of broadening his spirit, he should know.

My reverie was broken by Freddie's bounding up and launching himself, furiously, at Mordevaunt. I frowned and prepared to cry out, expecting a fight. But no: Freddie stood trembling, took off his crimson driving glove, and slapped Mordevaunt's face with it!

'What are you doing, Freddie?' I cried, furious now myself. The females did not know whether to squeal or giggle, so, practical souls, did both.

'You are a bounder and a thief, sir!' cried Freddie. 'You have insulted my Mistress! I challenge you for your honour! Swords, on the common – tomorrow, at dawn! I trust that suits you?'

Mordevaunt did not seem at all surprised, but raised an eyebrow.

'I believe the challenged party normally chooses the weapons,' he drawled. 'But swords are fine with me, sir. Tomorrow at dawn then, I shall await you.'

'To the death!' insisted Freddie.

'How else?' replied Mordevaunt. 'And I must say, a blowhard and a cur like yourself shall be no great loss when they carry your body off.'

They glowered at each other like two bulls, and for all the bombastic silliness of the thing, there was none the less something very thrilling that two strong males should fight over me. I leapt between them.

Enough!' I cried. 'Girls, prepare to return homeward! As for you two, I have never heard such stupidity! Where would you get a sword, Freddie?'

'I . . .'

'Don't answer! As for you, Mordevaunt –'

'A gentleman must accept his challenge, Mistress.'

'Mistress!' cried Freddie, aghast. 'Miss de Comynge is my Mistress!'

'Be quiet,' I commanded. 'You cannot fight a duel, you foolish chumps!'

'It is for your honour, Mistress!' they exclaimed simultaneously.

'I take care of my own honour. Besides, it is illegal. And worse, against academy rules, my proud chamberlain.'

'Oh,' said Freddie, nonplussed at the idea of offending St Agatha's, and hence myself. 'But Mistress, we must fight. He stole your flowers, and has insulted me.'

'This braggadocio is nothing but a soft-shelled crab,' said Mordevaunt disdainfully, 'and I'll fight him to teach him a lesson.'

I could see that as always, men must be accommodated in their idiotic pride, which is nevertheless rather touching, especially where it concerns a beloved lady.

'Very well,' I sighed, racking my brains for a solution. Then I thought again of my wrestling with sweet Mrs Turnpike in Cornwall.

'I have the answer,' I said. 'If you insist on fighting, it must be done according to rules. You shall wrestle for me, gentlemen.'

They looked at each other grimly, and nodded in agreement.

'Very well. Not at dawn, for that is rather uncivilised. And certainly not on Wimbledon Common. You will present yourselves at the summerhouse at ten o'clock tomorrow morning. I think you both have an idea where that is . . .'

Freddie and I were both silent on the drive home. Before we embarked, Connie said that she knew a shortcut and proposed to take the others that way. Her route, while hilly and tougher on the legs, would give the chaps' poor bottoms less painful 'saddle time'. Veronica knew the route as well and offered to accompany them and, with her in command, I assented. Sure enough, Connie and Veronica were back at St Agatha's before us, looking quite flushed and happy from their exertions.

I dismissed them all, and went to get a well-earned bath, for driving can be mucky work, with all the smuts and emissions from the petrol engine. Miss Chytte was there, and I ordered her to attend me. While she ran my bath, I stripped and casually tossed aside my leathers and underthings, and prepared to sink into the fragrant suds.

'Why, Mistress,' she said gleefully, 'have you been laced? What a tanning you must have taken! I wish I had been there for your games!'

I looked at my bottom in the mirror, wondering if Mordevaunt's tender thrashing was still apparent, but saw that my whole body was a mass of crimson weals, as though I had endured the most brutal of floggings! My belly, thighs and breasts were all livid and red. Then I realised that the dye from my costume had been soaked by the river water, and run over my skin and underthings. Miss Chytte thought I had been chastised and, mischievously, I did not disillusion her.

'Why, yes, Miss,' I said airily, 'I have had the most splendid time. I was thrashed by all my Swish girls. I bet them they couldn't dish out a proper punishment, so they took willow branches, stripped me naked, and laced me quite unmercifully all over my body! How lovely it was to writhe helplessly under their caning!'

'But did Freddie and the St Alcuin's lads see?'

'Why, they took part, and were the most severe of all. Especially that Mordevaunt. I thought he should thrash me to within an inch of my life. How I wriggled and squealed!'

'Gosh, Mistress,' said Miss Chytte, enviously.

I teased her, but there is truth even in our wildest fantasies, and now, as I relaxed in my bath, I realised how much I wished it had been so!

9

The Rules of Swish

The next morning, I saw that the breakfast table reserved for the Swish girls was in a state of high animation, centring round the beaming figures of Connie and Veronica, who seemed to be regaling their friends with some mirthful story. Naturally I was curious but had to attend to the wrestling match between my two young bucks. I went straight away to my office, rather nervous, and lit a cigarette. It being Sunday, I did not expect much business; naturally, I had scarcely a moment to myself.

I was puffing the fragrant smoke, when a knock came on the door. I cried, 'Enter!', forgetting that here I was in flagrant breach of the institution rules. It was Veronica. Suddenly I realised I was smoking and, deciding that coolness was best, continued as if it were quite natural. Veronica affected not to notice, but I knew Veronica missed nothing. Her business was to invite me to a sort of initiation ceremony for a new member of Swish, one evening later that week. It seemed that young Emily Beausire had been tried and found suitable, and was to be 'inducted'. Of course, as governess, I was to oversee the proceedings. I readily assented and Veronica handed me a document which she said was my copy of the rules of Swish. I thought this charming, but did not smile; instead I took it gravely as though it were a paper of state, and thanked her.

'Tell me, Veronica,' I said, 'what was causing so much merriment at your table this morning?' She had the grace to blush slightly.

'Oh, Connie and I had an amusing time yesterday, on our way back from East Molesey with those lads,' she said.

'I am glad to hear it. May I be let in on the secret? We Swish girls must share our confidences, mustn't we?'

'Well, it was funny, the couple we saw on the towpath, you know, the gentlemen with the boater and the lady in the pretty dress with the parasol, well, we saw them again.'

'What is funny about that?'

Veronica grinned.

'They were in the bushes; the gentlemen had the lady over his knee, with her skirts up and her knickers down, Miss, and he was spanking her bare bottom! And when they saw us looking, they both waved and smiled!'

'That is very nice, Veronica, but scarcely enough for uproarious laughter. What else?'

'Oh, the lads said that it was time we got the same, Miss.'

'And did you?'

'Yes, Miss.'

'The boys spanked your bare bottoms?'

'Very hard,' she giggled. An inch of ash fell from my cigarette, and I took a long puff, then stubbed it out.

'And?' I said.

'Well, Miss, Connie said that back home in Arizona, men were men and did not stop at a spanking, when they had gotten a lady all excited.'

'We say "got" in England, Veronica. Go on.'

'We were in the woods at Raynes Park, you see, and quite alone, and – well, Miss, you know what we saw in the summer house – I was very curious, and Connie said it was the loveliest thing in the world and, oh, Miss, I feel all giddy.'

'Sit down then, and continue. What did Connie say was the loveliest thing in the world?'

Veronica sat, and took a deep breath.

'Why, to be . . . poked, Miss. I think that is an American word.'

'You'll find it current on our side of the Atlantic,' I said drily. 'So you were poked, as you put it?'

'Yes, Miss. Connie went first, to show me. She lay down and took up her skirts, with her thighs spread and her lady's place all pink and bare and shiny, and I felt myself all wet in my own lady's place. Then Booter took down his trousers – how red and yummy his bare bottom looked – and his pego stood up stiff and hard. Then he put it inside Connie and moved very rapidly, bouncing up and down on her, and then he cried out most savagely, as though he were being hurt, but he wasn't, really, he was spending in her, Miss.'

'And you did likewise?'

'Connie took all of their pegos in her lady's place, first. It was thrilling, Miss! She squirmed and cried out, and her face was all red with happiness. Then it was my turn. Connie explained that with their balls emptied in her, it would take a long time for them to spend again, and I would enjoy a lovely long poke. I was all wet – down there, you know – and I couldn't wait to feel a pego inside me. It was heavenly, Miss!'

'And who took you, Veronica?'

'It was Mordevaunt, Miss.'

I felt an icy tingle in my heart.

'Did he make you spend?

'Yes. Oh, how I cried out as I felt him spend his spunk in me! Then the others took me too, but they did not make me spend, although I had their spunk as well. And when they had done me, they poked Connie again. In the bumhole. That made her wild, and she told me that it was a surefire way to spend, so I stroked Mordevaunt's pego until he was hard again, and begged him to poke me there, in my bumhole, and Connie was right.

'It hurt a little at first, and I thought he wouldn't get in, my hole was so tight, but suddenly, when he was about an inch inside me, he gave a great push and thrust all the way inside, all smooth and slippery. I felt like a stream with a lovely strong salmon swimming up me! While he was sliding in and out of me, so tight round his pego, he frigged me, on my little acorn, Miss, and she swelled up and hardened so beautifully. Then, when I felt his spunk all hot inside my bumhole, I spent again.' Veronica paused, breathless.

'Well,' I smiled, 'I am glad the day was so eventful. Do you think you would like to do poking again?'

'Oh, yes!' Her eyes sparkled.

'With other gentlemen?'

'I can't wait, Miss!'

'It is charming what a good spanking can do,' I smiled. And proceeded to explain in detail my plans for her and her comrades, which she heard with increasing excitement and pleasure. 'So I think you shall have plenty of occasions to indulge your new appetite. But tell me, does Second Lieutenant Arbuckle not cross your thoughts? Wouldn't you like to have poking with him?'

She frowned. 'I suppose so, Miss. But I thought that was love, not fun, and the two were different.'

'No, Veronica,' I said, and clasped her hand. 'You shall learn that the two are not different.'

The document Veronica had given me was written on cream paper, in green ink and meticulous copperplate script. I read:

RULES OF SWISH

1. Swish is an élite Society, consisting of the very best Girls at St Agatha's and hence the World.

2. Any Girl wishing to join Swish must be Passed by a unanimous decision of the other Girls, and must undergo all Initiation Tests decided on by said Girls.

3. All Girls must obey the Academy Rules, and behave in a Ladylike Fashion at all times. Any Girl acting to bring Swish into disrepute shall be punished by her Peers: for a Serious Offence, one stroke of the Cane on the Bare Bottom from each Girl; for a Very Serious Offence, two strokes; for a Horribly Serious Offence, three strokes, together with any additional Chastisement thought Necessary.

4. All Girls must behave nicely towards others and respect their privacy, and must not Lord it over Girls not good enough for Swish.

5. Girls must share Cakes, Tuck, etc., freely with other Girls. Any Girl being stingy will get the Cane on her Bare Bottom.

6. Swish Girls may only Diddle with other Swish Girls. Any Girl caught Diddling with a non-Swish Girl will be Caned on the Bare Bottom as a Horribly Serious Offence, and the non-Swish girl reported to the Governess.

7. If two or three Girls are Diddling or being Lovey, and another Girl asks to join in, she may not be reasonably refused, otherwise she has the right to Cane the Girls who were being unreasonable.

8. The Mistress of Swish shall be the Governess of St Agatha's; the Vice-Mistress and Secretary shall be elected by the Assembly of Swish. If the vote is not unanimous, the selection is decided by Fighting. At General Meetings, any Swish Girl may challenge the Incumbent for either of these posts, to be decided by Fighting. Instead of Fighting, the Girls may choose the Ordeal of the Lash, and be Caned to see which of them can Stand it the Longest.

9. Any Girls caught Fighting without the auspices of the Society shall be tied together completely Bare with very Tight Straps, and flogged for a Horribly Serious Offence.

10. The Vice-Mistress may Cane any Girl's Bare Bottom up to three Strokes, without trial. The Vice-Mistress may be Caned only by unanimous consent of the Society, but she must take Double Punishment.

11. If Girls wish to Cane each other's Bottoms for Pleasure, or as part of Diddling, then they must invite everyone else to watch, if they want to.

12. The Code of Swish is to be respectful to one's Superiors and polite to one's Inferiors; to observe sound business practice in dealings with Others, and give Value for Money at all Times.

I was tremendously touched by their esprit de corps, and put the paper in my drawer. I had just lit another cigarette when the telephone rang. It was a parent who had heard of the existence of Swish – how fast news travels – and hoped his daughter would be considered for it. He said he was a friend of Major Dove. His daughter, a nice, mousy girl, was a Junior, and, of course, too young to be considered, but I guessed the real subject of his call.

'Well, sir, I had better interview you, hadn't I?' I said sternly. 'You may take tea with me next week.' I hurriedly scanned my diary, and named a date, to which he happily agreed.

'No more than tea?' he said hopefully. 'I was wondering if I might meet one of the Swish girls, er, you know . . .'

'Oh, I think we can arrange a lot more than tea, sir,' I said drily. 'But you must know that my girls are fond of presents, and so indeed, am I, for the taking up of my time. In addition, we are very strict here, and sticklers for etiquette. If a gentleman's demeanour displeases us, why, we make him pay a severe penalty on the spot.'

'Well, I am not very good at the social graces, Miss. I feel awfully certain I should offend in some way.'

'Then you should certainly be punished for your ill manners.'

'How, exactly?'

'It is, of course, up to the Swish girl who entertains you. I dare say she might want to give you a thrashing, sir.'

'A hard one?'

'All thrashings at St Agatha's are hard. Hence, the cane or birch is applied without mercy to the bare bottoms of those who break our rules.'

'The bare bottom, you say?' He could hardly contain his excitement.

'It is our tradition, sir. And I must warn you that for very serious offences, the young woman, or the gentleman, is stripped entirely naked for the beating, which may even take place under the critical eye of other females. I shall expect you at the appointed time, sir, and be punctual, for if you are just one minute late . . .'

I put the phone down, grinning gleefully, only to have it ring again, for another, identical conversation. And this was repeated right up to ten o'clock. My diary was crowded, and now it was time for me to meet my sweet combatants for their wrestling match, whose prospect thrilled me every bit as much as my lustful assignations for the coming week!

10

A Naked Duel

It was a summery day, though not yet Easter, and I was dressed accordingly in a nice white pleated skirt that swirled prettily round my ankles, and a white blouse. Under my blouse I had a lacy white bodice, which pushed my bare breasts up so that my nipples were rather naughtily visible against the thin fabric of my blouse. I thought the boys' combat would be the fiercer if they saw what they were fighting for! I took a floppy straw hat with flowers in the brim and a parasol, and felt like a lady in one of M. Renoir's paintings as I set off to the summerhouse, for all the world as if I were going for a thoughtful stroll in the woods. The two lads were awaiting me, both in their Sunday best, and glowering at each other. They both doffed their top hats at my approach and bowed stiffly.

'Well!' I said briskly. 'What a nice day we have for our little *affaire d'honneur*, eh, gentlemen? Let us go in and start the proceedings.'

'It is a fight to the death, Mistress,' said Freddie melodramatically as we ascended the steps.

'Nonsense, Freddie, it is a fight which will stop when I say so,' I retorted. 'I am the referee, and my decision is final.'

They stood in the cool room, looking at each other uncertaintly.

'Well, what are you waiting for? Let me see you stripped, if you please. The wrestling shall be Graeco-Roman style, that is, no holds barred, and you shall of course fight naked.'

They looked somewhat nonplussed at that, but turned their backs and began to remove coats and trousers. Freddie had no restrainer this morning, and I saw they both wore my panties! That made them glower even more fiercely.

'Come on,' I said. 'Strip off. I want you nude, like the wrestlers of old.'

Gingerly, they lowered their panties and stood before me, two naked Greek gods, and already I felt my heart pounding in excitement at the thought of those lithe bodies grappling for my honour. Men are frequently uneasy when naked with each other, unlike women, who take to shared nudity quite merrily, and I told them so, and that they should not be so silly.

'When you are struggling on that mat,' I said, 'you will be too busy sweating and straining to be embarrassed, and you will be very glad of the freedom nudity allows. Now, the winner shall be he who obtains the other's spoken submission, or who, in my own judgement, shows himself obviously superior. I shall call a minute's pause every four minutes. I don't want to be here all day however, while you dance around each other, so to make things brisk I have got this little encouragement for you to grapple closely and get down to business.'

From my bag, I took one of my golden body chains, about two feet long. The large hoops at each end were designed to clamp onto a lady's nipples – it was one of Miss Chytte's mysterious Sapphic gifts from Paris – and I found that they clipped quite neatly around the balls and penis of each combatant! They were taken aback but could not protest, and my two naked wrestlers were now bound together by the very manhood which inspired them!

'You will shake hands,' I ordered, 'and when I say "Begin!" – well, then you will begin.'

They shook hands and nodded to each other, and then I gave the word. Mordevaunt was the first to strike: slippery as an eel, he got his arm round Freddie's neck and tried to pull him to the coarse raffia mat on which they fought. Freddie fell, but twisted himself under his opponent, and kicked him in the belly so that Mordevaunt flipped over on his back. It was all thrillingly fast, as if they had been born to the gladiators' arena. Mordevaunt was trapped, with Freddie sitting on him, his balls pressed against his bare belly, trying to catch Mordevaunt's flailing arms. Those arms soon dealt a chop to Freddie's neck, which toppled him, dragging Mordevaunt after with the straining golden link.

Now Mordevaunt bestrode Freddie, squatting on the small of his back, the chain binding them so fiercely, and pulling so at their poor balls, that I thought it must break. But it was as sturdy as they; at each fall or pinion, each twist or stranglehold, the chain held them together, their bodies now slippery with sweat, so that they looked like two eels writhing in some strange courtship. I felt giddy; my sex was becoming wet as I watched the two magnificent bodies struggling like impassioned lovers, and I remembered suddenly I should call a pause.

They broke, and stood hands on hips, gasping for breath, still locked by my ingenious chain. Then the second round commenced, and the combat continued as hard as before, each with hatred in his eyes, giving and expecting no quarter. I found it difficult to concentrate on the technicality of who was supreme: to me, they were both supreme, and I imagined myself somehow between them, bound to them by a chain, and wrestling with them. I was giddy with a tingling desire. It had seemed cool in the summerhouse but now I felt flushed, and unconsciously my hand strayed to my blouse, where I unfastened my top button, then my second button, baring some inches of naked breast-flesh. I suppose I thought they would not notice: they did notice, and redoubled the passion of their contest, gouging and kicking and twisting until my alarm at their ferocity was quite surpassed by my melting desire, for both of those handsome stallions!

The play of their naked sinewy bodies; one tan, the other pale, was breathtaking to behold. All modesty was gone and they struggled like lovers, their balls and cocks slamming against each other's, or squashed to back, belly or neck, as they writhed in a merciless dance of power. My quim gushed with desire and I undid every button of my blouse and swept it aside, baring my full naked breasts. I caressed my stiffening nipples to a sweet hardness as I watched them, and at last called for another pause.

This time they stood with their backs to me, and I felt disappointed, and ordered them to turn round. They did so, and before their eyes, I coolly caressed my naked breasts, opening and crossing my moist thighs. Their cocks stood half-erect! That was the reason for their modesty. I said nothing, gazed at both of them with cruel rapture, and bade them continue. The air was electric with desire; the harder their struggle, it seemed, the harder their cocks grew, until both saplings stood proud and quivering in that vicelike golden grip.

I could not bear it; I was too far gone in desire to care for propriety. I raised my skirt above my waist and allowed my fingers to play on my quim, through the spreading wet patch on my panties. It was not enough; I undid my garter straps, pulled down the panties, and wriggled out of them and in full view of the sweating fighters, spread the lips of my quim and began to frig my clit with slow, sure, spine-tingling strokes. Their cocks stood rock-hard, their faces creased in hatred and lust, and when I called the next pause, they were two rampant naked males, fighting for a naked woman, and we were three animals in that hot room. I swallowed, continuing to frig myself, faster and faster now and then I held up my panties soaking with my love-juice.

'A trophy for the valiant victor,' I whispered. 'Continue, my bucks, and let me hear you squeal.'

The fight continued, with neither their ardour nor their cocks showing signs of wilting. Panting, I unfastened my skirt and slipped out of it, leaving me naked but for my white silk stockings and lace garter belt. I raised my legs so that my booted feet touched my shoulders, and spread the lips of my glistening wet cunt as wide as I could, all the time rubbing my engorged clit with slow, shuddering caresses that made me gasp and moan in time with the panting of my wrestlers.

Their contest did not slacken; it seemed that it could go on forever. I could not wait; I wanted them, wanted both proud cocks inside me. Their penises strained against their golden bonds, hard and glistening as they clashed and rubbed in a savage caress. I had never thought to get such excitement from such a spectacle; two erect naked males fighting and embracing, their cocks and balls rubbing as though in passion, and I wondered if this was how men pleasured each other in those ways society condemns. It was only a hair's breadth for Freddie's swollen cock to slip between the taut cleft of his opponent's buttocks, find the succulent little anus-bud, and ... the delirious fantasy overwhelmed me, and the tingling of my clit burst into a fierce orgasm, which made me squirm and moan with short, yelping gasps. My body glowed: I felt like a goddess.

'Enough!' I cried. 'I declare the wrestling over! Approach me, that I may unbind you.'

Slowly, the boys disentangled themselves and walked awkwardly to my chair, where I gracefully folded my legs down, but held my thighs wide so that my swollen cunt-lips were naked for them. I reached out and unfastened the golden chain from their stiff cocks, stroking their balls as I did so.

'But who is the winner, Mistress?' gasped Mordevaunt.

'The wrestling is over, but not the contest,' I said, smiling fiercely. 'You have fought like men, and now you will love like men!'

I took Freddie by his penis and guided him to the mat, where I made him lie on his back. While Mordevaunt watched in lustful apprehension, I lowered my thighs and straddled Freddie, until the tip of his cock was caressing my quim. Then with one thrust, I sank onto him, and felt his engorged cock penetrate my cunt to the hilt. I squatted on Freddie thus, and bent over so that my naked teats were pressed against his chest.

Then I clutched the cheeks of my arse with both hands, and spread them so that my tender arse-bud was exposed. Freddie, underneath me, began to writhe, fucking my cunt with a gentle rotation, as Mordevaunt silently positioned himself on all fours over us and tickled my anus with his throbbing shiny glans.

'Yes ...' I moaned. 'Oh, yes. Fuck me, my men. Fuck me in my cunt and my arsehole, so soft and tight for your cocks. Fuck me so hard ...'

I felt Mordevaunt's cock inch its way into my tight anus, and I spread my bud as wide as I could, almost painfully, until at last with a powerful thrust his penis was gliding smooth and beautiful all the way to the root of my anus. I had never conceived such loveliness was possible, to be filled in both my intimate places by the two cocks I loved most in the world.

Both stallions began to buck me now, harder and harder, making me writhe with sweet pain as my body felt she would burst under their tender onslaught. My cunt was full, and my gentle anus, and I felt my very soul was bursting with love as the sweet hard maleness of the two bucks flowed through my pinioned body. I was trapped between two rampant, bucking cocks, embraced by arms whose straining muscles I bit and sucked as they locked me.

'Oh, Mistress,' sighed Freddie. 'Your cunt is so sweet, I shall fuck her forever.'

'Mistress,' said Mordevaunt. 'It is I who shall pleasure you in your lovely hole till you can take no more.'

Each thought he must last longer than the other, to win the contest! I realised that each one had his hands clasped to the other's bottom, pressing him closer to my body as he fucked me, and the delicious intimacy of this, far from seeming unnatural, was glorious and thrilling and so perfect! And as we clasped each other, I felt myself shudder again in a sweeter, longer spend than before, intensified by the hot jets of spunk which my writhing and moans at last milked from the hard cocks that pleasured me so fiercely, and Freddie and Mordevaunt joined their voices to mine, and I had my wish, I heard them squeal!

We lay there for a time, each boy kissing my body with loving lips, and I said:

'Well, Freddie, do you think Mordevaunt a bounder?'

'No, Mistress.'

'And you, Mordevaunt, is Mr Whimble a braggadocio and a cur?'

'In no way.'

'Then,' I said, as we untwined our limbs and rose, 'I think we can all be friends.'

'But who has won the contest?' cried Freddie. I put my arms round their necks, and kissed them both, and said:

'Why, we all have, you chump!'

'Then who shall have the panties?'

'Why you both will,' I said gaily. 'You shall take turns!'

'Well, Whimble,' said Mordevaunt, as we dressed, 'I suppose you aren't such a bad wrestler.'

'Nor you, Mordevaunt.'

'Bet you're no good at ping-pong, though.'

'Ping-pong!' exclaimed Freddie. 'Why, I am the champion of Cornwall at ping-pong!'

I could not recall Freddie's ever having expressed the slightest interest in this unmuddy game.

'We'll see about that!' cried Mordevaunt. 'I challenge you, for first possession of our Mistress's panties.'

'A fight to the death?'

'Agreed!'

And, after bowing their goodbyes, the pair walked jauntily back to the great house, their arms around each other's shoulders.

It was only when they were out of earshot that I had a premonition I was not alone. I was startled to hear a decorous sound of clapping, followed by bursts of female giggles. I looked round, and saw my Swish girls emerge from their hiding place on the verandah!

'Congratulations, Miss,' said Veronica Dove, 'for you are now a fully-fledged member of Swish, and here is your own membership badge!'

She handed me a brooch like her own, a little birch made of hairs, except that all the hairs were of different colours.

'It was my idea, Miss,' said Connie Sunday. 'We each plucked three hairs from our lady's place for your ornament.'

'Why ... thank you,' I said, blushing furiously as I realised the girls had watched the whole lustful proceedings. 'But my gratitude does not make me less stern about this infraction of discipline. You are out of bounds, girls! I think you will agree that your entertainment has earned you a caning!'

'Miss Chytte gave us permission, Miss,' said Vanessa Lumsden innocently.

'It was a very pretty entertainment,' added Phoebe Ford-Taylor.

'Nevertheless, you have infringed the code of Swish, which I have read, by ... by invading the privacy of others,' I blurted. 'That, as I remember, merits severe punishment.'

'Then it must be discussed at our inaugural meeting, Miss, which you are to attend,' said Veronica sweetly. 'As must the equally serious matter of a Swish member caught at the unladylike practice of smoking.'

'Well, who can that be?'

'Why, you, Miss,' said Veronica. 'When I visited your study this morning.'

'Oh – really, Veronica!'

'Miss Chytte gave me six strokes of a willow cane on my bare bum for smoking,' said Amanda Nightingale. 'Gosh, how they smarted!'

'I am your Governess! You're not suggesting –'

'It shall be put on the agenda, Miss,' said Veronica with an angel's smile and a pretty curtsey.

And then, neatly arrayed in twos, my obedient group accompanied me back to St Agatha's.

11

Connie In Leather

One morning, on impulse, and to gratify a curiosity which had been gnawing at me, I ordered Connie Sunday to attend me at my morning bath. Her trim body most pretty in her uniform, she ensured the bath was at the correct temperature and supplied with frothing oils. Then she watched me undress and took my robe as I sank into the luxurious suds.

'Well, Connie,' I said brightly. 'Veronica has told me you enjoyed your little trip to Raynes Park with the St Alcuin's students.' Her mouth opened.

'Before you say anything, Connie, be aware that Veronica has told me everything and, far from being displeased, I am rather delighted – and curious. Arizona must be such an exotic place! Tell me, have you had many such experiences? The Wild West sounds so thrilling to our English ears!'

She bit her lip, and sighed. 'You bring back sweet memories, Miss. I'm just a little homesick! Well, my dad has a ranch not far from Bisbee, just across the line from Mexico. Me and my brothers lived there with him –'

'My brothers and I, Connie.'

'My brothers and I, Miss. Well, my mom's long gone, you see, and I kind of grew up like a boy. Bisbee's a copper town and my dad owns the copper mine as well as the spread at Mesa Grande. I used to go down the mine with my brothers, I really liked it down there, it was so hot and smelled so weird, and all the miners were stripped to the waist, you know – all gleaming and muscly and sweaty, and I found it kind of exciting. They were Mexicans, vaqueros from Naca across the line, and so I got to know them.

'As well as mining, they worked with the steers when it was the season, roping and branding and corralling, and such. I used to ride my pony a lot, and I used to pass by their camp, and one day I heard the most terrible squealing and commotion, so I went to have a look. I recognised some of the boys from the mine; they were young fellows, all dark with lovely white teeth, not like the grizzly old fellows that were the regular cowboys. Anyway, they were branding horses, and that was the commotion. They were naked to the waist, like in the mine, and they were passing around a bottle of tequila, and were all a bit merry, I think. The poor horses were lying there in a row, all trussed up, and whinnying fit to bust. I saw the branding irons red-hot in the fire, and there was a horrid smell of sizzled meat.

'Course, they said, "Hello, little señorita, come take a look as your dad's mark goes on his horses", and I dismounted. They all looked at me with – you know, that look – 'cos I was bare-legged, and had only a light gingham dress on, and riding boots, which I guess looked odd with my flimsy dress. Anyway, I said I thought it was terribly cruel, and couldn't property be marked some kinder way, and they laughed a lot and said I didn't know the ways of the west, and such. Well, it was only a couple of years ago, I was just sixteen. I knew about branding, but I had always shivered at the thought of it, and pretended it didn't happen. My brothers ribbed me terribly. Once they gave me a plate of pan-fried "prairie oysters", and when I ate them, they told me what they were.'

'And what were they, Connie?'

'Why, bull's balls, Miss. When they cut them with a knife ... Ugh!'

'What did they taste like?'

'Quite nice, actually. Yes, like fried oysters!'

'Go on with the branding.'

'I watched as they branded one poor pony on his flank. It was so cruel! But I didn't go ... I was fascinated. And I must say, when they took off the ropes, the colt bounced around quite carefree, as though his pain were quite forgotten. I mean he didn't kick at them or anything. Well, they were passing round the tequila bottle a lot, and offered me some, and I guess I shouldn't have, but I wanted to show I was one of the boys. It was horrible, like kerosene! But after a while I felt sort of loose and warm and giggly. They said, didn't father expect me, and I said no, I wasn't expected till suppertime. I should have known better.

'The leader of the boys, his name was Jaime; a big handsome Mex with long shiny hair tied in a red bandana, he took my arm, and said I should learn that branding was nothing at all! I didn't like this one bit. I tried to get loose, but he held onto me, and then before I knew it they had my dress over my head, and I was wearing only panties, no bodice or anything to cover my teats. I was mortified! Worse was to come. They started to banter about what to do with me. One said it would be fun to make me ride the rail, and I cried out, real scared, because I'd seen that. It was one of the town girls, caught stealing, and my dad had her whipped for it while she rode a rail.'

'You'd better explain, Connie,' I interrupted. 'The mores of the New World are infinitely mysterious to me.'

'Oh ... riding a rail is where the girl has to squat on top of a fence, with no panties on under her skirt. Well, this girl had to ride the rail for two hours, her wrists tied above her to the hanging branch, and wearing only a thin shirt in the sun. You can imagine how it hurts! Your bare lady's place and the cheeks of your bottom pressed to the hard wood. Then, after the two hours, she got whipped five times, which made her wriggle so. I guess riding the rail must have been pretty darned uncomfortable! Well, I didn't want that. Luckily, they decided against it, and all the time I'm squirming and squealing. So, at last they took my dress off and tied me to a tree. And, suddenly, I realised that I was excited! I stopped squealing, and acted dumb, wanting to see what they would do. They tied my wrists behind my back, then looped a rope around my waist and hoisted me up so that I dangled helplessly with my toes barely touching the ground. They laughed and drank as though I was just an animal, and Miss, I am ashamed to say, I could feel my heart thumping in terror, and at the same time I could feel myself getting wet in my lady's place!

'They started touching me – my teats, my buttocks and my thighs, and they said I was too skinny, and my teats weren't big enough, and I was mad at them! Then Jaime took a big length of rawhide and dipped it in a water bucket till it was sopping wet, and began to loop it round my belly. He did that, winding it so tight, till I was trussed like a chicken, with the wet leather forcing my teats up and my waist in until I thought I shouldn't breathe any more! He said my teats were proper teats now, and when I looked down, I saw them all bunched up and pretty, like ripe melons, and I got a wet feeling in my quim again! They went on drinking, and watched me, as the sun dried that raw leather, and as it dried, it tightened and tightened until I thought my bottom and my teats would burst, they were forced out so big and round and swelling! And I felt I was lovely for them!

'They didn't stop there; they took off my boots and lifted my legs, then bent my ankles forward and right around the back of my neck, and tied them together, so that I was dangling a good three feet from the ground, quite helpless and bare-ass naked! My rear stuck out behind me, and my squashed teats hung under me like a cow's udders, for all the world to see, and Miss, I could feel my quim just gushing with excitement! It was so thrilling to be trussed and helpless like that, under the eyes of those gorgeous cruel naked boys! But I was right scared, for they were talking about branding me!

'I started to cry out again, and this time they gagged me by stuffing my own panties in my mouth! Jaime said I should be whipped into obedience, and the next thing I knew, he took up a cruel rawhide stockwhip and I felt a terrible smarting on my bare buttocks where he had lashed me! I couldn't cry out. He lashed my naked rump again and again, then they all took turns, and each stroke of the whip sent me skidding back and forth like a puppet on my leash! It felt as though my whole body was on fire. I was weeping so that my panties were quite wet with my tears and all the time, the terrible crack of that whip landed again and again like a fury on my bare, bulging arse.

'I was so scared, Miss, I lost control of myself, and released my water, and that excited their lust still more! For it wasn't just water; my thighs were all wet with my love-juice too, for in that devilish helpless truss, I felt more excited than I could imagine, to be their naked, helpless plaything. Miss, I . . . I felt like a woman! And I did not – could not – resist what happened next.

'The whipping continued; most pitiless. My bare nates were smarting terribly, and I found to my horror that it was thrilling to be thrashed thus, to feel my bottom all glowing and hot! And, Miss, my whole body trembled, and as that cruel lash descended on my naked behind . . . I spent! It was a lovely, lovely wash of pleasure that surged through me, much better than I had ever known by diddling myself! They saw it, and laughed some more, but I didn't care. The whipping stopped.

'They went to the fire, and I smelled the branding iron as it came nearer. Jaime was stroking my flogged arse. He said that it was time to make me a real cowgirl, the señorita de papa, and brand my naked bottom.'

'God! How barbaric men seem in your transatlantic wilderness!' I exclaimed. But all this time my fingers were busy under the bath suds, frigging my engorged clit; my cunt flowing with moisture as I heard Connie's thrilling tale . . .

'I felt the hot iron come closer and closer to my bottom and, Miss, I didn't squeal or squirm or anything! I was transfixed by fear, but also by a terrible thrill – the thought of being branded as a man's property, his slave, his animal! But just as the hot iron was singeing my mink-hairs, Jaime threw it aside, and laughed fit to burst! Suddenly my hips were grasped and pulled back, and I felt something at my bumhole! It was Jaime's naked cock, and he tickled me there, stroking me back and forth, across the tip of his manhood. It was so exciting, I thought I must spend again – which I did, when I felt his shaft thrust most brutally all the way inside my anus! He fucked me there, Miss, very hard, diddling my stiff clit with his whipping hand, and I writhed and groaned and loved it as his spunk bathed me!'

By now, I was writhing myself in excitement; Connie's story of being trussed by half-naked cowboys had awakened a keen desire in me, and a pang of envy!

'So you escaped branding! I'm glad you enjoyed your ... escapade, Connie, but still, to take a girl by force is not the done thing in this country!'

'Oh, they didn't really take me by force, Miss,' she smiled, blushing. 'You see, the knots that bound me were only bowlines; I could have snuck out any time, and got away, if ... if I'd really wanted to! And, damn them, they knew it! Deep down, I wanted to be tied and ass-fucked! That is why I am here, Miss, because my dad found out, and sent me to England, to learn manners, and such.'

'But surely the episode was not your fault, Connie?'

'Not that episode; but, you see, I went back to the vaqueros, again and again! And each time I let them love me in the bum-hole, and let them whip and tie me, and at last I let Jaime take me in my cunt, and I was so happy! I guess it showed, for my dad made me tell him the truth, and then he rounded up all of the boys to watch me being punished for it. First, he stripped me bare-ass naked, and gave me seven strokes of the bullwhip, real hard! Then he wanted to turn the boys over to the law in Bisbee, but I begged them to let them go back to Mexico and never come to Arizona again, for the law in Bisbee is nothing but lynch law.

'Jaime was so brave, he offered to be punished for all of them, he offered to take a branding, which for a Mexican is the worst, most humiliating punishment. But my dad said no, he wouldn't brand a man like an animal, although I figured branding was better than a noose. And, Miss, I went down on my knees and offered to do it myself, to brand my sweet Jaime, if none of the men were brave enough to do it! And Jaime agreed, saying he would be proud to bear my mark! But my dad said no, he wasn't to be branded, but he could take the punishment as ringleader, and wear my mark too. For I myself was to whip him, and if he took that, they could all flee the country.

'Miss, I whipped my lover! He was tied naked to a tree-trunk, and I had to give him not just seven, but eighteen strokes with that cruel bullwhip, and he took my beating without making a sound! He looked at me so proud and loving, straight in the eye, and I knew he was a real man! My body was all glowing, and not just from the pain of my whipping. For Miss, as I whipped my lover, I saw his naked cock rise for me, and I came over all in a tizzy. And Miss, my cunt was dripping and my belly fluttered and ... I spent! Straight away, they went back to Mexico, and I never saw them again,' she concluded sadly.

I was close to spending myself. My cunt was deliciously wet, my clitty tingling with hard excitement!

'Do you miss your home, Connie?' I said softly.

'Oh, yes, Miss,' she said.

'I think St Agatha's may be able to offer you some consolation,' I said. 'Go to the closet, and remove the lilac corset you will see there. It is the smallest one I possess. You may remove your blouse and strap yourself into it.'

Connie's face glowed as she obeyed. Loosing her pert young teats, she then strapped the tight silk on the whalebone frame around her waist.

'Oh,' she gasped. 'It's so tight I'll never manage it!'

'Not rawhide, but the best we can do. Here,' I said, rising from my bath, 'I'll help you.'

Soon I had her corsed so that her pert little teats and trim bottom bulged as sweet as pomegranates, and she gasped for breath.

'God, Miss,' she panted, 'that is so thrilling! How I wish you had a tree to tie me to, and a bullwhip to lace my bare bottom!'

'We shall see what we can do, Connie,' I replied. 'First, you may dry me and dress me, and then we shall visit St Agatha's secret chamber.'

I made sure her hands lingered on my intimate parts as she towelled me, and she was well aware of my wet cunt as the towel slithered between my thighs, all wet with love-oil. Then I led her along dark, winding corridors, down to the oubliette. Her eyes opened in wonder as I opened the door.

'Gosh! I never knew such an exciting place existed,' she murmured.

Here eyes ranged across the array of instruments of correction, all lovingly shined and polished, and her face was pink with anticipation.

'Oh, Miss,' she blurted. 'It breathes beauty! I'm all ashiver at the thought of ...'

'Of what, Connie?'

'Why, of the things that St Agatha's girls had to suffer in ages past! How cruel, yet how beautiful!' She looked at the whips, and flogging posts, at the thongs and fetters which lined the walls of my little dungeon, and her eyes sparkled with desire. At that moment I knew I had to possess her.

I had baulked at making love to one of my students, although how I longed, for example, to embrace Veronica; to make her dance to my cane, then feel her naked breasts pressed to mine, and my lips on hers as we sweetly frigged each other's soaking cunts! But I had been cautious for too long, I now knew. I wanted the lithe body of Connie Sunday. She looked at me with big eyes, and she knew it, too.

Wordlessly, I undid her tie and the buttons of her blouse, and stripped her to her tight lilac corset, above which her breasts bulged so beautifully. I refrained from kissing her nipples, which were already stiff, for I knew things must be done in order. She let me bend to unfasten her skirt, and strip her of it, then unlace her boots, and roll down her calf socks. She stepped out of her boots and socks, and was nude but for her corset and blue panties. With trembling fingers, I hooked her panties and rolled them down over her creamy hips. The top of her curly blonde mink peeped coyly, then, with no sound in the room but our own harsh breathing, I revealed the ripe swelling of her young mound, and the thick, glistening petals of her cunt. She stepped out of her panties, her face quite red and her lips heavy with desire.

'What is to be done with me, Miss?' she asked.

Her curious locution pleased me. I longed to embrace her and kiss her lips, then to kneel and plunge my tongue inside those hanging, fleshy petals from which her clitty was already peeping, wet and stiff.

'You shall be trussed, I think,' I said. 'In old England, you may recapture the joys of your American home, dear Connie.'

I motioned her to a device which had already aroused Mr Izzard's scientific interest. Bolted to the floor stood a thick teak slab about four feet high, consisting of two separate pieces which were fastened by a groove, so that its height could be adjusted. All along its length dangled stout leather straps with buckles, and at its base were two footrests with metal clamps. Connie placed her bare feet in these, and I fastened the clamps across the insteps of her feet, locking her in place.

Then I fastened each of the straps across her legs, adjusting the height of the pole so that it came up just to her sex-lips. Her legs were a shiny wall of black leather; she could not move a muscle.

'So tight,' she murmured. 'So lovely, Miss ...'

'That corset is a loose thing, Connie,' I said. 'We must tighten you there as well.'

'Loose! Why ... Oh yes, Miss, it's far too loose.'

A similar rigid slab extended from its bolts in the ceiling; placing Connie's back against it, I adjusted the height so that it came down to the base of her spine. Then began the work of trussing her arms and torso with the numerous leather straps, so close that one seemed to merge with the other, giving her the appearance of wearing a second, leather skin.

Her corset had made her flesh bulge, and now, as I tightly buckled her, it was the corset which bulged! She gasped with little whimpers as I trussed her belly, then the ribcage, drawing the thongs as tightly as I could, and pinioning her arms straight and helpless by her sides under the cruel straps.

'I wish Mr Whimble were here,' I panted, 'for his muscles would have you well tightened!'

'I can't move at all, Miss,' said Connie. It's divine, you know.'

And in truth, I was envious. To be trussed helpless and naked, as a plaything or doll, stock still and a mere object in the total power of a master or mistress, made me giddy with desire, and my quim was very wet as I finished tightening the straps. The last one went across the top of her breasts, forcing the sweet teat-flesh to stand out still further; her rock-hard nipples like bursting plums, and each breast forced to point at an opposite angle, as though she carried two hard, shiny artillery shells beneath her shoulders.

I stood back to survey my handiwork: Connie was quite immobilised, her body a gleaming, straining wall of buckled leather, which came up to her armpits. Apart from her buttocks and pubis, only her hands, shoulders and head were bare. I quickly unfastened the top thigh strap, and tucked her hands in there before fastening it as tightly as before. Now even her hands were helpless. Connie was a gleaming monolith, the penis of a giant carved in black marble.

'Thank you, Miss! Oh, thank you! I feel like a goddess! So helpless and straight for you! Why, I can't bend or move a muscle, or anything! And my teats, they are like gorgeous jewels growing from me! It is so good!'

The extreme tightness of the thigh and belly straps had in fact forced her fesses out very hard and bulbous, like the pictures I had seen of steatopygous Hottentot women; in the same way, her mons was pushed up and out so that she bulged like a peach, with the pendulous cunt-petals standing swollen and pretty between her pressed thighs, and the clitty stiff as a button between them. A rivulet of her juice glistened all the way down her black leather thighs.

'Aren't you going to give my arse a lacing, Miss?' she said timidly. 'I am sure I deserve it.'

'It would be sweet punishment indeed not to lace you,' I laughed. 'But there's more, Connie.' I unfolded another leather fitting from the wooden slab: it was a blindfold which I tied snugly over Connie's eyes, fastening it behind her head. She trembled violently as she cried:

'God, Miss, I think I shall spend, I am so tense! It is so good! I am your thing, your helpless slave!'

She could see nothing. At last, I could lift my own skirts

and, holding them under my arms, I lowered my panties and began to frig my engorged stiff clit. The sight of my trussed slave maddened me with desire; I felt a surge of rage at this girl for making me so helpless with lust! I could feel a spend not far off. Panting, I took off my skirt and panties altogether, and took a thick four-foot willow cane from the rack. The tip was splayed, and I passed the jagged edges across Connie's lips. She shuddered.

'This is the cane that shall flog you, Connie,' I said as coolly as my excitement would allow. 'You are right that you deserve punishment; the very insolence of asking that question is your crime. I propose to give you six strokes with the cane, on your naked bottom – and one for luck!'

'Please ... yes, Miss. Oh please,' she whimpered. 'Can't you see how wet I am in my quim? I think I shall burst!'

Standing behind that straining, engorged rump, the arse-skin tight as a drum, I raised my cane and lashed her fiercely on her unprotected bum cheeks. She groaned, and her arse-globes twitched, but no further movement was possible. Trussed as she was, she could neither squirm nor shudder to dissipate the smarting pain of her bare-buttock whipping. The second stroke followed, and the third, and her groaning grew to a loud, keening wail, almost as though she were singing. I was breathless with my eagerness to finish the flogging, and the strokes followed very rapidly, scarcely allowing her, or myself, time to draw breath between each cut. At last I had delivered the seventh stroke for 'luck', and could no longer contain my desire. I knelt by her crimson buttocks and, placing my hands on her labia, pressed her to me as I smothered her bare arse with fervent kisses.

Now her moaning had turned to a sigh, of pure delight.

'Oh, Miss, bring me off,' she sobbed. 'Make me spend, I beg you. Such a sweet lacing, and such cruel torment to have my quim so wet and hot for you! Oh lick me, Miss, kiss me on my cunt, please, oh please.'

I could not resist. Giving her arse a last kiss, and then quite a hard bite, which made her jump and squeal with pleasure, I moved to kneel before her glistening mink.

Feverishly, I undid the straps that bound her feet, and then, clasping her buttocks, I pressed my lips to the swollen red cunt-petals, and kissed them as fervently as I had kissed her flogged buttocks.

My tongue speedily locked onto her swollen clitty, and flicked hard and rapid over its tender, shiny surface, making her give little squeals of delight. She moaned with joy, and I felt her trussed belly begin to heave; at the same time I had my own soaking cunt firmly pressed to her bare toes, and was rubbing powerfully, so that her toes tickled my clit, sending shudders of pleasure up my spine and making my stiff nips tingle unbearably. Her love-juice was a cascade, spurting over my lips and cunt. I drank thirstily of her salty sweetness as I tongue-frigged her clitty, and my buttocks pumped, like those of a man fucking, as I pummelled her toes with my own stiff damsel. It was heaven, and we both cried out, our cunts gushing, as we reached our spends. Connie could not move a muscle, but her orgasm sent an electric shiver through her whole body, and her moan became a scream of pure ecstacy.

I sank to the floor, and kissed her feet which were soaking with my own love-juice; then rose to caress her nipples with tender bites through their leather prison; finally, my lips met hers in the sweetest of kisses, our tongues embracing as our bodies pressed. I began the slow task of releasing her. Connie's lips and cheeks were bright red.

'Miss,' she said faintly. 'That was the most . . . the most fantastic orgasm I have ever had. It was as though all the lovely joy, all the energy of my climax, was kept boiling inside me, because I couldn't move in my cruel straps to let it free. Oh, when shall I be punished again, Miss? Will I have to do something naughty? I hate to be naughty.'

'Why, no, I think not, Connie,' I said. I referred to my diary full of appointments with gentlemen. 'Perhaps you would like a gentleman to "chat" with you as I have? There are many gentlemen who would be kind to you in this way, and perhaps remind you of your dear Mexican Jaime.'

'Yes please, Miss!' cried Connie, free at last, and jumped into my arms to embrace me with tearful gratitude.

'Good!' I said briskly. 'Well, on to the day's business, Connie. Lessons start shortly, you know.'

'Yes, Miss,' she said in a subdued voice. 'Double French, I think.'

'Splendid! Then you will be just about at the chapter where Henri binds Yvette, who is gagged and blindfolded, with steel thongs to the funnel of the Ostend Ferry. I am sure you'll enjoy that!' Her eyes lit up.

Our American cousins certainly have a lot of jolly good things, I said to myself, as I locked the door behind us. I'll have Miss Chytte order some tequila. It must be quite powerful stuff . . .

12

The Governess Bound

The day of the Swish 'conclave', where, amongst other business, Emily Beausire was to be admitted as a member, I allowed Veronica Dove an exeat to visit her father in Knightsbridge. She was to be back at St Agatha's by tea time. She was collected by carriage, all dressed in her finest silks, and I knew that a meeting with Second Lieutenant Arbuckle would undoubtedly be on the agenda. In fact, I suspected that her meeting with her father would be quite brief! She took with her a package for him, containing one pair of my very soiled panties, with instructions that he was to wear them on duty at all times. She returned early from her outing, and appeared somewhat disconsolate. I took her aside for a quiet word.

'Well, Veronica, are you looking forward to our Swish meeting?'

She brightened up a little, as though she had forgotten.

'Oh yes, Miss, it will be nice to be with girls again, among my friends.'

'And is Second Lieutenant Arbuckle no longer your friend? Don't pretend your day out was not to see him.'

She blushed.

'Yes, Miss, I admit it. I thought I loved him, but now I don't know at all! Men are such strange creatures.'

I pressed her to explain.

'I gave your package to papa, Miss, and I wonder what could have been in it, to make him go all red, and smile such a soppy smile!' Veronica's lips curled in her familiar knowing grin for a moment, then she frowned again. 'I spent most of the day with Second Lieutenant Arbuckle. We went riding in the Row, which was lovely and then took luncheon at the Trocadero. I had a glass of wine and felt rather merry, and then he said it would be great sport to attend the Marlborough Street Magistrates' Court, so I agreed.'

'That is Mr Justice Ruttle's court,' I said. 'Jane Ruttle's father – the birching judge.' Veronica shuddered.

'Yes, Miss, I can believe it,' she said. 'All the sentences were birching – it was quite horrid. Fifteen strokes, and six months at hard labour; and most of the victims were men guilty of nothing more than im ... impor ...'

'Importuning, you mean? Yes, there are men who like the company of other men, Veronica, and they do the same things to each other as gentlemen do to us. With modifications, of course.'

'Well, I can't see the harm in that,' she said. 'Although, why would a gentleman want to put his pego in another gentleman, when he could put it in a lady?'

'As you say, men are very strange. But as to your beau, Arbuckle?'

'Oh, I don't know if he's my beau! I'm so confused! You see, after the court, which Arbuckle thought was topping fun, he invited me back to the barracks to see him do some work, as he put it. I was curious and agreed with pleasure. But the work ... well, it was not part of his duties, I know that. It was secret and shameful. He took me to a place far underground, smirking and giggling all the while, and there ... there, I watched him flog a man with the cat-o'-nine-tails!'

'But that is contrary to regulations!' I exclaimed.

'Yes, he said I was not to tell papa – but the common soldier was a proper villain, and it was the only punishment he understood. The poor man was held by two burly sergeants, and Arbuckle flogged him, laughing and grinning at me as he did so. It was so horrid! The room smelled of fear and pain and hatred. He asked me if I didn't find the spectacle amusing, but I said I had a headache, and asked to come home. And he said all his other young ladies liked to watch him flog his men! His other young ladies! Why are men so cruel, Miss?'

'Veronica,' I sighed, 'there are cruel things in this wicked world, and some men think their cruelty impresses us. But you have taken a caning from me, girl, and on your naked bottom. Was that cruel?'

'No, Miss! I was proud to take your beating, because I deserved it, and because there was kindness in it even as the cane made my bare bum sting!'

'Well, that is the difference, Veronica,' I said tenderly, stroking her cheek. 'Here at St Agatha's, you are beaten because we love you.'

I had it in the back of my mind to deal with this insolent subaltern, for upsetting one of my girls, but put the thought aside as I prepared for the evening's mysterious ceremony. What impishness had my girls dreamed up? It was obvious from their rulebook that they took themselves quite seriously. I dressed myself in black silk, ankle-length and stern; but underneath I wore the corset that had so delighted Miss Chytte.

My experiences with her and Connie had made me curious about the effects of tightening, and I gasped with shocked pleasure as I laced the devilish frame around my belly. It hugged me like a vice, and that hug sent a million tickles through my breasts and clit! I felt like a new woman, looked at myself in the glass, and I was! My breasts, large as they were, thrust up beautifully now like giant, straining melons. My buttocks were pushed smartly out by the impossibly narrow wasp waist thong, so that I felt trussed like a lovely slave in some Roman or African market. It was deliciously naughty! And to compound my naughtiness, I snapped on the tightest garter belt I could find, my best black silk stockings, and ... no panties. I had a pair of lace-up boots which were higher than my normal wear, going up above the knee, and I put those on as well. The effect of these constraints was to be felt very quickly in my sex, which began to moisten and tremble. As I made my way to the classroom where the ceremony was to be held, I felt as though all eyes were on my swelling teats and bum, and responded to every casual, 'good-evening, Miss,' with a maiden's fiery blush!

I was agreeably surprised to find the classroom lit by

candles, giving our meeting a mysterious solemnity. Veronica had chosen a room in a wing of the academy deserted at this hour, so that our deliberations could proceed in seclusion. The desks were arranged in a circle, and all the girls were seated when I entered. They rose and bowed, all wearing their Sunday best. Veronica indicated my chair, between her own and Connie's.

It was difficult to see in the smoky flicker of the candlelight, but each girl had a candle on the desk in front of her, throwing her face into sinister relief. I saw that there was one vacant seat left, presumably to be occupied by Emily Beausire upon her acceptance. Emily stood, head bowed, behind me.

'Welcome, Mistress,' said Veronica, in a portentous voice.

'Welcome, Mistress,' the others chorussed.

'Why, thank you,' I said. 'Well, I won't get in the way. Carry on, Veronica, since you seem to be the, ah, Vice-Mistress.' Veronica consulted papers on her desk.

'The first item on the agenda is the ratification of official appointments,' she announced, and I wondered where she had got these big words. 'Veronica Dove, that is, me –'

'That is I, Veronica,' I said automatically.

'Yes, Mistress, that is, I –'

'We know it's you, silly!' cried Prudence Proudfoot.

'Silence!' hissed Veronica. 'Well, I, or me, have been nominated as Vice-Mistress without opposition. May I take it that the election is carried unanimously?' She glared around the tables to suggest that it had jolly well better be. And so it was. There were murmurs of assent, and Veronica declared herself Vice-Mistress of Swish.

'Next,' she said, 'the office of Society Secretary. It is the job of the secretary to take the minutes of our conclaves, and to ensure that the log book of the society's activities is kept up to date.'

This was new to me, and I interrupted to ask her to explain.

'Why, all doings must be recorded, Mistress,' she said. 'Girls must give an account of themselves in their own writing when they make the acquaintance of a gentleman, for the instruction of their Swish comrades in years and centuries to come. Also, of course, all punishments, disputes, etcetera, must be described in detail.'

'You should address me as Miss, you know,' I interrupted.

'In class, Mistress, you are Miss,' replied Veronica sternly. 'But here you are the Mistress of Swish. So we must call you Mistress. One candidature for secretary has been proposed, that of Connie Sunday, which I may say has my approval.' She glared anew. 'Carried?'

'That sounds jolly good to me,' I said brightly, and Veronica gave me an icy look.

'The role of Mistress, Mistress, is ceremonial; business is conducted by elected officials,' she said very formally.

'Oh,' I said. 'Yes, of course.'

At that point we heard the soft elegant tones of Phoebe Ford-Taylor, my excellent telephone operator.

'I say, I rather wanted to be secretary!' she exclaimed. 'I'm always getting good marks in English.'

'So is Connie,' said Veronica.

'But she's . . . she's not even English!'

'Why, Phoebe!' I cried. 'Speaking ceremonially, Vice-Mistress, I wish to say that is a most unladylike statement.'

'Lots of people aren't English,' said Amanda Nightingale. 'That doesn't make them rotters, I mean, not really.'

'I heartily agree,' said Veronica. 'The ideals of Swish, and of course St Agatha's, are universal! I take it Connie is elected?'

There was a murmur of assent, and Phoebe flushed with embarrassment and anger.

'Well, it says in the rules, which you drew up, Miss know-it-all Veronica Dove, that I can challenge her to fight! And I do! So there!'

'Do you accept the challenge, Connie?' Connie licked her lips.

'You're darn tootin' I do,' she said.

'I thought Tootin' was a railway station in some ghastly suburb,' said Florence Bages, and everybody giggled.

'Silence!' ordered Veronica. 'Phoebe and Connie shall wrestle for it, here and now! Girls, you are to strip, if you please, and take your places in the centre of our tables.'

'Strip?' said Phoebe. 'You mean, we must fight in our underthings?'

'No,' answered Veronica, 'I think you shall fight completely nude.'

Connie was already undressing, and the sheepish Phoebe followed suit, until both girls stood naked in the makeshift arena. I was pleasantly reminded of my own escapades with Mrs Turnpike, and of my more recent, thrilling supervision of the two young men's naked duel, and I admit that the sight of those two bare bodies ready for combat made me feel slightly moist in my sex. I could see why Phoebe was embarrassed. I knew she was ample of bosom, but now I saw her breasts were larger even than my own. Untrammelled by clothing, those ripe dugs hung in their splendid nudity well down over her ribcage. My sex suddenly became quite wet indeed as I thought of the effect my tight corset should have on those lovely swelling teats, forcing them out and up like twin mountain tops.

There was a tiger's glint in Connie's eye, and Phoebe looked uncertain, as though she regretted her challenge, but the die was cast.

'You will fight to a submission,' said Veronica. 'No scratching or gouging, or pulling hair, but anything else is all right.' She looked at me, and I nodded in agreement, as eager as the rest of them to observe this naked tussle! As I expected, the contest did not last long. Connie's eyes were burning to avenge the insult to her non-Englishness.

'Begin!' cried Veronica.

At once, Connie delivered a lightning kick to Phoebe's breasts, which knocked her off balance and made her squeal in outrage. Connie followed this by taking a very sharp, and no doubt painful, hold of those big, flapping mammaries, pinching Phoebe's nipples tightly with her fists and using her breasts as a slingshot to whirl her opponent round and send her crashing into the tables, whence she sank moaning to the floor, clutching her sore bosom. There was no mercy, however; Connie threw herself on the larger girl and spreadeagled her, then sat on top of her and pummelled her quite savagely, as though punishing Phoebe's delicious big teats for being bigger than her own taut young peaches.

'That's not fair!' wailed Phoebe, trying to dislodge Connie with feeble punches of her own.

'It is perfectly fair,' said Veronica. 'She is not scratching, nor pulling hair.'

I felt a fluttering all up my spine, and in my belly, and I knew that my clit was stiffening in excitement; I felt a fierce urge to slip my hand inside my dress and frig my naked quim ... or invite Veronica, who was as flushed as I was, to do it for me! There were gasps of pleasure from my bright-eyed girls as they watched the lithe young American savagely pummel her naked rival, then, with a jump, turn round so that she was sitting on top of the squirming Phoebe, her bottom to her face. Swiftly, she pulled up Phoebe's legs, making her squeal quite horribly and, leaning on them with all the weight of her own body, forced them up so that Phoebe's feet were pressed back against her shoulders. Connie had raised herself entirely from the floor, her legs stretched out like a ballerina's, and she lowered herself so that her thighs pinioned Phoebe's, rendering her immobile, with her quim squashed firmly against Phoebe's breasts. It was a delicious, and lustful position, had it not been for purposes of war.

Phoebe's bottom and the backs of her thighs were now stretched in their full nudity beneath Connie's gaze. Phoebe battered ineffectually at Connie's muscular back, but could not move under the grip of those powerful, straining thighs. Connie wriggled cruelly back and forth on her naked, pressed teats, making her moan with pain and indignation. Then, Connie raised both arms high in the air and brought her palms down, to deliver a mighty slap on each of Phoebe's squirming bare flanks!

'Spank her! Spank her bum!' cried the Swish girls, and Connie did just that.

With a sure aim and strong arms, she spanked Phoebe's

naked bottom, and the backs of her thighs too, until they were glowing red, and Phoebe's cries were quite uncontrolled.

'Submit! Submit!' cried the girls.

As she spanked, Connie was rocking back and forth on Phoebe's breasts, which I thought cruel torment indeed, until I realised from Connie's little moans that she was rubbing her own clitty against those magnificent nipples. She was subtly frigging herself on Phoebe's breasts as she ferociously spanked the girl's naked buttocks!

Phoebe had stopped pummelling Connie's back, and her squeals had turned to low moans which sounded like moans of pleasure. Her bottom still squirmed as she endured her spanking, but it seemed to me that now she was writhing in joy, thrusting to meet the hard palms of her spanker rather than to flee them. The two girls now were oblivious of their audience. I could not bear it any longer, and let my hand stray under my desk to the tight fabric of my dress, and through it I found my quim wet and gushing; the clitty hard and throbbing inside my cunt-petals, and I began to frig myself rapidly. There was not a girl but did the same!

Suddenly Connie discontinued her spanking, and thrust her body forward so that her mouth was on Phoebe's exposed, squirming pussy-lips. I thought that in her frenzy she was going to bite the girl's cunt, which was not allowed, but no – she began to lick and kiss Phoebe there as though she were kissing the lips of her face. At the same time she shifted her own quim so that she sat directly on top of Phoebe's mouth, and I saw Phoebe's tongue darting in and out of Connie's glistening wet slit. The two opponents were gamahuching each other with every sign of voluptuous tenderness!

They stretched languorously now, embracing each other's bottoms, all thoughts of fighting forgotten; and this sweet caress continued until both girls cried out as their entwined bodies heaved prettily in a climax. I was not far from spending myself, but I desisted reluctantly from my frigging although my cunt was a veritable sea of love-juice, as the two girls rose shakily from the floor, and with coos of friendship embraced.

'Gosh!' cried Phoebe, her face flushed with joy. 'I submit, Connie. I certainly do! And I'm sorry I was horrid to you!'

Connie squeezed her tightly, which pressed their two wet cunts firmly and lovingly together, and kissed her on the cheek.

'Why, you could never be horrid to me, Phoebe,' she said. 'How can a Swish girl be horrid to another?'

Smiling, the two girls parted, picked up their clothes, and hurriedly dressed. When they had resumed their seats, Veronica passed her sheaf of papers across my desk to Connie, who said with a grin, her voice trembling only a little:

'As secretary, I now move to the next item on the agenda: the induction of the girl Emily Beausire.'

'Will Emily Beausire please step into the centre,' said Veronica.

The girl shuffled uncertainly into the arena where the combat had taken place, and stood, head bowed and hands behind her back, her eyes darting suspiciously round. She was a slender girl, not of striking beauty, but with a certain lithe strength in her lanky frame. Her hair was mousy, not well groomed, her mouth quite pouting, almost sullen, with thick fleshy lips gracing her bony skull. She had a charm, I was not sure how: what the French, as usual having a word for it, call *joli-laide*. Her big brown eyes scanned us incuriously.

'Emily, you wish to join our society,' said Veronica.

'My daddy wanted me to,' the girl replied sullenly.

'Well, have you read our rules? Are you ready to obey them?'

'Suppose so.' Emily yawned.

'Respect others, give value for money, and take punishment like a St Agatha's girl?'

'Suppose so.'

'Emily, have you already experienced punishment here at St Agatha's?'

'Got a caning from Miss Chytte.'

I reflected that Miss Chytte was certainly a model of assiduity, where corporal punishment was concerned.

'How many?'

'Six, I think. I don't remember. It wasn't much of a caning.'

'Bare bum?'

'Yes.'

'And you say it wasn't much!'

'It didn't seem like much.' Emily yawned again. 'At my old place I used to get ten on the bare bum.'

'I suppose that didn't seem like much either,' said Veronica sarcastically.

'No, it didn't.'

'Well!' cried Veronica, somewhat flushed. 'I think it is time for your initiation, Miss Beausire. Are you ready?'

'Suppose so.'

'Hmm!' Veronica stepped smartly to her side, and produced a cloth, with which she blindfolded the girl. Emily displayed no reaction.

'Now,' said Veronica, breathing heavily, 'you are to learn what it is to be a Swish girl, Emily. You are blindfolded because you are about to receive a severe caning. You must show your mettle. The caning shall be on your bare bottom and you shall receive a stroke from each member present. You will kneel, please, and lift your skirt, then lower your panties. At any moment you may halt the test, if you cannot take it. Is that understood?'

'Suppose so,' said Emily, yawning again.

Casually, she lifted her skirts and knelt, crouching with her naked bum in the air as though with the ease of long practise. She wore no panties.

'Naked under your skirt!' I cried. 'That is against the rules of St Agatha's. You shall come to my study tomorrow at nine, Emily, to explain yourself and receive a further caning.'

'Yes, Miss,' she sighed. 'But couldn't I take them all now? It would save time, I mean.'

'What?' I blurted. 'Take an extra four – that would make thirteen strokes in all, Emily!'

'You think that unlucky? I don't,' she said insolently. My blood raced, and I felt a strong desire to tan that luxurious bottom bright red, until she squirmed heartily.

'Very well!' I cried. 'You shall take one from each of the members of Swish, and then four from me, for your offence of going without panties!'

'After the lacing,' added Veronica, 'you must bestow the Kiss of Swish – only then can you be admitted to our ranks.'

'The Kiss?' I whispered to her. 'What is that?' She grinned mischievously.

'You shall see, Mistress, and I hope you shall enjoy . . .'

It fell to me to deliver the first stroke to Emily's lovely bare backside, which swelled quite strikingly out of her thin frame and bony, slender back. I took a willow cane from Veronica – I was glad to see it was only a thin one, not three feet long – and lashed her rump as gently as I could without seeming 'soppy'. The cane was then passed to Veronica, who dealt the most savage of lashes, and to Connie, who outdid her in the ferocity of her stroke, landing it on exactly the same crimson place. Throughout this, Emily crouched unflinching, her bare bottom spread wide for the cane's touch, and her eyes dreamy, as though she were elsewhere.

Each of the girls took her turn at lashing Emily's motionless arse-globes, and though the porcelain white skin was beginning to glow a pretty crimson, she made neither sound nor jerk as the cane whistled and cracked on her naked buttocks. Finally, her ceremonial lacing was over, and it was my turn to take the cane once more, to deliver her punishment for going pantiless. I raised the lash with fury in my heart – how dare she be so serene – and a noticeable moistening of my quim, for those flogged buttocks were quite delicious in the flickering candlelight.

'Tomorrow, I shall explain why we have rules, Emily,' I said sternly. 'But for the meantime, you'll take a tight four to teach you that it is wise to obey them.' And with that, I whipped her with four of the hardest cuts I could manage, in rapid succession (about one a second), and all in the same crimson place at the centre of her bottom. The damned girl made not a squeak! Panting, I laid the cane aside, as nonplussed as the rest at the girl's indifference to her savage flogging. And an idea took root in my mind.

'Now for the Kiss of Swish,' said Veronica, enjoying my puzzled expression. 'Quite simply, Emily, you must stay in your position, and must kiss each of your sisters in turn, beginning with me, and ending with you, Mistress.'

With that, she placed herself in front of Emily's face, and to my amazement, raised her own skirts and lowered her panties (regulation blue, I was glad to see), then spread the cheeks of her bare buttocks and pressed her snub little anus bud directly onto Emily's lips!

'You may kiss me now, Emily,' she said, and Emily puckered her lips and delivered a warm, juicy kiss right on Veronica's bum-hole.

This ritual was repeated with each of my girls, and Emily kissed their arses with evident delight, adding little slurpings and lickings of her tongue: evidently disappointed when one anus was removed and there was a short interval before it was replaced by another. At last it was my turn. All eyes were upon me. I gulped, raised my skirts (rather embarrassed because I, too, was pantiless), and exposed my bare arse to Emily's lips.

She kissed my bum-hole with a lovely sucking kiss and, not only that, she wiggled her tongue right inside my anus to a depth of about an inch, and tickled me most delectably and lovingly, until my sex swam with gushing wetness! It was all I could do to tear my arse away from her caress, feeling a delicious little tickle as her tongue plopped out of my anus. Panting, and quite flushed, I adjusted my dress, and reoccupied my place. Veronica grinned and removed Emily's blindfold, then kissed her full on the lips that had just tickled my most intimate part.

'Congratulations, Emily,' she said, 'you are now one of us!' And everyone clapped politely.

'Well, I suppose that is nice,' said Emily, 'but I thought you said I was to get a severe lacing. I mean, did you all change your minds?'

I was overjoyed at Emily's blank reaction to her stern flogging. When I had made the acquaintance of Miss Chytte in Cornwall, she had astonished me by her tolerance of the lash, and she had explained that her hide was toughened by years of familiarity with naked whippings. Here was a girl who seemed just the same! The next day, I had a busy schedule of visitors, and I was pleased that I could offer gentlemen a martinet, that is, a girl so inured to floggings that she can patiently take any number of strokes from their impassioned canes. Such a girl is always in demand in houses of pleasure, for many gentlemen love to chastise a girl's bare bottom, as well as, or even instead of, having their own chastised. I resolved to explain more than the Academy rules to Emily when I had an intimate conversation on the morrow.

'Well!' I said brightly, once more their principal. 'That seems to be quite satisfactory! I shall be getting along, and I expect you girls have some prep to attend to.'

'Please sit down. Mistress,' said Veronica coolly. 'The secretary must deal with "any other business".'

I sat down, smiling politely.

'Any other business,' drawled sweet little Connie. 'Item: a Swish girl found flagrantly smoking in the presence of a comrade, namely, Miss de Comynge, witnessed by Veronica Dove. Item to be considered a Serious Offence.'

'Wait!' I cried. 'This is preposterous! Veronica, whatever can you mean? You burst into my study – I mean, really – I was smoking. Why, girl, you are insolent!'

'So you admit the offence, Mistress,' said Veronica. 'Remember that here, you are not Governess, you are Mistress of Swish, and must set an example. Have you any reason why you should not endure punishment?'

I knew very well what my punishment would be. I was about to be very cross, and tell them all not to be so silly, and then I looked at the bright eyes and flushed faces of my girls, and suddenly I thought of my bare bottom exposed in humiliation to their lash; of the delicious needles of white-hot pain stabbing my naked backside as they caned me, and my cunt gushed with hot liquid! I wanted to take their beating; to be helpless under their cruel whipping; to be one of them! I bit my lip, and looked at Veronica, and whispered:

'I'll take it, Miss. Please punish me. Please whip my bare bottom. Yes, I accept it gladly, with all my heart.'

Veronica smiled.

'You are our Mistress,' she said slowly, 'and so we shall have to make an example of you.' She nodded to Connie and I realised that the two were in cahoots, and had planned the whole thing! This was to be the high point of the ceremony, and I suppose I should have felt flattered, had my heart not thumped so as my clit tingled in little spasms of excitement, and my cunt flowed with my hot juices. How I wanted them to strip me, and tie me tight, lace my naked bottom until my skin screamed with the beauty of pain!

I bowed my head and obeyed. I was made to strip, as I had hoped, down to my corset and underthings. I removed my stockings and garter belt – 'No panties!' said Veronica drily – and was about to unlace my tight yellow corset when she told me to halt.

'Not the corset, Mistress,' she said. 'You are so deliciously tight; how big and ripe your bum cheeks and bubbies look! And so we shall make you tighter for your punishment. How that bum will swell to receive her lacing! The skin will be stretched so, every lash will feel like a hundred!'

'Yes, oh yes, please,' I heard myself murmur.

From the recesses of the classroom, Connie fetched the material of my trussing. Over my corset, I received a garment of black leather, like a waistcoat, but a thousand times tighter. My arms were pinioned and trapped by my sides; I thought I should stop breathing as I felt the cruel buckles lock into place behind my back, thrusting my teats up until I could almost take my engorged nipples in my mouth! My bottom, too, was squeezed out until she felt as big and tender as the blossom of a dandelion. I felt that one stroke from a cane, and she would burst. Next, a blindfold was placed around my head, also of fragrant leather, covering my eyes, so that I was in trembling darkness. My mouth and nose were free, but soon I felt a large metal ball placed inside my mouth, opening my jaws painfully wide, and strapped harshly into place by a thong around the back of my head. I could neither see nor speak; I thought myself completely helpless, and ... and I was thrilled!

But more was to come: my feet were strapped into metal cuffs, with the clink of chains, and suddenly I felt myself lifted by strong young arms and twisted until I was upside down. I heard the rumbling of a pulley, and then was jerked off my feet and lifted into the air. It was one of those frames which teachers use in class to move heavy charts and blackboards. My legs were forced wider and wider apart until I thought I should split. I could hear the inching of gear-wheels; I could feel the cool air on my stretched cunt-petals, open to the world's gaze; I fancied my head was at least two feet from the floor, swinging helplessly. I could not prevent my cunt from gushing with love-juice, as the realisation of my utter helplessness overwhelmed me, filling my body with an electric pleasure. I was trussed and gagged, in darkness, my intimate woman's places exposed quite shamelessly, my arse bulging naked from my bonds for the most savage of beatings. Dimly, as though from afar, I heard Veronica's voice:

'The offender shall receive a stroke of the cane from each of her sisters, to be administered to the naked buttocks.'

I wanted to ask – but of course could not – why I was thus strapped, when I should gladly have bent over and bared my naked rump to their sweet cane. But at Veronica's next words I understood the purpose of my trussing. Her voice was cruel and icy.

'The offender, being our Mistress, shall receive special punishment in addition, namely, a caning on the naked breasts and lady's place.'

Those harsh words struck terror in my heart. It was monstrous! They had gone too far! To be caned on the bare breasts was horrid enough, but on my naked, helpless cunt, it was unthinkable! I began to moan and shake in fevered protest, but of course to no effect. I was a prisoner!

All at once, the cane descended on my bared nates, and I felt its red-hot sting suffuse my body. Each girl was taking her turn to stroke me, and delivering the cut as hard as she could. And there was worse to come – a caning on my bare cunt!

I sobbed behind my cruel mask and gag, yet even as I shook with terror, and the pain of my vicious caning, my quim still gushed with moisture, and I realised to my horror that I adored what was to happen! I counted the strokes on my bottom; there should be nine, nine of the cruellest caresses I had ever felt; yet I was sure I was not mistaken – there were ten! My bottom smarted like molten gold; I was on fire; my mind swirled, and I wanted more of the lash, more pain, more of the fire which reduced me to an unwavering point of pure, glorious agony. Yes – let them cane my cunt! Oh God! I could take it! I wanted it, longed to tell them that I desired to be flogged so intimately, so cruelly!

'Now, the offender shall receive her punishment on teats and on cunt,' said Veronica. I felt an impact on my bare breasts and gasped, for it was not the savage cut of a cane. At the same time, my cunt tingled to a caress on her engorged, naked lips, and it was the same caress. Again and again I felt the slaps descend on my swollen nipples and cunt-petals, tickling them, teasing them with the ecstacy of their touch. My cunt and breasts were being whipped by a feather!

I gushed with moisture (awfully embarrassed to think it was trickling all over my tight leather corset!), and my clit and nipples throbbed like hot stiff irons, as though my whole body consisted of nothing but my burning buttocks and those hard buds of pleasure. I longed to cry out with joy; I could not. My cunt cried for me, weeping sweet oily tears of salty love-juice as my whole body at last convulsed in a spasm of orgasm and, under the tickle of that feather whipping on my breasts and clit, I spent until I thought I should faint.

I was released from my bonds by soft hands, and righted, with the girls holding me until I got my breath and balance.

'Oh Veronica,' I blurted at last, my cheeks wet with tears of joy. 'What a cruel minx you are!'

'You took your punishment like a Swish girl, Mistress,' she said solemnly, 'so now you are truly one of us.'

'But you cheated!' I cried in mock-indignation. 'I had ten strokes of that lovely, wicked cane, not nine! Eight of you, plus Emily – nine girls! I didn't give myself a cut, surely?'

'There are eleven members of Swish, actually Mistress, for my own little ceremony took place yesterday.' I looked round, and saw Miss Chytte.

'Who else would know how to deal with such a fractious girl as you, Mistress?' she said, smiling.

'You see?' said Veronica. 'We have whipped our Mistress with love.'

Naked, but for my yellow corset, I drew myself up to my full height, and with my hands on my hips, answered:

'The conclave, I believe, has now ended, and so I am once more the Governess of St Agatha's. Therefore you shall address me as "Miss"'.

'Yes, Miss,' chorussed my girls.

13

To Worship a Queen

'Why, we have a number of discerning young ladies, sir,' I said, 'who will be pleased to take tea with you. At St Agatha's, we strive to build the whole woman, complete with all social graces.'

'I see. Very good.' said my client (he was nothing less), rubbing the pale spot on his neck where, I surmised, a clergyman's dog-collar normally resided.

I opened my album of the photographs which Mr Izzard had tastefully mounted in red Morocco. This album purported to be a kind of prospectus of St Agatha's; in fact, it showed my Swish girls in all sorts of activities, poses, and states of dress or undress, including the merry photographs I had taken of them *au naturel* on our lovely day at East Molesey. The girls also appeared *au naturel* in the very graphic pictures of Deirdre and her surgery, especially her demonstrations of Mr Izzard's colonic irrigation machine. And – rather charming, I thought – where those girls who had chosen to have their minks shaved were undergoing that operation at Deirdre's capable hands, before selecting one of the lush, daring pubic wigs – the *visons d'amour* – which Mme Izzard had so thoughtfully woven for us! I was tempted to have Miss Chytte shave me, as she always begged to do, and try one myself in the fetching shape of a bird or a tulip, or a mink of extraordinary growth, although I thought my own natural mink second to none in lushness.

Of course, my favourite section of photographs illustrated the disciplinary practices of St Agatha's. Here, the girls were not entirely nude, but the relevant parts of their anatomy were. And, in vivid close-up, their blushing naked bums revealed that our playful posed scenes of chastisement were in fact 'the real thing'.

'You may care to take a look and select the young lady you would like to entertain,' I said. 'However, please do not touch the book. I shall turn the pages at your direction.' I showed him the photographs of my girls in their uniform; then came poses in full evening dress, naturally of a rather gay nature; gradually, as he became more at ease with the nature of his business, the choice of photographs became more and more intimate. He looked at the photos, and murmured:

'Her, perhaps, or her ...'

When he had named four possibilities, I passed to the section of gay frocks. That narrowed it down to two. The gentleman was getting very red in the face. He was quite good-looking, of 'a certain age' and, of course, wore a wedding ring. He was not one of the parents; a telephone call had announced him as a friend of a friend of a friend.

All my girls, I knew, were by this time well prepared for their lustful entertainment of my carefully vetted gentlemen. However I was glad when his choice centred on Emily Beausire. He licked his lips at the photos of her with panties down around the knees, and her skirt and blouse tucked neatly up her back, receiving a quite severe tawsing with every expression of dreamy indifference.

'She looks like a girl who can take it,' he said.

'All our young ladies can take it, sir,' I said sweetly. 'And dish it out too.'

'She is quite boyish,' he continued. 'Her derrière ... quite trim; one would almost imagine ...'

'She is no boy, sir, I assure you,' I replied briskly, 'as a close inspection of her very ample female bottom will reveal.'

'I am curious,' he concluded. 'Most curious. She looks a charming lad – I mean, a charming young woman.'

The matter was concluded. It was not long before I was able discreetly to escort Emily and our guest to a private room, having made small talk and taken tea with the reverend gentleman, if such he was, in my study. Emily seemed quite knowledgeable about ecclesiastical architecture in Wiltshire, though our guest seemed more interested in church choirs and the boys who sang in them. As soon as Emily was arranged over a chair with her bottom bared, and about to receive an agreed lacing of ten cane-strokes on her naked behind while she sang a delicate Kyrie eleison (at which she proved surprisingly good), I left them to their own devices. The sweet notes echoed past me as I made my departure, punctuated by the whistle of the cane and the satisfying crack on Emily's willing buttocks. I must say I felt a pang of envy!

I as "madame", was left unsolicited, as it were; but I did not see why my own charms should be denied the opportunity of extracting largesse from the willing customers of St Agatha's. Deirdre and Marlene too, I noted, were keen to demonstrate their lustful prowess: once a gay girl, always so. Well, I had one customer already, my faithful Major Dove, and my appetites resolved me to call on him and his lady wife very shortly. I was curious to see what passions I could unlock from the genteel strong box of her soul.

This resolve was increased as I supervised my girls, in impish succession, depart in their finest frocks or (for gentlemen whose tastes ran that way) their smartest uniforms, towards a private chamber of lustful pleasure, and afterwards read their dutiful descriptions in the Swish diary.

I confess that I could not read their sweet effusions of prose without feeling an effusion myself, that is, a hot wetness in my cunt, as I thought of their sweet pretence at innocence in the embraces of their rampant male clients; the shyness and blushing with which they accepted presents and coins!

The deal, as Connie put it, was that I received the payment for their services by tariff, of which they received a small percentage, which was kept in their own bank account until the end of term. They could, of course, keep any gewgaws or sovereigns which their charms could extract from their besotted customers in private, and they were very good at it, judging by the jewels and golden things I was obliged to order them not to wear during lessons. Such is the métier of the gay girl through the ages, and long may it be so!

In truth, my initiation into Swish had unnerved me somewhat. I loved to whip, both females and males: this proclivity, or gift, I freely admit to, thinking it a pity more souls do not own up to themselves that they secretly crave to wield or receive the lash. I also loved the caress of Miss Chytte's whip on my own naked flesh, had gasped with pleasure as the boy Mordevaunt caned my bare bottom so hard and so sweetly in the maze at Hampton Court and, of course, all that time ago when Freddie had first whipped me to orgasm with my own birch, naked on the sands by the wild ocean.

Yet, even in these painful tendernesses, I had felt myself somehow, in my deepest heart, to be in control of the loved person who flogged me. When I was trussed and punished by my Swish girls, bound, gagged, and whipped so beautifully on my naked breasts and cunt by Miss Chytte's ticklish feather, I had for the first time experienced a gushing, shuddering spend in a situation over which I had no control at all. I had been helpless; bound so unbearably tight that I thought my bonds were squeezing every last drop of ecstasy from my whipped body. And it was true!

And I was frightened. Frightened that in my deepest soul I was not the stern mistress of my imagination, but a girl who could not resist the cruellest of bindings; the harshest of floggings, in a quest for pleasure that transcended the smarting caress of the bare buttocks or back. I had never gone so far before on the sweet road of utter humiliation and denial of the self.

Since my trussed beating at the hands of Swish, I felt I knew intimately what my gentlemen desired to feel at the hands of the women who whipped them, and intended to put this understanding to good use! But, I wondered, if a gentleman wished to flog me – tie me, gag me, put me in his lustful power, entirely helpless – would I have the strength prudently to resist, or would my fluttering heart and gushing quim speak for me? As I read the scripts of my charges, I realised the truth, that I thought myself a hard woman, but every woman is hard.

These were Emily's words of her clerical encounter:

The gentleman and Miss de Comynge made sure my bare bottom was well presented, and then she left, and I got ten with a willow cane, which didn't hurt much. He got me to sing church things, which seemed to excite him, also the thought that my naked fesses were a boy's. Well, clerical gentlemen are sometimes like that, so I started to talk like a boy, and said gosh and damn and even bloody, which got him well going, to be sure. When he had finished caning me, he said I must be punished some more for my naughty language, so I said gosh and bloody some more, and let him poke me in the bum-hole. His prick was really hard, and I quite enjoyed it, though I pretended I didn't, and squealed; said damn, bloody etc. He spent in my bum-hole and I pretended to cry, whereupon he gave me a sovereign and told me to get a chocolate cake. (Note to the Vice-Mistress, I have got a nice cake from the shop in the High Street and only took one slice for myself).

Then he said that he was a naughty boy too, and deserved a spanking on his bare bottom, and I said that would cost him another chocolate cake, so I got another sovereign and bent him over my knee with his trousers down round his ankles, and spanked him very hard on his bum, which went all red. He squealed a lot and I do not think he was pretending. My hand was quite sore from the spanking, though not as sore as him I think. I was tired of all his squealing so I thought it a lark to shut him up, and I got up and took off my panties, then stuffed them in his mouth, and he was whining and moaning so much I couldn't be bothered to spank him anymore, so I took the cane which he had used on me, and gave him six with it on his bare bum, and he seemed to think it hurt, but his pego stood up again and he begged me to rub it till the spunk came, which I did, and then he kissed my boots and I let him keep my panties as a souvenir. He was quite a generous gentleman though somewhat confused.

I smiled as I read; how like my own dear Major Dove he sounded, although of course the only boy's bottom that interested the Major was his own whip-blushed buttocks as

I flogged them for him! Emily called to mind a better-spoken version of dear Tess! I read on, to see what Phoebe Ford-Taylor had been up to. Her tone had a little more *froideur* than the down-to-earth Emily's:

On Miss de Comynge's instructions, I put on my best dress, which was pale blue satin, down to my ankles, and a high neck with a white lace trim which I thought very fetching. It was very tight around my bosoms, and I was afraid I had grown out of it, but Miss de Comynge assured me gentlemen would find it very nice. Also, I had white kid gloves and a purse to match, and underneath I had on blue silk bloomers, also with a lace trim, and light grey calf-boots. Miss Deirdre had shaved my mink until my lady's place was quite bare, also around my bottom and bum-hole, which I thought rather nice, but Miss de Comynge told me to wear one of Mme Izzard's wigs, that is, a hairpiece to cover my mink, brown like my own hair but at least twice the size of my own mink, and awfully bushy, so I was glad I wore bloomers, and not tight panties, for it would have been itchy and uncomfortable.

My gentleman was young and quite handsome, with a nice frock coat, cravat, etc., and he took my arm like a gallant as we went to take our tea in the private room. I was carrying a little cane, for Miss de Comynge said that I must be prepared to chastise a gentleman who had been naughty. On the way, we passed Jane Ruttle, who gave me a horrid look, I am not sure she is really a St Agatha's girl. Tess served us tea and was rather saucy in a frilly maid's uniform, although Tess always looks saucy whatever she wears, and winked at me, which I did not like, and I felt like giving her a caning for cheek, but then I thought she might enjoy it like the minx she is.

Well, the gentleman did not desire chastisement, for he said the exercise should make me far too hot and I may perspire in an unladylike fashion, and didn't I feel too hot in my tight dress? I saw his eyes were on my bosoms, and I agreed that it was very hot, and would be more comfortable to be at my ease. But I said I had no bodice or corset under my dress, so if I lowered it, he should see my naked bosoms.

He said he would like to see them, so I unlaced my dress and sat with it on my lap, and sipped my tea with my bosoms bare!

The gentleman went all red in the face and I saw there was a bulge where his manhood lay. I thought this quite exciting, and put down my teacup and began to stroke my bubbies and nips, rubbing them quite hard till they stood up all stiff, and his manhood stood up quite visibly, and it seemed very large.

I asked him if he was not uncomfortable and he removed his shirt, and his bare chest was quite hairy, which I remarked on. He said he envied me my smooth bubbies and would like to touch them, to which I assented, pretending to be coy but in truth quite excited, and feeling wetness inside my bloomers from my lady's place. Then I decided to be completely at ease and took off my dress and bloomers altogether, and sat there wearing nothing but my blue silk stockings and my white garter belt with the straps loose.

He began to stroke my naked bubbies and said that they were the biggest he had ever seen, and the most beautiful bubbies on earth, and that my mink was just as beautiful, and wanted to know if it was all my own. I told him the truth, which he seemed to find very exciting, and he begged me to show him my shaven mount, which I agreed to. Then he was very excited and stripped off his lower garments and I saw his prick lovely and hard, with a shiny red knob that I wanted to stroke. He let me do this and put his fingers against my lady's place and began to caress me there, making me all wet with oily stuff.

All the time he was touching my bubbies and I let him pinch my nips quite hard, which made them very stiff and tingly. He asked if I would give him a 'bubby-fuck', and I did not know what this meant, so he showed me, putting his stiff manhood right between my teats and making me squeeze him and rub my teats together on his hard thing until he started to groan, and creamy stuff came out of his pee-hole, which was very exciting, especially as his fingers were busy in my lady's place, stroking my damsel, which was all hard and throbby, and just as I watched him spend his spunk on my bare bubbies, I had a spend too, which was very nice, and when I licked up his spend from my nips and bubbies, he was so pleased he gave me ten shillings, which I spent on cakes for me and my chums. He was a very nice gentleman, really, and I agreed to be friendly to him often.

I made a mental note to warn my Swish girls against the dangers to the figure of overindulgence in cakes! Next, Dotti van de Ven recounted in her terse Boer idiom:

My gentleman was brown of skin and told me he knew my country well, then produced a flask of home-made peach brandy, which he offered, saying it would make me nostalgic for the Transvaal, and frisky as a springbok. I had some and felt warm and happy, thinking of my distant veldt, and then he said he loved to ride the springbok, and I laughed and said, 'Ach, man, such a thing is impossible.' He said it meant a special thing in Kleinwinkeldorp, and would show me. Well, I had some more peach brandy and very soon I had taken off all my clothes except for my shoes and stockings, and he was as naked as I, and sitting on top of me as though he was riding a horse!

'Giddy-up,' he said, and I had to carry him round and round the room while he lashed my bottom with a crop, which was quite nice and hot. I could feel his naked balls pressed to the small of my back, and he was moaning, so I knew he was frigging himself. Then I threw him off and this time it was I who mounted him, and I made sure he had a better thrashing than I had taken, for when I had ridden him to a lather, his cock spurted his spunk all over the parquet floor!

I was feeling naughty by now and my quim was all wet from rubbing against his buttocks where I bestrode him, so I said that for ten shillings I would clean up the spunk, and he agreed, tucking a note into my wet quim! Then I knelt down and licked up all his spunk from the floor while he spanked my bottom with his bare hand, and frigged my clit until my juice was running all down my thighs, and I spent too, and it was lovely! After that I saw he had a trembling pego again, so I sucked him until he was as stiff as a eucalyptus tree and then I opened the cheeks of my arse and guided his pego into my bum-hole, where he poked me until he spent a second time. I liked the feel of his pole in my bottom so much that

I frigged myself while he was poking, which he thought super, and he gave me another ten shillings and told me not to tell! I liked that gentleman and hope to have tea with him again, even though he comes from a rude place like Kleinwinkeldorp.

As I was contemplating using these narratives as translations into Latin or French prose, Tess came in with my tea. She chuckled coarsely. I followed her eyes, and found that my fingers were unconsciously stroking my excited cunt through my dress!

Tess looked at me with her usual knowing smirk.

'Well, Tess?' I said, blushing as she saw the wet patch at my thighs.

'Having fun, Miss?' she said cheekily.

'You will pour the tea, and mind your own business, Tess,' I said. But my voice was insincere; she was wearing her favourite frilly French uniform, with her camisole very carelessly laced, so that an already generous cleavage was enlarged to show almost all of her milky teats and the red paps which crowned them so prettily. My reading, and my gentle cunt stroking, had made my quim all wet, and the sight of Tess's breasts – and her lush behind, as she bent over to pour my tea – did nothing to help matters.

I still had quite a lot to read; I sighed. Tess knew why I sighed and grinning wordlessly, she unleashed what little of her bosom was covered, and pressed her naked breasts to my face.

'Oh Tess,' I sighed, quite overcome, as my lips and tongue found her hardening nipples, which she obligingly thrust into my hungry mouth. I chewed and sucked on her nipples for a little while, to her evident satisfaction, for she placed my hand underneath her skirts and directed my fingers to her moist cunt.

'I know you, Miss,' she said with tender simplicity.

'What, again no panties?' I said weakly. 'Oh Tess, I'll have to give you a proper thrashing.'

'Now, Miss?'

'No . . . no, I must read, I'm busy. Tess, why are you so wicked?'

'It is my Cornish blood, Miss,' she said with great gravity, and knelt before me. 'But here, you read, Miss, while I attend to your wet little damsel. It must be exciting stuff, for she's all stiff! I'm not one for book-learning, but maybe I should try and better myself.'

With that, she plunged her head between my thighs, with a muffled reproach:

'You ain't wearing panties neither, Miss!'

And then I felt her probing tongue sending tingles of pleasure up my spine as she expertly tongued my stiff clit. Well, I thought, if I am to read, I may as well experience what I read about. I stroked Tess's hair as I delved into the narrative of Connie Sunday, which was typically brusque and to the point:

I don't believe in beating about the bush. My gentleman looked fit enough, in an English sort of a way, and as he was fiddling around with pouring my coffee (tea for him – ugh), I slipped out of all my clothes and stood in front of him buck naked. 'There,' I said, 'that's what an American girl looks like, now I want to know if an Englishman is virile enough to satisfy me.'

He almost choked on his darned tea! I sat on his lap and made him kiss my teats, then chew them real hard, and put my hand on his cock, and I fair got him going, because he had a stiffener fit to bust his pants. I told him to get naked, real fast, because I wanted that cock inside me, and was he man enough to hogtie me and whip my ass. He went all red and I pulled his pants off him. He had lilac panties, just like an Englishman, and I laughed so much he got all mad, like I hoped he would, and put me over his knee and began to spank my bare ass with his panties round his ankles.

I took a fair larruping, and my bum cheeks were nice and hot, and then I jumped off him and told him he had to tie me proper. But he got all embarrassed, like he was expecting some nice polite English cissy girl, so I told him I was going to whip some sense into him. I made him strip as naked as I was, and he was all trembling, but that cock stood like a redwood, and I was gushing from my cunt, I wanted him inside there so bad! I kneeled down and started to suck his pole like a stick of candy, and he moaned and groaned some, so I said I'd make him groan properly, and got my cane and made him touch his toes like boys do for punishment.

Then I gave him six of the best, English style – the English are real good at some things – nice and tight, always right in the middle of his cheeks. He yelped and squirmed something beautiful, as I made his ass glow all lovely and crimson. When I'd given him six, he stood up, and there were tears running down his face, and he was real mad, and told me he hadn't bargained for that.

So I made him lie down on his back and said I'd wipe his tears away, and I did. I squatted over his face and lowered my naked cunt and asshole right onto his nose and lips, and sat on him, rocking back and forward for a while, and rubbing his face with my full weight on him. He groaned and squirmed and I thought he was in pain from my weight, but his cock was standing up real stiff and I had some fun by flicking the tip of his bulb with my fingernails, which made him gurgle under my wet cunt.

He tried to put my hand on him and make me frig him, but I was too playful, and wouldn't do it, so he was all frustrated. I guess some men like having a girl sit on their face so they can be squashed by her naked quim, all wet and everything. When I let him up, he said I was wicked to make fun of him and let his pego stay so lonely without even a tickle. Well, I said, you'd better tickle me with a good thrashing then, but you'd better truss me good or I'll holler and kick like a mule.

He was so excited and mad at the same time, he did a lovely job. I had my own panties for a gag, then I lay on my side while he belted my wrists and ankles together in front of me. I was properly hog tied, and my cunt was so wet I could hardly bear it! Then he took the cane and lashed me with a good half dozen on my naked rear and made me all tingly and hot and flowing with love-juice so I could hardly breathe with the delight of it. And then he asked had I had enough, and I shook my head, no! That threw him. I took another six on the ass, and what a show I put on for him, writhing and squirming and shuddering at each cut, and I wasn't acting!

At last I told him to get that stiff pole inside my cunt and roger me, or I would explode, and he got the message and gave me the hardest fucking I've had since I left Arizona. I spent almost at once as I felt his pego thrust hard into my cunt, and then he rolled me around the floor on the end of his cock, fucking me all the time, as though I were a sweeping brush! And when I stopped rolling, he would dive for my clit and rub her real hard, so I spent two more times before he had finished fucking me! Then he gave me ten shillings and said I was very forward but he liked me, and I said he wasn't so bad for an Englishman, and we ended all lovey-dovey. I would have liked being tied harder, but he was OK, I guess.

As I read, Tess had her hands firmly clasped on my buttocks and was scratching them with her unmanicured fingernails, which was rather nice; especially as her tongue was slapping my stiff clit and sending little waves of giddy pleasure through my belly. My cunt was sopping wet, and I could feel my juice trickling on my bare thighs, which made it difficult to concentrate on my reading.

'You're all juicy and flowing, Miss,' said Tess. 'There must be something good in that reading of yours.' As though her sturdy gamahuching had nothing to do with it!

'Oh there is, Tess.' I described the piquant account of Connie sitting on the gentleman's face, which indeed reminded me of a similar event in Cornwall, when I had almost smothered Freddie with my bum and my wet cunt on his mouth and nose.

'Why, that is "queening", Miss, and a right good sport it is too. The Cornish gentlemen are very fond of it, and sometimes they like me to moo like a cow when I am on their faces. It is quite lovely to have a man helpless like that. Why, what's wrong, Miss? Did I hurt you?'

'No, Tess, how could your sweet lips hurt me?' I gasped, for her words had caused my loins to buck suddenly as a tremor of lust thrilled my cunt and belly. I took her head, and lifted her away from my thighs.

'And what is it about queening that men like so?'

'Why, all men long to worship a queen, and feel their eyes and lips crushed by her beauty, Miss.'

'Tess,' I said, 'would you do that to a lady? To me? Would you queen me, please, now?'

'With pleasure, Miss,' laughed Tess. 'But how can you read with my arse on your face?'

'Well, you shall read to me, Tess,' I said, as I lay down on the sofa with my skirts lifted to expose my quim. For I did not mean her to be finished there, and my upturned visage awaited the kiss of her bare bottom. Nimbly, she hoisted her own skirts and squatted over me.

'I can read,' she said proudly, 'as long as there ain't too many big words.' She took the book from me and opened it at my page.

'Sit hard on me, Tess,' I gasped, 'and please, with your stockinged toes, continue your lovely work on my quim and clitty.'

Tess lowered her buttocks and thighs until her anus bud was tickling my nose, and the wet hairs of her unshaven minge straggled across my chin. And then her weight was full on me; her cunt was already as wet as my own, and my lips kissed the swollen petals eagerly as my tongue found her throbbing little damsel in her fleshy nest. My nose was flattened in the cleft of her buttocks and I could feel her hard little anus bud pucker as my face wriggled against her.

She squealed in delighted surprise, and began to rock on top of my face with a sinuous rhythm, as though she were riding me. At the same time I felt her draw up her thighs, so that my body took the whole weight of hers, and then she inserted her toes into my throbbing wet quim. Her big toe speedily found my stiff clitoris, and caressed her with steady strokes, causing my belly to flutter as my nipples tingled and stiffened, and under those soaking, hairy folds of cunt-flesh, I thought myself trapped beneath a heavenly ocean. Tess began to read the words of Veronica Dove, to my great curiosity, for as my trusted Veronica more and more took charge of the assignations, I was not always aware of every visitor's name:

I was surprised when my gentleman introduced himself, but not so surprised, really, and he explained gravely that he wanted to see if I gave value for money. I tried to maintain a businesslike hauteur. We went to the private room, and I made sure I swished my cane in the air, to let him know what he was in for, whether he liked it or not, for I was not going to let slip the opportunity of tanning that juicy pair of fesses so tight and inviting under the trouser cloth. When we sat down and were having our tea, I must say we were both a bit shy, which was a nice feeling, really!

We made some small talk, and I at last asked him directly what he wanted, and he came over all blushy, which was nice too.

'Well, I think you know, Miss,' he said.

'Sir,' I said, 'you are here as a client, and must spell things out.'

'Oh,' he said, 'I should like to look at you.'

I asked if he meant, look at my naked body, and he blushed again, though he scarcely needed to, and nodded yes. I stood up and began to unlace my tight silk dress, and he stood too and begged to be allowed to do it for me. He stood as tall as I did, and he unlaced me with such nimble fingers that it almost seemed he was undressing himself.

All the time his breath was very hot and hard against my cheek, and I began to feel wet in my quim, being undressed by a man. When I was stripped to my corset – very tight, and blue silk, like my dress – I stood before him in corset, blue silk stockings and panties, and my black patent leather boots. My tight corset squeezed my naked teats very high and forward, with my nips pointing at him very proudly, and getting all stiff and tingly under his gaze. It is so thrilling to be naked and fiercely inspected by a man's shining eyes!

With trembling fingers he reached for the straps of my corset and unfastened me, then laid the garment reverently aside as I breathed a sigh of relief and made a little coo of pleasure as he ran his wandering fingers over the harsh marks the corset had left on my back and tummy.

'Oh you poor Miss,' he said, 'to suffer so much for beauty.'

I laughed and said it was sweet suffering, and wasn't his suffering sweet too, for his cock was ramrod stiff under those tight trousers. And he smiled a lovely smile!

Next, he knelt and unfastened my boots and slipped them from my feet, with a soft kiss to their toes, and then he undid

185

my garter straps and slid my stockings down over my toes, and kissed my bare feet too. I was tingling by now, and longed for him to divest me of my panties, and bestow a kiss on my lady's place, which I had shaved quite bare for the occasion, thinking it exciting for men, though uncertain why. I was soon to find out. He removed my panties and kissed them, too, where there was a wet patch, and then I stood quite naked before him, and smiled, and said did he like what he saw, and wasn't I to be favoured with a view of his own charms?

'A shaven cunt,' he said, all dreamy, 'how beautiful, how pure!'

He asked me to sit down with my legs apart, and hold the petals of my cunt open for him so that he could gaze on the shiny pink flesh within. I did so with pleasure, spreading my thighs and holding my cunt-petals as wide as I could, and I could feel the wetness flowing from them as he watched. He murmured that I was as lovely as an oyster or a conch shell, and I had to say I did not know what a conch shell was.

'Why,' he said, 'I should love to show you, one day. They are lovely whorled shells that you find on sandy beaches, and they are all pink and translucent inside, like a moist cunt.'

He said a shaven mount was exciting because the lady was proud enough of her beauty to show herself fully naked, without even the natural adornment of hair, and that a lady's cunt was the sweetest, most mysterious place on earth, and stuff like that, which I found rather touching, because no girl finds her cunt mysterious, although it is nice that men should.

I asked him if he did not intend to fuck me in my cunt which was now so wet for him, and that if he delayed much, I should thrash his bottom for disappointing me. His eyes glistened and he assured me that it would be an honour to bare his nates to my cane, but first, he wanted to dress in my clothes for his beating, if I would permit. I was flabbergasted and burst out laughing, but when I saw his face all sad, I touched his hand and said of course he could dress as me, if he wanted. He smiled and said he wanted to be me for a little while, which I found not just sentimental, but suddenly thrilling.

I watched as he denuded himself; he wore no panties, the naughty boy, and his cock was stiff as a tree. I longed to suck him, then feel him cleave my wet cunt. My thighs were still spread and, to excite him more, I began to frig myself gently, rubbing my clitty with slow, measured strokes, and making my fingers all wet with my love-juice which, before his popping eyes, I smeared on my nipples and mouth, grinning at him lustfully all the while. With trembling hands he put on my stockings, then garter belt, panties and boots, and reached for my corset.

I said he should never fit, and he said he would if I laced him. I said humorously that I should lace him twice then, for his adorable bare bottom would be jumping under my cane before long. I helped him get into the corset and it squeezed him as much as it squeezed me, though he had no bubbies to swell above it, but it did make the cheeks of his arse poke out most tight and beguiling. Finally he slipped into my dress and he was trembling with such excitement that I could scarcely fasten him up. But I did, and there he was, as pretty as a picture, and I hoped I looked as pretty when I was dressed. His stiff cock made my dress bulge, which I found very exciting, so I began to stroke him, as he ran his hands down the dress that clung to his body quite sheer, for he was a little broader than myself.

I saw that I should have to take matters in hand and, naked as I was, I ordered him sternly to bend over and touch his toes. He did so, and I pulled his dress – I mean my dress – right up to his shoulders, and lowered the panties so that I had a perfect vision of his bare buttocks. I could not resist. As he stood, all taut and straining for his beating, I knelt and spread the cheeks of his arse wide, then covered them with kisses which were quite sincere, and tongued his sweet hard anus bud, which made him wriggle and moan. Then I told him he was to take six from my cane, on his bare bottom, and he agreed with a little whimper.

I stood up and began his flogging, making the strokes as hard as I could, and raising a gorgeous crimson blush on those dusky arse-globes. As I flogged him I thought – wished – it was my own bare bottom taking that merciless stroking.

His cock stood stiff and shiny and when I had given him six, he gasped, having previously uttered not a sound. I clasped his cock in my fingers and pulled him towards the chair, where I made him sit down, and lowered myself, brushing his naked cock with my belly, to position myself across his knee.

I told him that he must fuck me, but to make me properly wet I needed to take a spanking on my bare nates, which was a white lie for my quim was already gushing. He laid the palm of his hand on my buttocks very hard, about thirty times, and I did not trouble to keep silent but squealed and wriggled and clenched my cheeks as they smarted, which made his blows all the more vigorous.

At last I could wait no more; I lay down on the divan with my thighs apart, and guided his cock between my swollen cunt-petals, and into my wet slit, where he gave me the most vigorous poking imaginable. As I came nearer and nearer to spending, I breathed the aroma of my own dress; my own perfume, and it excited me still more, so that when I felt the first spurt of his lovely hot cream in my throbbing cunt, I was tipped over into a chasm of pleasure that had me shuddering and scratching his neck as I smothered his lips with kisses.

When it was over and we lay in each other's arms, I thought it very tender that he should wish to dress as me, for in all of our amorous sports, kissing and smiling and fucking, do we not desire to become for a moment the loved person? When we bare our cunts to receive a man's hard cock inside us, do we not desire to absorb his strength and smell and male vigour, to become a part of his thrusting body? And just the same, does a male not desire, by fucking his woman, to bathe himself in her soft wet sweetness and, at the moment of his spending inside her cunt, to become her for a moment? So it seemed quite natural that Mordevaunt should wish to wear my clothes as I beat him and as we fucked. For – yes – my client was none other than Peter Mordevaunt, of St Alcuin's!

Veronica was taunting me, knowing I should read these words, and I felt a pang of jealousy! But my emotion was mixed with a stab of utter desire, as I imagined the sweet body of my faun dressed as my beloved Veronica, and fucking the tender quim that I longed to caress with my own lips, breasts and cunt-petals! Tess sensed that her reading had brought me to the edge of my climax and she lowered her thighs to squeeze my face very tightly, while my clitty now received the ministrations of her deft, tickling fingers. Squashed under her delicious cunt and buttocks, I thought that Tess was a queen in her way and, my mind awhirl with lustful imaginings, I bucked under her like one of Connie's western ponies as she stroked me to a breathless, whinnying orgasm.

I was so overjoyed with my queening that I wanted to show Tess the discreet photograph album of my Swish girls. I had a warm, wild idea of putting her in it, and Miss Chytte's maid Verity too, and of course Marlene and Deirdre, who had already hinted that their desirable cunts were going to waste.

Of course, they could not be members of Swish unless unanimously elected and I thought such approval would be unlikely, with the vestiges of snobbism which (perhaps healthily) inspired my girls. But I could have a second book, a sort of below-stairs catalogue; for there are plenty of gentlemen who like what Marlene pithily referred to as "rough trade". The tone of my second lustful catalogue could, and would have to be, much earthier, and I thought of enlisting the pupils of St Alcuin's to stage some lustful scenes with my staff, in which very little would be left to the clients' imaginations.

These and other fancies flicked through my imagination, as I rummaged for my book, but I could not find it; borrowed, I supposed, by Miss Chytte or Veronica, so I consigned it to the "rear bunsen" as Miss Warren, our science mistress, liked to say.

14

The Dungeon of St Agatha's

I did not mention to Veronica that I had read of her encounter with Mordevaunt. I was nervous, wondering if she had written it with me in mind, as a sort of veiled love letter, to excite my jealousy. Did Veronica long for my embraces as I longed for hers? She looked so like her father, with the same rugged, handsome features, though, in her, softened to a peaches-and-cream girl's beauty.

I did not know if Veronica suspected our relation, nor what she thought of it if she did, but I knew it was only a matter of time before one of our sessions of chastisement should lead to more than a caress of his throbbing member; the jetting of his hot sperm that begged to be released over my lips or breasts. In short, to a full fuck. Why should I not release the man from his marriage vows, a constrained fidelity to his frosty spouse imposed by our material and, I venture, hypocritical society? Take the man's body, take his daughter's too. And, yes, his wife's! The thought of fucking the whole handsome family, each in turn and each in their way, made me giddy with desire.

And, a bargain being a bargain, they should take my body for themselves. The lustful bargain is unique in that there need be neither winners nor losers, or at least, all win, by gaining pleasure. To take a whole family in this way – well, I knew how lustful father and daughter were, but Thalia, Mrs Dove, remained a closed box, whose treasures I proposed to unleash both to herself and the world. Would she respond to my caresses, I wondered. And to what degree of passion? She might yield to a gentle masturbation; to kissing and frigging under rustling skirts, perhaps even to a rigorous whipping on the bloomers or bare buttocks, leading to a full naked gamahuche! Marriage and our bourgeois proprieties are noble institutions, in that they lead to social stability and material progress. I do not think the wondrous automobile could have been invented by a man sated with unbridled fucking, and thus depleted of his inventive powers! Yet in the sternest conformity, the naked human beast begs for release; and that is the healthy and therapeutic nature of the house of pleasure, or the bacchanalian orgy of classical times.

They order things differently on the continent. A Parisian husband and wife would never dream of asking what the other was doing between five and seven, and the 'cinq-à-sept', the time for lustful assignations or visits to the bordello, is an institution as sacred and healthy as marriage itself, which is ever enriched by the spice of naughtiness.

The burghers of Frankfurt, Munich, Amsterdam and Venice enjoy a week's carnival every year, when masks are worn and faces (and bodies) are painted. No one asks his or her companion's name! There are many apocryphal stories of ladies and gentlemen who have woken up, and found to their dismay that they have spent a night of unbridled passion with their own spouse!

That was why I had installed my Turkish baths, which were popular with all. The bath, in which our naked bodies are wreathed in the elements of heat and water, is a kind of womb in which differences of class, wealth, even sensibility are dissolved in the pervasive steam. It cleanses our skins as it cleanses our minds of taboos and inhibitions. There, we are but hot, naked flesh. Innocent animals free to caress in friendship rather than in power.

My oubliette provided the same innocence for those gentlemen who longed to strip away the anxieties of the world and become a helpless individual, trussed and flogged by my merciless lash. I was their avenging goddess. For the brief time of their chastisement, I was their whole world; there was nothing for them but their bonds and the searing, pure pain of my lash on their naked skin. In earlier times, doctors were fond of purgatives and I see the role of the flagellant woman as providing a purgative for the soul;

the washing of fears and doubts that the Greeks called catharsis.

And, as my experience at the Swish conclave had shown me, the sternest mistress (for so I think of myself) needs the same purgation from time to time; to feel her own body bound and whipped, and the cares of dominance washed from her by the lash.

I alone had the keys to my oubliette, or dungeon. I alone undertook the chastisement of those males whose tensions were such that they required the most severe treatment. The painting in my study, depicting the torments of dear Sicilian St Agatha, was generally useful in guiding our conversation. Some gentlemen asked directly, even carefully, to be ministered to in my dungeon. Others, poor sweet lambs, hummed and hawed, and blushed and fidgeted, until I had to take them by their hand and look very coolly into their eyes, and suggest it to them. For the art of salesmanship, hence good business, is not, as some wrongly think, to foist unwanted wares on a hapless sucker (Connie's American parlance is very catching!), but to discern what the customers really want in their hearts and then provide it to their satisfaction. That is when the repeat business comes in! And as any businesswoman will tell you, eighty percent of profit comes from repeat business.

'Sir,' I would say, very kind and mellow in my demeanour. 'You have admitted that you have been naughty, and deserve a chastisement.'

'Oh yes, Miss, very naughty,' they would blurt.

'And I suppose your nanny or matron would in such circumstances sentence you to a full six strokes of the cane, on your bare bum?'

'She would, I suppose, yes!' And their eyes would light up.

'Well, I am not sure if you could stand such punishment. I am a very stern mistress, and my tuition is quite expensive.'

'Money, Miss, is not a problem. And as for your severity, why, I can stand any punishment, even six on the bare bum, if you thought it necessary.'

'What if I thought more was necessary? If six cane strokes would not begin to atone for your naughtiness?'

'Oh ...' (gulping). 'I am yours to command, Miss.'

And so I would lead them to my oubliette, where I would chain or strap them, whimpering, to my flogging post or pillory for their chastisement. In truth it was scarcely more severe than a normal bare-bottom caning, but it was the imagination which made their ordeal so much more thrilling; the feeling of utter helplessness as I bound them.

My oubliette contained corrective devices admirably adapted to my lustful ends: there were restrainers to discipline penis, balls and anus; a variety of corsets and gags; even leather suitings that would encase the victim in a second shiny skin of miraculous tightness and discomfort. Quite a few liked to be cruelly trussed in corsets, stays and so on. That is, to pretend they were women. In any case I attired myself for the event in a very similar costume to their own, which excited them still more. And, I admit, I myself enjoyed being laced into the tightest of corsets, or long, very slinky but uncomfortable boots which hugged my thighs right up to my peeping cunt-petals.

Thus accoutred, I would whip them very severely, with a scourge or many-thonged flagrum, or even with the simple cane on their bare, adorably trembling bottom. My severity was more in the word than the deed, that is, in their imagination, which is the key to the art of lustful pleasure. How much is the pleasure of naughtiness heightened by the very knowledge that it is naughty!

Thus, between each stroke of the whip, I would coo my most ladylike obscenities in their ears, explain that they were my slaves, and that I proposed to flay the very skin from their bodies, and that no one could hear their cries for help (which was actually true). How they blubbed and whimpered and begged, and how stiff their cocks stood, restrained or not, as I whispered my threats of humiliation and torment! Of course, the beatings they took were no harsher than those I enjoyed myself but, in the delighted fever of their minds, they had suffered the degradation of a thousand slaves!

As always, a business must have a good insurance policy. Thus Mr Izzard had furnished my oubliette with an ingenious array of photographic equipment, concealed artfully so that by pressing discreet switches with my foot or elbow, I could record in snapshots the enjoyments of my customers. The cameras would work in conditions of low light, but I made sure all the same that at least part of my proceedings were illuminated with harsh oil lamps, so that the ecstatic faces of my gentlemen were recorded for my archives. It does not do to be too careful; many of the gentlemen used obvious aliases, although I had a good idea who they were, or even recognised them from the public prints. Some were parents who would come with wives in tow, and part of the gentlemen's chastisement was the knowledge that as they writhed under the lash, their wives were at that very moment writhing naked under the amorous attentions of the young men from St Alcuin's. This added extraordinarily to their pleasure, as did my teasing:

'Just think, sir,' I would hiss, as my whip cracked painfully across their bare buttocks, 'your lady wife is seeing the sights of my academy, and you know how lustful young men are.'

'Why, Miss, she has gone to look at the buildings and classrooms, thinking I am occupied on similar business. Nothing more, surely?'

'You deceive yourself, sir. Even as we speak, and as I administer the chastisement to your bare bum which you so richly deserve,' – and I would give him two or three cuts in rapid fire, making him yelp – 'your wife is removing her dress, under the lustful eye of young Booter, or Phipps, or even the virile Mordevaunt, who has a pego far bigger than your puny morsel, sir. There!' I lashed hard.

'Ooo! God, Miss, that hurt!'

'Another cut for the feebleness of your manhood, you cur! Yes, at this moment your lady, the faithful wife of your bosom, is showing her corsets and panties to the eyes of my lads. Her bubbies are squashed up from her tight corset, aren't they, and she can see their manhoods bulge as they watch her unlace herself; stripping off the corset until her teats hang bare and the nipples are swollen with desire for those stiff young cocks. She slides off her panties, or her bloomers, showing them her lush curly mink, already wet with her love-juice; now she is naked for them, lying on the floor amid the dirt and dust, so desperate is she for a fuck!

'One by one they take her, sir, their hard cocks penetrating her anus, her dripping cunt, her open mouth. She gasps at the size of young Mordevaunt's engine, at the hard muscle of his smooth body, and shivers at the touch of his skin, perfumed by the sweetest of manly aromas! Surely that monstrous, swollen manhood must split her tight, wet quim clean in two! But no. She sighs and squirms as Mordevaunt thrusts his stiff cock firmly to the neck of her womb, and she clasps his pumping hard buttocks as he fucks her so ruthlessly and so divinely, and cries out in her own spend as she feels his hot cream spurt fast inside her; inside your own wife's body, sir! And when one cock is spent, another takes his place; she is giddy, at every touch of a cock or lip or fingers on her throbbing clit, she spends, sir. Her swollen cunt gushes with love-juice and she spends as she never thought to spend before!' (I must admit that I always seemed to dwell on the role of Mordevaunt in these proceedings, and my own cunt gushed wet as I did so.)

'Oh God! No! It cannot be true!'

My whip would descend again, to stifle his words in a squeal of pain.

'It is true, you worm! You vermin! Think of it! Your wife squirming under those juicy young cocks, as you are now squirming under my lash! It is true, isn't it, sir?'

'Yes! God, yes! It is true! Don't stop, please! Flog me till I can take no more! I deserve to be punished for my beastliness! My wife – Ooo!' (as my lash cut him) – 'you say, in her mouth? In her bumhole? It cannot be, surely.'

'This cut from my whip, sir –'

'Oo! God, Miss! Oh God! Oh, the smarting!'

'This cut says that I speak the truth. In the bumhole, in the mouth, and in the cunt, sir. The cunt that you thought to possess for yourself. So the next time you pleasure your lady, if pleasure it can be called, you must think of those lusty male cocks that have filled each of her holes and made her spend in an ecstasy never before imagined under your limp embrace, sir! There! The final cut!'

'Ah! Ah! Ah!'

And as often as not, my gentlemen would spend at only the slightest touch of my fingers to his quivering pee-hole, in some cases spurting his sperm without any caress other than the whip's! And the delicious part of my cruel tauntings was that I spoke only the truth!

On just one occasion did I have a problematic client, and that was a gentlemen of distinguished bearing who came straight to the point, demanded to be treated in the oubliette, and offered twice what my tariff demanded. This rather took me aback, for my tariff was high enough already. I had a pleasant way of making the extraction of money as painless as possible, by typing up an account and disguising the whole proceedings as a kind of medical bill, dealt with in a very matter-of-fact way, as though it were a business transaction as morally neutral as any other, which of course it was. This saved my gentlemen any embarrassment at revealing their most secret cravings and they were rather tickled to be presented with a bill after their treatments, itemised like any tailor's or wine merchant's statement of account: *Item: one severe colonic irrigation; item: one correction with birch, twelve strokes; item* . . . and so forth.

This particular awkward customer would have none of such amiabilities, but threw money at me, which of course I accepted, and demanded the best treatment.

'All our treatment is the best, sir,' I said primly, but led him to the oubliette. The strange thing was that he wore a mask over his face! Not a leather mask, such as we used in our chastising games, but a light linen cloth which he explained was to conceal the healing scars of an operation, something to do with wounds he had received in some accident. Of course I did not believe this, thinking that he must have something to hide, so when he demanded to be stripped and trussed with the most severe restraints available, I invited him to try our 'special' mask of black leather, with built-in gag. This would make it necessary to remove his own mask, and I promised not to look. I kept my promise as he changed masks, but of course my camera was under no such promise, and when I saw his photograph later there was not a blemish on his face. I did not know what worried him so; although there was something vaguely familiar about him. Nevertheless I was sure he was no household name to the public.

Before he was clamped into his gag, he gave me instructions as to his treatment. He wanted a punishment more severe that I cared to inflict, involving the very cruel pinching of his cock and balls, the filling of his anus with a shaft almost too big for the most spacious cunt, and certainly so for the tender bum-hole. I baulked at these requests but was prepared to try and please him. But then he demanded that I flog his bare buttocks with fifty strokes of my harshest birch. At first I thought he said fifteen, and said cheerfully:

'Fifteen stingers, then, you wicked boy! Oh, how I'll make your bare bum squirm! I'll redden him till you squeal!'

'No! No, Miss!' he howled in exasperation. 'I said fifty! And fifty you shall give me!'

I began to feel uneasy.

'Why, sir, that is too harsh a punishment. A full fifty! Sir, our chastisements are intended to purify the body, not to damage it! It is too much – I won't do it.'

'Then fetch a girl who can!'

His cold manner displeased me.

'None of my girls will oblige such a request, sir. Such cruelty is alien to us all, for discipline untempered by tenderness is no discipline. What you are demanding is unmitigated cruelty and I have no wish to know your reasons. No, sir, I won't oblige you. In fact, you shall have your money back, and you shall leave at once, for you have the wrong idea of St Agatha's, I am afraid.'

Thankfully, he made no trouble, and agreed to be gone, but gave a mournful cry:

'Oh, who, who, shall deliver me?'

I thought this rather curious but released him and, masked again, he stormed off, his face (what I could see of it) red with rage and frustration, and I thought what a sorry man he must be.

Apart from that one incident, I enjoyed my scenes in the oubliette, not least because I often found my quim moistening most generously as I flogged the naked body of a gentleman. Especially if he was quite young and handsome, which a surprising number were. Occasionally, I allowed our treatments to extend to a fuck, which was usually quite brief, due to the excitement caused by the punishment. I was often obliged to frig myself to a spend afterwards, before their eyes. As I rubbed my clit, I would sneer all the while at their lack of virility which, oddly enough, sometimes made them hard again, so that they were able to fuck me a second, and more satisfying time.

The photo book remained unaccountably lost, but that was no hardship, for we had tremendous fun with Mr Izzard making a new one. Also a below-stairs book. How we enjoyed the pictures of Marlene, Verity and Tess squirming naked as the nozzles of Deirdre's colonic irrigation machine caressed their innermost areas in a triple lavage!

Many of the gentlemen, and ladies too, were coyly excited by this hygienic procedure, and it was to their great satisfaction that I proposed a complete irrigation before their chastisement. Their satisfaction was even greater when the young lady who was to entertain them took a lavage alongside, and great sport was had trying to see who could outlast the other!

Certain of the girls took to this aqueous diversion in great spirit, notably Dotti van de Ven and Imogen Gandy. It was a delight to hear Dotti's guttural moans of pleasure as her sturdy Boer rump writhed under the probing ministrations of Deirdre's anal tube. And Imogen Gandy, a pretty but I thought, rather retiring soul (I tried to persuade her that her very large bosoms, like Phoebe Ford-Taylor's, were no disadvantage in social matters), became a positive fury as the hot fluid coursed through her, twisting and whimpering as though she were grappling with a vigorous lover and not a rubber tube, however intimately it caressed the depths of her anus.

I love all things aquatic: swimming, bathing, splashing with friends, and preferably in the nude. We are, it seems, made mostly of water, so what is more natural than to bathe ourself in the life-giving fluid, like happy little fishes in life's ocean? Gentlemen often remark that a lady's cunt is like a lovely sea, and I suppose we all have this urge to immerse ourselves in our primordial home. I decided therefore to try this new water sport, and duly presented myself at surgery.

Veronica and Connie were there, and also Phoebe and Imogen, who seemed to have become chums. (Like attracts like, and perhaps the two felt they belonged to a sort of sorority of the big-breasted.)

They greeted me with mischievous giggles and comments such as: 'It is always painful the first time, Miss', and so forth.

I smiled regally as I doffed my skirts and panties, like the others, and knotted my blouse high over my waist, then stood meekly with naked legs and sex before Deirdre's stern gaze. She ordered me however, to strip completely naked, as though I were no more than some errant pupil, and quite foolish.

The other girls stripped as though from custom, so I did the same and, nude, was ordered to turn round and present my arse for inspection, which I did. Then I felt my cheeks spread, and a finger poked inside my bum-hole to its fullest extent! I blushed and squirmed ever so slightly, for it was rather exciting, and I realised that was the attraction of the colonic irrigation: to have one's bum-hole well filled, by stiff cock or spurting water, is so nice!

Deirdre wriggled her finger round, and pronounced that I was fit to take a number three tube. I did not know what this meant.

'Give her a five!' cried Connie.

'Oh, she'll take a six, with that elastic bum-hole of hers,' purred Veronica.

'No, it is her first time, so it shall be a three,' said Deirdre sternly. 'You, Connie, haven't even got to the five yet, so if you don't hold your tongue you might get – you might get a seven!'

This silenced the girls and I dared not think what a seven might be like. There were five places on the machine, with footrests and handlebars and a padded saddle for our bellies. We faced outwards, our bums towards the steaming tank of hot fluid, and when we were in position, Deirdre fiddled with levers. To my astonishment, I felt the machine move under me, spreading my thighs and buttocks wide and forcing my bottom uncomfortably high, with my anus bud fully exposed. It was rather like riding a bicycle, really, only with obvious differences.

Deirdre applied lubricating cream to our bottoms in turn, and then deftly inserted a length of rubber tubing. I gasped at the shock; it seemed bigger and harder than any penis, and if this was a number three, I dreaded to think what a number seven must be like. The girls, however, prattled merrily, used to this anal discipline by now. The tube snaked into my tight anus as though there were no end to its fearsome length, and at last I felt the nozzle squat tightly against the very doorway to my belly! I wondered that the girls could take their punishment so calmly, for punishment it was, quite different from a vigorous arse-fucking with a hot, living cock.

The insertions complete to Deirdre's satisfaction, she permitted herself the hint of a smile, baring her white teeth most piquantly against her crimson lips and gleaming black skin.

'Well, we are honoured by Miss de Comynge's presence, girls, so I'll explain the drill to her. I'm going to turn the tap, Miss, and you'll feel yourself filling up with the cleansing liquid. All the girls will be filled at once; it's the beauty of Mr Izzard's machine. But you must hold it in, that's most important, so it can do its work. Relax only when I give the word. Understood?'

'Yes, Deirdre,' I said, trying to sound cheerful.

I could see that Imogen Gandy, beside me, had knotted

her brow in concentration, and that her lips were quite flushed as though in erotic excitement. Well, there was something erotic about this clinical operation, the inhuman tube inserted into my tenderest part as though I were some biological specimen on a surgeon's table. It was that feeling of naked helplessness which can be so thrilling to a girl and, evidently, to a gentleman as well, and I must confess I felt a slight erotic tickle myself. With a deft motion, Deirdre opened the taps, and the machine gurgled into life.

I had never felt anything like it! I groaned out loud as a jet of warm water spurted into my anus with, it seemed, the force of a volcano!

'Gosh, Deirdre,' I gasped. 'Are you always so rough? I hope I haven't got to hold it too long, I don't think my belly could stand it, she's quite bursting!'

Deirdre laughed rather cruelly, and so did the others, for she said that the irrigation had only just begun and the first draught was only to warm up my tummy. I was about to protest when she opened another tap, and this time a jet of water hosed my belly that made the first seem benign. It was very hot, and felt as though molten lava was searing my very vitals! I scarcely had the energy to groan, since the fierce hot flood delivered such a shock to my belly, but I felt tears well up in my eyes. In anguish, I looked round to Imogen Gandy, for moral support I suppose, and was surprised to see her with eyes tightly closed, writhing as though in a lover's caress, and murmuring hoarsely: 'Oh yes, yes. Oh, yes . . .'

This jet was followed by another, even more scalding than the first! I was boiling hot now, and dripping with sweat, and I could see why we had to be naked, for our blouses would have been quite spoiled. The merciless liquid surged through me until I thought my poor tummy should explode and I heard myself beg Deirdre to stop, which caused everyone to laugh uproariously. The second jet was allowed to slop around my innards and I fought to prevent my sphincter from expelling it. I was becoming not quite accustomed, but grudgingly tolerant, to this boiling ocean that lapped my insides, when suddenly there was a third spurt, hotter and more devastating than the last. I groaned in my discomfort, and writhed around on my saddle, wondering what malign god had singled me out for such torment.

'Ah!' sighed Veronica. 'That's better!'

'A proper irrigation at last!' agreed Connie.

'God, yes. Yes, I'm so full,' gasped Imogen Gandy beside me, her heavy teats flopping and sliding quite fetchingly as she writhed under the anal tube's stern caress.

'Mmm,' said Phoebe. 'Absolutely scrumptious.'

I could not believe my ears.

'How long must we ... you know?' I stammered.

'Oh, a good while, I hope,' said Veronica. 'As long as Matron doesn't chase us away. But you won't, will you, Matron? You'll let us stay with our pretty tubes up our bums and your lovely water washing our tummies, won't you? Miss de Comynge would be so disappointed!'

I was quite speechless as I listened to their cheerful gossip, as though they were taking tea instead of having their insides flushed away by liquid fire! It seemed that every muscle in my body was straining in the effort to hold the fiery liquid inside me.

'Well, it's better than being poked in the bum-hole by some of the gentlemen.'

'No it ain't!'

'Isn't, Connie,' I gasped rather feebly.

'Isn't, then, Miss. Nothing's as good as being poked in the bum-hole, except being royally fucked in the quim.'

This brought ironic cheers from the group of squirming, tubed girls.

'Or a good birching on the bare bum,' said Veronica thoughtfully.

'Ooh, yes!'

'I do like it when a gentlemen wants to birch my naked bottom, although I like birching them too.' This from Phoebe Ford-Taylor. 'And,' she added smugly, 'I can do something you lot can't, I can give them a teat-fuck.'

There was a chorus of boos.

'I can do it too! My teats are quite big enough. And shaped better.'

202

'No you can't! No they aren't!'

'Sour grapes!'

'Girls!' I moaned. 'You all have nice bosoms, so don't quarrel over a few inches of flesh. What I want to know is, when may I free my bowels of their harsh invader, this hot fluid?'

'Oh, not for ages, Miss,' said Veronica airily. 'Why, Mr Whimble I believe, can take a number five tube for hours without complaint.'

'And Mordevaunt takes a number six! Doesn't he, Veronica?' cried Connie impishly, making Veronica blush a lovely pink.

'Anyway, Miss, you mustn't be a cissy. That would be letting down the honour of Swish, and might earn you a juicy hard caning.'

'Anything would be better than this!' I groaned.

'Imogen doesn't think so! Do you, Immy? Look at her, she's huffing and puffing as though she's going to spend, or pee!'

'Or both!'

More laughter. Then Veronica said slyly:

'Imogen likes to teat-fuck, too, doesn't she? And we know who likes it as well. Imogen likes to teat-fuck him, and be buggered by him, and suck his cock to a spurt, and oh, everything that a gentleman's money can buy. Only he doesn't need to give her any, 'cos she loves him so.'

'Oo, oo! Lovey-dovey, soppy Imogen Gandy!' came the cry.

But Imogen was oblivious. Naturally, I wondered who Imogen's lucky sweetheart was, for she was a well-formed girl, firm of arse and bosom, with a warm personality under her charming reserve. Little of that reserve showed now. I had seen her at irrigation before, but her writhing then was not half so frantic. Perhaps Veronica's jibe had excited her. Her face was quite red and she looked as though she was going to explode. I was irked: the other girls were teasing me, because they knew who Imogen's sweetheart was, and wanted me to make a goose of myself by asking. So I did not.

Instead, I watched aghast as Deirdre's hand moved to the taps again and this time I felt a whoosh of water so icy that I cried out. Its numbing chill flooded my entrails until I felt like a balloon on the point of bursting into a million fragments of tortured flesh! Yet as the sting of the hot water was replaced by a pressure, like a thousand needles of ice puncturing my anus, and my sweats turned to shivers, I suddenly felt a great calm; a feeling of repose and satiety, as though my anus had indeed enjoyed a good hard fuck.

'Isn't it lovely, Miss? Just like a man's cock pleasuring your bum-hole,' said Veronica. 'Just imagine what the number seven would be like, Miss! Even Imogen can't take that!'

And Veronica was right. When Deirdre pulled the tubes sharply from our arses and told us we could evacuate, the pleasure was so heavenly I thought I should faint. It made all the torment of the lavage seem worthwhile, and it seemed that the other girls felt the same, judging from their moans of delight as the liquid flowed squirming and slithering from their tight anuses. But no one could outdo Imogen Gandy, who writhed and groaned as though Hercules himself were tonguing her clit. She was lost in a world of her own, as the lavage flowed from her squirming bum and, as I shuddered beside her, I heard her murmur, lost in some fantasy of love:

'Oh, your cock, sir. Oh, Mr Whimble. Oh, oh, oh, Freddie . . .'

At least, I hoped it was a fantasy, but something made me suspect it wasn't.

15

In the Steam Bath

Most people have private ways of resolving inner conflict and worries. A brisk walk is one, or a lapse into gluttonous consumption of chocolate and cakes or, more commendably, a vigorous bout of love making. I was never averse to the first or the last, but my method was to contemplate my picture of St Agatha in her various excruciations, and wonder how she would deal with a given situation, and what was going on behind that serene smile as she endured the most persuasive of chastisements.

It was the centrepiece of the tableau which rivetted my attention (and Freddie had commented on my interest). The young Agatha was receiving a whipping; evidently one of the fiercest, judging by the straining muscles and stern expression of her male tormentor. He wore only a brief loincloth, while Agatha herself took the beating naked. Her wrists and ankles were tied by leather thongs, rendering her immobile, except that she was cased in the most beautiful golden harness, whose glittering chains bit tightly into her trussed body. A halter was fastened to a body-casing of criss-crossed gold links which imprisoned her naked breasts and buttocks. This snaked cruelly across her pubis and anus, making these tender and most intimate parts swell ripe and helpless to receive the strokes of the whip. I trembled as I looked on it, for it was a costume to dream of.

Such contemplation was aided by a glorious session in my Turkish bath, where naked in the fierce heat, one can put the trifling cares of this world in proper perspective and solve them gracefully. It became my practice to enjoy a soak in the Turkish bath every day; sometimes twice. Generally first thing in the morning, when Freddie and Miss

Chytte would attend me, and in the evening, when I could blissfully wash away the stresses of the busy day. Sunday mornings were especially nice, for then the girls of Swish and my chaps from St Alcuin's, and of course my intimate staff members, would assemble for a leisurely chinwag while everybody was at church. I say that the lads visited the bath, but I instructed that there was to be no naughtiness, and they were as good as gold, so that I did not make them wear restrainers. It is piquant that in the heat of the steam bath, the very artlessness of our nudity can free us from lustful thoughts, particularly the gentlemen, whose erectile propensities are effectively calmed. And it is so agreeable to talk when naked, free of the accoutrements of power and status of which our clothing, consciously or not, is a statement.

On weekdays, however, I would invite certain of my gentlemen customers to the steam bath, there to mingle chastely with the young ladies who should later entertain them: a casual seraglio in which the gentleman's choice of companion was not confused by hasty and perhaps misguided lusts. Naked, he viewed companions who were casually naked too, and thus chose in tranquillity. I made sure that on these sessions we were attended by one or two of the St Alcuin's students, not just because I loved to have a pretty naked lad massage me; pour hot water; and act as some harem slave of old Stamboul, but because it put the customers at their ease and made the whole transaction seem normal and businesslike.

One regular visitor was the 'Greyhound King of East London' whom I remembered from our open day, and who seemed to have struck up an attachment with Freddie. How he regaled us with stories of his time in the East (did they have greyhounds in China? I do know the Chinese are great gamblers), where such bathhouses are normal venues for the discussion of business and of sensual pleasures which are an open part of daily life! He was very heavily muscled, which I thought rather exciting, and wondered if he would invite me to be his companion one day, or if I should be bold enough to suggest myself. It seemed that development of the musculature is regarded as an art East of Suez, and the body beautiful is held in high esteem for males as well as females, as in Ancient Greece.

He gave us rather thrilling descriptions of the strenuous exercises, wrestling and so on, he would practise with the native men, all, of course, naked (I thought of Freddie and Mordevaunt at their sweet combat). He told of their merriments in the bathhouse, where they would relax with wine and the most fragrant of 'houris', as he called the naked serving-girls, who seemed to think their calling a most honourable one, and were pleased to tend the egos of the men with cooing endearments as to the grace of their bodies, and the most lascivious caresses as reward for their manly exertions. All these attentions were provided with smiles and friendship, and talked about quite openly in public, even in polite society.

How furtive our English ways seem in comparison! Here, a man is rather embarrassed at having a good body, pretending it is an unintended by-product of hunting, riding, and manly sports. He does however take great pride in being covered by horrid swathes of ape-like hair, to show he is not vain. My greyhound man was shaven over his entire body, including the pubis, which he explained was the custom out East, where body hair is thought unsightly. Miss Chytte would eye my lush mink and grin, and I knew she wanted me to be bare! It would be exciting; I should let her do it to me, soon.

There was a tremor in my heart whenever I heard such exotic tales, or when Dotti van de Ven or Connie Sunday described the beauty of the vast deserts and plains of their native continents. I had a longing for the most daring of erotic delights, but I found now that I desired to travel; to find them in the souks and pleasure-domes and jasmine-scented gardens of distant lands.

In our bath, surrounded by the loveliest naked girls I could imagine, my traveller would make his choice of companion with the merest smile, and as she then waited on him, with soaps and oils, he would chatter merrily with Freddie, who would have the temerity to order me about as though I were his own slave, and make me attend him and oil his body and scrub him. I pretended to resent this but in fact I adored it! Men must be allowed to show off in front of other men. It made me giddy with pleasure to be, just for little while, the naked slave of my handsome master!

And that was the cause of my present confusion. Freddie shared my bed and obeyed my commands as always, but of late our relations had lacked the ardour of our first passion. I suppose this is normal and happens to all couples, although, heaven knows we had enough sport and curious divertissements to keep the spice in any marriage for a hundred years. Nevertheless there comes a time when eyes roam, and the cries of Imogen Gandy – I remembered how Freddie had blushed as he suggsted she would be a suitable member of Swish – suggested to me that Freddie's eyes had roamed to her.

It was not the fact that he was fucking her – why, he could fuck anybody he wished, with my blessing! What perturbed me was the fact that Freddie had not sought that blessing. They say there are two things that cannot be hidden: love, and a cough. Freddie had never been prone to coughing, but . . .

It was with determination in my heart that I made my way to the Turkish bath that Sunday morning. I had slept alone the night before, my decision drawing anxious frowns from both Miss Chytte and Freddie. I had Tess serve me breakfast in my room. The good girl, fearing that I was ailing, shyly bared her breasts and clasped my face to her, to cuddle me into a good humour. Tess thought it unnatural to sleep alone. I sighed and kissed her, and said not now. I suppose tetchiness is a third thing one cannot hide.

The bath was quite full when I entered and I smelled the sumptuous aroma of steam and hot coals; the perfume of sweating bodies; and the music of birch twigs gently slapping bare flesh. I received murmurs of welcome and Miss Chytte rushed to take my clothing and give me towels and soap.

'We were afraid you wouldn't come, Mistress,' she whispered.

'Why ever shouldn't I?' I replied.

'Oh, we thought perhaps there was something the matter.'

'Who is this "we", I wonder?'

I looked round; Freddie was there, sitting beside Imogen Gandy, and rather sweetly wearing my panties. I supposed he had vanquished Mordevaunt in some ping-pong battle. Peering into the swirling steam at the throng of bodies, I recognised most of the Swish girls and both the Izzards. Mme Izzard with her arm happily around her spouse, whose own fingers were absent-mindedly stroking his wife's shaven sex.

Marriage seemed such a contented state of affairs! For a moment, I wondered if it were not time to take the plunge which a woman feels she must eventually take, and investigate it. I squatted in the commode for a few minutes — there was a row of five *évacuateuses à la turque* like the ones in my own bathroom, but not quite so ornate. Even sybarites must keep an eye on costs. Mme Izzard detached herself form her husband's caress, and came to squat beside me.

'What is wrong, cherie?' she said with Gallic bluntness. 'It is a matter of love? The tetchiness amoureux?'

'Heavens, Mme Izzard,' I said with feigned indifference. 'The approach of summer has made your imagination fervid! Why, I see you have shaved your mink. How pretty! Although your mink before was quite the fullest I've seen.'

'Thank you for the compliments,' she said, 'but you shall not distract me. A shaven sex is to be cool in summer, and I think you are not cool, Miss.'

'Well,' I laughed, 'I must shave my mink, then.'

'Aha, the English jest! I think that will not be enough, Miss. Your Freddie, he has been making the sheep's eyes at another, yes? The hot weather, no doubt. Be advised that in questions of the love, the full frontal assault is always desirable, not the moue and the pout. The ball must be placed firmly on the other foot, Miss de Comynge! You are a St Agatha's girl!'

With that, Mme Izzard noisily concluded her toilette and

went to the shower-baths, before plunging into the ice-cold bathing pool. After a few moments I followed suit, allowing Miss Chytte to soap me before immersing myself, already perspiring freely in that humid heat, into the freezing water of the pool, in which ice shards still floated, being constantly replenished by the girls sentenced to chip at the ice block.

Then I took my seat, between Freddie and Imogen Gandy, who made space for me when they saw my intended destination.

'How nice!' I said briskly. 'Imogen, dear, you look as lovely as a dozen roses, all red and glistening with dewdrops.'

She grinned shyly. I did like Imogen, she was a lovely sloe-eyed beauty, with proud young breasts and a lovely ripe bottom that looked so tempting as she squirmed under Deirdre's merciless irrigation tube! I think my irritation, or, to be candid, my tinge of that despicable emotion, jealousy, was partly anger at Freddie for enjoying those charms as yet untasted by me. I put my arm around Imogen and kissed her cheek.

'You are very pretty, Imogen,' I said.

'Thank you, Miss,' she replied with a shy smile.

'And your bottom is so pretty – I think Mr Whimble will agree – she is a very fine specimen, but I think she must have taken an awful pummelling from Matron's irrigation tube the other day.'

'Oh, I am accustomed to it, Miss.'

'Yes, I'll wager you are. But I was worried. Such groans and squirming, as though your bottom was taking a lacing from my cane!'

'Scarcely as hard as that, Miss,' she said with a giggle, and shivered. 'You lay it on quite forcefully.'

'Thank you,' I said. 'Now stand up, Imogen, and let me see your bottom, if you please. I want to inspect your little anus bud, to make sure she is all right.'

Imogen obeyed, kneeling on the hard wooden bench, and presenting to me the cheeks of her arse, which I spread. I put my finger in her bum-hole and she gave a little jump.

'Oh! Did I hurt you? It must be very tender there, so I think you shouldn't sit bare bum on these hard benches. There might be a chafing or inflammation. Here. Mr Whimble shall lend you those pretty panties of his, won't you, sir?'

'Yes, Mistress,' said Freddie shyly, and stripped off my panties, then handed them to Imogen, who put them on with a smile of delight. They were truly my prettiest pair and suited her wonderfully. I told her so as she sat down again. Freddie's naked cock now hung all tiny and shrivelled in the damp heat and I longed to stroke him there and make him big again, but desisted, and said brightly:

'Well! I have good news for us all. It is Mr Whimble's birthday shortly before term's end – I'll bet you had forgotten your own birthday, Freddie – and we are going to have a big party. All our favoured parents and, ah, special friends, shall be there. Perhaps even the nobility, or the press!'

'But, Mistress –' Freddie began, and I tapped him smartly on the funny bone of his elbow, which shut him up.

'It shall be a fancy-dress party,' I continued, and there were oohs of delight from the company.

'I am glad my plan meets with your approval,' I said. 'And I welcome any ideas. I shall appoint an entertainment committee to arrange matters. I shall shortly be going away on business for a few days, so, Veronica, you shall be in charge.'

'Yes, Miss,' said Veronica, who was splashing in the cold pool.

'What fun!' cried Imogen. 'Don't you think so, Fre – Mr Whimble?'

'Oh yes,' said Freddie, still grimacing from my tap on his funny bone. 'Absolutely topping.'

'You see, ladies and gentlemen,' I said in a ringing voice – as far as I could ring through all that steam. 'I want to show that we at St Agatha's both work hard and play hard, as I believe they say in Arizona. We must show ourselves united in our happiness, bound by our loyalty to St Agatha's and each other. An educational establishment is like a ship.' (This is the sort of thing principals are supposed to say.) 'We must all pull equally on our oars. Anyone slacking is letting the side down, isn't she?'

There were murmurs of, 'Yes, Miss', which is the sort of thing pupils are supposed to say.

'And of course,' I continued, 'anyone who doesn't pull her weight, or, worse, tries to upset another girl out of spite or thoughtlessness, is a rotter and must be punished, mustn't she?'

There were cries of, 'Hear hear!' and 'Voilà!'

'A ship can only sail true if the keel is even, good discipline is maintained, and the captain's orders obeyed. That is why the cane is always on hand to chastise the bare bottom of an erring crew member.' Rueful groans and smiles. 'And order is most important in the field of personal relationships, which must be conducted in a spirit of fair play and businesslike honesty, like all other transactions. A girl, therefore, who would cause grief or disappointment to another or, without official permission, take something that is not hers, is guilty of a very serious offence: tactlessness. The most horrid and unladylike thing imaginable.'

There was a lusty cry of, 'hear, hear!', and no cry was lustier than Imogen Gandy's. I squeezed her shoulder and kissed her on the cheek. Then whispered in her ear:

'I am glad you agree, Imogen, for I think you know what I am driving at.'

'Miss?' she stammered.

I stroked the top of her bottom through my panties.

'My panties aren't too tight?' I said pleasantly.

'N ... no, Miss. They are lovely. I wish I could keep them!' she said with nervous gaiety.

'That is easily arranged,' I said. 'And you shall keep them.'

Out loud I said, 'Happily, the acceptance of punishment provides what the Greeks call catharsis for any transgressor, who may arise with her buttocks stinging from her chastisement cleansed and virtuous. And that, to conclude, is the moral rock upon which our noble academy is founded, ladies and gentlemen.'

I musn't overdo things! There was clapping, and I nodded and thanked them. I began to stroke Imogen's hair, and noticed she was trembling despite the heat.

'You really are the prettiest girl imaginable, Imogen,' I said softly, 'and we all love you very much. That is why I should not like you to feel bad, that perhaps you might have done a bad thing, for regret is a most insidious emotion. That is why we purge ourselves with chastisement of the body. Why, girl, you are shivering, is something the matter?

'I . . . I don't know, Miss.'

'I think I do. But you must be the one to tell me.'

Freddie, beside me, was still grimacing, though no longer, I thought, from the blow to his funny bone. I gave him another one to justify his lugubrious expression.

'Have you caused hurt to someone you love, Imogen?' I said.

'Oh, I hope not, Miss. It is so difficult. I don't know what to think.'

'Well, that is what I am here for,' I said. 'You may tell me, but only if you like.'

'She bit her lip, and sighed. Then she blurted:

'Oh Miss, it is Freddie, I mean Mr Whimble. I meant no harm. I don't think he meant any, but you have been looking so . . . so distraught, ever since we took our irrigations together and I cried out indiscreetly, for I was spending, Miss. As I felt the hot liquid surge through me I imagined it was Mr Whimble's spunk spurting in my bumhole, for . . . for he has done that to me, and I enjoyed it. And wanted more. And he poked me there, and in my lady's place too, Miss.'

I stroked her hair, and kissed her tenderly.

'Well!' I said brightly. 'I dare say we don't need to go into details. (I knew I should extract them from Freddie later, painlessly or otherwise.) Imogen began to sob.

'No, Imogen, don't cry,' I said, stroking her hair. 'Please don't. It is horrid.'

'But I've been horrid,' she moaned. 'I have made love with a staff member of St Agatha's, and without your permission, Miss! I know Mr Whimble is your friend. Oh, I've offended against the honour of Swish, I have committed a terribly serious offence!'

'Imogen, you have been foolish, that is all,' I said, soothing her. 'My distress is small, compared to your peace of mind and happiness.'

'Then, Miss for my peace of mind, I must be severely punished,' she said vehemently.

'Well, I won't pretend not to be glad you said so, Imogen, for it shows you have proper pluck. What do you suggest?'

'You must flog me, Miss. Flog me here and now, on my bare bum. Please do it to me!'

'Very well, Imogen, you shall be flogged. But not on your bare bottom, no. I think I shall whip you on your panties. They are mine, you see, and therefore I shan't want to lace you too hard, for fear of ripping them.'

'But you must! As hard as you can!'

'Imogen,' I laughed, 'you won't be saying that when you feel the birch on your poor bottom.' She gasped, and her eyes widened in fear.

'Yes, Imogen,' I whispered, brushing her lips with mine. 'The birch . . .'

Imogen was very brave. She stood and announced that as she had been guilty of an offence against her comrades and St Agatha's, which Miss de Comynge forbade her to name, she had requested to be punished immediately, and would receive a birching on her buttocks, covered only in the panties she wore. There was some excitement at the prospect of witnessing her punishment (how we long to experience, whether vicariously or in the flesh, what most terrifies us), and everyone helped her collect the birch twigs which, flimsy enough when used singly to stimulate the skin while bathing, nevertheless formed a fearsome instrument of correction when a dozen were bound together. It was this flogging tool which Imogen gravely presented to me.

'Please tell me how you wish to take me, Miss,' she said in a sweet small voice.

'Why, lying flat on the bench, I think. On your tummy with your legs splayed. I suggest you hold on tight to the bench legs while you are beaten.'

Imogen positioned herself thus and I was presented with the perfect globes of her buttocks gleaming in my tight wet panties.

'But, Imogen, you haven't told me what punishment you deserve.'

'Why, you said a birching, Miss, and I am ready for it.'

'But how many, Imogen?' I said quietly, but so that all could hear. 'Part of your chastisement and the joy it shall bring, is that you must determine your own beating. Perhaps you would think four strokes appropriate?'

There was a pause, and we heard Imogen gulp.

'I . . . I should like eight strokes, Miss,' she said.

'Eight strokes with a dozen birch twigs!' I gasped. 'Are you sure?' In truth, I hoped she was sure, for I was cruelly delighted at the thought of her bottom writhing under a vengeful lash.

'Yes please, Miss.'

I thought a moment. 'Very well,' I said. 'And to sweeten your punishment, Imogen, it shall be Mr Whimble who flogs you.'

Freddie started. 'Mistress!' he cried. 'I cannot – please – I beg you. Do not be so cruel!'

'It is you who shall have to be cruel, sir, as you make your damsel's bottom squirm under your birch,' I said sweetly. 'Now,' I handed him the birch, 'please begin the chastisement.'

Freddie lifted his arm and delivered a half-hearted stroke to Imogen's buttocks, with an expression of unease on his face.

'That is not hard enough, sir,' I murmured. 'You will hold the birch with both hands, please, and lift your arms to their fullest before delivering each stroke with all your strength. If I judge any stroke insufficient, you shall get three times the stroke, with my own birch, whose kiss is far harsher.'

Freddie shivered, and did as he was told. At the second

cut, Imogen groaned, and her bottom flinched most beautifully. The third cut made her whisper, 'Oh, God!' through gritted teeth, her eyes screwed tight, and her tender buttocks dancing now in their torment.

'Think, Imogen, this is the baby of birches, and still you squirm and bleat!' I said cruelly. 'Five more lovely strokes to go, my girl, until you have taken the eight you begged for.'

'Oh Miss,' she sobbed. 'Oh please . . .'

'Please what? Don't you want to take them? Just say the word, Imogen, and the punishment will stop and you may hand in your Swish badge.'

'I'll take them, Miss.'

I nodded and Freddie delivered another cut, but I mischievously judged it half-hearted, and told him he had earned three for his pusillanimity.

'Come, Freddie, you've made her bum squirm with your rogering in her tender little arsehole,' I taunted. 'Let us see if you are man enough to give her the punishment she wants, and deserves!'

His response was to make the fourth cut a veritable lightning bolt; the birch twigs slapped her twitching buttocks and seemed to cling there, basking in their stinging kiss, and I saw that there was bare flesh peeping through the fabric of my panties.

The fifth stroke landed, and again I deemed it insufficient, earning Freddie a further three from my own birch. The sixth and seventh were better, following each other in rapid succession, as though he wanted to end both his and Imogen's discomfort as quickly as possible. Her naked body now trembled in shivering spasms and her voice was a high keening moan deep in her throat. I breathed hoarsely, feeling excitement glow in my body and my quim moisten at the sweetness of the vengeful spectacle.

Before Freddie could deliver the eighth stroke, I seized the birch and raised my own arms to deliver the tightest, juiciest cut imaginable, which finally made her squeal out loud before sinking in a torrent of sobs. There was scarcely an inch of pantie that was not torn to gaping holes, revealing her pretty buttocks all livid and crimson. I reached down and stroked her hair, then caressed her naked buttocks through the holes in her panties.

'There, Imogen, it is over, and you have taken your punishment well. I said you might have the panties to keep, and so you shall, though I'm afraid Mr Whimble's strength has caused them no little damage. Perhaps you will treasure the garment as a souvenir of your bravery under the lash of St Agatha.'

Imogen smiled weakly. 'Yes, Miss,' she whispered, sitting up and removing the torn garment, then holding it to her heaving breast. 'I shall.'

'It remains to be seen whether Mr Whimble is as brave for his own chastisement. For there are two transgressors here whose tactlessness must be purged.'

'You are going to beat me here, Mistress?' blurted Freddie. 'Must I fetch your birch?'

'No, Freddie,' I said, 'that will come later. I don't want you being brave to impress the women – and you may dwell on the delicious prospect of six hard birch strokes on your naked bottom. No panties for you, boy! But here, we must make your punishment fit the crime.'

At that moment Deirdre entered the bathhouse, exactly at the time I had appointed. With her, she wheeled a clanking, gurgling instrument which was one of Mr Izzard's transportable irrigation machines. She grinned with delight as she stripped off her clothes and, proud in her splendid nudity, began to connect the taps and nozzles of her appliance. Her body shone as she worked. I invited her to pause for a cold bath but she said she would relax better when her work was in progress.

'Now, Freddie,' I said. 'You have made rather a chump of yourself over young Imogen and caused her no end of distress, so I think that now you must be treated as a chump. You will bend over and touch your toes, and receive a good bare bum spanking.' He did so, smirking slightly at the ease of his penalty. 'A bare bum spanking,' I added, 'from every single female in this room.'

'Gosh,' said Freddie.

The girls sang with eager laughter.

'I shall go first,' I said, 'to show you how it is done, not that I think anyone needs showing.'

I positioned myself behind Freddie and made him spread his legs wide, so that his prick and balls were nicely visible between his thighs, then began to slap his naked buttocks very hard. I worked methodically, making sure all of his straining bum skin was well covered, and soon his nates were suffused by a delicious pink, and he began to tense and squirm at each blow. The force of my spanks made his balls swing, but this became less obvious as they tightened: in no time, the boy had a massive erection!

It was quite exhilarating to spank him naked, feeling my breasts sway at each stroke and the sweat bathing me in that fierce heat. I delivered quite a few 'uppercuts', that is, on the tender skin of his lower buttocks and inner thighs, and how he flinched at that! It was all I could do not to swipe him on those delicious tight balls and make him really squirm. I thought of those buttocks pumping into Imogen, his cock sliding in and out of her anus, and I became all wet, and furious too. I wanted to spank the very skin from his bum! But after about thirty spanks, I stopped, to let the others have their turn and, panting, dived into the cold pool.

Veronica took over Freddie's chastisement and her spanking was even tighter and more methodical than mine. He was wriggling nicely now, most uncomfortable in that humiliating position, and his bare bum was bright red.

'You have heard of sailors being flogged round the fleet, Freddie,' I called merrily. 'Well, you can boast that you were spanked round the academy!'

This caused great amusement, and indeed a festive air was taking hold of our gathering. Deirdre finished setting up her machine and noticing Freddie's proud penis, tut-tutted; then she fetched handfuls of ice shards from the bathing pool and, kneeling before him, clamped them hard against his balls and cock which made him cry out as he was being spanked, but did nothing to lessen the vigour of his erection, much to everyone's secret delight.

One by one the girls took their turn, including a giggling Miss Chytte and a demure Mme Izzard, to the hearty applause of her husband. Freddie's eyes were shut tight in his distress and his bottom was as red and trembling as a jelly. His face was very flushed, so I threw a pail of icy water over him, which made everyone roar with laughter.

Deirdre's turn came, and it was marvellous to watch her magnificent black body as she stroked the poor trembling young man. She spanked him with both hands at once, each palm descending sure and harsh on his backside, so that he received sixty spanks and not thirty.

'Oh!' he cried. 'That's not fair! Who is treating me so cruelly?'

'You have no say in what is fair, sir,' I said. And just then a figure I had not observed before emerged from the steam. It was Peter Mordevaunt. He grinned at me and put a finger to his lips, then pointed to poor Freddie's quivering nates. I understood him and shook my head.

'No! I hissed. 'You are no girl, Mordevaunt!'

He disappeared into the steam again and re-emerged wearing Imogen's ripped panties!

'Now I'm a girl,' he whispered with a broad wink, and I was unable to say more, because I was trembling myself in a delicious fit of the giggles.

The girls and I watched enthralled as young Mordevaunt spanked the naked bottom of his chum and rival, and I have never seen a more vicious or exuberant spanking. I supposed it was a bit naughty to watch one naked lad spank another, but it was quite thrilling, and the spectacle made my quim so wet that I had to dive into the pool again to calm myself, where I was followed by almost everyone else. We all knew what desire we felt at that sight! In the delightful intimacy of the bathhouse, any petty repressions of the pleasurable impulse are quickly dissolved by the caress of that healing steam!

At last the spanking was complete (I observed that no spanker was more enthusiastic than Imogen Gandy), and Freddie was permitted to stand up, panting and gasping as he gingerly rubbed his flaming buttocks.

'God, Miss, that was quite a walloping! I thought a spanking was easy as pie, but you women know how to hurt a chap with your palms! Especially that last set! God, it was tight! Which of you . . . ?'

'No Freddie, that would be telling,' I replied gaily; but Freddie's eye roamed around the company, and fell on Mordevaunt, who could not conceal his cheeky grin.

'You!' he roared, and raised his fist, then made to leap at his friend.

'Freddie!' I cried. 'Stand still!'

He obeyed, grimacing fearfully, and growling threats and curses at Mordevaunt, whose own helpless laughter was quite drowned by the chorus of mirth from the rest of us. And at last, Freddie himself smiled, then slapped his thigh, and roared with laughter along with us. So we were all in a merry mood as Freddie obeyed my instruction to take his place on Mr Izzard's portable irrigation machine.

His buttocks were clamped and spread, as I remembered. Deirdre's grin was positively fiendish as she showed Freddie the tube which was to bring him his delightful catharsis. He went pale, even in that heat, as he saw the giant bulb, not unlike the glans of a man's cock, only with an aperture as wide as a half-crown!

'No . . .' he groaned, and his cock shrivelled as though by magic.

'Yes,' said Deirdre. 'The number seven, Mr Whimble, sir.'

How he squirmed, the silly boy! We were obliged to strap his wrists in the cuffs thoughtfully built onto the machine, and it took both Veronica and Miss Chytte to hold his buttocks wide enough to insert the monstrous tube. Deirdre pushed with all her might, as though it were a battering ram at an enemy's gate. Freddie jerked and squealed, but at last the glans of the tube had disappeared into his stretched anus and, with a powerful shove, Deirdre plunged the tube into him right to the kernel of his belly. Then she briskly opened the floodgates, and Freddie's contortions of both face and body were wonderful to behold.

'Ah . . . Ah . . . Ah . . .' was all he could say; such was

the pressure of the scalding cleanser that no words would come. At last he was full and found his tongue.

'I'm bursting! I can't hold it, Miss,' he moaned piteously.

'But you must,' barked Deirdre. 'For now it's my turn to have a dip in the pool!'

And as Deirdre splashed happily in the water, poor Freddie huffed and groaned as he strove to prevent his straining sphincter from evacuating any of his fluid. I was breathless with a strange excitement, and my hand crept to my naked quim, there to rub, unconsciously I suppose, my awakening clitty, which now tingled and was stiff as I watched my lover's torment. My cunt began to gush quite copiously; I saw dimly in the haze that many of my girls caressed themselves also, thrilled by the spectacle of this tamed, tortured male writhing naked before them. My heart leapt and I seized my birch.

'Can't you take it, sir?' I cried. 'I'll show you! You are due six strokes of the birch for your imperfect attentions to Imogen's bottom. Well, you shall take them here and now, sir. And that shall really give you a cause for whimpering!'

There was a murmur of eager agreement. I lifted the birch, and laced Freddie's already crimson buttocks with six firm, heavy strokes, putting all the strength of my flogging arm into the beating, while with my other hand I caressed my quim and clit to the very plateau of orgasm. As I dealt him the last vicious cut, I crossed the edge of that plateau and my belly danced in a sweet fiery spend as my blurred eyes watched his adorable bottom all red and pumping under my birch, in a paroxysm of quivering, as though he were fucking me.

We were all in a state of high excitement as Deirdre returned to complete the lavage by filling his anus with ice-water, which he was also obliged to hold for an agonisingly long time. Through the steam, I saw my girls caress themselves or each other, and I think all off them came to a spend, judging by their gasps. But those gasps were nothing to Freddie's roar of relief and anguish as he was finally permitted to evacuate, which he did with a seemingly endless, spurting shudder. We were all breathless, Freddie included, but too hot in body and spirit to stop the corrective entertainment. I helped Freddie to rise from his place of suffering, and said loudly:

'Your correction is not complete, sir. I want that cock hard again, sir.' I began to stroke his balls and penis very tenderly. 'For the last part of your punishment is that you must fuck all of us women one after the other. You must fuck each one of us to a spend, mind and we shall milk every last drop of spunk from these fine balls, sir, so that you will think twice about putting your cock which belongs to me, your Mistress, where he has no business to be.'

Freddie groaned again, gasping in discomfort as he rubbed his tender anus bud. But I noticed that at my words his penis was hard again.

'Well, then,' I said. 'Who is to be first?'

'Let me open my cunt to this man's fucking,' said a tremulous voice. It was my Sapphic slave, Miss Chytte.

16

Silk Stockings and Panties

My surprise was scarcely greater than my delight.

'Why, Miss Chytte!' I cried. 'Yes, you may take a fucking from Freddie! Oh, how sweet! How pleased I am! I know you've had him once, on my orders, you remember, on the coach to Exeter.'

'That was a hurried affair, an *amour de politesse*, Miss.' She smiled, 'and I've decided at last that I must have strong meat inside me, for I have seen the pleasure it gives, if properly done. I have become all wet in my quim watching Freddie taking his spanking, and especially, well, that other boy, all bare and his muscles so soft in the dim light.'

Mordevaunt emerged from the steam behind her. He was nude, but now his penis stood very hard; he looked shyly at Miss Chytte and I saw his hands glistened with her love-juice. I smacked my lips and smiled, and put my arms around them both, while Freddie, erect also, glowered at Mordevaunt.

'I shall take Miss Chytte, with the greatest of pleasure, Mistress,' Freddie chirped. 'And the others too. It shall be no punishment, and this blowhard Mordevaunt shall have to watch how a real man fucks!'

'Without the braggadocio, Freddie,' I warned. 'And don't forget, all the girls will be watching too.' He grinned very cheekily.

'Yes, Miss, and I shall show them a thing or two. My bottom is on fire from my lacing, and for my relief, my balls long to spurt into all your lovely cunts, my ladies!'

'Actually,' said Miss Chytte, 'it is the thought of the girls watching me as I'm being fucked which is so exciting, Mistress, and has convinced me to feel the caress of a man's cock with joy and desire, as well as the knowledge that it will please you, and make you all wet as you watch me. It will, won't it?'

'You know it will, Miss,' I said.

'Then it is now or never, I think.' Miss Chytte abruptly stood with her legs apart and her fingers stretched wide the lips of her shiny shaven quim to show the glistening pink flesh inside. I noticed that her cunt-petals were already quite red and swollen.

'This, then, sir, is the mysterious place that your cock longs to visit? I think mine is as tight and wet as any, and I invite you to take me,' she declared to Freddie.

With that, Freddie gallantly kissed her hand and gave her his arm, then escorted her to a row of cushions which formed a makeshift love-bed.

'Remember, Freddie, you must bring her to a spend, whether or not you spend yourself,' I warned. 'And knowing Miss Chytte's tastes . . .'

'I'll make her spend, Miss,' he crowed, with a smug leer in the direction of Mordevaunt, whose cock seemed to have softened somewhat.

Gently, Freddie laid Miss Chytte on her back. For a woman so versed in the arts of erotic pleasure, she seemed strangely subdued when faced with a man's rampant cock. He proceeded to kiss her with great tenderness, not on her mouth, but on her cunt, where I saw his tongue vigorously flicking her little red damsel. Miss Chytte moaned and stroked Freddie's head, pressing him tightly to her open cunt, and then he withdrew suddenly, and, still grinning, squatted and put her over his thigh, causing her to smile delightedly as she realised what was coming.

A man's job in lovemaking is always to guess the wishes of his lady! So I did not hesitate in handing Freddie the birch. He was able to flog her lightly from his squatting position, lashing her naked buttocks five or six times with short, whippy cuts that had her squirming in ecstasy. All the time, his fingers were busy between her thighs, tickling and stroking her clit, which I imagined to be well stiff and tingling, judging by the rivulet of love-juice that adorned her thighs. At last he set her on her hands and knees and took her doggy-fashion while his hand pleasured her wet slit, pausing for an occasional volley of slaps to her already reddened arse, and it was not long before Miss Chytte's sighs grew to moans of enchantment, and then shrieks of delight as her spend engulfed her.

'I'm spending, Miss, oh, I'm spending! Take all my hot spunk . . .!' cried Freddie, and gasped harshly as his sperm came inside her. We all applauded and Freddie stood up and bowed! Even Mordevaunt, whose penis, I was glad to see, had been restored to full erection by the joyful spectacle, clapped Freddie chummily on the back.

The girls jostled for who should be next; it was Connie. Freddie, correctly guessing her wishes, took her from the front but made her lie supine while his hand clamped her wrists above her head, and thrust into her by slamming the full weight of his body onto hers at every stroke, as though he were a wrestler felling an opponent. It was not long before Connie, too, achieved her spend but I was not sure if Freddie had spurted in her.

Our mood was festive; as girl followed girl, to be fucked by Freddie's seemingly inexhaustible manhood. Fingers strayed to cunts and breasts and lips, and after a while there was no longer any pretence of modesty and our Turkish bath resembled more an orgy-house of ancient Pompeii. Naked bodies writhed, entwined in the most intimate of embraces, like a chorus of bacchantes surrounding the virile naked power of their lustful god.

I saw Mme Izzard bucking with delight under Freddie's body, which seemed to grow more powerful the more he fucked. Mordevaunt was beside me; without hesitation, I knelt and plunged my mouth on his throbbing cock, sucking him until he moaned. Then I forced him down on top of me: that stiff beauty slid into my wet slit as smoothly as butter, and with his lips to mine, he brought me to a glorious spend with the most vigorous fucking imaginable. Now it was his turn to grin at Freddie! When Mordevaunt's seed had washed my womb, I took Mr Izzard's hand, and made him lie on me, and he murmured that he had dreamed of no less for years, ever since he had known me as a schoolgirl.

In truth, he did have a nice penis. Quite slender compared to Mordevaunt or Freddie but cosy and comforting as he slid in and out of my throbbing cunt in a friendly, almost avuncular way, so that my spend, when she came, was no tumult but rather a warm soft bath of pleasure.

I was giddy with desire, as were we all. I felt lips on mine; a girl's, I was not sure whose. Then other lips on the petals of my lady's place and a sweet hot tongue probing my slit and tickling my engorged damsel; a third mouth nibbling at my breasts and nipples. A shaven mink presented herself, squatting over my face, and I eagerly sank my lip on hers, clasping the full, ripe buttocks to my face. I think it was Veronica; I did not care. I saw Miss Chytte in a deep embrace, *soixante-neuf*, with Connie; both women vigorously gamahuching the other's wet cunt and clitty. From time to time I would receive the pleasure of a hard spanking on my bare bum, or even, delicately and thrillingly, on my naked breasts, from hands no less sweet for being unseen and I was sure Miss Chytte had her share of spanking me! I was in seventh heaven, overwhelmed by the salty odour of wet slit, the delicate aroma of soft breasts and eager mouth, all the perfumes of love.

And when at last we orgiasts were sated, as even the most fervent orgiasts must be, Freddie's cock stood as hard as ever, glistening with the love-juice of a dozen women. He grinned a great grin of triumph, and I thought I had never desired him as much as I did then. Sighing and sweating, we all plunged ourselves into the cold pool and laughed at our joyful naughtiness, holding hands and stroking each other in lustful complicity, until the gong rang for luncheon. I hoped Maxence had produced something specially nice!

Shakespeare generally has a word for it. The Bard, having no original ideas of his own, nor any sense of humour (which amounts to the same thing), made his money by expressing the most commonplace truths in poetic finery. Thus, when he opined that appetite grows by what it feeds on, he certainly hit the nail on its head. I could not wait for bedtime! That night I summoned both Freddie and

Miss Chytte to my bed, together for the first time, and we sported until dawn. I was ruthless with my slaves, subjecting them to whippings fiercer than I had thought myself capable of; making them gamahuche and fuck me and each other, in cunt, mouth and anus; all three of us locked in a triple embrace, until I lost count of the number of times I spent. A woman's body is capable of feeling such ecstasy, if given the right slaves to take her there!

Still Freddie's cock was a ramrod, to my, and pleasingly, to Miss Chytte's delight. My Sapphic slave was certainly making up for lost time in her enjoyment of the male caress, although of course, as she had predicted, she required a sturdy flogging to complete her enjoyment of any coupling. She did not realise that Freddie's perpetual stiffness, despite his impressive spending a mere two or three times, was not the usual thing at all! I ordered Freddie to tell us what he was up to and, smirking, he confessed that his greyhound friend had told him some of the 'tricks' he had learned out East. These involved Yogic discipline, Yin and Yang, Karma and Dharma, and other mysteries, by which a man can learn to pleasure a woman inexhaustibly. This information only quickened my desire to see the wonders of the world and all the fascinating men that must be in it!

Towards morning, as we lay entwined, Freddie asked me where I was going on my business trip, and couldn't he come with me.

'To a city in the Midlands,' I said mysteriously. 'But only for a few days. You must stay here; I am sure Miss Chytte would be lonely without your caress.'

'You mean, Miss Chytte and I may –'

'I positively command it, Freddie. I trust you are not going to be so foolish as to stray beyond my orders, however wet and willing dear Imogen, or others, may seem.'

'I've learned my lesson, Mistress. You are going to Birmingham?'

'Not Birmingham. Worse!' I told a little white lie.

'Then I shan't mind staying in London.'

Dawn was breaking, and in the pale pink half-light, I identified what it was about Freddie that had puzzled me.

'Why, Freddie,' I cried, 'you have shaved off your mustache, or pretence at one.'

He blushed. 'Yes, Mistress.'

'I thought Imogen Gandy rather liked it,' I said sarcastically.

'She did, Mistress. That is why I have shaved it off.'

I gave him a hearty cuddle and a kiss. 'You are my sweet boy, Freddie.'

'There is only one thing, Mistress . . . this birthday party for me.'

'Aren't you pleased?'

'Yes, but, well, it isn't actually my birthday.'

I sat up in bed and gave his nose a playful whack with one of my teats. 'If I say it is your birthday, then it is your birthday. Is that clear, slave?'

Like a little boy, Freddie hugged me to him and buried his face between my breasts. 'Yes, Mistress,' whispered the future Lord Whimble.

'*My darling Tweakums*,' read Miss Chytte. She paused to grin. 'Are you Tweakums, Mistress? I didn't know you had a nickname.'

'Enough persiflage, Miss,' I said severely. 'You wished to be acquainted with my business in Oxford, so read and find out.'

The Midland city where I had spent an agreeable two days was indeed Oxford. A delightful place full of honey-coloured spires, and clotted cream teas at the Randolph Hotel; this letter was the pleasing result of my promotional visit. It came with two others: one, a letter from Dr Hamm in Africa, with a splendid photograph of himself in the peak of health and surrounded by eight or possibly nine beaming, naked females who appeared to be his new wives! The other letter was the product of a diseased mind, calling me a whore of Babylon, a Jezebel, and other epithets beloved of those who preach the milk of human kindness. It warned me that if I did not cease my sinful ways forthwith, Nemesis was at hand. I did not discard the unsigned letter, for I had the glimmering of an idea whence it might have come.

Miss Chytte read on:

'*How I long to see you soon and kiss your bubbikins, and your lovely little clitty-poo, and feel my botty all hot and stingy from your lovely spanking! Sweet Tweakums, you are the sweetest, tweakiest lady in the whole world, whether ancient or modern! I am wearing your frilly panties as I write, isn't that naughty, and I deserve a spanking, don't I? Please come soon and we can cuddle and tweak and kiss and you can dress me as a girly if you like, to spank me and make my botty all pink and glowing for you! I can hardly wait till October when you will bring our new scholars, Mr Mordevaunt and Lord Whimble. Are they frisky too? My lady wife is very fond of giving tea to frisky scholars from dear St Alcuin's, and I am glad our college has tied scholarships for such virile men, for I love to watch! You don't mind if I wear your panties as I do? If you mind, then of course my backside must suffer. Please, please write, oh heavenly Miss de Comynge, my eternal sweetest Tweakums.*

From your devoted slave, Kissums.'

The letter was written on printed notepaper, headed: The Rt Hon. Angus Gutteridge, Regius Professor of Mesopotamian Archaeology at the University of Oxford, Dean of Studies, Christ Church College.

'So Freddie and Mordevaunt will be leaving us for Oxford? How thrilling, but how sad to see then go.'

'Well, it isn't far, you goose, and think of the visits we shall have. Freddie is going up to read politics, philosophy, ancient history, philology, French, German, Russian, Latin, Greek and Mesopotamian archaeology.'

'What, all at once?'

'That is the way things are done at Oxford. It is a very learned place, Miss Chytte, and an Oxford man is the most learned there is.'

'So it would seem ... Tweakums.'

I smiled. 'I think it best to keep this letter between ourselves, don't you ... Slave?'

'Of course, Mistress. It is just that you seem so clever at getting what you want from men. Kissums!'

'That is because, be they professors or pot washers, men

are all the same. Well, Oxford is settled; now we must set about making our grand end-of-term fancy-dress party absolutely perfect. I think I should have a progress report from Veronica.'

I decided to call on Veronica in her study, and found her strangely disconsolate.

'Well, now, what have you got arranged for our end-of-term party, Veronica?' I said brightly, after kissing her cheek.

'Party? Oh, the party, Miss. Yes, I ... I've been thinking.' It was evident from her expression that she was not thinking of the business.

'You soppy thing,' I said. Do I detect your poor heart brooding? Is it Mordevaunt?'

She shook her head. 'Mordevaunt is such lovely fun, Miss, but this is different.'

'Then, that soldier you were, and evidently still are, sweet on?' She blushed, and nodded.

'Hmm, the infamous Arbuckle,' I said.

'He wrote me a billet-doux, Miss, full of all manner of sweetnesses. He begs to see me again and says that he is a reformed character, and, oh, I don't know. Here I am, a gay girl – not that I don't adore the fun – but will he think ill of me? Oh ...' she sighed.

'A soldier is no stranger to gay girls! And as for Arbuckle, well, no man is ever a reformed character, Veronica. You will learn that a man's character cannot be changed, it can only be controlled, most efficaciously by the discipline of a lady's stern and loving rod.' She sighed again. 'Well,' I said, 'I can see you are in no mood for business. I had you appointed to take tea with the Bishop of Ribblesdale this afternoon, but I suppose you are *hors de combat* just now. And don't worry about the party, I shall oversee the arrangements myself.'

'Party?' she said blankly.

'Yes, party. Everybody who is anybody will be there, and plenty of people who aren't anybody, too. Lots and lots of parents, even, I suppose, that dreadful Judge Ruttle. It will be such fun! Your mama and papa will be there and,

Veronica, I shall invite Second Lieutenant Arbuckle!' I tickled her under the chin and stroked her hair. 'But you'll see that Arbuckle isn't for you, I'll make sure of it.'

'Never, Miss!'

'I'll offer you a wager, if you are so sure of yourself. If I prove my point and release you from this infatuation, you'll bare your bum to me and take a sound birching: six strokes, as six is such a nice round number. And that will clear your heart and your head. But if I'm proved wrong, then I shall gracefully concede defeat, and you may tan my own naked bottom for my presumption.'

This seemed to cheer Veronica, for she smiled with some of her usual zeal. 'Miss, it shall be a pleasure to see your bum squirm under the birch. And as part of the wager, Arbuckle may watch as I flog you. Do you agree?' I nodded, and we solemnly shook hands.

For weeks I lived, breathed and dreamed of my party. I was glad to have taken over the Entertainment Committee from the love-struck Veronica, for I realised how fiercely I wanted it to succeed. It was Freddie's party, but it was mine, really. I had never had a party before! The business of St Agatha's and Swish continued, of course, but I left things more and more in the hands of Miss Chytte. I prudently decided to hold the party a week after the end of term when the majority of girls would be safely home in their shires, and only my trusted intimates would be left to help set up the stages, decorations and playthings for my entertainments.

My own excitement speedily suffused the whole group of invitees and I had all the girls avidly plotting their costumes. They tried out little gewgaws of jewellery, tight corsets, daring panties, shoes and stockings, or ingeniously embroidered frilly things on the gentlemen they entertained, which had the welcome effect of intriguing my clients. This, I believe, is known as 'market research'.

The great day of my party dawned! It was to be an all-day affair, with the guests beginning to arrive around noon for a buffet luncheon alfresco, followed by various games, entertainments and invigorating visits to the Turkish bath, for those who wished, and discreet entertainments in our private rooms for those that could pay.

Before dinner the company would change into fancy dress and the gala would become a proper party; there was to be a grand banquet at which Maxence had promised to excel himself, then more musical entertainments, less sedate in nature (my girls, I knew, had deviously prepared some little surprises), lasting at least until midnight, by which time decent English folk expect to be in bed. I wanted to mark my own coming of age in the world as a woman of wealth and respectability, a living testimonial to our profitable English virtues of lustfulness and hypocrisy!

The girls were in a great tizzy, jealously guarding the secrets of their costumes from each other, though not from me. All seemed to see themselves as colourful females from history and mythology, generally of a 'dominant' nature. Connie wanted to be Eve in the Garden of Eden, since the costume would be so simple, but I told her sternly that she was missing the point. Miss Chytte chose to be Sappho (of course) and Mme Izzard, Marie Antoinette (equally of course), on the grounds that it would permit her to eat unlimited cake. I ordained that the servants should be kitted as ladies of ancient Greece, Babylon and especially Egypt, where complete nudity was visible under the loveliest diaphanous silk robes and tunics.

My fondness for the ancient world in general is due no little to the absence of our modern puritanism concerning the unclothed body. To most of the ancients, nudity was normal and admirable, and when a garment was worn to denote status or rank the body was naked underneath. Priestesses, brides and mourners at funerals were nude, and shaven, since in nudity, the spirit is bared before the gods.

Caesar informs us that our virile British ancestors shaved their entire bodies below their necks, and certainly the attraction of a shaven pubis, in both male and female, is that nature's creation is in no way covered up, even by a coating of pretty hairs. And what part of nature's creation is lovelier when naked than a cunt, or a penis and his balls?

Undergarments, however pretty we may find them, were unknown until very recently, and it is a tribute to our female genius that our inventive sex has transformed these supposedly joyless items into naughty and tantalising advertisements for the naked pleasures they conceal!

The St Alcuin's lads naturally chose to be great heroes or martial men, except for Booter who wanted to be St Augustine, "because he sinned an awful lot". Freddie was eager to be something grand from the military Whimble history, but I told him I had a super surprise for him, and he would not know until we were about to don our costumes before dinner. Marlene and Deirdre hinted darkly that at last they would show us what 'real whorin'' was all about.

It was a glorious sunny Saturday and shortly before noon the carriages and automobiles began to disgorge their eager cargos. Every guest had access to a private dressing room, into which the absent girls' studies had been converted, much to the pleasure of the ladies. A sumptuous buffet awaited us on the lawns, with champagne, of course, and all sorts of salads and crustaceans and things in aspic. For the afternoon, Tess and her comrades wore their normal maid's uniforms, leaving the diaphanous antique creations for the sensual evening. But Tess's adorable sluttishness – a button undone, a strap unclipped, a stocking that dropped – managed, as always, to make the most lumpen garment look sensuous. Miss Chytte's Verity favoured the apple-cheeked English milkmaid look, as opposed to Tess's naughty French maid, and the very innocence of her smock emphasised the gay ripeness of the flesh beneath.

I myself wore a rather stern costume, of my finest blue silk, with a very tight blue corset underneath, which I wore for naughtiness rather than necessity. I felt very proud and wicked as I knew the gentlemen's hungry eyes feasted on my swelling bubbies and bottom. The afternoon passed very pleasantly, with croquet, and tinkly tea-time music, and of course constant refreshments of the clotted cream variety; as always, no lady was to be left cakeless. The press, as I had promised, was there in the shape of Mr N. B. Izzard, to whom his cousin Mr Izzard introduced me.

'Nobby Izzard, the bloodhound of Fleet Street,' he said proudly, and the pleasant-featured Nobby smiled and shook my hand. I told him I had enjoyed his last piece, and hoped he was always as truthful!

'Why, truth is my middle name, Miss N. B. – nothing but!' He laughed jovially, and I permitted him to kiss my fingertips.

I proceeded to nod and chat with many old friends, including the good Mr Beausire, whose lucrative bottom had become no stranger to my cane. His daughter Emily was radiant beside him, and his enthusiasm for St Agatha's and all things Agathean knew no bounds.

'But d'ye know – here's a funny thing – I was over in Paris, buying a few frocks and things for the wife, you know' (I forebore to remind him that his wife was sadly deceased, but let him burble) 'and I picked up some two centime paper, because I saw a curious headline. It just shows what a depraved lot these froggies are. Here, Miss –' And he thrust at me a crumpled page. I translated:

ENGLISH BEAUTY, 'LA FLAGELLANTE', THE QUEEN OF PARIS SOCIETY

'For months now, the exotic dancer known as "La Flagellante" has entranced the Parisian beau monde with her renditions of classical pieces such as the Dance of the Seven Veils, etc., performed at intimate soirées and cabarets where counts and dukes jostle for the privilege of escorting her to a late supper, or perhaps home. She is seen in the best boxes at the opera or the Jockey Club at Longchamps, and is never without a gorgeous new frock or necklace!

'Her background is as mysterious as her beauty. She claims to have been a slave girl in the harem of the Sultan of Marrakesh, where she was cruelly beaten and subjected to the most lustful indignities. The high point of her dance is the revelation of her body completely naked, where spectators are awed by the sight of marks of numerous whippings on her back and buttocks, and it is typical of our superb French aesthetic sense that these marks of tribulation enhance rather than mar her beauty in the eyes of her admirers.

'Our special correspondent in London, Mr Napoleon Bonaparte Izzard, now reveals that "La Flagellante" is none other than Lucinda Charmley-Boddis, disgraced daughter of one of England's noble families. She fled her cruel homeland to the tolerant arms of la belle France, after suffering the most brutal of English boarding-school upbringings at the notorious academy of St Agatha's, where young ladies are incessantly flogged on their naked bottoms!

'How fitting that the victim of English hypocrisy should find glittering success in France, where our fine sensibilities see beauty even in the marks of humiliation! If flagellation is the English vice, its appreciation is surely the French virtue!' etc, etc.

'How interesting,' I said to Mr Beausire, who, I suspected, expected a free whipping for his trouble. 'So you see that St Agatha's can benefit even the most incorrigible girls, sir!' I took the cutting and thrust it at Mr Izzard, smiling hugely as I asked him to explain how a non-existent girl could become the toast of Paris.

'Why, this is true, Miss, I swear! The girl calls herself Lucinda Charmley-Boddis!' he blurted. 'I know I was little poetic with the truth in my last piece, but that's what you wanted, wasn't it?'

'It was, and I am well pleased.'

'For all we know, she is Lucinda Charmley-Boddis, and she might as well be, for she has the marks on her bottom to prove it! Who knows what she gets up to with those French dukes? Anyway, that's the power of the pen,' he added proudly. 'Life imitates art, you see?'

'I am delighted that a girl has had the enterprise to profit from your delicious fiction, Mr Napoleon Bonaparte Izzard,' I said slyly. He looked round with a nervous expression.

'Actually, Miss, I prefer to be called N.B. The patriotic readers of the Intelligencer might not like my real name. Dad was an admirer of the first Emperor, and thought the wrong side won at Waterloo.'

'So it wouldn't really do if your editor found out?'

'I should think not!'

I gave him my other hand to kiss, and smiled regally. 'Then I am sure you shall write nothing but kindnesses about St Agatha's, Napoleon dear,' I said. 'For wouldn't it be awful if he did?' My Mr Izzard laughed, and his charming cousin grinned ruefully, and had the grace to blush!

At about four o'clock tea was served, indoors in the conservatory, and after that most of the guests retired to their dressing rooms to rest. Some guests already had to take their leave, but still others had yet to arrive; among them the Dove party which I had made sure would include Second Lieutenant Arbuckle. I took Freddie to my room for a nap, and to kit ourselves in our fancy-dress costumes. He was very excited when he saw an officer's scarlet full-dress uniform laid out on my bed, complete with all the tassels and medal ribbons and golden trimmings which young people find so thrilling.

'Gosh,' he said, as we undressed for bed. 'What regiment is that, Mistress?'

'Why, the First Cornish Heavy Horse,' I said on the spur of the moment. (Actually, I had had it run up by Mrs Danziger the theatrical costumier and pubic wig specialist in the Bethnal Green Road!) 'But that is not for you, Freddie, it is for me!'

'Oh,' he said, disappointed, as we snuggled naked together between my sheets. 'Then what am I going to wear?'

'Why, this,' I said, indicating my discarded silks. 'You are going to be me, Freddie, and I am going to be you.'

It is delicious to cuddle naked with a loved one, yet not make love! Freddie was excited; his hard penis stroked my naked belly as though begging to be allowed inside, but I would not let him, even though I was wet for him! The trembling frustration of such a chaste embrace adds piquancy to a loving friendship and makes the joys of complete loving even greater when they do come. We dozed in each other's arms for an hour, until it was time to bathe and dress. We squatted side by side on my Turkish commodes, holding hands, and after this delightful intimacy we soaked in my bath for a while, with Freddie's penis in its normal state of erection.

'Well, I think it must be the restrainer, if that's the way you feel,' I said cheerfully. 'For it would never do to have the governess of St Agatha's make her dress bulge with a stiff cock. The number four, perhaps.'

'Yes, Mistress,' he said dolefully. 'It is just that it is awfully exciting – the thought of dressing in your clothes, of being you, whom I adore, in front of others!'

'And they will take you for me, Freddie,' I said seriously. 'Fancy dress is not obligatory – some guests will just wear a token badge or flower, I suppose – so those that recognise us will be charmed, and those that don't will be mightily impressed! It shall be such a lark!'

I told him to rise, for I wanted to shave his pubis quite naked, which I did, baring not just his cock and balls but also shaving every inch of his body. Then, to his surprise, I ordered him to do the same to me. I lay back, half out of the soapy water, as he shaved my mink right off, and then my legs and armpits. It was gorgeous to have this erect male serving me thus, applying to my naked skin the most vicious of shaving blades, yet whose caress was pure tenderness.

We towelled and dried each other, feeling all giggly and naughty, then returned to the bedroom, where he feasted his eyes in astonishment as I applied rouge to my nipples, to my cunt-petals, to my anus bud and to my very clitoris. His poor penis looked as though it would burst, as he sighed with lust!

'Now I really am a scarlet woman!' I said. 'And you are to be my scarlet man, dear Freddie.'

He lay down and I began to paint his face like a woman's. I then applied the rouge to his nipples and anus, and, taking his cock and drawing back his foreskin very hard, I painted the whole bulb of his penis, and his naked balls a fiery scarlet.

'There!' I said, 'we are both as pretty as pictures, though I think you have the edge on me. How we men envy women, that they may adorn themselves so beautifully!'

It only remained to clothe Freddie in the golden chain which Miss Chytte liked so much, and which wound around my waist attached to big rings which clamped onto my nipples and cunt-lips. In this case, Freddie's nipples were attended to – I was excited to see that they hardened and stood up just like a girl's – and the ring which adorned my labia fitted snugly around his balls.

I could not help parting his cheeks and delivering a soft kiss and a little lick of my tongue to his rouged anus, it looked so adorable, and afterwards one kiss on each tense buttock. He shivered with pleasure, which was very nice. Over his cock-chain I fitted a restrainer, taking great delight in his groans as I pushed the bulging tongue very tightly in his anus, and buckled his stiff cock hard under the leather flap, so that the tightness of the restraint made him soften to an engorgement I supposed just about bearable.

Next, there was a corset for each of us, with slightly different aims, but equally delicious effects. Mine was long and narrow, and flattened my bubbies in the manner of a Greek apodesmos, so that I looked like a rather virile man and not a full-breasted woman. Freddie's, however, was my impossibly wasp-waisted affair in blue satin backed with vicious whalebone rods. After his piteous squeals as I sternly laced him into it, crushing his gold chain against his skin, he looked scrumptious, with his teats all squashed and pushed out, and his bottom compressed into two jutting peaches just like my own!

'Gosh, Mistress, do women put themselves through this torture by choice?' he gasped.

'Yes, Freddie, indeed they do,' I replied. 'It is because they wish to look pretty for gentlemen.'

'It's worth it, then,' he said cheekily, which earned him a slap on his tight round bottom, making him squeak playfully like a girl.

The blue silk stockings came next, then the matching panties, and finally the dress, which fitted him as tightly as a glove. It was a very near thing – but it fitted none the less! A lush perruque, made by Mme Izzard with the cuttings of my very own hair, completed him, and when I stepped back to look at my work, I told him to his shy delight he was quite the most desirable package of womanhood imaginable.

He helped me lace myself into my own corset, with little clucks of disapproval or sighs of admiration, just like a real girl. I do not think he was acting: how profoundly we change with our apparel! Then, he rolled up my stockings, held my panties as I stepped into them, and fussed an unconscionable time to see they were snug around the cleft of my bottom and my shaven mons. His fussing was not entirely feminine, for he made sure his fingers enjoyed a lavish exploration of my bare bottom and my quim, whose oily wetness I thought it pointless to conceal.

As for my hair, it was cut shorter than usual so that I was able to fold it up, leaving my neck bare, and shape it to look like a male, rather boyish, coiffure; the upswept front overlapping the long back locks. I would pass myself as a young, beardless subaltern, my delicately tan skin giving me the aspect of one who had served in sunny parts. We looked at each other in the mirror and embraced, with a deep kiss, so that some of his rouge came off on my lips.

'Oh, sir,' he said, simpering. 'I wager you have been kissing all the girls. Oh, you must not trifle with my affections, sir!'

'Is that what we girls sound like?' I laughed. And he blushed.

'Well, so I believe from hearsay, Mistress.'

The gong rang; then as a final touch, I pinned a Swish badge to each of our breasts, then gave Freddie my arm, and the proudest beau in the world escorted his lady in to dinner.

The effect of our entrance was quite magical; my uniform drew smiles of approval while I could see Freddie, dressed as me, excited appreciative, nay lustful looks from ladies and gentlemen alike. Those that knew our trick smiled privately, while the others looked in admiration.

'Why, Miss, you are not in fancy dress,' teased the Greyhound King of East London, who was fetchingly attired as the Ace of Spades. (I wasn't certain if he knew or not.)

'Oh, too busy, I'm afraid,' said Freddie, reddening deeply, but managing quite a sweet imitation of a girl's contralto voice. I wondered if I sounded like that: everyone else seemed to think so!

The majority were in costume, those uncostumed wearing a token brooch or flower, and many wore masks. The great dining table was set in a quadrangle round the refectory, and sparkling with silver and crystal and linen white as snow. There was no hierarchy of places, for we were all in disguise, and in theory unknown to each other. The place cards were set by disguise, so that Lucrezia Borgia sat next to the Emperor Caligula, Attila the Hun next to Joan of Arc, and so on. I found myself beside the Ace of Spades and Robin Hood who, as I knew, was none other than Major Dove. We chatted politely about military matters for a while, and I affected to have seen service in South Africa, fighting the Zulus. I found it quite easy to lower my voice into a kind of boyish trill and it was quite a while before Major Dove felt the penny drop.

'Why, Mistress!' he blurted. 'I'd never have guessed! You are so ... lifelike!'

'Well, I hope I am normally lifelike, Major,' I said.

'But then, I mean, who are you?' and he pointed to Freddie, who was talking animatedly to Mrs Dove, in the guise of Maid Marian.

'Mr Whimble, of course. Isn't he pretty?'

Major Dove licked his lips, and said merrily: 'Dashed pretty, Mistress. I think he should be careful. Ha ha!'

'Well, he is safe with Mrs Dove, I am sure.'

'Yes, I dare say he is,' he said thoughtfully. I put my hand on his wrist.

'In that case,' I whispered, 'come to my study after dinner, and enjoy a liqueur? I mean you and Mrs Dove.'

Then I turned my attention to my other neighbour, the Greyhound King of East London, who made me laugh with his rather risqué stories of life in the East. It seemed he had indeed been in the army, and he knew many of my guests, including the Doves and even Second Lieutenant Arbuckle, though he was not, I suspected, of such exalted rank.

17

Masquerade

He certainly knew a lot about greyhounds, though, and told me that his estate at Chipping Ongar had been bought with the proceeds of the track: he mentioned a yacht, and a little place he had at San Remo, and another on Corfu. I assured him sincerely that a sea trip from San Remo to Corfu had always been my idea of heaven.

Wine flowed copiously, accompanying a meal whose Belgian splendour quite distracted from conversation. We had snails and lobsters and things with truffles in them, and the good food and wine had their usual convivial effect, so that the tone of the gathering rapidly proceeded from droll to risqué to outrageous. The daring costumes of my serving girls, with their thinly-veiled nudity, helped marvellously to whet our sensual appetites, with Freddie sternly explaining to any doubtful ladies that such garb was 'classical', and therefore all right. Tess, of course, managed to add a louche aspect to the simplest transparent Egyptian shift, under which her nipple rouge had contrived to smear itself jammily on her naked breasts, and one of her shoulder-straps had broken. She was perfect!

How powerful are masks and disguises in freeing the lustful impuses of the soul! The only *invité* who did not seem to partake of the gaiety was Mr Justice Ruttle, who sat as though willing himself to be gloomy, his only concession to fancy dress a violet flower in his buttonhole, which is the colour of penitence.

It was exciting to see Freddie taken for myself, and equally so that I was taken for Freddie. I received many smiles, and even winks, both from chummy gentlemen and from curious ladies. Our meal was concluded with my favourite profiteroles, and then generous pourings of port

241

and brandy; at St Agatha's, I explained, the custom was for the gentlemen to withdraw, leaving the ladies to ribald chatter over port, but Miss de Comynge had kindly consented to waive the rules on this occasion.

Suddenly, the lights were dimmed, except for those on the dais above us, and Veronica Dove announced that the St Agatha's Players would perform a short masque telling the story of St Agatha of Sicily. This was a pleasant surprise to me as much as to the company, and I watched eagerly as the girls of Swish appeared on the dais clad in beautiful antique costumes scarcely less revealing than the serving girls'. Most of the piece was conducted in mime, to the accompaniment of tinkly lute music from Phoebe Ford-Taylor. Veronica herself played the brutal prefect Quintilian, who, enamoured of the virgin Agatha, subjects her to the cruellest tortures to make her yield to him.

In mime, these barbarities assumed an eerie, spiritual beauty, as it is the job of art to transform pain into enchantment. Agatha was played by Connie Sunday, and the few words were stock expressions of melodramatic passion from her lover, and equally melodramatic refusal by Agatha. Thrilled, we watched Connie writhe under branding iron and whip, or scream silently in rack and pillory, until the moment when, in neat contrast to the true story (in which Agatha finally dies still virgin), she yields her virginity on the promise that henceforth it is Quintilian who shall be her slave! The final scene shows Agatha turning the tables on her Roman tormentor, and giving him a sound lacing with his own whip, after which the pair fall into each other's arms for a conclusion of passionate lovemaking, whose performance I suspected was entirely authentic. The moral was fairly clear and true, that by submitting to the lash, each has gained love, and lost a futile obstinacy which they are far better without. The company applauded heartily, faces gleaming with a lustful fervour inspired by more than wine.

There was a pause while the Merton Brass and Wind Ensemble trudged forward to set up their instruments for the evening's dancing, and I took the opportunity to squeeze Major Dove's balls rather hard, and instruct him to bring Mrs Dove to my study for some fine brandy.

'Well,' said Mrs Dove suspiciously, 'I must admit I had my misgivings about coming here. I'm not sure it's natural, all this fancy dress: you as a gentleman, Miss de Comynge; and Mr Whimble as a girl. Although I grant you both look handsome. I'm quite confused who I should be addressing!'

'You may take me as myself,' I said with a smile. And Freddie smiled too as he sipped his brandy.

'I suppose the dinner was nice,' she said nervously, but I mustn't let all this wine and brandy go to my head. The play was a bit too artistic for my simple tastes, really. Still, the girls seemed to enjoy it.'

Major Dove took a hearty gulp of his cognac, which seemed to cheer him up from his gloom at the close proximity of his wife.

'And what are those simple tastes, Mrs Dove?' I said quietly.

'Why . . . nice things. Normal, well brought-up things.'

'You know that here at St Agatha's, to be normal and well brought-up means to submit to frequent corporal chastisement, like our illustrious Agatha. Your daughter Veronica will tell you so.'

'Well, yes . . . but I don't like to think of such things,' she replied uncomfortably, taking a sip of brandy and coughing gently.

'Of such things as your daughter's bottom bared to the cane?'

'Well, she is happy here, I suppose it must be good for her.'

'It is good for all of us, Mrs Dove. It is good for me, and Mr Whimble here. Oh, yes, he is a trusted staff member, but when I have occasion to be displeased with him, his naked bottom feels my birch!'

'Rather!' said Freddie, and Mrs Dove's face went even redder.

'It is even good for Major Dove.'

'What!' she cried. 'Are you suggesting that I . . . that I beat him?'

'No, Mrs Dove – may I call you Thalia? Such a pretty name. No, it is I who raise the crimson blushes on his buttocks, buttocks which I believe you have had opportunity to inspect, on my orders.'

'But those marks were from the saddle of a fractious horse!'

'No, Thalia, they were from my very own cane, a beating lovingly applied, and lovingly taken on your husband's naked backside.'

I rose suddenly from the sofa, and went to my rack of corrective instruments.

'Oh, I don't know what to think! This is scandalous!'

'Ignore what you think, and consult your feelings, Thalia. I observe you are agitated; does your belly not tickle and your thighs moisten at the thought of your naked husband taking a flogging from me, over this very sofa?' I swished my cane in the air.

'Say it isn't true, dear!' But Thalia made no move to rise.

'You know it is true, Thalia,' said Major Dove quietly.

'It is true, because he cannot receive the treatment, the corrective chastisement, that he and all men deserve, from the wife of his bosom,' I said cosily. 'And, moreover, that wife refuses to take a proper spanking herself, when she deserves it, as all girls do. Admit it, Thalia, did you not find our play more than interesting? Did the spectacle of your daughter flogging her naked captive not thrill you? And I assure you that those floggings were not mere acting. Do you deny that you no longer embrace your husband, because you fear to admit, fear to beg for, what you most desire?'

'No! Perhaps . . . Oh, I don't know! You aren't fair!'

This time, Thalia drained her brandy glass, and did not cough. I flicked up the hem of her tiny green tunic with the tip of my cane, and looked her in the eyes. Her breathing was hoarse.

'Very pretty,' I purred. 'And Thalia, I am sure your bottom will be just as pretty a red after you have taken a lacing from this sweet little cane. Look how she bends and hums, longing to caress your naked buttocks, my dear. And I see in your eyes that you long to feel her caress.'

She swallowed, and Freddie nimbly refilled her glass. Shakily, she drank, and took a deep breath.

'This is so sudden,' she murmured, but I knew the fight and pretend outrage had gone from her. I put my hand on her thigh.

'No, Thalia,' I said, kissing her cheek. 'You have known for a long time, and been frightened by that knowledge of your deepest self. You must not be frightened; here, you are among friends. You shall take a naked beating, now, Thalia, you know you will, for it is time. And your beating will free you of guilt and anguish, and make you a happy girl again. But you must ask.'

Tears welled in her eyes.

'Yes,' she whispered, after a long pause. 'Please flog me, Miss. Flog my naked bottom, and let my husband watch, for I deserve it.'

'I shan't flog you, Thalia,' I said with a smile. 'It shall be Mr Whimble who does that. He's dressed as me, and for this precious moment, he is me. I, in my soldier's uniform, shall flog Major Dove.'

Numbly, Thalia rose and bent over the sofa and allowed Freddie to lower her tights and panties, while I did the same to Major Dove. His panties were of course the ones I had given him. As I unrolled them, his penis sprang stiff from their bands. Gently, I placed their arms round each other's waist, and then Freddie and I raised our canes.

'It shall be six strokes each,' I said softly. 'And you'll get six tight ones, Thalia, for Mr Whimble shan't spare you.'

'Please don't spare my bottom, sir,' she whispered.

The beating began in silence, broken only by the whistle of our canes on the bare bottoms of the man and his wife. We flogged in unison, and Thalia took it with surprising meekness; only the third, particularly harsh stroke from Freddie caused her to moan gently. Major Dove took his flogging in utter silence, but by the end of the set, both bottoms were squirming and clenching nicely, and blushed a hearty crimson. I saw that my dress bulged with Freddie's erection, despite the restrainer he wore, and my own quim was gushing with thrilling moisture. I looked at

Thalia's bare thighs, and there was a tell-tale trickle of shining love-juice seeping from her soaking wet mink!

I nodded to Freddie. In silence, he raised his dress and unfastened his restrainer, while I gently stroked Major Dove's poor red bottom and kissed him there, then made him stand while I took his place on the sofa and lowered my breeches and panties to reveal my naked arse.

'Fuck me, sir,' I ordered. 'It is time at last for that, too. Fuck me as my slave fucks your wife, sir. This is a masquerade, and we are all, for this brief moment, someone else.'

Freddie began to thrust very slowly but hard into Thalia. As he fucked, her moans grew louder and louder, and her bottom wriggled and danced beside my own. I watched Freddie's magnificent gleaming shaft slide so powerfully and strongly in and out of her and thought that timeless beauty could never cease to thrill and enchant me. Freddie watched me, his Mistress, fucked by the Major's powerful cock, and as our eyes met in a smile, I knew he was thinking the same. Nor has the magic of fucking ever ceased, or ever shall!

When Thalia had been brought to a writhing, squealing spend and at the same time I felt the Major's spunk hot against my womb, we disengaged, and Major and Mrs Dove fell into a loving embrace. His cock, like Freddie's had subsided only a little. I took both men by the balls, and tickled them once more to full erection, then I made Thalia kneel and kiss each cock, taking the glans full in her mouth to suck and caress it. The denouement was simple and beautiful; Freddie and I fucked, gently and slowly, while we watched the newly amorous spouses couple on the rug in the most passionate fucking imaginable!

Dresses smoothed, and tights replaced, we enjoyed a restorative brandy, poured by Freddie's only slightly trembling hands.

'Well,' I said. 'Now you have felt the power of masquerade, I have another revelation for you. Second Lieutenant Arbuckle is here, I think.'

'You ordered me to bring him, Mistress,' said the Major.

'He is a bad egg; he is sweet on Veronica, and I don't like it.'

'Then you shall witness me making him unsweet on Veronica,' I said, and instructed Freddie to take them to my dungeon, while I went in search of the Second Lieutenant.

I was rather excited as I went back to my room for an important 'fitting', partly because it was something I had long planned, and partly because of the thrill that Freddie and the Doves would be in hiding to observe my little subterfuge. I imagined St Agatha's as a wonderful gloomy castle of the Middle Ages, full of spies and intrigues! I swiftly unwrapped Mr Izzard's package, lowered my breeches and panties, and inserted the curious appliance. I left my panties aside, for I had no need of them, rolled up my breeches and surveyed myself in the glass. There between my legs was a splendid bulge, like a man's cock, and I was at last the very picture of a soldier! Strapped around my waist was a leather pantie, and into my anus fitted a large tongue, like that of a uro-genitary restrainer, but soft like a penis. To this was attached, by a cable fitted snugly between my fesses, a real penis, or at least an admirable facsimile of one, which dangled like the real thing, complete with spacious balls.

I gave a practice squeeze with my anus muscle, and my penis stirred! Another, harder squeeze, and he stood half-stiff, and finally a concerted pressure in my bum-hole on the ingenious control lever pumped my surrogate cock to a wonderful erection that strained against my breeches as if to split them! Mr Izzard had been generous in his estimate of a soldier's manly proportions, and my cock was bigger even than Freddie's. Thus equipped, I practised raising and lowering my lovely drawbridge, and when I had got used to the different pressures required, I sallied forth into the refectory, which the music of my Merton terpsichoreans had turned into the gayest of ballrooms. The place was quite a pandemonium; couples whirled, or openly embraced, all secure, as they thought, behind their masks and disguises, just like the carnival at Venice.

There was a constant stream of new arrivals, ladies and gentlemen in the most glittering costumes, and the late arrivals, I noticed, were all of them masked, so that the Venetian air was very pronounced. One striking couple arrived as Harlequin and Pierrette, and were greeted by Miss Chytte. The gentleman mumbled something about a late sitting at the Lords, and I thought I knew the voice. Miss Chytte however seemed too busy to notice, and I don't think they noticed her, all dressed in Greek robes, with flowers and berries, and her breasts daringly painted, but I knew them when they asked for Miss de Comynge and Mr Whimble: it was Lord and Lady Whimble, all the way up from Cornwall! I was so pleased to see them that I hurried to get my business over with and sidled past them. I saw Lady Whimble's eye stray to the generous bulge in my breeches but I was unrecognised.

Arbuckle was easy to recognise, by face and manner. He was slightly in his cups, and acting the blowhard with a group of unimpressed ladies, who took my cheery arrival as an excuse to get away. He didn't seem awfully perturbed, but grinned from a face that was quite handsome, but somehow florid and shifty, with hard, unfriendly eyes – we women always look to the eyes – that I saw would warm no lady's heart, and nor, if my analysis was correct, did their owner really wish to.

'Arbuckle, old man!' I cried jovially. 'Don't believe we've met. Heard so much about you. Whimble, First Cornish Heavy Horse.'

We shook hands; his grip was moist, and lasted longer than seemed normal.

'Glad to know you, Whimble! Cracking do! Bags of fillies, what?'

'Yes,' I drawled, accepting one of his cigars and a glass of brandy, 'if you like that sort of thing. Damned women, always noisy, always squealing and squawling about something! Weak creatures, too. Show 'em a touch of the crop and they burst into tears! Not like your Zulu woman: proud and silent, the Zulus.'

'So you were in Africa?'

'Yes, rather at the sharp end, old chum. In the Karoo, fighting brother Zulu. Splendid warriors, bloodthirsty and proud, you feel sort of honoured to fight them. And they can stand up to a good flogging better than any man I know. Not a peep out of them, which is more than you can say for the ORs we get these days.'

'Oh, some of 'em can take it,' said Arbuckle, his eyes glittering now. 'I like to put 'em through their paces down at Knightsbridge. You should see them squirm! Come down and watch sometime. They pretend it's against the rules, but that's all rot. A soldier who can't take fifteen with the birch ain't a soldier.'

'Fifteen!' I cried. 'Why, a Zulu buck can take thirty without a squeak! And d'you know, Arbuckle,' I leaned conspiratorially forward, 'we whip 'em naked, of course. And when they get the lash, their Jolly Roger stands up hard! Ain't that something? And they have them as big as cannons, I assure you!' Arbuckle smiled.

'You are quite well endowed yourself, sir, if you don't mind.'

I smiled and looked him in the eyes, which met my gaze, as I lazily pretended to scratch my balls, making sure I squeezed and rubbed my cock quite blatantly, which is of course quite normal male behaviour. I saw that his own bulge was quite pronounced, and nodded at it.

'We seem to be two of a kind, then, Arbuckle, for you're handsomely taken care of in that department. In fact you've quite a name for yourself, or so Veronica Dove tells me. She seems to have a bit of a pash for you, old boy.'

He laughed cruelly. 'Oh, that snively little thing! I just play her along, you know. To oil into her papa's good books, and get promotion.'

'Well,' I said, restraining my anger. 'I'm just here to help with the admin side until my next posting, but I've seen that these St Agatha's girls take their lacings like a fellow. We even have a special dungeon, where . . . but I shouldn't really tell you.' I gave a squeeze with my anus, and felt my breeches strain as my cock swelled.

Arbuckle put his arm on my shoulders, and looked

down at my bulge. 'Come on, old sport, you can tell me.' His mouth was very close. 'In fact, why not show me? We can slip away from the party for a bit; it'll be a lark.'

I squeezed with my anus again, and my make-believe cock stiffened quite alarmingly, so that I feared I had overdone it.

'Well, why not?' I said, with brandy merriment. 'Come on, then, Arbuckle.' And I led him away from the dance, to my dungeon. As we negotiated the narrow staircase, his hand brushed against my cock.

'I say,' cried Arbuckle, open-mouthed, as I illuminated the chamber to show him my treasures. 'What a splendid show! I wish I had some of these things to tame my damned soldiery, the brutes!'

'But if it ain't allowed, old boy ...' I murmured.

'Oh pshaw!' he said. 'Why, I wouldn't give 'em a tanning I couldn't take myself! I went to a hard school!'

'How hard?' I asked slyly. 'Hard enough for this?' and I indicated my sombre whipping post.

'Why, I've been "posted" many a time,' he replied airily.

'I bet you don't dare show me.'

'What, let you beat me? We were naked, you know.'

'Of course not. Let's just pretend – for a lark, Arbuckle. Just show me how you would stand to take it. Go on, strip off, we're all chaps together, aren't we? I haven't seen a naked chap in that lovely whipping stance for ages, not since I gave those Zulus what for. My, they were big bucks! How I loved seeing their muscles clench as I laced them; and their big smooth bums squirming!'

Arbuckle needed no further encouragement. He stripped off his uniform and stood quite naked before me, his cock blatantly stiff.

'There!' he said. 'I don't think these Zulus of yours have anything to show me!'

'Why, no, Arbuckle,' I said. 'That's quite a monster you have.'

'Let's compare, then, Whimble,' he said with a smirk. 'Come on, I'm in the buff, let's have a look at you and that rampant big engine I see swelling under your breeches.'

'Swelling?' I laughed. 'Why, you haven't seen him swell yet! He's still soft!' At that, Arbuckle's cock leapt to full erection.

'Won't you show me?' he said coyly. 'We could have some ... fun.'

'Oh all right, then. But I'm shy, when I have fun with a chap. Why not turn around and stand in the whipping frame while I get my bags off: on tiptoe, with your bum all tight; as if I'm to lace you.'

He did as I asked, and stood with his back to me and his hands against the dangling cuffs.

'Well, why don't you lace me then, Whimble? A flogging contest.'

'All right.' I pressed my body to his back, so that my fully erect cock was against the cleft of his buttocks, and he shivered.

'Whimble, you're a good chap,' he said in a voice weak with desire. 'How about this – the chap who cries halt to his beating has to bend over for the winner. I mean, for a good bumming, you know?'

'That sounds most equitable,' I said, unable to conceal my sneer. But by then it didn't matter, for I reached up and snapped the cuffs smartly on his wrists. He was trapped and helpless.

'I say!' he cried. 'Steady on! It's only a bit of fun!'

'Is it a bit of fun when you flog those poor soldiers, for refusing your bumming, Arbuckle? Or those Indians, terrified of starving, and obliged to submit to your lash?' My conversation with the Greyhound King, old India hand, had indeed been instructive. I stroked his quivering bottom, quite tenderly. 'Don't worry, Arbuckle, this is my fun.' He gulped as I lowered my breeches, and with my false cock pumped to full erection, I nuzzled it against his bare arse.

'Oh yes!' he cried. 'God, it's huge! Bigger than I've ever had! Please, Whimble, be a sport, put it in my bum. Give me a good arse-fucking, I beg you. Fuck me till I squeal! You're a gentleman, you're one of us, you understand!'

'Hmmm,' I said, withdrawing to pick up a heavy birch

from the rack of implements. 'I think I'll beat you first, Arbuckle. A nice fifteen with this will have you frisky for a bumming.' I stroked his arse with the tips of the birch and he shuddered.

'Fifteen!' he cried. 'No ... no, you don't understand. I couldn't take that!'

'Yet you expected your men to take it.'

'That's different! They are common scum!'

'And you, sir, are a common coward, and I'm going to beat you for it. You have the nerve to sneer at Veronica Dove; why, she would bare her bottom for such a beating and smile.' I lifted the birch and lashed the flogging post an inch from his naked bottom. It made a fearsome whistle and landed with a fierce crack. He jumped.

'God! No! Anything! Please don't beat me with that!'

'But it's all in fun, Arbuckle,' I said. 'Not like the whippings you give your men, for you are punishing them for your hatred of your depraved self, aren't you? Punishment must be with love, not hatred, Arbuckle. And because I love this tight little bum, I'm going to skin him with a juicy fifteen, before I split you in half with the hardest bumming you've ever had. You want it, don't you?' He was silent, save for his tortured breathing.

'Please, Whimble ... bum me, with that huge cock, sir. Not the flogging – please, that was just a game. But God, I beg you, fuck my arsehole hard!'

I stroked his buttocks again with the birch.

'I think it is time for you to stop playing games that hurt others,' I said. 'You won't be a soldier any longer, my friend, for you'll go straight back to Knightsbridge and resign your commission.'

'What madness is this?' he babbled. 'Let me go, this instant!'

'It is no madness, Second Lieutenant Arbuckle,' thundered Major Dove, as he emerged from his hiding place. There was a new authority, a new virility in his voice and bearing as he loosened Arbuckle's bonds and made the snivelling officer face him. 'Your sword, please.'

Arbuckle handed him his sword with trembling fingers,

watched by myself, Freddie and Mrs Dove. As I adjusted my uniform, Arbuckle gasped with fury as he realised the truth, but it was too late, for Major Dove had him by the scruff of the neck and held him bent over with his arse up.

'I'm going to thrash you, sir, for your damned impudence and depravity. And if I ever see you near my daughter again, or at Knightsbridge at all, well, it will be far worse for you. Do you accept your thrashing, and a discreet departure from the regiment?'

'Oh God,' sobbed the broken Arbuckle. 'Yes, sir, I must accept. Oh please don't hurt me too terribly!'

We all sneered in contempt at his blubbing, as Major Dove told him he would take six cuts, as six was a nice round number. He then dealt him six lashes with the flat of his own sword on his bare buttocks. Then the Major broke the sword over his knee and threw it at the whimpering wretch's feet. Grinning fiercely, he offered an arm to myself and Thalia.

'Not really the thing to mix soldier's business with pleasure,' he said. 'Shall we rejoin the company, dear ladies?'

18

Kisses for the Governess

'Well, Mistress,' whispered Veronica. 'I believe you have won your wager. I'm to get a lacing, because you proved me wrong about – about that rotter, whose name I won't say. And the sooner the better; I shan't feel cleansed until I get my birching. You promised me a good six on the bare bum!'

'Tomorrow, then.'

'Oh Mistress, I can't wait! My bum's itching for a tickle!'

I looked round and saw my guests dancing, drinking and flirting – and stealing off in surreptitious pairings to the private rooms! The party was in full swing.

'You must wait, Veronica. I have to circulate among the guests!'

'Awww . . .'

'And, Veronica, you must eschew these American expressions you get from Connie. The correct English is "Ooo . . ." '

Miss Chytte and Mr Izzard seemed to be jointly in charge of ceremonies, so I was happy to watch from the sidelines. Mr Izzard was arrayed not unlike her, in a Grecian robe of many-layered silk, which gave him the pleasant aspect of a rushing, shimmery stream. I asked him who he was: Julius Caesar, Alexander the Great?

'Why, a colonic irrigation, Miss,' he said proudly. 'Don't I look just like running water?'

Prizes were being awarded, or else sold at auction (for Mr Izzard's 'St Agatha's Appeal Fund!') for the most glittering costumes, or the most acrobatic feats of dancing. It was amazing how lively and inventive my respectable guests had become in the childlike freedom of mask and disguise! Mr Izzard's prizes were quite inventive, too. One offering was a 'special exercise bicycle', one of those machines which are fixed to the floor and give exercise without the inconvenience of actual travel. Vanessa Lumsden, dressed fetchingly as a Mayan princess, demonstrated; pedalling away with increasing fury as she got redder and redder in the face, finally exploding in an extraordinary yelp, which nearly toppled her from her saddle. She got off the machine, very flushed and pleased with herself, and we all clapped as we saw that Mr Izzard had replaced the saddle with one of his own invention, namely a huge cock like the one I had strapped to my waist!

Needless to say, the bidding was very heavy for that prize, as for the little sets of glittering 'Easter eggs' which were smilingly demonstrated by Imogen Gandy and Amanda Nightingale. The evening was far gone in wine and lasciviousness; I was unaware of the time, and we seemed to inhabit a magical world of pure freedom, naughtiness and desire. So when it was clear that the Easter eggs were a chain of caressing balls to be worn inside a lady's vagina, the ladies jostled to accede to my suggestion that the prizes be awarded to the ladies who could take the soundest spanking!

As Imogen and Amanda played with themselves, and each other, to show the wondrous pleasures to be had from these 'quim-balls', the ladies raised their skirts and lowered their panties (if they even had any) to bare their bums for sound spankings from Connie, Veronica or Phoebe Ford-Taylor. And soon the music was prettily punctuated by the sound of slaps and delighted squeals. The sight of the girl's naked minks and the squirming bare bottoms of the most respectable of matrons, excited no disquiet, but rather the reverse, encouraging our guests to throw aside every vestige of caution in their pursuit of lustful pleasure.

Rapturous glee greeted my suggestion that an extra prize, a badge conferring honorary membership of Swish, would be awarded to any lady who could take, not just a spanking, but a brisk three with a willow cane on the bare bum! How the gentlemen pushed their wives forward. And how the ladies giggled as they bared their nates to my cane, as they supposed themselves to be beaten by a dashing and conspicuously virile, army officer, and squealed with pretend anguish as they rubbed their sore red bums and proudly showed them to their friends! The more staid had long ago departed; my merry-makers would evidently be here well past the appointed hour of midnight, and I was glad I had got a new ice block for cooling champagne, and copious supplies of drink from my merchant in St James'.

Couples whirled to the splendidly lively music, in polkas, sambas, rumbas and other exotic dances with 'a' at the end. And at last – I was sure – there, in full view of others, a couple's lustful embrace had turned into the most lustful of all. The gentleman held his lady up with her legs curled around his back, and her skirts decorously billowing around their bucking loins: they were actually fucking! Naturally, I began to feel rather hot myself. I danced with several ladies, who thought I was a gentleman, and rubbed against my pumped-up cock with lust in their eyes; and with gentlemen who realised I was a lady (at least, I hoped they did!) and mischievously addressed their probing fingers to my tightly-strapped teats. Tess, Verity and the other maids performed winningly, as they had been promised a handsome bonus, fighting their way through the swirl of merriment to deliver precious champagne to those who were thirsty from dancing and, frequently now, from fucking!

Tess was superb; both her shoulder straps had managed to break, and she had given up the unequal battle of holding up her chiton, so that she now passed, Grecian, through the crowd with her magnificent rouged teats entirely naked, and open to the caresses of every gentleman with curious fingers. And, being Tess, whenever her nipples and breasts were caressed, she smiled politely and curtseyed!

'Gosh, Miss,' she gasped in delight. 'Aren't the gentlemen so nice and friendly!' And she showed me her tray awash with pound notes. 'I've even got a few gold sovereigns,' she confided, 'but I have the gentlemen put them up my bum for safe-keeping. Although,' she added doubtfully, 'most people seem to know the way there.'

'You look awfully sweet, Tess,' I said. 'And as I am a gentleman for the moment, I think I'll see if you are telling the truth.' I bent to kiss Tess on her shining breasts, all smeared with nipple-rouge, and my fingers dived under her waistband, to caress the cool melons of her arse before I squeezed two fingers into her elastic anus, where I felt a whole stack of coins!

'I like these ancient revelries,' said Tess, 'for the gentlemen treat me with respect.' She touched my swollen false cock, and sighed. 'Would that he were real, Miss! What is it like, being a gentleman?'

'Almost as nice as being a lady,' I said. 'Here, I'll show you.'

I was so inflamed with gaiety by now that I bent Tess over, there and then, and lifted her chiton to expose her full bare bum. And then, as I delivered a sound slapping to her quivering globes, I had my false cock against the bud of her anus. I thrust with all my might; she moaned and bucked, and at last the mighty engine plunged to the hilt into her belly. At once, she began the most enthusiastic frigging of her clit, begging me to bugger her as hard as I could.

I obliged, frigging my own damsel most luxuriously at the same time, as with my free hand I reddened Tess's quivering arse, and rapidly brought her to a sweet groaning spend. When my cock had plopped from her arsehole, she stood up and curtseyed, blushing with pleasure, and thanked me, but said she had to be about her work. Throughout our sport, Tess had not put down her serving tray of brimming champagne glasses!

Deirdre was wonderfully attired, as Maebh, the Irish goddess of lust (she assured me there was such a thing), with a touch of Cleopatra and the Queen of Sheba thrown in for good measure. She made frequent trips in the direction of the private rooms, with flushed gentlemen in tow, before which expeditions I saw her tuck something glittering beneath the folds of her robe. She always averred to distrust paper money, as it got spoiled in the places she liked to keep her savings. Marlene was happily at the same trade, and her costume, with Caledonian frugality, was a thin tartan robe and nothing else.

In the midst of this orgiastic joy (for orgiastic it had become), a sombre figure appeared at my side. I did not recognise him, for he was smiling! It was Justice Ruttle and his smile was a gaunt affair that betokened only pain. He was accompanied by a nervous man in a brown suit, whose only fancy dress was a shiny badge like that of the Metropolitan Police. I was merrily going to offer him a replacement Swish badge, if he would take a spanking for it, when I realised to my dismay that it was a real Metropolitan Police badge.

'Well, Miss de Comynge,' said Ruttle, in a voice I recognised, as I suspected I would. 'I think I have seen enough. I shall be leaving soon, and shall never set foot here again, nor shall my daughter, Jane. My friend, Chief Superintendent Lines, insisted that the matter must be pursued discreetly, as so many personages of the highest society seem to be involved in these satanic proceedings, and the scandal must not be allowed to reach the public prints.

'As a judge, of course, I cannot interfere with the operations of the police, but it is foolish to think we do not have our channels of communication. There is a warrant for your arrest, Miss, as I propose to take out private proceedings against you, as a common whoremonger and brothel-keeper! How I should like to deal with you in my own court, and how I regret that female offenders may not be sentenced to the birch! At any rate, you had fair warning.'

'Ah, so it was you who wrote that perverted letter, Mr Ruttle! I suspected as much,' I said coolly. In fact, I knew as much. There had always been something shifty about that family. 'Very well!' I laughed. 'Arrest me! And arrest half the members of Parliament, and the Church of England, and the Queen's Bench, along with me!' I gestured grandly at my cavorting guests, many of whom seemed to have dispensed with all disguise save their face-coverings.

'It should not be necessary,' said Ruttle, glowering. 'If you agree to close these proceedings forthwith and leave this establishment, and this country, forever, then I shall show mercy.'

'My dear judge,' I said. 'I cannot resign from what is my personal property. And as for a prosecution, what witnesses shall you have? I have a dozen lords, bishops, and senior judges here; I emphasised the word senior, to his displeasure, 'who will testify that you have brutally interrupted a charity event of tea, cakes and hymn-singing!'

My Merton terpsichoreans obligingly struck up a rousing rendition of 'Big-bummed Bathsheba from Bangalore'.

'Pah! I have all the evidence I need, in this!' And he drew from his coat the secret book of St Agatha's, my photographic 'catalogue' of all my Swish girls which had gone missing not long before!

'Yes,' he smiled viciously, 'my daughter, Jane, clearly borrowed your catalogue of depravity. It shall be enough to hang you, Miss, unless you agree to leave St Agatha's and go and live abroad, in the cesspools of, of . . . foreignness which are your true home!' He was rather startled at my calm reaction.

'So, your daughter is taught to thieve, eh? Not surprising, since her father seems to be a lunatic. It seems I have no option but to agree, sir, but I ask you to accompany me to my study, where I must show you some matter pertaining to your alleged case, after which I may go quietly, as Chief Superintendent Lines would no doubt say.'

'It can do no harm, sir,' said the policeman, 'to be discreet.'

I beckoned to Deirdre that she should accompany us as a witness, and together we retreated, more or less unnoticed, through the gaiety of happy embracing couples, which caused Ruttle's nose to wrinkle.

Once we were seated in my study, I became quite steely and businesslike, and opened my desk.

'You are not obliged to stay, Chief Superintendent,' I said to the poor man. 'You are obviously more at home dealing with housebreakers and coiners and other delinquents,' (I stopped myself saying 'of your own humble class'), 'than with the affairs of a great academy, whose traditions, like the tradition of the highest society which nurtures her, are not readily comprehensible to those of a less refined sensibility.'

Lines and Ruttle gaped uncertainly as I withdrew my own album from my drawer and opened the photographs to their gaze. Ruttle turned pale and, astonishingly, the policeman blushed.

'Yes, Mr Ruttle, you yourself make quite an interesting study, especially when trussed bizarrely, naked in my dungeon, begging for a flogging so severe that even I refused to deliver it!'

Mr Izzard's camera had indeed caught the wretched man as he took off his mask to don my flogging costume. Judge Ruttle was, as I had always suspected, our mysterious masked man!

'I refused your perverted wishes, sir, because here at St Agatha's, we chastise to make better; you wished to be flogged to make you worse. We chastise in love. You, from your bench, order birchings in hate, because you hate yourself. Unable to find meaning in pleasure, you seek to prevent others from doing so. When you sentence those poor tarts and buggers to be flogged, you are really punishing yourself, for the crime of existing at all!'

I was in fine flow, when Chief Superintendent Lines got up in embarrassment.

'Sir,' he said. 'A humble copper is out of his depth here. If you wish to bring a private prosecution, that is up to you, but I don't think you can count on any help from the Met. The doings of the upper classes are best settled amongst themselves. And after all, it is they who pay our pensions. I'm more at home with my forgers and burglars, and keeping Berkeley Square and Carlton Terrace safe for high-class folk to live in, so that they can leave their homes and enjoy themselves at St Agatha's and such. So if you don't mind, I shall excuse myself.'

He tipped his hat and bowed most courteously, and I thought I detected a wink as Deirdre opened the door for him!

'Well, Mr Ruttle,' I said. 'A private prosecution, is it? I think not.'

He stared at his likeness and gaped in silence. The Sunday Intelligencer, with whom we have amicable relations, would be very happy to see these pictures of the famous birching judge, in leather accoutrements, trussed in my flogging dungeon!' He found his tongue.

'Curse you!' he howled. 'Very well, I have no choice, I shall have to let the matter rest. But be assured I shall lose no opportunity to tell the truth about this sink of iniquity.'

'Sir, I don't think you would know the truth if you fell into it,' I said sternly. 'You shall let the matter rest, sir, but we shall not let ours rest. It is the merciful function of St Agatha's to administer virtuous correction to those who need it most!'

At that, I nodded to Deirdre, and with a sure, strong grasp, she picked up the squealing form of the birching judge and carried him kicking in the direction of surgery.

I made my way back to the merrymaking, to find it even merrier than before. The company had decided that the bushes and lawns on this hot night were a perfect place for naked revelry, and there were plenty of lusty celebrants outside, too impatient or too fond of nature to seek the seclusion of the private rooms. Far away, I could see lights flickering in the summerhouse and the shadows of bodies in vibrant amorous motion. I felt the whole of St Agatha's to be one living, passionate creature.

In the refectory itself, gentlemen no less than ladies queued to bare their bottoms to the canes of Freddie (still radiant, as me), Veronica, and the young women, even though there were no more prizes, so that the dais swayed in a veritable ballet of naked buttocks quivering under the caress of a dozen lashes! I was so pleased that my first ever party was such a success! Suddenly I felt an all too familiar hand stroke my bottom.

'What a marvellous party, Mr Whimble,' purred a lady's soft voice. I looked round, smiling, and saw the disguise of Pierrette, worn by none other than Lady Whimble.

'Only,' she continued, 'I don't think you are Mr Whimble, are you? I think you are Miss de Comynge, that naughty governess who ran away from Rakeslit Hall and took my son with her to this delightful den of depravity!'

'Why, Your Ladyship,' I said. 'How nice of you to come! Where is His Lordship?'

She gestured vaguely towards the lawns. 'Outside, being muddy with some London temptress, I expect. Is Whimble still as muddy as ever? I dare say he has plenty of occasion here in Wimbledon. We are in town a lot, of late. Things have changed at Rakeslit and I believe we have you to thank for it, Miss. You got us out of that dreadful rustic torpor, with our silly pagan rites and turnip-growing sacrifices and whatnot; all run by that appalling Reverend Turnpike, who had me at any rate under his spell for a long time.'

I thought back to the lustful vicar, who had introduced me to the delights of nude modelling and (in the interests of art, of course), naked wrestling with his lovely wife Hetty.

'I don't think he was all that appalling, Milady,' I said thoughtfully. 'Perhaps a little overkeen on his fertility rites.'

'Be that as it may,' she said. 'The Turnpikes are now, I believe, ensconced in New Zealand, where he has something to do with sheep, though what exactly, I shudder to imagine. We have you to thank, Miss, for your sound common sense. You were a breath of fresh air in our dung-strewn arcadia. Rakeslit is now run on proper business principles, and we are the largest producer of clotted cream west of the Tamar! Also, Whimble has started to take his aristocratic duties seriously, and visits the Lords conscientiously. We did not call before, because, well, we were not sure we would be warmly received.'

At that, I threw my arms around Lady Whimble and embraced her.

'Milady, how sweet it is to see you! Have you seen Freddie?'

'The boy is dressed as you! How piquant – yes, we spoke briefly. He's busy, the muddy beast, with all those ladies' bottoms! He said that he has a gift for you, which you will receive later, with due ceremony. But before that, we have some unfinished business, Miss. Let us go somewhere private, as it would not be seemly to conduct it in front of Freddie.'

I took her hand and led her to the Turkish bath which, if not exactly private, for it was full of naked, sometimes writhing bodies, at least afforded the anonymity of nudity.

We stripped and I was thrilled to see that Lady Whimble was still the slim, delicious figure I had known; I complimented her and she replied that I was as voluptuous as ever. She remarked on my ingenious false penis and told me to keep it on, as it was so charming. When we were seated and beginning to feel the sweat cleanse our pores, she slyly put her hand on my quim, under the balls, and began to stroke my clit very tenderly. I gulped and responded, and we stayed in this loving embrace, making our quims wetter and wetter. Her clitoris swelled and stiffened until she was quite enormous; thrillingly so. I remembered that milady had told me she had once been foolishly ashamed of her unusually distended love-member! At last I asked what this unfinished business was.

'Why, you left my employ without your month's notice, Miss. I believe I am entitled to some compensation.' Her tone was joking. 'You remember that before you left you had agreed to stay on as my personal assistant? And that part of your duties would be to attend to my bottom with a sound whipping every week?'

'I do remember, milady,' I said, giddy and wet in my lady's place as I recalled the scene of pleasure we had enjoyed before my unfortunately hasty departure. 'Do you wish, then, to claim your due? I have at my disposal a sound assortment of disciplinary tools, to serve your bottom.'

'Excellent! Then we can start right away,' she said, pressing me between my legs and rubbing the swollen lips together in their bath of oil, to my quivers of pleasure.

'Now, you are twelve weeks in arrears, Miss de Comynge, so that makes twelve whippings for my hungry bare bottom, doesn't it?' I smiled in agreement, enjoying our little game. 'That makes, let me see, at a thousand lashes per beating, a total of twelve thousand lashes.'

I started in surprise. 'Milady, that is a bit thick! No one can take a thousand lashes all at once! You make me shudder!'

'Oh but I insist, and a Mistress's decision is final. You owe me twelve thousand lashes! But I will be generous and not take them all at once. We may go to your chamber, Miss, and start now, with a tight juicy six on my wet bottom. Six is such a nice round number.'

'But milady, at six strokes per session that would mean I owed you a lacing whenever you pleased, for the rest of your life!'

'Yes, it does rather look like that, doesn't it?' she said, smiling sweetly.

I took her to my study, and once more we were naked for each other; after a long, silent embrace, our breasts and lips kissing, she languidly stretched herself over my sofa. I tell myself not to become attached to things in this transient world, yet that sofa, over which I had taken my own first caning, now possessed great symbolism for me. I had taken Freddie, her son, there; Mordevaunt, and Veronica Dove, and her father too, and I wondered if the worn leather somehow contained a spirit, as in the Indian philosophies expounded by my Greyhound King, so that each bottom bared for a flogging was enriched by the aura of former chastisements. Such mystical thoughts were cut short by Lady Whimble's impatient wiggling of her naked bottom, and her coos for a beating, without which, as she had confessed to me at Rakeslit, she was unable to achieve a climax.

She was already on tiptoe, her thighs and buttocks straining and taut. I took my hardest yew cane and dealt her six strokes in rapid rhythm, my cunt growing wetter at each slap of the wood on her moist, gleaming arse, and each soft groan that shook her breast. When it was over, I clapped my hand between her legs, and felt her slit gushing with hot moisture. She rose, and embraced me, our breasts, lips and quims presed tight, and we sank to my rug in the most loving of caresses. First, I put in my 'penis' and gave Lady Whimble a vigorous fucking, followed by an equally vigorous bumming. From her moans of pleasure as her fingers pressed my hand to her stiff damsel, I could not tell which she enjoyed more. After I had fucked and caressed her thus for a good ten or twelve minutes, we placed ourselves in the sweet position of sixty-nine, so that our tongues licked our throbbing clits, and our hands stroked and squeezed our arses until we both squealed with joy in panting wet spends.

'That was lovely, Miss,' she purred as I stroked her hair. 'It is so long since I was flogged as only you know how! Well, your debt is diminished somewhat, for now you owe me a mere eleven thousand, nine hundred and ninety-four lashes!'

We re-emerged from my study, as Lady Whimble said that we must find out what Freddie's gift was. The time seemed to be almost three in the morning; the gaiety was at its height, and there was no sign of flagging energy. Champagne and sex are a wonderful stimulant!

'Yes,' said Freddie, when we caught him. 'Your gift, Mistress. I meant it to be a surprise!'

'Well, it is a surprise, you clot,' I said, 'because I don't know what it is!'

'Ah! No, you don't, do you?'

He conferred with Miss Chytte, and Tess was sent to fetch the precious thing, while I waited on tenterhooks. She brought back a bulky package wrapped and ribboned in exquisite silk, and handed it to Freddie, who called for silence. The band stopped and every eye was upon me. Freddie went all red.

'My Lords, Ladies and, er, gentlemen,' he said. 'I'm not much of a one for making, er, speeches, so let us give thanks to, er, Miss de Comynge, who has enriched our lives with so many instructive pleasures, and may do so, we hope, er, for absolutely ages and ages!'

He handed me the package and I opened it with mounting excitement. I gasped when I saw a dazzling mesh of pure, glistening gold chains, a garment designed to enclose its wearer's naked body in utter beauty. I held it up, to loud cheers. It was pure, twenty-four carat gold, and must have weighed three pounds at least.

'Ladies and gentlemen – and, er, Lords. The Golden Harnesss of St Agatha!' cried Freddie. The band struck up 'For She's A Jolly Good Fellow', and everyone sang lustily. I felt a lump in my throat, which is *de rigueur* at such moments. Miss Chytte kissed me, Lady Whimble kissed me, Veronica and Thalia and Major Dove kissed me, then all my students, and it seemed that I had never been kissed so much nor so fondly.

'It's only a replica, actually,' blurted Freddie. 'I know how much you like it, in that funny picture of yours, Mistress, so I had it made up in Bond Street.'

'Oh Freddie, my sweet slave, it is divine!' I cried. Already, I was stripping myself naked for my gift. 'I must wear it at once! But pure gold ... how can you possibly afford it?'

Freddie blushed and cleared his throat.

'Oh, er, ha, hum,' he said, or words to that effect. 'My chum Rudiger' – he indicated the Greyhound King of East London, who bowed – 'introduced me to his infallible system for winning at the track. That's how he has all that money, you know, he bets at Walthamstow and White City, and all the greyhound tracks.'

'And I thought he bred greyhounds!' I gasped, then burst out laughing. 'So he's a gambler!'

'The very best,' said Freddie. 'You see, it's called the system of seven. You add up all the races on the card and bet on trap number seven. Then fourteen, twenty-one, and so on, doubling the bet each time. If there are only five traps in the first, for example, you don't bet, but bet on trap two in the next race, which makes seven. Then add up to fourteen, then twenty-one, then twenty-eight. It works, as you can see, Mistress!'

But I hardly heard him. I stood naked as eager hands wrapped me in the golden harness, the chains snaking so tightly across my intimate body that they seemed alive, and energising. Tight! My teats and bottom were squeezed out like hard melons, reminding me of my induction into Swish. There was not an inch of my naked skin that did not feel the bite of that gorgeous harness. My quim flowed so hot with my love-juice that I felt ready to spend at the sheer touch of that gold and, when I moved, I felt the caress of a thousand tongues. Finally, the sweetest touch, a band of solid gold was fastened tightly across my lips, with a gold ball filling my mouth to gag me. I raised my arms in the air in a gesture of triumph. Veronica stepped shyly to my side. Her legs and buttocks were naked. She handed me my young birch.

'Remember, Mistress?' she said. 'You owe me six of the best, as our wager. Only, henceforth, I suggest that a St Agatha's lacing should be seven of the best.' I raised my eyebrows in puzzlement. 'For luck, Mistress. Six may be a nice round number, but seven must be the lucky number of St Agatha's, for it has earned you the golden harness.'

I nodded. Veronica bent over, her bottom bared to me and, trussed and gagged (Oh how tight and delicious were my bonds!), I lashed her buttocks seven times with my birch. She took each cut with a lovely little shiver and sighed with relief when the seventh had kissed her blushing cheeks. Then I took Freddie's arm and handed him the leash that dangled from the waist of my harness. He understood. He removed my gag, freeing my mouth, and used the band to clamp my wrists tightly behind my back, so that the gold ball caressed the cleft of my buttocks. Then he led me from the dais by my golden leash, and I knelt to the floor like a captive slave, then walked through my lustful crowd on all fours, holding my birch in my teeth, and my naked bottom high in the air, so that my anus bud and the glistening hot petals of my cunt were presented for the adoration of all.

And I was used! Every naked cock that I passed stood for me, and I bent my head to the floor in submission to take him in the anus or quim, while my buttocks danced to the cuts of that sturdy birch. The band played slow, sensuous music that seemed to come from a long-buried temple, or glade of orgiasts in ancient times. I felt that my body was a tool of pure pleasure, a parcel of flesh to be used in sacrifice to the joys and lusts of all my loves.

Everyone used me, filled me, possessed me. My lips and

tongue sucked the cocks and wet quims that spread before my face, and my anus and cunt writhed under a never-ending coupling. I felt myself to be a fish swimming in an ocean of desire and gratification, as if one eternally hard cock fucked me, one eternal cunt bathed my lips with her moisture, and one eternal birch laid sweet fire on my flesh; I was the core of a universe of lust, an eternal hot fountain of unutterable delight, in which the whole world bathed.

I remember that I was at last carried in triumph from the hall, to the loving cheers of the company I had pleasured. My head was as light as a rainbow. Then I was in my bed; Freddie was beside me and Miss Chytte and Mordevaunt and Veronica. Naked, we embraced and cuddled, bathing in our own radiance, and our embraces were chaste. We did not copulate but, caressing each other in silence with easy tenderness, we watched the dawn come up before we fell into a sated, blissful sleep.

It was quite late in the morning when golden sunshine (and Tess) awoke us. Tess brought tea and the morning papers, and looked at us sprawled in our friendly bed with a little moue of disapproval; not that the five of us should lie so blatantly naked, but that she had not been invited to join in. She put the tea things on the side table and held up a newspaper.

Look at the Sunday Intenser!' she said. 'There's a bit about us in it!'

Her squeak of delight roused my sleepy lovers, and I heard Mordevaunt and Freddie groan and yawn. (Why is it that men can never do the simplest thing without groaning?)

I felt playful so I reached out and grabbed their cocks, finding them stiff as tent poles! Although I believe there is a reason why men are hard in the morning, whatever it is, it is a happy one for women!

'You are all hard, you naughty buggers!' I cried gaily.

'Mmm . . .' said Miss Chytte, and I felt her fingers groping on mine.

Veronica yawned and threw the sheet from her naked

breast. Mordevaunt planted a big soppy kiss on her nipple, which made her squeal happily. Soon we were caressing each other anew and I was happy to lie back and rub two gorgeous stiff cocks, while each woman had her mouth on my breast.

'Don't you want your tea?' asked Tess in a peeved voice.
'In a minute, Tess, we are just waking up.'
'And what about the papers?'
'Why don't you read to us out loud?'

Tess had a malicious gleam in her eye as she watched our friendly cuddling, and abruptly she hoisted her maid's frilly skirt, to reveal her bare mons and bottom, and I remarked that her mink was shaved smooth! She said that a kind gentleman had done it to her last night, and she was well pleased, and wished her mink would grow fast, for there were guineas to be made by having her shaved over and over!

'But you need something in your mouth of a morning, Miss,' she said. And promptly hoisted herself on the bed and sat down hard on my face, with her cunny and anus prettily squashed on my lips and nose!

'See? A good queening gets you up and about,' said Tess seriously. I wished to point out that this was rather illogical, but all I could say, smothered by that fragrant arse, was 'Mmm . . .'

Tess picked up the paper and applied her finger to the lines of print. And in true male fashion, my companions began to distract her with nips and kisses and licks to her breasts and bottom, which made everyone giggle, not least Tess.

'Ooo, stop it,' she cried, meaning, don't stop it. 'I must read the story.' She began:

'AT IT AGAIN AT ST AGATHA'S
'By N. B. Izzard, Court and Social Correspondent.'

At that moment the telephone rang beside my bed. Miss Chytte disengaged her lips from Tess's shaven mink and picked it up.

'Well, she said, 'Miss de Comynge has rather a lot on just now.' She listened for a few minutes and said, 'Yes, I'll give her the message,' and replaced the receiver. 'That was Deirdre, Mistress. She says simply that Mr Justice Ruttle has just left us, with something of a change of heart. It appears that a rigorous number seven irrigation over several hours, accompanied by sound bare-bum spankings, and hygienic sucking of his manly parts, have convinced him of the virtues of kindly chastisement and the St Agatha's way. Despite the intractability of his symptoms, Deirdre nobly agreed to charge him only three times normal tariff for the treatment, which included expert demonstration of the therapeutic powers of the female quim and bum-hole. She also took the liberty, during such a demonstration, of accepting Jane Ruttle back at the academy with slightly increased fees, i.e. double, for the strict regime of corporal discipline which her father now thinks essential for her.'

'Mmm, mmm,' I said, indicating approval. As I lay there with Tess's love-juice trickling over my chin, and my hand on the stiff cocks of my two young bucks, and my toes tickling Veronica's and Miss Chytte's. I thought back on the events of my recent life and felt absurdly happy. I had the golden harness of St Agatha lovingly wrapped up in my drawer, next to the presents I had for Mordevaunt and Freddie. Veronica had been saved from her false beau; Nemesis, in the shape of Judge Ruttle, had appeared to spoil the moment of my greatest happiness, and now had been happily tamed. Now it was the holidays, a glorious sunny few weeks of freedom.

'I say,' cried Freddie, 'can't I have a go at this queening?'

'And me!' said Mordevaunt.

'Yes!' said Veronica and Miss Chytte together.

I levered Tess's rump off my face and helped her squat on Miss Chytte, while I bounded up and went to my closet. There I took out my presents for my fellows and they looked in puzzled delight.

'An Oxford scholar's gown?' said Mordevaunt.

'Yes – you are both of you going up to Christ Church

in October, to read philosophy and history and, well, oodles and oodles of things.'

And to their delight I told them how I had arranged the matter of the St Alcuin's tied scholarships. Tess began determinedly to read, squirming gently on Miss Chytte's face, which exhibited every sign of satisfaction at being queened so heartily.

'Well, it was high jinks last night at posh St Agatha's, the ladies' college for naughty rich girls who need their bottoms spanked! Your intrepid reporter paid a brief visit and witnessed the most extraordinary fun before he had to make an excuse and leave.'

Freddie jumped up and grabbed his gown, putting it on in front of the mirror, and then Mordevaunt did the same.

'Don't we look swell!' crowded Freddie. 'We'll need to learn Latin! And,' he blushed, 'take a good supply of Mistress's panties.'

'I already know Latin, you goof,' said Mordevaunt smugly. Before they could start pummelling each other, I cried out:

'Mordevaunt! What is that . . . that growth between your legs?' He looked down at his pubis and blushed.

'Oh, I grew a moustache . . . to please you, Mistress,' he blurted.

He had shaved his mons, all except for a little comma of hair which curled cheekily up over his belly from the naked shaft of his penis and bare balls! 'I hope you don't mind.'

'Boys, and their moustaches!' I sighed. 'Of course I don't mind, Mordevaunt, it's lovely, so come back to bed and let me feel him.'

Soon I had two Oxford scholars beside me and two lovely stiff pricks, one with a moustache, throbbing gently in my hands.

'A masked ball sounds innocent enough,' read Tess, persevering, *'but not when the mysterious Miss de Comynge, governess of St Agatha's, organises it! From his vantage point in the bushes, your fearless reporter was able to discern scenes that would have put Nero or Caligula to shame! Men dressed as women and women as men; or undressed*

altogether. All dancing and drinking foreign wines and treating each other to vigorous spankings on their bare bottoms, which our upper classes seem to think is great sport! As well as that, I could distinctly see immorality openly taking place, with the full consent and even participation of the innocent or not so innocent young ladies. They seemed to think it topping fun to spank and even birch each other's naked buttocks or permit older ladies and gentlemen to administer the chastisement! Contacted by telephone, the elusive Miss de Comynge insisted that the evening was a wholly innocent one! She admitted that corporal chastisement on the naked buttocks had been depicted as part of a play about the martyrdom of St Agatha and that I had mistakenly assumed antique togas to be women's clothing! Come off it, Miss de C! If all those bottoms wriggling under the birch were part of a play, then I'm the Rajah of Jubbulpoor! What a way for the upper classes to bring up the daughters of the Empire!'

Mordevaunt now took matters into his own hands and hoisted Tess onto his own face for a queening. At the same time I began to frig both his and Freddie's cocks rather firmly, which had them both squirming. Miss Chytte's face, now glistening with Tess's love-juice, met mine in a lovely sloppy kiss and we tongued each other as her fingers found my throbbing little damsel. I felt Freddie's teeth on my nipples as I stroked his shaven balls and cock, and Veronica's hands caressing my bottom and belly, and I knew that we should all be spending before long, even Tess, who writhed quite delectably on the probing tongue of Mordevaunt.

'I think that N. B. Izzard is making it all up!' she said indignantly. 'Why, I heard him telephoning the paper from your very study, Miss! And he didn't make excuses and sneak away!'

'How do you know, Tess?' I panted, as my clit tingled under my slave's caress.

'Because he's still in my bed, the lazy sod! He sent me out to make his breakfast!'

Our conversation came to a halt there as we all fell into the friendliest of morning embraces, warm in the afterglow of our dreamtime. Mordevaunt's cock took me in my quim, as Freddie's caressed my anus and bummed me most vigorously; then it was the turn of Tess, Veronica and Miss Chytte, to receive those stiff, rampant young scholars in each and every orifice, while I used my palms to good effect to deliver a hearty spanking to whichever bottom stayed still long enough; at last, having come to our several spends, we all lay in a tousle, with Tess wailing that the tea would be cold and she would have to make it all over again.

'Don't worry about that, Tess. We have a splendid long holiday in front of us. What do you know about sailing, Miss Chytte?'

'Nothing, Mistress.'

'Freddie? Mordevaunt? Veronica?'

'Nothing.'

'Well, you had better learn, because I think we are going to sail from San Remo to Corfu,' I said.

'I once rowed a rowing boat across Padstow Bay,' said Tess proudly. 'But it leaked and I had to swim to Trebetherick, and the yokels could see all through my wet dress!'

'I don't think we need to worry about dresses on "The Maid of Walthamstow", wet or otherwise,' I said. 'Just think, we can have three glorious weeks on Rudiger's yacht with no clothes on, and nothing to do but enjoy ourselves! I think we all deserve a break!'

Everybody agreed happily, and then the telephone rang again. I picked it up.

'St Agatha's Academy, Miss de Comynge speaking.'

'Ah, yes. Tattersall here, of the Northamptonshire Tattersalls, don't you know. Thing is, I read about you in some tuppenny paper this morning, one of the servants left it lying about. And, well, I have this rather headstrong daughter, and I wonder if there might be a place for her at St Agatha's . . .?'

Nexus

NEXUS BACKLIST

This information is correct at time of printing. For up-to-date information, please visit our website at www.nexus-books.co.uk

All books are priced at £5.99 unless another price is given.

Nexus books with a contemporary setting

ACCIDENTS WILL HAPPEN	Lucy Golden ISBN 0 352 33596 3	☐
ANGEL	Lindsay Gordon ISBN 0 352 33590 4	☐
BARE BEHIND £6.99	Penny Birch ISBN 0 352 33721 4	☐
BEAST	Wendy Swanscombe ISBN 0 352 33649 8	☐
THE BLACK FLAME	Lisette Ashton ISBN 0 352 33668 4	☐
BROUGHT TO HEEL	Arabella Knight ISBN 0 352 33508 4	☐
CAGED!	Yolanda Celbridge ISBN 0 352 33650 1	☐
CANDY IN CAPTIVITY	Arabella Knight ISBN 0 352 33495 9	☐
CAPTIVES OF THE PRIVATE HOUSE	Esme Ombreux ISBN 0 352 33619 6	☐
CHERI CHASTISED £6.99	Yolanda Celbridge ISBN 0 352 33707 9	☐
DANCE OF SUBMISSION	Lisette Ashton ISBN 0 352 33450 9	☐
DIRTY LAUNDRY £6.99	Penny Birch ISBN 0 352 33680 3	☐
DISCIPLINED SKIN	Wendy Swanscombe ISBN 0 352 33541 6	☐

DISPLAYS OF EXPERIENCE	Lucy Golden ISBN 0 352 33505 X	☐
DISPLAYS OF PENITENTS £6.99	Lucy Golden ISBN 0 352 33646 3	☐
DRAWN TO DISCIPLINE	Tara Black ISBN 0 352 33626 9	☐
EDEN UNVEILED	Maria del Rey ISBN 0 352 32542 4	☐
AN EDUCATION IN THE PRIVATE HOUSE	Esme Ombreux ISBN 0 352 33525 4	☐
EMMA'S SECRET DOMINATION	Hilary James ISBN 0 352 33226 3	☐
GISELLE	Jean Aveline ISBN 0 352 33440 1	☐
GROOMING LUCY	Yvonne Marshall ISBN 0 352 33529 7	☐
HEART OF DESIRE	Maria del Rey ISBN 0 352 32900 9	☐
HIS MISTRESS'S VOICE	G. C. Scott ISBN 0 352 33425 8	☐
IN FOR A PENNY	Penny Birch ISBN 0 352 33449 5	☐
INTIMATE INSTRUCTION	Arabella Knight ISBN 0 352 33618 8	☐
THE LAST STRAW	Christina Shelly ISBN 0 352 33643 9	☐
NURSES ENSLAVED	Yolanda Celbridge ISBN 0 352 33601 3	☐
THE ORDER	Nadine Somers ISBN 0 352 33460 6	☐
THE PALACE OF EROS £4.99	Delver Maddingley ISBN 0 352 32921 1	☐
PALE PLEASURES £6.99	Wendy Swanscombe ISBN 0 352 33702 8	☐
PEACHES AND CREAM £6.99	Aishling Morgan ISBN 0 352 33672 2	☐

PEEPING AT PAMELA	Yolanda Celbridge ISBN 0 352 33538 6	☐
PENNY PIECES	Penny Birch ISBN 0 352 33631 5	☐
PET TRAINING IN THE PRIVATE HOUSE	Esme Ombreux ISBN 0 352 33655 2	☐
REGIME £6.99	Penny Birch ISBN 0 352 33666 8	☐
RITUAL STRIPES £6.99	Tara Black ISBN 0 352 33701 X	☐
SEE-THROUGH	Lindsay Gordon ISBN 0 352 33656 0	☐
SILKEN SLAVERY	Christina Shelly ISBN 0 352 33708 7	☐
SKIN SLAVE	Yolanda Celbridge ISBN 0 352 33507 6	☐
SLAVE ACTS £6.99	Jennifer Jane Pope ISBN 0 352 33665 X	☐
THE SLAVE AUCTION	Lisette Ashton ISBN 0 352 33481 9	☐
SLAVE GENESIS	Jennifer Jane Pope ISBN 0 352 33503 3	☐
SLAVE REVELATIONS	Jennifer Jane Pope ISBN 0 352 33627 7	☐
SLAVE SENTENCE	Lisette Ashton ISBN 0 352 33494 0	☐
SOLDIER GIRLS	Yolanda Celbridge ISBN 0 352 33586 6	☐
THE SUBMISSION GALLERY	Lindsay Gordon ISBN 0 352 33370 7	☐
SURRENDER	Laura Bowen ISBN 0 352 33524 6	☐
THE TAMING OF TRUDI £6.99	Yolanda Celbridge ISBN 0 352 33673 0	☐
TEASING CHARLOTTE £6.99	Yvonne Marshall ISBN 0 352 33681 1	☐
TEMPER TANTRUMS	Penny Birch ISBN 0 352 33647 1	☐

THE TORTURE CHAMBER	Lisette Ashton ISBN 0 352 33530 0	☐
UNIFORM DOLL £6.99	Penny Birch ISBN 0 352 33698 6	☐
WHIP HAND £6.99	G. C. Scott ISBN 0 352 33694 3	☐
THE YOUNG WIFE	Stephanie Calvin ISBN 0 352 33502 5	☐

Nexus books with Ancient and Fantasy settings

CAPTIVE	Aishling Morgan ISBN 0 352 33585 8	☐
DEEP BLUE	Aishling Morgan ISBN 0 352 33600 5	☐
DUNGEONS OF LIDIR	Aran Ashe ISBN 0 352 33506 8	☐
INNOCENT £6.99	Aishling Morgan ISBN 0 352 33699 4	☐
MAIDEN	Aishling Morgan ISBN 0 352 33466 5	☐
NYMPHS OF DIONYSUS £4.99	Susan Tinoff ISBN 0 352 33150 X	☐
PLEASURE TOY	Aishling Morgan ISBN 0 352 33634 X	☐
SLAVE MINES OF TORMUNIL £6.99	Aran Ashe ISBN 0 352 33695 1	☐
THE SLAVE OF LIDIR	Aran Ashe ISBN 0 352 33504 1	☐
TIGER, TIGER	Aishling Morgan ISBN 0 352 33455 X	☐

Period

CONFESSION OF AN ENGLISH SLAVE	Yolanda Celbridge ISBN 0 352 33433 9	☐
THE MASTER OF CASTLELEIGH	Jacqueline Bellevois ISBN 0 352 32644 7	☐
PURITY	Aishling Morgan ISBN 0 352 33510 6	☐
VELVET SKIN	Aishling Morgan ISBN 0 352 33660 9	☐

Samplers and collections

NEW EROTICA 5	Various ISBN 0 352 33540 8	☐
EROTICON 1	Various ISBN 0 352 33593 9	☐
EROTICON 2	Various ISBN 0 352 33594 7	☐
EROTICON 3	Various ISBN 0 352 33597 1	☐
EROTICON 4	Various ISBN 0 352 33602 1	☐
THE NEXUS LETTERS	Various ISBN 0 352 33621 8	☐
SATURNALIA £7.99	ed. Paul Scott ISBN 0 352 33717 6	☐
MY SECRET GARDEN SHED £7.99	ed. Paul Scott ISBN 0 352 33725 7	☐

Nexus Classics

A new imprint dedicated to putting the finest works of erotic fiction back in print.

AMANDA IN THE PRIVATE HOUSE £6.99	Esme Ombreux ISBN 0 352 33705 2	☐
BAD PENNY	Penny Birch ISBN 0 352 33661 7	☐
BRAT £6.99	Penny Birch ISBN 0 352 33674 9	☐
DARK DELIGHTS £6.99	Maria del Rey ISBN 0 352 33667 6	☐
DARK DESIRES	Maria del Rey ISBN 0 352 33648 X	☐
DISPLAYS OF INNOCENTS £6.99	Lucy Golden ISBN 0 352 33679 X	☐
DISCIPLINE OF THE PRIVATE HOUSE £6.99	Esme Ombreux ISBN 0 352 33459 2	☐
EDEN UNVEILED	Maria del Rey ISBN 0 352 33542 4	☐

HIS MISTRESS'S VOICE	G. C. Scott ISBN 0 352 33425 8	☐
THE INDIGNITIES OF ISABELLE £6.99	Penny Birch writing as Cruella ISBN 0 352 33696 X	☐
LETTERS TO CHLOE	Stefan Gerrard ISBN 0 352 33632 3	☐
MEMOIRS OF A CORNISH GOVERNESS £6.99	Yolanda Celbridge ISBN 0 352 33722 2	☐
ONE WEEK IN THE PRIVATE HOUSE £6.99	Esme Ombreux ISBN 0 352 33706 0	☐
PARADISE BAY	Maria del Rey ISBN 0 352 33645 5	☐
PENNY IN HARNESS	Penny Birch ISBN 0 352 33651 X	☐
THE PLEASURE PRINCIPLE	Maria del Rey ISBN 0 352 33482 7	☐
PLEASURE ISLAND	Aran Ashe ISBN 0 352 33628 5	☐
SISTERS OF SEVERCY	Jean Aveline ISBN 0 352 33620 X	☐
A TASTE OF AMBER	Penny Birch ISBN 0 352 33654 4	☐

------ ✂ ----------------------------

Please send me the books I have ticked above.

Name ....

Address ....

....

....

.... Post code....................

Send to: **Cash Sales, Nexus Books, Thames Wharf Studios, Rainville Road, London W6 9HA**

US customers: for prices and details of how to order books for delivery by mail, call 1-800-343-4499.

Please enclose a cheque or postal order, made payable to **Nexus Books Ltd**, to the value of the books you have ordered plus postage and packing costs as follows:

UK and BFPO – £1.00 for the first book, 50p for each subsequent book.

Overseas (including Republic of Ireland) – £2.00 for the first book, £1.00 for each subsequent book.

If you would prefer to pay by VISA, ACCESS/MASTERCARD, AMEX, DINERS CLUB or SWITCH, please write your card number and expiry date here:

....

Please allow up to 28 days for delivery.

Signature ....

Our privacy policy.

We will not disclose information you supply us to any other parties. We will not disclose any information which identifies you personally to any person without your express consent.

From time to time we may send out information about Nexus books and special offers. Please tick here if you do *not* wish to receive Nexus information. ☐

------ ✂ ----------------------------